5/24

ONE
PERFECT
COUPLE

ALSO BY RUTH WARE

ONE PERFECT COUPLE

RUTH WARE

S

SCOUT PRESS

New York   London   Toronto   Sydney   New Delhi

Scout Press
An Imprint of Simon & Schuster, LLC
1230 Avenue of the Americas
New York, NY 10020

First Scout Press hardcover edition May 2024

SCOUT PRESS and colophon are registered trademarks of Simon & Schuster, LLC

Simon & Schuster: Celebrating 100 Years of Publishing in 2024

For information about special discounts for bulk purchases, please contact Simon & Schuster Special Sales at 1-866-506-1949 or business@simonandschuster.com.

The Simon & Schuster Speakers Bureau can bring authors to your live event. For more information or to book an event, contact the Simon & Schuster Speakers Bureau at 1-866-248-3049 or visit our website at www.simonspeakers.com.

Interior design by Jaime Putorti

Manufactured in the United States of America

10 9 8 7 6 5 4 3 2 1

Library of Congress Cataloging-in-Publication Data is available.

ISBN 978-1-6680-2559-8
ISBN 978-1-6680-2561-1 (ebook)

RAPID
READS
WARE

To Ian, my absolute favourite scientist.
Thank you for being you.

ONE
PERFECT
COUPLE

PROLOGUE

He is fighting. He is fighting for his life—but so is she. She is neck-deep in the water; there is salt in her eyes, water in her lungs, and she is gasping, choking, unable to breathe.

His body is hard and muscled and stronger than she had ever imagined possible, thrashing like a pinned beast beneath the water.

And as she struggles against him, she knows two things, knows them to be piercingly, desperately true—one: it is him or her, and if she lets go, she will be the one drowning under the waves.

And two: to kill someone this way, you have to want them to die with every ounce of your being.

The question is: Does she? Does she want him to die?

PART ONE

THE CALM

02/15—02:13 a.m.

Hello. Hello?

CHAPTER 1

"I CANNOT, REPEAT cannot, go to a desert island," I said. I didn't look up at Nico, who was hovering behind my chair. Instead, I continued to stare at the computer screen, trying to make sense of the spreadsheet in front of me. One thing was for sure: the data definitely didn't show the kind of correlation Professor Bianchi had been hoping for when he hired me. This was my third attempt, and I could no longer ignore the sinking feeling in my stomach. Something was very wrong.

"But Lyla, I'm telling you, it's the opportunity of a lifetime. Reality TV. *Reality TV.*"

"It could be the opportunity of the millennium, Nic. I can't go with you. How am I going to get the time off?" Was there a pattern I wasn't seeing? Maybe if I tried adding in the previous results? "But don't let me hold you back; you go. I'll cheer you on from here."

"Were you not listening?" Nico asked, the pleading in his voice now tinged with a touch of testiness. "I can't go on my own. It's a *couple's* TV show. Lyla, I don't ask for much, but Ari thinks this is make-or-break for my career. I won't get a chance like this again. You know how long I've been banging my head against the wall, auditioning for God knows what— This could be it. This could be my big break."

I pulled up the spreadsheet of the last batch of samples, clicked to plot the data again, and as the graph filled out, Nico exploded.

"Lyla! For fuck's sake, are you even listening to me? This is the turning point of my career and you can't turn off your laptop for thirty seconds?"

I took a deep breath. My mother's voice sounded in my ear: *Get your head out of your phone, Lyla....*

I saved the file and swung my chair round to face my boyfriend.

"I'm sorry. You're right. I wasn't listening. Tell me about it properly."

"It's a new reality show. Not much of a prize, because it's being done on a shoestring budget for a brand-new streaming channel, but it's going to be their flagship launch original, and if it takes off the exposure could be through the roof. And Ari knows the producer, Baz. They went to uni together. Ari says he can get me in through the back door. Us, I mean."

"And, sorry, what's the concept?"

"Five couples on a desert island. Elimination format, counting down over ten weeks. I'm not sure where, Ari was saying something about Indonesia? It's kind of *Love Island* meets *Survivor*—you have to stay coupled up to stay in. Sun, sand, sea . . . come on, Lil! It's just what we both need. A proper holiday."

"But it's not a holiday, is it? And how long did you say this would take? Ten *weeks*? Starting when?"

Nico shrugged.

"No idea, but it sounded like they're in a hurry. Ari was asking about my calendar over the next couple of months. I told him there was nothing I couldn't move."

I sighed.

"I'm really sorry, Nico, maybe *your* calendar is empty, but mine isn't. There's no way I can just bugger off for the remainder of my contract, you know I can't. Professor Bianchi would sack me, and then how would we pay the rent?"

Not with Nico's meager snippets of income as an aspiring actor and part-time barista, was the unspoken coda, though I didn't say it. But Nico was shaking his head.

"But Lyla, that's the point. If I got this, it'd be real exposure. I could be a household name by the end of the series, we'd be talking TV roles, film, ads—you name it. It'd be proper money—regular money. *House-buying* money. I could take some of the pressure off you. Come on, Lil, think about it. Please?"

He pushed my laptop out of the way and moved to sit on the desk in front of me, holding out his arms, and I leaned into his embrace, resting my forehead on his chest, feeling the familiar mix of exasperation and love.

I loved Nico, I really did. And not just because he was funny, charming, and extremely hot—definitely an eight or nine to my six. But he was also an incurable optimist, whereas I was a very firm rationalist. His habit of convincing himself that every rainbow ended in a pot of gold just for him—a habit that had seemed so endearing when we first met—had started to grate after two years together. Two years of me footing the bills and doing the admin and generally acting the grown-up, while Nico chased opportunities that somehow never *quite* materialized.

This sounded like another one of his pie-in-the-sky dreams, just like the West End musical of *Twilight* that turned out no one had cleared the rights to, and just like his plan to become a YouTube acting coach. There had been so many schemes that had come to nothing, so many shows canceled before their first episode and pilots that never got off the ground. But if I pointed any of that out, *I* would be the bad guy. I'd be the person who had denied Nico his chance.

"Can I at least tell Ari you'll meet with the producers?" Nico said, his breath warm against the top of my head. I shut my eyes, knowing that if I looked at him, at his brown puppy-dog eyes and pleading expression, I'd be lost. What I *wanted* to say was that there seemed precious little chance of this getting past the first meeting, when the producers would presumably meet me and realize I wasn't the big-boobed hottie they were looking for. Reality TV wasn't exactly my usual entertainment fare, but I'd watched enough to know there was a certain physical type for female contestants, and that I didn't fit it. Nico—with his gym-toned body and salon-tanned skin—he was different. He'd have fitted in fine on *The Bachelorette* or *Perfect Match*. But me? Were they really going to look at a thirtysomething scientist with fingers stained purple from protein gels, and a permanent frown line from squinting into a microscope, and think, *We want to see her jogging down the beach in a skimpy bikini*? Unlikely.

On the other hand . . . if it was never going to happen . . . would it really matter if I strung Nico along for a bit longer? Then, when I got rejected, or the whole thing finally stalled in development, this Baz guy could be the baddie, and I'd get to be the supportive girlfriend. Until the next hopelessly naive scheme materialized, anyway.

I opened my eyes, trying to think what to say, but instead I found my gaze straying to the glowing screen of my laptop. I couldn't read the figures because Nico had shoved the computer to the far side of my desk. But that didn't matter. They were there, and I knew it. Inconvenient. Incontrovertible. Unignorable.

"Please?" Nico said, breaking into my thoughts, and I realized that he was still waiting on my answer. I looked up at him. At his big brown eyes, fringed with impossibly long lashes—like a young George Michael. I felt something inside me giving way . . . melting. Oh God, I was going to say yes, and we both knew it.

"Okay," I said at last, feeling my face crack into a reluctant smile. For a moment Nico just stared at me, then he gave a whooping holler and lifted me off my feet, crushing me in a giant bear hug.

"Thank you, thank you, oh my God, *thank you*. I love you, Lyla Santiago!"

"I love you too," I said, laughing down at him. "But you have to get on the show first, okay? So don't count your chickens! I don't want you to be disappointed if you don't get in."

"I'll get in," Nico said, setting me down and kissing me firmly on the lips, one hand on either side of my face, his smile so wide it crinkled up his tanned cheeks. "Don't you worry about that, Lil. I'll get in. We both will. How could they resist?"

I looked up at him, at his broad grin, his white teeth, his sparkling dark eyes, and I thought, how, indeed, could they resist? No one could say no to Nico. I just had to hope Professor Bianchi would feel the same way.

02/15—02:13 a.m.

Hello? I'm not sure how this thing works, but this is Lyla, to the *Over Easy*, over.

02/15—02:14 a.m.

Hello, is anyone receiving this? This is Lyla to the *Over Easy*, please come in. Over.

CHAPTER 2

"OH DEAR." PROFESSOR Bianchi's face had gone from cheerful to depressed as I talked him through the latest batch of data. The findings left by Tony, my predecessor, had been—well, *exciting* was an understatement. If they'd proven reproduceable, they would have represented a major breakthrough in chikungunya, my specialist area. But they weren't proving reproduceable, and that was a problem.

The annoying thing was that Tony was long gone. He'd published his thesis to rippling excitement and had promptly been headhunted by a private lab for a permanent position. I'd been hired by the university on a one-year contract to tie up the loose ends. My task was supposed to be simple: repeat Tony's experiments with a wider range of samples and prove that the results held up. The problem was, they didn't. I'd repeated and repeated and repeated until I was blue in the face, but after the third attempt, I'd had to admit it. The effect Tony had found wasn't just weaker, it wasn't there at all.

In theory, I'd done my job. Pat on the back. Great work, Lyla. And in theory, disproving a false lead was as valuable and important as finding something new. The problem was that in practice, we all knew that wasn't how it worked. Grant funding didn't go to the scientists who found out something *didn't* work. It went to the groups with sexy new discoveries and results that got everyone talking. No one wanted to publish a paper meticulously outlining the anatomy of a damp squib, no matter how good the research.

In my darker moments, sleepless, at 3 a.m., I'd blamed Tony. Perhaps he'd written his method up wrong. Maybe he'd even faked his results? But in my heart of hearts, and with my scientist's head on, looking at the data, I knew it wasn't Tony's fault. He'd thrown a dozen dice and they'd all returned sixes. Just one of those things, and when I tried again on a much bigger scale, the pattern hadn't held. But I was the one having to break the bad news, and deal with the fallout.

Up until a few weeks ago, I hadn't been worried about the fact that my contract at the university was about to expire—Professor Bianchi had more or less assured me that obtaining further funding was a formality. Now . . . well, now I could tell from his expression that I should be polishing up my CV. And I wasn't looking forward to explaining at interviews the fact that I'd spent a full twelve months working on a highly exciting project and had absolutely fuck all to show for it.

"You'd better write it up," Professor Bianchi said a little wearily. "And then we'll have to see whether there's anything that can be salvaged from it. Maybe something will come out of Gregor's animal modeling."

I bit my lip and nodded.

"I'm sorry," I said again, and Professor Bianchi shrugged, the philosophical shrug of a man with tenure who'd wanted this to work out, but hadn't hung his career on it.

"Not your fault, Lyla."

"What do you think it means for the funding renewal?"

"Ah. Good point. Your contract's up next month, isn't it?"

"March, in fact," I said quietly. "Ten weeks."

Professor Bianchi nodded.

"I'll speak to the grant committee. But . . ."

He trailed off. *Don't make any big purchases in the meantime*, was the strong implication.

I forced a smile.

"Sure. Thanks. Listen, I . . ." I swallowed. Now wasn't the time I'd have chosen to ask for time off, but in a way it didn't matter. I could write up the paper just as well on Nico's desert island as I could here, and I might as well take my holiday entitlement before the contract ended. "Would now be a bad time for me to take some leave? Nico, my boyfriend, he's been invited on this—" I stopped. I wasn't 100 percent sure Professor Bianchi knew what a reality TV show was. The one time I'd referred to *Big Brother*, he'd assumed I was talking about George Orwell. And it didn't exactly fit with the responsible in-demand professional image I was trying to project. "On a work trip," I finished. "He's asked me to come along. I can write the paper there; it's probably easier than trying to fit it in around lab work."

"Sure," Professor Bianchi said, and his face . . . did I imagine a flicker of relief? "Of course. And hopefully by the time you come back I'll have heard from the grant committee. Thanks again, Lyla, for all your work on this. I know it's never easy coming in with disappointing results."

"You're welcome," I said. And then, since the interview was plainly over, I showed myself out of his office.

I SPENT THE bus ride back to east London watching the winter rain trickle down the steamed-up windows and considering my choices. I was thirty-two. All around me friends from university were buying up houses, settling down, having kids. My mum's jokes about grandbabies had started to become slightly pointed. But here I was, stuck in a cycle of short-term post-docs that didn't seem to be going any-where. Once, I'd dreamed of heading up my own team, my own *lab*, even. Talks about the dearth of women in STEM had made it all seem so possible—funding committees were crying out for driven female scientists, we were told.

In truth though, there'd been a healthy proportion of women in my cohort, at least when I started out. My first two bosses in the lab had been women. But the funding committees didn't look any more kindly on us than they did on the men, and as the years ground on, more and more of my colleagues had been forced out by the reality of life in academic research. Maternity leave didn't mesh well with funding deadlines and the pressurized race to results. Babies didn't mix with tissue cultures that needed constant tending, cell lines that had to be split at ten o'clock at night, five in the morning, endless round-the-clock work, or else they'd wither and die. And mortgage providers didn't like the uncertainty of short-term contracts. Every time I started a new job there was a narrow window of security when I was out of the probation period, but not yet under statutory notice of redundancy—and it never seemed to be long enough to get a foot on the ladder. Combined with Nico's feast-or-famine line of work (and there'd been precious little feasting over the two-and-a-half years we'd been together), it made for a stressful existence. And the longer I'd been in the field, the more I realized that there was a tick-ing clock, and not just one relating to babies. The career pyramid for science was shallow—many researchers, very few lab heads—and the competition was astonishingly fierce. If you didn't tick certain boxes by the time you were in your thirties, you just weren't going to make it.

Maybe it was time to throw in the towel, admit once and for all that the dreams I'd held when I left uni were never going to happen. That I was never going to be able to fund my own lab. That Professor Lyla Santiago was never going to exist, would never give the keynote address at a prestigious academic conference, or be interviewed on *This Week in Virology*. With every year that ticked by, it was looking increasingly likely that I'd be forever a lowly post-doc, scrabbling around for my next short-term contract. And maybe it was time to face up to that and figure out what to do.

It didn't help that Nico was only twenty-eight, and decidedly not ready to settle down in any way. He'd barely changed from the cute, wannabe actor I'd met almost three years ago, at a friend's "Valentine's Day Massacre" horror-themed party for pissed-off singletons. He'd been a disturbingly sexy Freddie Krueger; I'd cheated and borrowed a lab coat from work, spattered it with some fake blood. We'd mixed Bloody Marys in the kitchen, watched *Friday the 13*th on my friend's couch, shrieking and hugging each other during the jump scares, and ended up snogging in the bathroom. The next day my friend had ribbed me about pulling out of my league.

For six months I'd almost forgotten his existence, the only reminder the occasional thirst-trap photos he posted on Instagram. They were . . . I mean, they were easy on the eye, I had to admit it, and they made a nice break to my workday. I'd be flicking through my phone on coffee break, and there would be Nico, sweatily tousled at the gym, all crunched abs and tangled dark hair. On the bus back from the university, there he'd be again, sprawled on a beach in the Algarve, tiny swimshorts stretched across his hips, smirking up at the camera from behind mirrored shades.

For half a year that was it—me single, bored, head down at work, barely thinking about the handsome actor I'd groped in my friend's bathroom. And then one day, out of the blue, I posted an Instagram photo of myself. It was uncharacteristic. My normal feed was dinners I'd cooked and funny memes about the hell of working in academia. But I'd ordered a dress online and when it turned up it was almost comically undersized, the skirt just skimming my thighs, my boobs spilling out of the top. I posted it as a funny "what I ordered / what I got" pic, but I was aware that, while I wasn't going to keep the dress, it also wasn't exactly unflattering. It was about as un-me as it was possible to get, but it also squeezed me in the right places, and my tits did look pretty awesome.

The first comment was from Nico—just a string of chili peppers that made me laugh.

And the second was a reply from him to his own comment. It just said "Drink?"

A drink turned into drinks, which turned into dancing, which turned into tequila slammers and drunken snogging and, eventually, a shared Uber (which Nico promised to split, but never did). Nico, it turned out, lived around the corner from me in a house share in Dalston, but that night we ended up at my place—and, well, somehow he never quite moved out.

Two and a half years later, I was older, wiser, and considerably more jaded—facing up to the realities of living in one of the most expensive cities in the world on a researcher's salary. My rent had gone up. My pay had not. I had started to think about plan B. Maybe even plan C. But Nico was still dreaming of Tinseltown, still refusing to sell his dinner jacket in case he one day needed to attend the BAFTAs or the Grammys. Nico was still fighting, still hustling for his dreams, and most days that was part of what I liked about him—his relentless optimism, his faith that one day his ship would come in.

But on a day like today, the grayest kind of gray London day, when even the sun seemed to have given up and gone back to bed, that optimism was a little hard to take.

When I got off the bus at Hackney Wick, the rain had turned to a stinging sleet, and I realized I'd left my umbrella at the lab. I half jogged the twenty minutes from the bus-stop, trying to shield my laptop from the worst of it, then stumped wearily up the three flights to our little flat in the rafters of a Victorian terrace house. When I had first brought Nico here, we'd run up, laughing, only stopping to kiss on the landing turns. Now I was chilled to the bone, and each flight felt steeper than the last. I had to will myself up the last set to my front door, and when I finally reached the top, it took me three tries for my numb fingers to get the key in the lock.

"I'm home!" I called as I peeled off my wet coat, though the flat was so small—just a bedroom, a bathroom, and an everything-else-room—that I didn't really need to raise my voice.

The words had hardly left my lips when Nico appeared, mobile pressed to his ear, motioning me to keep quiet.

"Of course," he was saying, in what I thought of as his *actor* voice, deeper, smoother, and more assured than he would have sounded on the phone to his mum or a mate. "Sure. Absolutely. Absolutely." There was a long pause, with the person on the other side evidently saying something, and Nico nodding with an attentive expression on his tanned, handsome face that was totally wasted on the person on the other end. At last, after a short back-and-forth of goodbyes, he hung up and danced down the hallway to throw his arms around me, lifting me up and whirling me around.

"Nico!" I managed. His grip was suffocatingly strong, and in the narrow hallway my foot caught the mirror as he swung me round, making it swing dangerously against the wall. "Nico, for God's sake, put me *down!*"

He set me on my feet, but I could see that my reaction hadn't dented his mood. He was grinning all over his face, his dark eyes quite literally sparkling with excitement. That expression had always seemed like the worst kind of cliché to me—from a scientific point of view, it's not possible for eyes to change their reflective properties because something fun has happened—but I had to admit it was the only apt description for Nico right now.

"That was Baz," he said. "The producer of *One Perfect Couple.*"

"The producer of what?"

"That's its name." Nico flicked his fringe out of his eyes. "The show. I told you."

"You didn't, but okay."

"I *did*. But anyway, that's not the point. The point is I sent him some pics and he *loves* both of us—"

"Wait, you sent over photos of me?" I was taken aback, but Nico was barely listening.

"—and he definitely wants to set up a meeting. He said we're exactly the kind of couple they're looking for. They want real authenticity, not the usual *Love Island* types."

"Real authenticity?" I looked down at myself—crumpled T-shirt, wet jeans, old trainers for working in the lab. "Is that code for *needs a wax and to lose five pounds off her arse*?"

"Actually, he said you reminded him of Zooey Deschanel," Nico said. "And by the way, your arse is perfect."

"I notice you didn't comment on the wax."

"Look, stop taking the piss. *You're* perfect, okay? I think so, and Baz agrees. He really likes that you're a scientist. He said having a boffin on the show would be good for ratings, and as far as your arse goes, he said you were g—" He stopped, stumbled over whatever he'd been about to say, and then finished, "Very good-looking."

"Okay, clearly that's not what he actually said, Nico. Spit it out."

"I, um . . . I can't remember his exact words," Nico said, but his ears were reddening, his invariable tell whenever he was lying, and I began to tickle him, digging my fingers into his ribs and the soft skin beneath his collar.

"Nico, what did he say?"

"Stop it!" he ordered, ducking away from me and trying not to laugh. "Lyla! I'm warning you—"

"So tell me what he said! If I'm going on this show—"

"If?"

"*If.* I have a right to know what the producer thinks of me. Or should I ask him?"

"Stop tickling me!"

"I'll stop when you tell me what he said!"

"All right, all right! He said you were . . . *girl-next-door fuckable.*" He spoke the words slightly shame-facedly, acknowledging my reaction even before my expression of disgust had formed.

"What? That's gross!"

"He didn't mean it that way," Nico added hastily, aware that he'd made a faux pas and anxious that I didn't turn against the idea of going on the show. "He said I'm *fantasy first boyfriend,* if it makes you feel better."

"What? No! It doesn't make me feel better! That's gross too, you're twenty-eight. You shouldn't be anyone's first boyfriend!"

"Fantasy, Lil! That's the point. You know, when you're thirteen and you want a kissable poster on your bedroom wall—someone sexy but not too threatening. Zac Efron. Jacob Elordi. Personally, I think I'm a bit too old as well." He threw a glance at what I knew was his own reflection in the mirror over my shoulder, appraising the laugh lines that were just starting to form at the corners of his eyes. "But you know, he's just talking *types,* not saying that's how *he* thinks of us."

"Still." I was barely mollified. *Girl-next-door* fuckable. Girl-next-door *fuckable*? Was it a compliment? No matter which word I put the stress on, it didn't feel like one. "What else did he say? Any news on dates?"

Nico nodded.

"They want to move fast. It's for a new reality TV network that's launching later this year, so they've got a really tight deadline to get everything filmed and tied up."

"Which means?" I followed him into the room that doubled as our living room and kitchen and watched as he put on the kettle.

"Your guess is as good as mine, but it sounded like they want to start filming in a matter of weeks. He kept saying the word *asap*." He pronounced it as two syllables, *ay-sap*. "*I'll get my assistant onto you asap. The researchers will be in touch asap.* That kind of thing."

"Oh." I was calculating in my head. "I mean . . . from my perspective that's probably a good thing. I can get the time off now, but in a couple of months, who knows. Where are they filming?"

"Well, that's the best bit—they're aiming for the *Love Island* audience, so it's being filmed on this exclusive boutique resort in the Indian Ocean, which sounds pretty sweet."

"Wow." I was impressed in spite of myself. "I thought Ari said they didn't have much budget?"

"I don't think they do. Baz let slip that the resort's owned by an old school pal of his. It sounds like it's kind of a new venture—I'm actually not sure it's open to the public yet—and I got the distinct impression Baz is getting it for free . . . like, PR? You know, if people see the show they're going to want to travel to the island, that kind of thing."

"Are we going to turn up and find they're still building it?"

"Baz's assistant sent me some pictures of the island," Nico said, not quite answering my question, but not quite evading it either. He turned off the kettle and opened his phone, passing it to me. While he put teabags in mugs and poured the water, I clicked on the WhatsApp link—to a site dubiously named "Effing Productions"—and a gallery opened up, the screen turning an almost unbelievable shade of blue that seemed so out of place in our dark little attic that I blinked.

"Wow! Sorry, that has to be a filter."

"Right? Wait until you get to the coral."

As I flicked through the pictures, even I had to admit it was not just a filter making this place look good. White sand. Palm trees. Water so clear you could see the fish swimming through it. A scattering of little straw-roofed huts . . . four or five? Maybe six. It was hard to tell, as they were mostly identical and were cleverly situated among the palms so that each looked completely private. Only one stood out—a villa like ones I'd seen in pictures of the Maldives, out over the shimmering water on wooden stilts. Hammocks swung from porches, and inside were white beds scattered with rose petals and immaculate pebble-tiled bathrooms with rainforest showerheads. It was a stark contrast from bleak, rainy east London.

"Holy fuck, Nico. It looks incredible."

"Doesn't it?" Nico was smirking. He knew he'd scored a hit with the pictures. "It's elimination, so we have to commit to minimum two weeks, maximum ten, plus the winner has to agree to do PR on return to the UK. I don't totally understand the format, but from what I could make out, each week there's some kind of challenge, and I think the loser is out, and the winner can pick who they couple up with, so the couples shake up every week."

If there had been a soundtrack to our conversation, this would have been followed by a record scratch.

"I'm sorry, *what?* You very much did not mention the recoupling part."

"Didn't I?" Nico looked a little uncomfortable, and more than a little guilty. Judging by his expression, Baz absolutely *had* mentioned it, and he'd deliberately failed to tell me. "I mean, it's not a big deal. It's just for the cameras."

"Are you telling me this is *Love Island,* only the twist is wife swapping?"

"I mean, I don't think anyone taking part is married, so technically—" Nico began, and then saw from my expression that this particular argument was not the one that was going to win me over, and hastily changed tack. "But the point is, it's just to mix things up. You don't *actually* have to shag the person you're coupled up with. It just means you're a couple within the show's format. You could choose to stay coupled with the person you enter the show with, but obviously they're not going to want everyone to do that. I imagine couples who stick together too closely are going to find themselves eliminated in the tasks."

"You mean they'll rig the outcome to get rid of faithful couples?" I knew my voice sounded shocked, and I could hear the primness, but somehow I couldn't stop myself. Nico rolled his eyes.

"Lil, these things are *always* rigged. It's not *Jeopardy!*—nobody's watching this to see how good your general knowledge is. They want drama. They want big characters. They want screaming arguments and people shagging in the Jacuzzi for the cameras. Anyone boring is going to get the axe."

"So is that what you'll be doing after I'm gone? Shagging in the Jacuzzi?"

"What? No! Stop twisting my words. I didn't *say* that. I said it has to *look* like that. I'm not going to be shagging anyone. But yeah, maybe I'll shed a few tears after you've gone, talk about how you were my soulmate, cry on some girl's shoulder while she strokes my hair. I'm a fantasy first boyfriend, remember? That's what they'll want from me."

"And I'm girl-next-door fuckable," I said with a touch of bitterness. "So what does that leave me doing? Fucking the guy in the next villa?"

"Over my dead body," Nico said, and now he gripped me by the waist, kissing the side of my neck. "Seriously, Lil, this is an acting job. That's why they're contacting acting agents. You're not an actor and they know it—they'll be fine with you failing the first task, maybe the second—you'll be on a plane home within a fortnight. And I'll melt everyone's hearts with how broken I am after you've gone, make a strategic friend-zone alliance with some heart-of-gold influencer, and lose with good grace in the final. And then I'll come home as the abs that launched a thousand TikToks."

"Ugh." I pulled myself out of his grip and picked up the tea he'd left on the side, nursing it as I walked to the window, more to give myself time to think than because I really wanted it. "Nico, I don't know. I really wish you'd explained all this before I spoke to Professor Bianchi."

"Wait, you spoke to him?" Nico's face lit up. I nodded, almost reluctantly.

"I did."

"And what did he say?"

"He said I could have two weeks, if I wrote up the chikungunya results while I was there."

"You're kidding?" Nico's face had split into a wide, exuberant grin, and now he advanced towards me, his arms held out, and an expression that made me hold out my brimming cup of hot tea.

"Do not even think about bear-hugging me again. I don't want third-degree burns!"

"But you've got the time off? We're really doing this?"

"Wife swapping?"

"Going on the trip of a lifetime, you idiot!" Nico said. I tried not to smile, but it was impossible not to—Nico's excitement was so transparent and so infectious that I felt the corners of my mouth twitch in spite of myself.

"Lyla?"

"I don't know. I need time to think."

"Think about what? About an all-expenses-paid trip to paradise?" He fished his phone out of his back pocket and held it up in front of me; the tiny island, white and green, glowing like a pearl-crusted emerald in a sea of blue. "Are you *really* going to turn this down, Lil?"

I turned my head away from the screen, away from Nico's pleading face, but it was a mistake—what faced me instead was the soot-streaked skylight lashed with rain.

Why was I holding out on this? What did I really have here other than a shitty job and a shitty commute and absolutely fuck all to look forward to? I couldn't even hold up Christmas as a carrot to myself—

it was January, and the gray London winter stretched out in front of me like a prison sentence—a prison sentence with the unemployment queue waiting at the far end.

Could this really solve everything? If it actually got made—and I was doubtful about that; Nico had been in enough "sure things" for me to know how shaky these promises were—then Nico was right, this really could transform his prospects. And if it didn't . . . well, it would be two weeks in one of those adorable little huts.

"At least let Ari set up a meeting with Baz," Nico begged, and I turned my gaze away from the skylight and looked at him, really looked, for the first time in what felt like a long time. I'd been expecting Nico's trademark knee-weakening smile, but what I got was something far more devastating. He looked . . . worried. And I realized, maybe for the first time, that Nico's eternal optimism wasn't as effortless as it looked. That maybe he was facing the same crunch point that I was, the same realization that if the next roll of the dice didn't come good, he might be out of the game. Maybe this was a last chance for both of us.

I felt myself giving way.

"Okay. I'll talk to Baz."

"Yes!" Nico punched the air. "I fucking love you, Lyla!"

"It's just a meeting! They might not even want me."

"Of course they'll want you. How could anyone not want you? You're a fucking scientific genius *and* you're hot. What more could anyone want?"

A scientific genius wouldn't have ended up in a research dead end with a publication record that had holes in it the size of the Grand Canyon, I thought a little wearily. But Nico was still speaking.

". . . and you know what—I know you can only take two weeks off, but I don't care. *We're* the perfect couple, no matter who takes that prize."

"We are," I said. I put down the cup, stood on tiptoe, and kissed

Nico on the lips, feeling his wide smile against my mouth, irrepress-
ible even as he kissed me back.

"This is going to change everything." He spoke the words close to
my ear as he gathered me into him, squeezing me tight. "I can feel it
in my bones."

I could only hope he was right.

02/15—02:14 a.m.

Over Easy, can you hear me? The wind is really picking up and I'm getting seriously concerned. Is there any kind of storm shelter on the island?

02/15—02:16 a.m.

Over Easy, if you're receiving this, please come in, this is urgent. The storm is getting really bad and I think we might need to evacuate. In fact just now— Oh God!

CHAPTER 3

IT'S ALWAYS DIFFICULT explaining what you do as a scientist to outsiders—spike proteins and viral entry pathways isn't everyone's cup of tea at the best of times, even post-Covid when everyone and their uncle fancied themselves as a virologist. It's doubly hard when you're on a Zoom call with a group of producers who keep talking off mic. When Baz called me a "boffin" for the second time, I felt my patience snap.

"We tend to prefer scientist," I said, a little shortly.

"What's that?" Baz said, leaning into the camera. "I didn't catch that, sweetheart?" He had a strong Australian accent, and the screen-name at the bottom of his picture read *Baz—Effing Productions.*

"The boffin thing," I said. "It's just . . . you know, it's not how I tend to describe myself. I'd say scientist. Or, you know, virologist if you want to get down in the weeds."

"Ha," Baz said, grinning widely. He had an extremely '90s tongue piercing, which was distracting on camera. You could see it when he laughed, and he kept playing with it when other people were talking, clicking it against his teeth. "You're funny. I like that."

Funny? Before I could figure out how to explain not just that I wasn't joking, but that I didn't even know what the joke was supposed to be, the conversation moved on to questions about mine and Nico's relationship—how long we'd been together, where we saw ourselves in five years.

"We've been together three years," Nico said, squeezing my hand. I opened my mouth to correct him—we'd *met* three years ago, but we'd actually been together slightly over two, and even that was pushing it. But then I remembered, I wasn't at work, and I closed it again. No one was going to quiz us for supporting documentation and calculation methodology.

Nico was still talking and had moved on from first dates to his five-year plan.

"I mean . . . this is hard to answer without sounding either pathetically humble or delusionally ambitious, but I'm an actor—I want to be acting. I guess, you know, thinking about the career paths of people I admire, I see myself very much in the James McAvoy, Adam Driver kind of mold: indie word of mouth, critical acclaim, moving on to mainstream success, but keeping the artistic integrity. A bit of theater here and there, keeping myself artistically grounded, not letting success change my commitment to my craft . . ."

In the corner of the screen I saw Ari shift in his seat.

". . . what I'm saying is, where's the *Skins* for my generation? Where are the edgy, authentic depictions of life in your thirties?"

"Uh . . . yeah." Baz had clearly tuned out and was looking at something his assistant was showing him. "And, uh, Leela, sweetheart, what about you?"

"Me?" I was taken aback. I should have seen the question coming but I'd been so preoccupied by Nico's answer that I'd failed to anticipate being asked the same thing. "Um, it's Lyla actually," I said slowly, buying myself time to think. It wasn't just that Nico's answer was sort of delusional—did he really think that he was on an Adam Driver career path? I might as well compare myself to Rosalind Franklin. It was also that not one word of his answer had featured me, or indeed any kind of homelife at all. "Five years. I mean, I—"

I stopped. Where *did* I see myself? In five years I would be thirty-seven. A few weeks ago I might have answered, if not confidently then at least optimistically, heading up a research team on something exciting—dengue, maybe; there was some exciting work on IgA antibodies coming out of the US—with a permanent academic post. I'd have bought a flat somewhere in east London, convenient for my mum to come and stay. Maybe even a little house, if I were prepared to commute. There might be kids on the horizon—if not actual babies, at least the idea of one, in the not-too-distant future.

Now, after the conversation I'd had the other day with Professor Bianchi, I honestly wasn't sure. It felt like I'd screwed my chances with this project, and I badly needed a few publication credits on my CV—the long gap with no papers was starting to look ominous. And how long would it take me to find another more promising project, get hired, complete the post-doc, write up a couple of papers and get them through the publication hurdles? Three years? That was pushing it. The chikungunya research had been supposed to give me a boost onto the next rung of the ladder. Unfortunately, that rung had just broken.

I realized every face on the screen was looking at me, waiting for my answer. Plus Nico.

Dammit. Nico. Where *was* Nico in all this exactly? Living in my terraced house in suburbia?

"Five years," I said again, feeling their eyes on me. "God. I . . . I don't totally know. I'm kind of at a crossroads, to be honest. I have to make some decisions."

"Really." Baz's eyes had focused again, and now he looked interested, his voice drawling as he stretched out the two syllables. "Is that so? What kind of decisions, sweetheart?"

Fuck. This was a conversation for me and Nico after a lot of wine, not for a sober Zoom call in the presence of Baz, Ari, and bunch of people I'd never even heard of.

"I just . . ." I swallowed, trying to stop my gaze from flickering nervously sideways to see how Nico was taking this. "I guess you could say my last project didn't go so well. I have to decide, I mean, I have to decide if science is still for me. It's a tough world. Your profile is really everything."

"Well, that's where we come in," Baz said. He was leaning forward. "Let's be honest, not everyone can win the pot, but you're all going to come out of this a hell of a lot more high-profile than you went in, if this show is the hit we think it's going to be."

I pressed my lips together, forcing a smile that somehow stretched my lips without feeling in the least bit genuine. The kind of profile I would get from *One Perfect Couple* wasn't going to matter a toss in the academic world. In fact, possibly the reverse. I couldn't imagine anyone taking my funding application seriously if they'd seen me frolicking in a bikini on a tropical beach. Fortunately, I didn't think grant committees were likely to be the core audience for a brand-new streaming channel focusing exclusively on reality TV.

Still, Baz's mention of "the pot" had given me the chance to pin down some of the more elusive variables still floating around the whole project.

"The pot you mentioned," I said. "How much is it exactly? And while we're on the subject, can you talk a bit more about the structure of the show? I'm unclear how this is all going to work."

"Sure," said one of the other producers smoothly, leaning in towards the camera. I got the impression that Baz was not much of a details guy. "So, the pot isn't fixed, but will be determined partly by how everyone does in the tasks—the idea is that you'll all be contributing to build it up. And then at the end . . . well, I can't talk too much about that, but there will be a mechanism for splitting it between the final contestants, or possibly not. It could be taken home by just one person. Those details are still confidential."

"Okay," I said, "but assuming everyone hit their targets and got the maximum possible, how much are we talking?"

There was a short, uncomfortable silence. The producer flicked his eyes at Baz, but before either of them could speak, Ari, Nico's agent, leaned forward and unmuted himself.

"Lyla, I think the thing is, as Baz mentioned, the prize here, at least as far as people like Nico are concerned, really isn't the money. Whatever the prize pot actually turns out to be, it's going to be small beans compared to the subsequent professional opportunities the show opens up."

"Sure," I said, "but—"

But then I felt Nico squeezing my hand. I looked at him. He was smiling, but there was an unmistakable, *let this go* behind the smile. I took a breath.

"Okay. I take that point. So, what about the format and so on?"

"It's elimination," the unnamed producer said. "Ten contestants at the start, and they'll get whittled down one by one, each week over nine weeks. There will be some strategic advantage to being in a couple for the tasks, so there'll be a recoupling opportunity each week, and you might find there's a few twists and turns to shake things up, but again, the details of that are top secret at this stage. All you need to know is five couples go in, one couple comes out. And it could be you!"

"But—" I started, but Baz was speaking, his microphone overriding mine, and he clearly felt like he was the one who was supposed to be asking the questions, not me.

"So we know about Nico, from Ari here"—he gestured at the place where Ari's face presumably was on his screen, although confusingly it was the opposite side from mine—"but let's hear a bit more about *you*, Leela. Would you call yourself a feminist?"

"A *feminist*?" I was puzzled. I wasn't sure what I'd been expecting on this Zoom call—questions about my relationship with Nico seemed fair game—but this was a surprise. What on earth was Baz trying to find out? "I mean . . . I guess so. I believe in gender equality. Doesn't everyone?"

"Define gender equality?"

"I guess . . . having the same pay for the same work . . . the same professional opportunities . . . the same bodily autonomy . . ." I was more and more mystified.

"And you wouldn't say you had that already?" Baz was leaning forward towards the camera, frowning, but he didn't look put off by my responses; if anything they seemed to have encouraged him.

"Well." I was completely at sea now. "I mean . . . I'm a scientist. If in doubt, I look at what the data is telling me, and according to the data, no, we definitely aren't there yet. In my own industry alone, less than a quarter of science professors in the UK are female, even though women make up nearly half the workforce."

"Citing your sources, I like that," Baz said with a grin, even though I hadn't cited any sources at all. Actually, my stats were from an article I'd read in *Nature* a few years ago, but Baz had no way of knowing that. What on earth was he on about? My jokey remark to Nico about needing a wax and to lose five pounds came back to me, and an image floated into my mind: Baz, turning to his assistant, concerned, *We gotta find out if she's a hairy Mary under that lab coat!* I stifled a laugh, and then hastily straightened my face, remembering that we were on camera. Fortunately, Baz was still talking. "And your politics. Would you say they're left of center . . . centrist . . . right . . . ?"

"I guess . . . center left? Sorry, is this relevant?"

"Sorry, sorry, you're right. I got offtrack," Baz said with a wave of his hand. "But finding out what makes you tick, what makes you different . . . sure, that's important. We don't want to end up with five identikit couples on the island, we want to get people from right across the spectrum. I suppose that's what we're going for with this show—that's what's going to sell it to Real TV. We want real couples—real authenticity, you know? None of this *Love Island* manufactured shite. We want real partnerships, tested to the hilt in the white heat of competition."

"If you're looking for authenticity, you've come to the right place," Nico said, putting his arm around me. "Lyla and me have that in spades, and we're in it to win. Right, Lil?"

"Right," I said, stretching my lips again in that fake smile. It felt like the meeting was coming to a conclusion without any of my questions being answered. Nothing had been clarified. There was no real information at all—just smoke and mirrors—and it was completely antithetical to the way I was used to working. Every fiber in me wanted to pin Baz down and get a proper answer from him. But I could feel Nico beside me practically begging me not to fuck this up for him—and I guessed this was probably just how TV worked. *Fake it till you make it*, wasn't that what they said about Hollywood? Or was that Silicon Valley? Either way, it was a long way from the world I knew—faking anything at all was the polar opposite of good science.

"Well"—Baz looked across at the colleague sitting next to him and raised one eyebrow, and when she nodded, he turned back to the camera—"I think we can safely say you'll be joining us on the island in a couple of weeks."

His words gave me a jolt like an electric shock. First of all, I hadn't agreed to this yet. This was only supposed to be a chat. Second, a couple of *weeks*? I shot a panicked look at Ari, and then at Nico, but he was looking excitedly at Baz, who was still speaking.

"My assistant Camille"—he indicated a blond girl sitting far back, almost out of frame, who leaned forward and gave a shy little wave—"will be in touch about booking flights and so on, so keep an eye out for her email. We'll be flying into Jakarta and then travelling by boat to the actual island, and I assume Ari's shown you the pictures? It's my mate's place—brand-new, you'll be the first-ever guests to stay there, and words really don't do it justice."

"It looks *incredible*," Nico said, very sincerely.

"Ari, Camille will send over the contracts and confidentiality agreements today," Baz said. "Are you happy for her to contact Leela and Nico direct about the flights? We really need to get booking those, and she'll need their passport numbers and all that bullshit."

"Sure, sure," Ari said expansively. "Camille, just drop me a line and I'll hook you guys up."

"Great. And in the meantime, Leela, Nico, get picking out your favorite bathers. We'll see you in paradise!"

"See you in paradise!" Nico shot back, his grin almost wider than his face, and I heard my own voice, like a pale echo repeating the phrase, with a good deal less conviction.

"See you in paradise."

And then the screen went dark.

There was a moment's silence. Then Nico turned to look at me, his face alight with enthusiasm.

"Well? What did you think?"

"I think that all went incredibly fast," I said a little edgily. "It was only supposed to be a chat, but everyone, including Ari, seemed to think it was a done deal."

"Well, hey." Nico looked a little flustered. "I mean . . . nothing's signed. But are you seriously going to turn this down? I mean, God, this is the real thing! We're going to be famous—properly famous! Think about what this would mean for my career!"

"I *am* thinking about that," I said. "That's the only reason I was on the call. But didn't you get a bit of a weird vibe from Baz?"

"From Baz?" Nico was taken aback. "What do you mean? I thought he was great."

"Really? I thought he came across as a bit of a . . ." I stopped, struggling to find the word. "I don't know. A bit of a chancer?"

The truth was, though I wouldn't have said it to Nico, on the call he'd reminded me of Ari, Nico's agent, who talked a very impressive talk but who somehow always had an excuse for why the money hadn't come through, or he hadn't done some very simple thing that Nico had asked. Nico had signed with him straight out of acting college on the promise of TV, riches, and stardom. Seven years later, Ari had yet to deliver anything more impressive than a few walk-on roles and a minor speaking part in *Holby City*, all of which I was fairly sure Nico could have got on his own. His much vaunted but never specified "contacts" had never seemed to come through—until now at least.

Because this was the thing: on paper, *One Perfect Couple* seemed to be the real deal. It *was* major, it *was* telly, and it *had* come about through one of Ari's contacts. Okay, there was probably no money involved—unless Nico won, which seemed statistically unlikely. But if the format caught on, there was every chance of this raising Nico's profile considerably and I had to give Ari props for that. There was just something about the whole thing that didn't seem right.

"A chancer?" Nico looked at me like I was mad. "In what way?"

"Well . . ." I scrabbled to try to remember one of the warning bells that had gone off during the call. Effing Productions. Calling me Leela. I didn't think Nico would care about any of those and I certainly couldn't say that he reminded me of Ari. "Okay . . . for example, what do you think Baz meant about selling it to Real TV?"

"What do you mean?"

"When he was talking about us being an authentic couple, he said, *that's what's going to sell it to Real TV.* But I thought they'd already sold it? Ari made it sound like it was a done deal. Their flagship show and all that."

Nico waved a hand.

"You're reading too much into it. It's just a figure of speech. He probably meant that's what Real will like about you and me."

"I guess. I just . . . I don't know. I was surprised no one from Real was on the call."

"They're busy people, Lyla. I mean, let's be clear, they're setting up a whole new TV network! It's not surprising they don't have time for meetings about flight times."

"Ugh." I stood up and walked to the window, staring out over the grimy rooftops. There was a dead pigeon lying in the gutter opposite and I turned away. "I just . . . I want to be supportive, Nico, I really do, but I just wish they'd answered a few more of my questions."

"Look." Nico came over to me and put his arms around me. He pressed my cheek against his chest, and I could feel how much he'd been working out, presumably with the prospect of *One Perfect Couple* in mind. "Look, Lyla, this isn't your comfort zone, I get that. TV's weird. It's not science-y types dotting every *i* and crossing every *t*—there's a lot of shifting parameters and building the plane on the fly. But it's not as seat-of-your-pants as it seems from the outside; there *is* a process to protect everyone involved. There's contracts and legalese and all the stuff that's Ari's job to worry about. That's what I pay him for—he's got years of experience and lawyers coming out the wazoo. He's not going to let us get caught up in anything that's not kosher."

But you don't actually pay him, I thought. *You don't make any money, and a percentage of nothing is nothing.* I couldn't say the words though. I wasn't that cruel.

"So . . . are we really doing this?" I asked instead. The question was more to myself than to Nico. But it was Nico who answered, looking down at me, his face incredulous.

"Hell yes we're doing this. Are you kidding? You don't turn an opportunity like this down."

I nodded. I was feeling slightly sick—but Nico was right. This *was* the crunch point of his career. If *One Perfect Couple* was the hit Nico hoped, it could change the whole direction of his life—and maybe mine. And just because my own career felt like it was heading for the rocks, it didn't mean I could deny Nico his chance.

"Lyla?" Nico said now, tipping my face up to look at him. "Lyla? Please tell me you *are* up for this?"

"Yes," I said weakly. "Yes, I'm up for this." And then, in an attempt to convince myself, "I am really up for this." And then, as the reality of what we were proposing sank in, "Fuck, I'll need to buy a bikini. I don't suppose my Speedo one-piece is going to cut it."

"A bikini?" Nico raised one eyebrow. "I think you mean biki*nis*, plural. In fact, you probably need a whole new wardrobe. Get yourself down to H&M with my credit card."

"What about you?" I said, ignoring the fact that Nico's credit card was so maxed out I'd be lucky to get a single pair of socks. "What does the fantasy first boyfriend wear on the beach? A crisp white T-shirt?"

Nico smirked.

"Maybe. But I'm not planning on wearing a top for much of the filming." He lifted up the hem of his shirt and pointed at his washboard stomach. "These abs didn't come cheap, you know."

"Of course," I said. Somehow, now that it was a done deal, now that I had actually said the words, *yes, I am up for this*, my nerves were fading a little. Nico was right. Ari wouldn't let us sign up for anything dodgy. And I needed to get away, we both did. "You owe it to all those hours in the gym. And your thirteen-year-old fan base, of course."

"Well, exactly," Nico said. He slid his arms down my back to my bum, squeezing my arse with both hands. "We can't all be girl-next-door fuckable, you know."

"Girl-next-door fuckable," I growled, nettled all over again by the stupidity of the term. "I'll give you girl-next-door fuckable."

"Oh, I've already *got* girl-next-door fuckable," Nico said, smirking. "She's right here, waiting to be fucked." He hoisted me up, his strong arms underneath my butt, and I wrapped my legs around his waist, laughing down at him.

"Is that so? That's quite the set of assumptions right there, mister."

"Well, there's only one way to test this hypothesis, Dr. Santiago," Nico said, grinning up at me as he walked me backwards to the bedroom door. "And I think I've got just enough time before the gym."

02/15—06:34 a.m.

Hello? Hello? Is anyone out there? This is an emergency Mayday call. We are stranded on an island in the Indian Ocean after the storm last night. I don't have any coordinates, but we flew into Jakarta and sailed southwest on a yacht called *Over Easy*. The yacht is gone and we have no idea what's happened to it. Several of our group are seriously injured and need medical help. I don't know how long the battery on this radio will last, but if anyone can hear me, please send help. I repeat, this is an emergency Mayday call for medical assistance. Can anyone hear me? Can anyone help? Over?

CHAPTER 4

THE NEXT FEW days were a whirlwind. Somehow, unbelievably, it seemed like we *were* actually doing this, and almost within hours, Ari was sending over draft contracts with terrifying nondisclosure clauses, and Camille was asking whether we'd prefer to fly out of Gatwick or Heathrow.

The strangest thing was that apart from me, everyone from Ari to Professor Bianchi was acting like this whole thing was perfectly normal. Professor Bianchi didn't seem to understand that this was any different from your regular last-minute winter break—although I hadn't exactly tried to spell it out. Ari appeared to think that dropping everything and flying to Indonesia on two weeks' notice was totally reasonable. And maybe it was, in his line of work.

Nico's friends messaged with sincere-sounding congratulations that unsuccessfully masked their professional jealousy. Mine made envious comments about free holidays and winter tans.

In fact, the only person who raised any doubts was my mum, who sounded bewildered when I outlined the situation to her over the phone, the weekend before we were due to fly out.

"A reality TV show? But, Lyla love, why? You don't even watch those programs."

"It's for Nico," I said, knowing as the words left my mouth how lame they sounded. "He really wants it."

"Is he having some kind of midlife crisis?"

I laughed.

"I'm not sure Nico would thank you for calling him middle-aged, Mum. But no, it's not that. It's a career move for him. If they go big, these reality TV shows can be great exposure."

"But why do you have to go?"

"Because—" I stopped. *Because it's a couple's TV show*, would have been the easy answer, although I wasn't honestly sure if I was allowed to say even that—everything about the format was supposed to be confidential according to the NDA I'd signed. But it wasn't really the truth, and it wasn't what my mum had meant. The fact that the format was couples was why I'd been invited. It wasn't why I'd said yes.

Why I'd said yes . . . well, I wasn't sure if I was ready to probe too deeply on that. Part of it was the knowledge that Nico and I were at a crunch point. Not a midlife crisis exactly, but we couldn't carry on like this, him banging his fist on a closed door, me increasingly resentful of supporting his dreams when my own were receding further and further. Nico needed a break—and so did I, just in different ways.

"I just think," my mum said, filling the silence, "that this is the wrong time for all of this. You're thirty-two, love, you and Nico should be settling down. And I can't imagine your boss is too pleased."

"Mum, Nico needs this, and I love him," I said. "And that's what you do for people when you love them. You support them."

"Well, we all need a break from the cold, and I suppose at least it's a free holiday," my mum said resignedly, and I laughed.

MY MUM'S REMARK about the cold came back to me the second the plane touched down in Jakarta. Of course I'd known on paper that February in Indonesia was a completely different climate to February in London, but somehow knowing that fact in theory didn't make the sauna blast of humid air any less shocking. We'd walked onto the airplane wearing raincoats, boots, and scarves. As I made my way down the steps to the tarmac, the sweat was soaking into my bra before I'd even reached the ground.

I'd made the mistake of trying to start the chikungunya paper on the connecting flight from Dubai, and now I felt almost drunk with tiredness, in contrast to Nico, who'd downed four gin-and-tonics and then slept for six solid hours, despite the cramped economy seat. He looked fresh and positively bouncing with excitement as he wheeled his carry-on to the air-conditioned bus, whereas I felt gray and drained. When I caught sight of my reflection in the bus window, I didn't look anything like a contestant on a reality TV show. I looked like what I was—a stressed, mildly hung over scientist who was trying to spin straw out of gold and form a publishable paper out of dog-crap results.

Luggage claim and customs were the usual nightmare of wailing babies and grown men pushing and shoving to get to a case that would come around the carousel again in less than five minutes. From the aggression of my fellow travelers, you'd have thought that the bags disappearing behind the plastic curtain were about to get incinerated, rather than popping out unharmed a few feet farther on.

But at last we were through passport control and blinking in the arrival hall, scanning the crowds for a familiar face, or at least a sign with a name we recognized. Camille's email had promised "meet and greet on arrival," but as we passed driver after driver, I realized she hadn't actually said what to look out for. Nico's *actual* surname was Rice, Nicholas Rice, in fact. Nico Reese was a stage name. But I couldn't see anything saying Reese/Santiago, Rice/Santiago, or even Effing Productions.

And then I turned and saw a bored-looking man in a suit, holding up a small whiteboard on which was scrawled NICO LILLA PERFECT COUPLE.

I nudged Nico.

"Do you think that's us?"

"A perfect couple?" A grin spread across Nico's face. "Hell yeah." He yanked his case sideways through the flow of irritated people, like someone fording a particularly turbulent river, and said "Here from the TV show? I'm Nico. This is Lyla."

"Hello, Pak!" The driver broke into a welcoming smile. "Welcome sir, welcome miss. Welcome to Indonesia. May I take your cases?"

THE TRAFFIC IN Jakarta turned out to be one jam after another, and in spite of the honking horns and stop-start junctions, I fell asleep before we got out of the city. I awoke as we went over a set of speed bumps, jolting my head against Nico's shoulder, and looked out of the window, wiping the drool off my cheek. The high-rise buildings and concrete sprawl of Jakarta were gone—replaced by a small harbor filled with bobbing yachts. The sun was high in the cloudless sky, and I could feel its heat despite the air-conditioning blowing in my face from the car's vents.

"Sir, miss, we are here," the driver said over his shoulder. The display on the dash said it was almost twelve noon. Nico put his arm around my shoulder and squeezed hard.

"Excited?"

Not really, was the honest answer. *Exhausted*, was the word I'd have chosen, closely followed by *hungry*, and *nervous*. But I knew that wasn't what Nico wanted me to say, so I smiled weakly.

"Yeah. Let the adventure begin."

There was a woman standing at the quayside with a clipboard, and now Nico unfastened his seat belt, opened the door, and slid out before the driver was able to hurry round to open it for him.

"Hi . . ." I heard indistinctly through the car door as I scrabbled around for my belongings. ". . . Nico . . . so great to meet you . . ." And then, as the driver opened the door, "Lyla, come and meet Camille!"

Camille—the girl from the Zoom call. So this was happening. It was *actually* happening. The realization was as shocking as the weather in Jakarta had been. Of course it was happening—it was what I had agreed to, wasn't it? And yet . . .

I pasted a frozen smile on my face and waved.

"Just a second!"

I'd lost a shoe at some point in the journey, and I had to fish around in the footwell. When I finally located it, under the seat in front, I straightened up to see Camille standing beside me, holding out her hand.

"Lyla! So great to finally meet you properly!"

"Camille, hi. Uh . . ." I shifted the shoe into my other hand, and then shook hers, rather awkwardly. I was horribly conscious of my disheveled state, and the fact that I'd been wearing the same clothes for two days and hadn't thought to reapply deodorant. "Really nice to put a face to a . . . well, I suppose we met on Zoom, but it's not the same, is it. Sorry I look such a . . ." I made a gesture towards my sleep-crumpled face and mussed hair, and Camille waved a hand.

"Oh! God, don't even. You must have been traveling for days. There'll be plenty of time to get freshened up before the meeting."

"Meeting?" Nico was instantly alert.

"You're the last to arrive! So as soon as you're ready, we're going to up-anchor, and then everyone will gather for a big roundtable Q&A on how this is all going to work. You can meet the other contestants, chat to Baz, ask anything you want . . . it's your chance to really settle in and get to know everyone."

I blinked. I had the disquieting sensation of having stepped onto a roller coaster that was starting before I was fully prepared.

Nico, on the other hand, was clearly already strapped in and ready for the ride.

"We're the last?" He looked put out, and I could see he was calculating how this might have affected his chances, and imagining the others busily forging alliances, making friends, and agreeing on strategies. "I didn't know that. How long has everyone else been here?"

"Uh . . . not too long," Camille said a little vaguely. "Baz and I have been here just over a week and the other contestants have been turning up on and off since then. Bayer and Angel were on the flight before yours, so they've only been here a couple of hours longer than you. I think Conor and Zana were the first to arrive."

"Great," Nico said a little snippily, but then I saw him rein himself in and force himself to be charming. "Well, last but not least, eh? I can't tell you how excited Lyla and I are to be here, aren't we, Lil?"

"Yeah, so excited," I managed weakly.

"Well, the feeling is *very* much mutual," Camille said warmly, and gave my arm a little squeeze. "Now, this beauty"—she gestured to the largest boat in the harbor, a big gin-palace-style yacht moored right by the quay—"is our ride." I looked across, taking in the glittering white and chrome, the stacked decks, the hot tub. *Over Easy* was painted on the hull in flowing letters, and below it in smaller writing *Kupang*, which I guessed was probably the home port, though I had no idea where Kupang was. A mahogany-and-chrome gangway stretched across the gap to the quay, and as I watched, a white-uniformed man began uncoiling one of the ropes lashing the boat to a bollard, preparing for . . . I'd been going to say *takeoff* but I was pretty sure that wasn't right. In the prow, somehow completing the picture, was a stunningly beautiful woman with long silver hair, leaning over the railings and smoking a cigarette. As I watched, she lifted her chin and blew a perfect smoke ring into the still air. It hung there for a moment, rising into the cloudless sky, and then dispersed.

"Isn't she gorgeous?" Camille said. For a moment I thought she was talking about the woman smoking, and the remark took me aback. It was true, but it also seemed a little objectifying. Then I realized she was talking about the ship.

"Um . . . yes, very impressive," I said, trying to echo her enthusiasm.

"I think they're pretty much ready to up-anchor, so let's grab your luggage and get you on board!"

I was just turning to help the driver with our cases when a voice came from behind me.

"Excuse me, miss, may I speak with you?"

I turned, thinking for a moment that the speaker was address-ing me, but it was one of the crew members, and he was talking to Camille.

"Of course," she said politely. "What is it?"

"The captain would like to discuss the weather reports. There is a storm coming in. Two, three days away, so it is possible it will—" He stopped, searching for the word and then finished. "—dissipate before it reaches us. But—"

"Let me stop you," Camille said with a smile. "This is a conver-sation for my boss, Mr. Ferrier. Shall I ask him to come up to the bridge?"

They moved off, still speaking earnestly.

Great, I thought, as Nico and I helped the driver heave the cases out of the car boot and onto the quay. A storm. Just what I wanted to hear. I just had to hope we'd be safely off the *Over Easy* and tucked up on the island before it hit.

"I'VE GOT TO be honest." Nico was looking around the very cramped cabin we'd been allocated for the boat ride. "This isn't exactly what I was anticipating."

As I followed his gaze around the little room, I saw what he meant—rather than a plush double suite, Camille had shown us into a small bunkroom that resembled a cross-channel ferry more than a luxury yacht. It didn't remotely match what I'd seen of the top deck, which meant, I was fairly sure, that this had to be the staff quarters.

There was a tiny salt-misted porthole, practically at the waterline, two narrow beds stacked on top of each other, and so little floor space that we had to edge around our suitcases.

Still, there *were* beds, and there was also a working shower, which was really all I cared about at this point. And, as a small silver lining, it was highly unlikely they'd be doing any filming in such a cramped space, which meant I was safe for the moment. There was barely room for a third person, let alone a TV camera.

"I guess we won't have to put up with it for long. Did she say how long we'd be on the sea?"

"No." Nico was looking thoughtful. "But the implication was definitely that we'd be sleeping here tonight. This island must be more remote than I imagined."

"Well, look, I need to shower before this bloody meeting." I rubbed my hands over my face. I couldn't think of anything I wanted less than to attend an all-hands debrief right now. I wanted to eat my own bodyweight in carbs and then sleep for approximately eleven hours. "I feel absolutely gross. Is that okay?"

"What?" Nico was looking at a folder he'd found on the bed. "Oh yeah, no problem. I'll jump in after you if there's time, but I feel fine."

I was about to respond, when the boat gave a sudden jolt. Nico looked up, his expression alert. I put out my hand, steadying myself against the wall. Seconds later came the shuddering roar of the engine kicking in. It ticked over for a few moments, and then the sound rose to a higher pitch, and we began to move. I felt my stomach pitch uneasily as the boat lifted against a wave and then rolled down. We hadn't even left the harbor.

"I guess this is us," Nico said. He grinned, teeth white against his five-o'clock shadow. "No going back now!"

"No going back," I echoed, but my own smile felt anything but sincere.

In the shower, with the hot water running down my scalp and

removing some of the sweat and grime, I felt a little better, but the strange shifting sensation continued, and more than once I had to brace myself as the ship caught an awkward wave. I was just rinsing the foam out of my hair when there was a banging on the door that made me jump.

"Who is it?"

"Nico!" he yelled. "And Camille. They're ready for us upstairs. Are you done?"

Ugh.

"Almost," I called back. I wound a towel around myself and looked about for a hair dryer. No bloody hair dryer. Not even the kind that was wired into the wall. And I hadn't brought one. Great. "You go up, I'll find you."

There was a murmur of voices and then Nico called back, "Okay. Apparently it's two flights up, then head towards the stern. See you there."

IT TOOK ME ten minutes to wrangle my long dark hair into something that looked slightly less like I'd been pulled through a hedge backwards and get into one of the new dresses I'd bought for the trip. As I made my way along the narrow corridor to the stairs Nico had mentioned, it was plain that this was no cross-channel ferry, but a much smaller boat without stabilizers. I held on to the banister with both hands as I began the climb, feeling an answering drop in my stomach every time the boat heaved itself up a wave and slapped down the other side.

At the top of the second flight, I had to take a minute to orientate myself and figure out which way was the front of the boat. Stern, Nico had said. That meant the front, right? No. The back. There was another juddering slap as the boat crested a wave and I felt nausea rise inside me, and took a long, deliberate breath through my nose, looking out of the window at the horizon as I did. The sea was the same bright blue as the sky, just a shade darker, and the sun was beating down with an enthusiasm that felt almost insulting. *Look!* it seemed to be saying. *It's not even stormy!*

Swallowing, I turned and groped my way along the corridor against the direction of the boat, following the faint sound of voices, barely audible above the noise of the waves and the hum of the engine, but growing louder the farther I went. At last, when I was almost at the very back of the boat, I got to a glass door leading onto a sort of patio filled with sun loungers, beanbags, and deck chairs, and shaded by an awning that was rippling in the brisk breeze. The seats were occupied by what I assumed must be the other contestants, all holding a glass in their hand and staring up at a woman in the middle of the circle, who had her back to me and appeared to be speaking.

Before I opened the door, I stood for a moment, taking in the scene, trying to assess the people who would be the competition for the duration of our stay on the island. On paper they probably looked like a fairly diverse crowd—different ages, different ethnicities, different body shapes—the men ranging from slim to stacked, the women from voluptuously curvy to model thin. The main thing that struck me, however, even from the other side of the glass, was that they were all, without exception, extremely good-looking, and most of them were beautifully turned out. Across the room was a woman, a girl really, with hair a lot like mine—long and dark, falling below her shoulder blades—but hers shone with a rich mahogany luster that mine had never achieved even on a good day. I felt another lurch in my stomach, but this one had nothing to do with the movement of the boat.

Then, from the other side of the glass, Nico turned and saw me, and his face lit up.

"Lyla!" I heard him say. "Come on out!"

Taking a deep breath, I pushed the door open and stepped outside.

After the air-conditioned chill of the boat, the heat was like a hug from a sweaty man, even with the brisk breeze, and I felt the perspiration under my arms prickle in response.

"Lyla!" The woman in the middle of the circle turned, and I saw she was Camille. She looked fresh as a daisy and completely unbothered by either the heat or the waves. As I approached, trying to keep my balance on the shifting deck, she picked up a glass from the nearby table and held it out to me. It was pink and fizzy—some kind of cocktail, I assumed, though it seemed a little early for that.

"Sorry I'm late," I said, taking the glass. Camille shook her head.

"Don't worry! We'd barely started. We were just raising a toast to . . . *One Perfect Couple!*"

"*One Perfect Couple!*" chorused the group, and there was a little cascade of melodic *chings!* as people tapped glasses, and the sound of laughter. A tall man with dark, slicked-back hair sitting opposite me threw his head back and downed his glass, the muscles in his throat working.

"Oh mon Dieu, c'est fort," said the woman sitting next to him, and I realized that I recognized her. She was the smoker I'd seen blowing rings over the prow when we'd first arrived, and now she made a face as she put down her glass. I took a cautious sip of mine. It tasted like prosecco . . . and something else that was probably aiming for crème de cassis but landing closer to grape juice.

"Right, first things first," Camille was saying, raising her voice above the chatter that had broken out. "Now Lyla is here, perhaps we could do a little getting-to-know-you exercise? Your name, something about your partner, and something fun about you. I'll go first— I'm actually single, so I'll make Baz my work boyfriend!" She laughed. "Um, so I'm Camille, I'm twenty-five, and I've been working for Baz for just over six months. Um . . . something about him is that he's an insomniac, which can make him a touch hard to work for when you wake up to sixteen emails in your inbox!" She gave another laugh, this one slightly tinkling and forced. "And . . . um . . . a fun thing about me . . . I'm allergic to watermelon." She smiled around the group as if waiting for a response, and then, when she didn't get one beyond polite smiles, she said, "Um . . . okay, Angel, shoot!"

Angel turned out to be the French woman who had commented on the strength of the cocktails. She was willowy thin with long silver-blond hair that streamed down her back, jutting cheek-bones, and dark eyes—something like a blond Zoë Kravitz. She was wearing a kind of billowy silk kaftan that would have been hard for someone less stunning than her to pull off—on me I was fairly sure it would have looked like a sack—but on her it somehow only emphasized her angular collarbones and slender wrists. Now she leaned back in her deck chair and spoke.

"My name is Angel, short for Angelique. I am—shockingly—French, you may not have guessed." There was a little ripple of laugh-ter from around the circle. "A fact about me, I wanted to be a Formula One racer when I was a little girl." More laughter, this time a little uncertain, as if no one was quite sure whether she was joking or not. "I have been with my boyfriend, Bayer, for two years, a fun fact about him . . . he detests wasps."

There was another round of laughter, this time more confidently. The big dark-haired man sitting beside her spread his hands and raised his eyebrows, making the piercing in his right brow wink in the sunshine.

"What?" He looked Italian maybe, or perhaps Turkish, but his accent was pure Vinnie Jones—the kind of guy you could have met working out in a gym in Hackney any day of the week. I could smell his aftershave from across the circle, and his T-shirt looked to be at least two sizes too small, presumably aimed at making his impres-sive biceps look even more pumped. But there was a self-deprecating twist to his grin that made me like him. He looked like he would be quick to take offense, but quick to laugh at himself too, if the joke was against him. "Am I wrong? Little bastards never met a pint of beer they didn't want to fucking drown themselves in. Anyway, I'm Bayer, been with my girl for two years, like she said. I'm twenty-eight. Fact about me, I can bench-press four hundred pounds." There was no laughter this time, only an impressed murmur from around the listeners, though the stat meant nothing to me. Was four hundred pounds a lot? I guessed it must be from the way he'd trotted it out. "Fact about Angel . . ." He paused, thinking. "She can get her ankles behind her head in yoga. Ain't as fun as it sounds, lads, trust me."

There was more laughter this time, a proper guffaw from some of the men, and Angel shot Bayer a look that was one part *you disgust me* to two parts *ha, ha very funny*, but I could sense the affection beneath. They felt like a good couple—like the kind of people who would be sending each other up in public but would have each other's backs if it came down to it.

We continued slowly around the circle, introducing ourselves, although the names and facts of each couple quickly began to blur into each other. There was Romi, who looked like she was going to fill the "bubbly blonde" casting niche. She did a lot of giggling and hair twirling during her brief intro, and she seemed like an odd match with her boyfriend, Joel. He was skinny and serious-looking with thick, angular glasses, and he forgot to give a fun fact at all—in fact, his introduction was very brief, as if he wanted to get it over with. Romi's fun fact was that she had 150,000 subscribers on YouTube, which seemed more like a flex than a fun piece of trivia, but I supposed no more than Bayer's.

Next came Santana, who was a stunning, curvaceous strawberry blonde, something like a redheaded Adele, with the poshest accent I'd ever heard in real life, and cleavage that made me feel better about having my own on display—it was a look that was definitely working for her. Her boyfriend, Dan, had surfer-dude, sun-streaked hair and was cute in a boy-band kind of way. Their fun fact was a joint one; they had matching tattoos of Mickey and Minnie Mouse, which seemed like a weird thing for two adults to admit, but the rest of the circle cooed and smiled appropriately.

The next couple were Conor and Zana. In a roomful of beautiful people, they were easily the standout, as much for the contrast of their good looks—different, but complementary as a couple in a way that Joel and Romi had not been. Neither gave their ages, but Conor looked to be late twenties or early thirties, tall and lean, with a close-shaved head, sharp cheekbones, and startling light-gray eyes, made all the more striking by his deep tan. He had the kind of feral grace that you saw in people who were extremely fit, and supremely in command of their own bodies. I found myself wondering if he was a professional athlete—a climber maybe, which would have fitted with his contained strength and the tan. But when he described himself, he said only that he was "in media," which could have meant anything. His fun fact was that he'd been born at 6:06 on the sixth of June.

Maybe it was Conor's air of complete confidence, but his girlfriend, Zana, looked much younger and much less self-possessed, barely out of uni I would have said, though that could have been partly down to her size. She was small, barely five foot, and almost ethereally slender, with a heart-shaped face, huge Bambi-like dark eyes fringed with sooty lashes, and long, shimmering chestnut hair that cascaded like waves over her shoulders—hair that I'd noticed and envied through the door. She spoke very quietly, and didn't give a fun fact about herself, and when she sat down, I got the impression that she was relieved to be out of the limelight.

It was then that I realized that everyone else had spoken—and Nico and I were up.

Nico stood up, holding my hand, and smiled around the circle.

"Hey guys, I'm Nico. I'm twenty-eight, and I'm an actor from East London. Lyla and I have been together almost three years"—again, I bit back the urge to correct him, but let it pass—"and our fun fact, and I guess it's a joint one like Dan and Santana—is that it's our third anniversary this week."

I did a double take, and then realized he was right. Well, if you counted our anniversary as the day we'd got off in my friend's bathroom. It was the second week of February—almost Valentine's Day. Three years. Three *years*. Even if I quibbled Nico's definition of "together," it sounded like a *lot*.

There were wolf whistles from around the group, and someone made a crack about it being time for Nico to propose maybe? I was so distracted that I stammered my way through my introduction, saying something about working in science, and then sat down, loosening my sweaty hand from Nico's as soon as I reasonably could and wiping it surreptitiously on the skirt of my red dress. *I am Lyla and I have no idea what I'm doing here*, was what I had really wanted to say, but it was the one thing I couldn't admit. *Fake it until you make it*, I heard again inside my head. But I wasn't a faker. I was a scientist—the absolute opposite of a faker—someone whose prime duty was to the truth. Could I really do this? Could I bullshit my way through the next two weeks? I took a gulp of my drink. It was disgustingly warm, and this time the sweetness made me shudder.

"That was so much fun!" Camille was saying. She had stood up and now she moved to the center of the circle, clapping enthusiastically as the others joined in. "I know it probably seemed a bit whirlwind, but trust me, there will be *lots* of opportunities to get to know each other on the island. And we have a whole evening on the boat for you to mingle. Now, before you all scatter to chat, there's one more bit of business we need to get through—and I'm sorry about this—but we have to take your phones. And your smart watches, laptops . . . basically any communication devices. So if you could, um, set your out of offices and so on and then, well, pop them in here." She gestured towards a box sitting beneath the table that had held the welcome drinks.

There was a long, shocked silence. Then Angel spoke, her voice stony.

"I am sorry, *what* did you say?"

"It was mentioned on the contract," Camille said apologetically. "But, um . . . yes, I can appreciate we maybe should have made that a little clearer in the initial talks. Sorry, it is completely standard practice on reality TV, I assure you."

Looking round the seating area, it seemed that I wasn't the only person who hadn't been aware of the rule. Santana was looking taken aback, and Dan had his arms folded in a very mulish way. It was Bayer who raised his voice over Camille's apologies.

"It's a fucking cheek is what it is. That's a brand-new Apple watch, that is. It's got all my biometric data on it. How am I gonna monitor my sleep patterns?"

"I know, I know, I'm really sorry," Camille said again. "I really am, I thought your agents had passed all this on—but honestly, it is standard. We can't have people communicating outside of the group, and obviously we don't want any leaks."

"But we all have signed an accord de confidentialité!" broke in Angel. Her accent was getting stronger with the upset. "That is what I do not understand. If you don't trust us to say not who is won, what good will taking our phones gonna do?"

"It's not about trust," Camille said, looking a little desperate. "And I can assure you the devices will be *totally* safe. Baz is putting them in his personal safe—"

"It was on the contracts you signed," broke in a deep voice, and turning, I saw that Baz had come around the corner of the deck and was standing, arms folded, just behind Camille. "And anyone who doesn't like it can fuck off and I'll sue you for breach of contract. Capiche?"

At his words, I felt a little shiver of outrage run through me. This was the first time I'd seen Baz since the Zoom call, when he'd been all *sweetheart* and *super*. The first time I'd ever met him in person, in fact. Now we were all safely signed up to his project, it was jarring how quickly he'd jumped from bonhomie to threats.

I could tell I wasn't the only person having these thoughts. There was a mutinous silence in the room. I could see the other couples looking at each other, signaling varying degrees of irritation and alarm. Even Camille seemed to have sensed the change in mood. She was looking extremely tense. I put my hand up, and then, when Baz didn't say anything, I coughed.

"Can I ask a question?"

"Sure." Baz folded his arms. "Fire away, Lola."

"*Lyla*," I said firmly. I had let him get my name wrong too many times on the Zoom call. "I've got a laptop in my bag. I need it to do work. Can I keep that, assuming it's not connected to the internet?"

"Sorry, no can do," Baz said dismissively.

"I'm in the same boat," Joel said, rather anxiously. "I mean, maybe if you don't give us the internet password—"

Baz cut him off.

"I said, no can do. And FYI, and this goes for everyone, there *will* be luggage and personal searches, so don't even think about trying to smuggle anything onto the island."

A little hum of indignation ran around the room. The relaxed, celebratory mood had completely dissipated.

"I'll need to call my mum," Nico said. He had crossed his arms, and I could feel his tenseness in his biceps, pressed against mine. "And my agent. I can't just go off-grid."

"Oh, of course, *totally*," Camille said. "And there's, like, a whole procedure with contacts and stuff. We have a dedicated number for families to check in with, and of course if anything crucial were to happen at home, we could pass that on."

"How do we know you'll tell us?" said Bayer, a little sulkily. "You could just sit on the information."

He had a point—and my respect for him went up a notch at his willingness to raise it.

"Um—I mean—" Camille looked a little desperate, and she cast an imploring look at Baz, who broke in brusquely.

"You don't. All you have is my guarantee that if it's something important, we'll tell you. And if that's not good enough for you, you can go home."

There was another silence. I could feel a strong undercurrent of resentment running around the room, but also something else—a sense of capitulation. Because the truth was, and we all knew it, everyone was here because they wanted to be, *needed* to be, or because their partner did. Every single one of these couples had someone who was hoping to make it big off the back of this opportunity, and no one could afford to turn down that chance.

"Well, I guess that settles that, then," Baz said, and he folded his arms.

Then Conor stood up. Standing, I realized he was even taller than I'd thought. He had a good six inches on Baz, and in the muted light filtering through the awning, his pale gray eyes looked almost uncanny.

"Your word is good enough for me, Baz," he said. "I left my phone in my room, but I'll get it to you as soon as possible, and so will Zana."

And then he smiled.

For a moment Baz didn't say anything. *Thanks*, would have been the natural response, but he didn't say it. He simply stood there, staring Conor down, unblinking. I looked from one man to the other, trying to figure out what the energy crackling between them meant. I've never been a body language kind of person—I prefer data, figures, cold hard facts. But now I wished I had Nico's gift for reading between the lines, because there was *something* going on here, and I couldn't for the life of me figure out what it was. Baz should have been grateful to Conor for backing him up—but he didn't look it. He was looking at Conor almost as if he disliked him. Was he pissed off at Conor for acting like Baz needed his support to get the group on his side? Or was there some other undercurrent—something that I was missing?

Conor, meanwhile, was acting . . . not quite conciliatory, but there was a touch of magnanimity in his voice, as if he was making it clear that he didn't *have* to comply but was choosing to.

What *was* going on here? Did these two know each other?

It was Baz who looked away first—down at his phone as if to underscore the fact that *he* at least didn't have to give up his tech.

"Good," he said, his voice almost a growl. "I'm glad that's clear. Now, if you'll excuse me, I've got a fuck of a lot to get sorted before we make land. I'm sorry I can't stick around, but you're in good hands with Camille."

Camille bobbed her head nervously, and Baz yanked open the door back inside and disappeared.

"Well, that was fucking weird," Dan said in a low voice. No one else seemed to react, but I glanced at him and our eyes met, united in our discomforted bewilderment. *What the fuck just happened?*

Camille cleared her throat.

"Well, anyway. As Baz said, glad that's cleared up, and so sorry if that wasn't made clear from the outset. I do assure you it's *totally* standard for reality TV. We want you communicating with each other, not head down over your phones! But, um . . . well, I'll let you finish your drinks, and then maybe everyone would like to grab their phones and turn them in, and I'll give out the latest version of the information pack—it's got lots of useful info on the other contestants, the rules, the welfare team . . . loads of good stuff. And if you've got any questions, I'll be in the breakout zone on the third deck."

There was absolute silence, then Conor began to walk towards the exit. Zana followed him without a word.

And with that, it was clear that the meeting was over.

02/16—2:28 p.m.

Hello, my name is Joel Richards, this is . . . God, I'm not sure. Maybe our third Mayday call? Please, if you can hear us, send urgent help. We're stranded on an island about twenty hours southwest of Indonesia. Twenty hours by boat, that is—we came here by boat. It was swept away in the storm, we don't know what happened to the crew. There are people here with serious injuries, life-threatening injuries, and my girlfriend— God . . . my girlfriend . . . Look, please, this is a Mayday call. If anyone can hear me, please respond or send help. We don't know how long they will last.

CHAPTER 5

BACK IN THE icebox chill of our little cabin, the motion of the ship was somehow even more noticeable.

"That was fucking weird," I said to Nico, who was hunched on his bunk with his phone, evidently making the most of his final hours plugged in.

"What was weird? Taking our phones? It's a dick move, but I just did a search on the contract and it looks like Camille was right, it *was* in there. Ari obviously didn't think to flag it up."

"Not that," I said, ignoring the question of Ari, though the fact that he hadn't thought it worthwhile mentioning that we'd be cut off from humanity for potentially ten weeks, made me wonder what else he hadn't brought up. "The whole thing with Baz and Conor. Didn't you think it was strange?"

"What whole thing?" Nico looked up from the screen for the first time, frowning.

"Did you really not think something was off between them? It was like they knew each other."

"So, maybe they do? Entertainment's a pretty small world. Look, sorry, I have to call Mum. If I'm going to be off radar for ten weeks—"

The boat went over another wave, and I nodded hastily.

"Of course. Look, you call her, I'm going to head up and turn in my devices."

"Don't you want to call anyone?"

I shrugged. I'd already told Professor Bianchi and my parents that I'd be gone for two weeks, and I had absolutely no intention of staying longer than that.

"I've already set my out of office. I've sent Mum a WhatsApp saying I'll be out of range and to call that number Camille gave if anything comes up, but I think they can cope." I looked at my phone. "Besides, it's seven p.m. there. She and Dad will be out at bridge."

Nico nodded, and I picked up my laptop and made my way back up the stairs to the outdoor area where we'd had the drinks.

When I got there, I found I wasn't the only person handing in their tech. Joel was in front of me, going through an impressive list of devices with Camille: his laptop, Romi's iPad, her phone, his smart-watch . . .

It was clear they were going to be some time, so rather than hover over them, I picked up a copy of the one of the information brochures lying on the table and took it around the corner of the deck to a shady lounge chair, with the aim of trying to fix the names and descriptions of the other contestants more firmly in my memory.

The first couple listed was Conor (31) and Zana (22), and the age gap made me do a double take. Was it weird that a thirty-one-year-old was dating a twenty-two-year-old? Not *that* much weirder than my four-year age gap with Nico, I guessed. Conor (whose bio said he was a "YouTuber and NFT trader") was grinning in his headshot, his cheeks crinkled in a wide, infectious smile that had me smiling back, almost in spite of myself. Zana, on the other hand, stared seriously out from under narrow, straight brows and described herself as a part-time model, which wasn't hard to believe. She didn't say what she did with the other part of her time.

Then there was the couple who had spoken first at the round circle—Bayer (28) and Angel (28). Bayer described himself as "a fitness instructor from North London," Angel as a "Pilates coach and influencer—not necessarily in that order," whatever that meant. Maybe she influenced people to do Pilates.

The next couple listed was Dan (25) and Santana (25). Dan's picture showed him laughing and topless, flexing for the camera in a way that looked a *tiny* bit narcissistic for my taste. His bio described him as a "swimsuit model." Santana was finger-combing her strawberry blonde hair, and her bio said that that she was a "champagne socialite." Another term that left me at sea. Was socialite a typo for socialist? Or was it her idea of a joke? Perhaps it was a fancy way of saying she was unemployed—though she didn't look it. In person she'd had the glowing, glossy look of someone with a lot of money.

Then there was Joel (33, "a teacher from south London," and the only contestant older than me) and Romi (31, "beauty influencer"). Their headshots reinforced the impression I'd had at the meeting of an oddly mismatched couple. Joel grinned shyly at the camera through thick blocky glasses that gave him an endearingly geeky look. He was handsome, in a kind of nerdcore way, but he looked like he'd be totally at home in one of the labs I worked in—a sharp contrast to Romi, who was made up to the nines with thick foundation, platinum hair, and lashes I was sure couldn't possibly be real. I tried to imagine her pipetting a tray of samples and failed—there was no way you'd be able to fit a pair of nitrile gloves over those nails, for a start.

Finally, I got to me and Nico. Nico (28, "actor and presenter") and Lyla (32, "doctor").

"Oh for fuck's sake," I said aloud.

"Sorry . . . did I . . . ?"

I looked up. Joel had come around the corner of the deck and was standing, looking a little anxious, at the foot of my lounger.

"Sorry, sorry, not you. I was just—I was reading the information pack and they've got my job wrong. I'm not a doctor—I mean, I am a doctor, I suppose, but not in the medical sense—I'm a PhD. I work on viruses. I bloody hope no one's going to expect me to do a tracheotomy while we're here."

Joel laughed.

"Join the club. They've got me down as a teacher—I'm actually a lecturer in journalism at St. Clements. I already told them once, when they sent the pack around the first time, but clearly they didn't bother correcting it."

"A lecturer?" I sat up and pushed my sunglasses up my nose. "No way! I thought I recognized a fellow academic. How do you find St. Clements?"

"Honestly? Bloody shit. I don't know about science, but my side it's all zero hours contracts and no job security. I imagine research is probably a bit better?"

I snorted.

"I wish. Well, I mean to be fair, it's not zero hours, but it's all short-term contracts so you're always budgeting from one twenty-four-month post-doc to another."

"Tell me about it," Joel said ruefully. Then he laughed, and for a moment we just sat there, or rather I sat and he stood, grinning at each other like idiots, savoring this weird moment of camaraderie in the middle of the Indian Ocean. It was Joel who broke the moment. "So . . . what brings a virologist on a reality TV show? Hoping to invest your prize money in cutting-edge Covid research?"

I laughed.

"I'm nothing as fashionable as Covid. I'm working on chikungunya at the moment." When Joel looked politely blank, I added, "It's a mosquito-borne disease, a bit like malaria, but not quite as deadly. There's no cure and no treatment. It's classed as a neglected tropical disease by the WHO, which basically means there's also no funding.

Anyway, as you can probably guess, I'm here for my boyfriend. He's the one with the hopes of breaking out. It's a weird format, isn't it—I get the impression that's how a fair number of us ended up here, dragged along by our more extroverted half."

"Guilty," Joel said, placing a hand on his chest and smiling again. He really had the most endearing smile. It crinkled his eyes at the corners and changed his rather solemn expression completely. "As you may have guessed, I was not the one who applied to go on this show. Romi—that's my girlfriend—she's the one with the dreams of the big time. If I'm honest though . . ." He paused, and then stopped.

"What?"

"Well . . . look, I'm conscious this probably sounds a bit snobbish, and I don't mean it to be, but I watch a lot of these shows with Romi—she's kind of a reality TV addict, Real TV's ideal subscriber—and there's a real type. They're all influencers and YouTubers and so on. They're only on it to make it big. I think it's what made shows like *Traitors* so compelling, because it was the kind of people you'd never get on *Love Island* or *Selling Sunset*. Just normal, regular people. And I think at the end of the day, that's what people want. Yes, they want the Real Housewives and the X Factors, but they also want normal people being normal—a bit like how *Big Brother* was when it first started, before people realized it could be a passport to fame. I think that's why they've gone with this format. It's quite canny actually."

"Huh." It was the first time I'd heard anyone offer a good explanation for what had seemed to me, ever since Nico explained it, a very strange setup—and Joel's theory made sense. It also explained why Baz had been so excited about my *authenticity*. It was code for exactly what Joel was talking about—the fact that I was a million miles from your usual reality TV contestant. "You could be right."

"And I guess there's something pretty compelling about watching real couples being torn apart in front of your eyes," Joel said, and now he wasn't smiling anymore. He looked, if anything, a little resigned.

"How do you mean?"

"Well, shows like *The Bachelor* and *Love Island*, yes, they're all hooking up, but it's mostly strategic, they've only known each other for a few days. There's no real emotional connection there. Whereas this show, if they succeed in breaking one of the couples up . . . yes, it's going to be a lot harder to do that, but if they manage, it's going to be car crash TV. A real long-term relationship ripping apart on-screen."

"God." A shiver ran through me now, realizing he was right. "Do you really think that's what they're going for?"

Joel shrugged.

"Honestly? I have no idea. But I don't imagine they'd be upset if it happens. And for the entertainers, the stakes are pretty high. If someone starts to feel their partner's weighing them down—" He stopped, raised one eyebrow. I felt a sickness that had nothing to do with the motion of the waves.

"Nico and I have a pact," I said slowly. "I can't take more than two weeks off work. I'm going to try to flunk one of the first few tasks, get eliminated. He's going to try to make a strategic alliance with one of the other singletons. But we agreed it—I can't see him really betraying me."

Joel smiled again, but this time his smile was different, still sympathetic, but it didn't reach his eyes.

"I'm sure you're right," he said.

"Setting up alliances already?" said a voice from behind Joel, and we both turned to see Conor standing there, arms folded. He was wearing swim shorts, and although he was smiling, I found it hard to keep my eyes on his face. Instead they kept straying to his torso, which was (a) impressively ripped, and (b) extensively tattooed, with what looked like two huge eagle wings spread across his abs.

Joel had evidently noticed the same thing, because he turned and said admiringly, "Nice ink, man."

"Thanks," Conor said. "You're Joel, right?"

"That's right. I know who you are of course."

"Yeah?" Conor looked disarmed and a little flattered. "You a fan?"

"Um . . ." To my surprise, Joel looked a little awkward. "I mean . . . it's more a professional interest I guess. I'm a lecturer in media. My girlfriend's a YouTuber though—Romi Ellison?"

He offered the name up as if Conor might have heard of her, but Conor only nodded encouragingly without any sign of recognition.

"Always pleased to hear about female fans," he said. "My audience has a rep for being very male, but I get a lot of correspondence from women."

"The NFT stuff was news to me," Joel said with a laugh. I had the slight, puzzling impression he was trying to change the subject, though I couldn't say why.

Conor rolled his eyes.

"It was news to me too. I made *one* video about buying bitcoin, and they've obviously extrapolated out from there to make out I'm some kind of tech kingpin. I think they've decided I'm their key to drawing in the NFT bros. Either that or they're trying to set me up as the douchebag. Every show needs a villain, right?"

The remark took me aback, but now he said it, I realized he was right. Every reality TV show *did* have a villain. Who was it going to be?

"I think you've got other qualities, mate," Joel was saying, a smile twitching at the corner of his mouth.

"Other qualities . . . ?" Conor said. Joel jerked a thumb towards his bare torso, and he laughed, a little sheepishly.

"In my defense, I was sunbathing. I'm not planning on walking around topless for the whole series."

"I think the production team'll be confiscating your shirts now you've shown them the goods," Joel said dryly.

Conor laughed properly at that, throwing back his head, and I decided I liked him. He wasn't what I'd expected somehow. I don't know why, but I'm always a little suspicious of extremely good-looking people. If they know it, it usually comes over as preening. If they seem like they don't know it, I don't believe them. No one can go through life being a ten to most people's five or six and be unaware of the fact. Conor seemed like the right combination of self-aware about his looks, but not dickish about it. And he seemed articulate too, which should maybe have been less of a surprise. I didn't really follow YouTubers, but I knew enough to figure out that it was hard to build up a success-ful following without having something interesting to say, and a fair amount of personal charm alongside.

"Sorry," I said now, standing up and smiling at Conor, "I feel I should know this, but I don't watch a lot of YouTube. What's your channel about?"

Conor shrugged.

"Politics . . . current affairs . . . general chat. I guess it's kind of like a talk show, except mostly I'm the only guest. I just talk about what I think people will be concerned about. Anything that's current. I have other people on sometimes."

"And you do all right?"

Joel laughed at that.

"You could say that. He's got ten million subscribers—"

"I'm sorry, *what*?" I broke in, too surprised for politeness. "Did you say *ten million subscribers*?"

Conor grinned a little sheepishly.

"I think it's about 10.4 now, but yeah, something in that region. And another five or so on TikTok."

"What the fuck are you doing on this show, then?" I blurted out, and Joel laughed. Conor smiled.

"I guess . . . one, the production company came to me, and I was flattered. And Zana was keen. Two, if I'm being completely honest—" He stopped, and for a moment there was something surprisingly vul-nerable in his expression. "I want what everyone wants: credibility.

YouTube's great, but there's still a snobbishness there from mainstream media."

"And you think this could send you mainstream?" Joel asked, a little skeptically. Conor shrugged again.

"Maybe, maybe not. At the end of the day, it's win-win for me. Worst-case scenario, nothing happens and I'm back to my regular subscribers. Best-case scenario, the show really breaks out and I get a talk show."

I nodded slowly. His logic made sense.

"What about you, then?" he asked. "What brings you to the island?"

"Oh, we're just along for the ride." I indicated Joel. "We're both academics. It was our partners who wanted to come."

"That's right." Conor looked like he was remembering something, "You're a doctor, aren't you?"

I groaned.

"No, I'm fucking not. I've got a PhD in virology, but I'm not a medical doctor. So *please* don't be expecting me to fix any broken legs while we're out there."

"Gotcha," Conor said. He grinned again, his teeth very white in the bright sunlight. "No broken legs."

"Joel!" The voice was sharp, and we all turned our heads to see Romi stalking along the deck. She had changed into the world's smallest white crochet bikini, a huge sunhat that was threatening to blow away in the stiff breeze, and teetering platform sandals that didn't look like the best idea as the ship pitched and rolled. "Joel, I've been looking for you everywhere. You said you'd meet me at the hot tub."

"I didn't," Joel said mildly, but with a touch of testiness in his voice. "You said *you* were going to the hot tub."

"Well, whatever, I've been waiting for you for hours. I couldn't even text you."

I suppressed a smile at that. Joel had handed in his devices not ten minutes before, so it was hard to take her complaints too seriously. I tried to break the tension with a laugh.

"I guess we've got to get used to that, haven't we?"

"Got to get used to what?" It was Nico, strolling along the deck wearing a pair of swimming shorts and a towel slung over his shoulder.

"Being without our phones," I said, but Romi had already turned to Nico and was speaking over the top of me.

"Hey, you're Nico, right? Did I see you on *Holby City*?"

It was the right question, and Nico instantly turned the full beam of his charming smile on Romi and regaled her with the details of his acting CV, while she gazed up at him, batting her lashes in a way that was frankly a little OTT. I wasn't bothered—I could tell she was only doing it to punish Joel for chatting to me instead of meeting her at the hot tub—but it was a puzzling contrast to her hostility to Joel.

"Shall we talk about this at the hot tub?" she was asking. "I'd love to hear how you got into acting."

"Of course," Nico said earnestly. "Lyla, are you coming?"

I smiled and shook my head.

"Thanks, but I can't think of anything worse in this heat."

"Guys?" Nico turned to Conor and Joel.

"Maybe later; I need to find Zana," Conor said. Nico nodded, and then he and Romi made their way up the deck. As they rounded the corner, I saw Romi put her hand on his arm, and then throw back her head and laugh at something he'd said.

"You've got a live one there, mate," Conor said dryly, and Joel sighed.

"She's pissed off at me. I'm not sure why. This whole *Perfect Couple* thing was her idea—but somehow nothing I do is right anymore. I don't earn enough, I don't compliment her enough, I don't support her career enough . . . I don't know what she wants anymore. I'm kind of worried—"

He stopped, seeming to think better of what he'd been about to say.

"Go on," Conor said. His voice was . . . curious. Sympathetic. Joel looked down at the ground.

"I guess . . . it's like . . . you know these things have a formula? All these preset types they're casting for."

I didn't, but I nodded.

"And in terms of the blokes, there's always the alpha males, the ones who're duking it out for the prize, the joker, the jock, and you know, the cuck. The nice guy who's there to be humiliated." He swallowed. "I guess . . . I guess I'm just wondering which one is me."

"Hey," Conor said awkwardly, and I tried to think how to fill the silence. I couldn't comment on how right he was about reality TV shows, because I hadn't watched enough to have an opinion. But I couldn't help thinking that in an American high school movie, Joel would have been cast as the geek. The guy who got his lunch tray smashed in his face. And that probably wasn't a very fun part to play.

"Look," I said at last, "the whole point about this, Baz's entire pitch to me and Nico, was about how this show isn't like all the others. It's supposed to be breaking down all that bullshit."

"Yeah," Joel said, though he didn't sound convinced. "I'm sure you're right. Well . . . I'm going to go and get some food. See you later?"

"I'd better head too," Conor said. He was looking at Joel and his face was . . . I couldn't pin it down. Not concerned exactly. Thoughtful. "Zana's waiting for me. Nice to meet you both. And, seriously Joel, mate, don't worry. I think you're overthinking this. She's probably just tired and jet-lagged—we all are."

"Yeah," Joel said. He gave a smile that tried for some of Conor's confidence and didn't quite get there. "You're probably right. Nice to meet you, Lyla."

"Nice to meet you," I echoed, and the two of them turned and walked away in opposite directions, leaving me holding my phone, and wondering.

02/17—3:31 p.m.

Hi, hello, can anyone hear this? Please will someone come in? Anyone? Over.

02/17—3:32 p.m.

Please. Please. I'm begging you. Over.

CHAPTER 6

"LAND AHOY!"

The shout rang out, piercing through my sleepy haze and yanking me to consciousness with a jerk. For a minute, I had no idea what the words meant. Land ahoy? Like in pirate movies?

And then I sat up, blinking against the strong light filtering through the tiny porthole, and remembered where I was—aboard the *Over Easy*, sailing towards Ever After Island.

It wasn't the real name obviously; that was an Indonesian name I couldn't remember, though one of the producers had mentioned it. But Ever After Island was what the production team were calling the island—after the show's tagline *Who'll get their happy ever after?*

I looked reflexively for my phone, before remembering that I'd handed it in to Camille yesterday. Instead, I leaned over the side of the bunk and peered at the little digital clock embedded in the plastic molding above the inbuilt side table. 7:02 a.m. Craning farther, I could see Nico was still out like a light in the bunk below. He had been up late drinking with the other cast members, whereas I'd flaked out after supper, jet-lagged into exhaustion. Now I was fully awake, and I felt the first stirrings of proper excitement . . . and nerves. This adventure was suddenly becoming real.

"Nico," I whispered, and then, when he didn't move, "Nico, are you awake? They just said they can see land."

Nico muttered something into his pillow that sounded like "Shallah down a mimma" and pulled the blanket over his head. I grinned, swung my legs over the side of the bunk, and ten minutes later I was showered, dressed, and up on deck, my wet hair still dripping down my back.

After the heat of yesterday, the air was refreshingly cool and clear, though I could feel a promise of fierceness to come in the sun's warmth, even at this early hour. Below me, two crew members were scrubbing the decks and chatting away to each other in Indonesian, and in the distance was a little slip of land, edging closer moment by moment. All my London worries—my job, Professor Bianchi, how I was going to write up the paper without my laptop—they all felt very far away. I could worry about that when I got back. If I was going to lose my job anyway, did it really matter if I did the paper now or in a few weeks? I could write it up in the evenings if I had to. And God knows, I needed a holiday. I couldn't remember the last time I'd had a proper break.

I was leaning over the side, staring at the little island in the middle distance, when a voice sounded from behind me.

"Lyla, right?"

I swung round, putting a hand to my chest. Standing there, smiling, was the tanned, handsome face of the guy with the Mickey Mouse tattoo. I could remember his girlfriend's name—Santana—it had stuck out to me for being unusual, but I couldn't for the life of me remember his.

"Oh God, you scared me! I thought I was the only one up." The name was hovering at the edge of my memory, then it came to me. "Dan, right?"

"Yup." He came up alongside me, shading his eyes as he gazed out over the horizon. He had a light tenor voice and a faint northern accent, though I couldn't place where. Liverpool, maybe. Or perhaps Manchester. It was so slight it was hard to tell. Standing next to him, I could tell that he bleached his hair—what had looked like sun streaks from a distance were clearly hairdresser highlights close-up. "So that's it, huh. Home for the next however long we survive."

"That's it," I echoed, following his gaze.

"Looked pretty sweet in the photographs," Dan said. "I tried to check it out on Tripadvisor, but apparently the resort is brand-new—they haven't even opened for business yet. Hope it lives up to the first impressions."

"Unlike the boat, you mean?" I said dryly. Dan laughed at that, a surprised "Hah!" that bubbled out of him irrepressibly. He put his hand over his mouth and grinned, looking a little guilty.

"I take it you had one of the shit cabins as well, then?"

I nodded, then shrugged.

"I mean, I'm not complaining. It just didn't really live up to . . . all this." I waved my hand at the teak decking and gleaming polished handrails.

"Well, I *am* complaining," Dan said. He tossed his head. "I don't want to come over the diva so soon into production, and I know Santana and I aren't exactly A-listers, but we *are* the talent. You'd think they'd give us something above the waterline at least. I bet that Connal guy got a suite."

"Conor?" I was surprised. "How come?"

"Oh, he's like best mates with Baz apparently. Dated his niece or something, that's what my agent was telling me."

"Best mates? They didn't seem very matey yesterday," I said doubtfully. And Zana was very definitely not Baz's niece, so clearly something had happened there. Dan shrugged.

"I dunno. I'm just passing on what I've been told. Didn't you think there was a definite sense of hierarchy at the meet and greet?"

I had to nod. There *had* been a feeling of that.

"Plus of course, he's fit as a ferret, which certainly doesn't hurt."
Dan sighed. He leaned over the rail, looking wistfully at the island,
which was getting closer by the minute, close enough now to see the
white sand edging the land. "I wish Elijah was here."

"Who's Elijah?"

"My boyfriend," Dan said, and then slapped his hand over his
mouth. "Fuck. I did *not* say that. You have to promise not to tell Baz!"

"Of course I won't," I said, puzzled. "But why does it matter?"

"Because we're supposed to be a couple, me and Santana."

"Wouldn't they let you on with Elijah, then?"

Dan shrugged.

"I didn't ask, mate. But I couldn't see it happening. It fucks up
the format, doesn't it, if you've got a same-sex couple buggering
up the maths? Love's only for the heteros, apparently."

"Well, that sucks," I said slowly, but I could see that he was right.
Love Island, *The Bachelor*, they were all relentlessly heteronormative.

"In some ways it makes it easier," Dan said. "I mean, don't get me
wrong, I'd like to have had Elijah here, but I wouldn't have enjoyed
watching him play the field if I got eliminated—and vice versa, I don't
think he'd have enjoyed sitting at home watching me try to cop off
with a load of hotties. But this way, he knows it's all for show. I'm not
going to be running off into the sunset with Santana. Not that she's
not fit, but I'm like a candy stick, me. If you snapped me in half, I'd
have *G-A-Y* running all the way through, and Elijah knows that."

"What about Santana?" I asked curiously. "Does she have a boyfriend?"

Dan shook his head.

"No, they broke up a few months ago. She's been pretty depressed
about it. That's why I signed us up, in fact—I wanted to give her something fun to think about, you know? It's a bit shit when the bloke you
think you're going to marry passes you up for a younger, skinnier
model." There was a silence while I tried to imagine who on earth

could possibly be more gorgeous than Santana, then Dan said with a laugh, "We really do have matching tattoos though, that bit was true. How does your man feel about all this? Isn't he jealous?"

"Nico?" I said, surprised. "I mean . . . no, I don't think jealous exactly. I agree, the whole format's a bit fucked-up. But like you said, it's only for show. He knows I'm not here to meet anyone. Besides, I'm not planning on hanging around."

"What d'you mean?"

"Well . . . keep it to yourself, but since you told me about Elijah . . . I only agreed to this to help Nico. I've got a job, and I've only got two weeks off. I'm going to have to try to flunk one of the early challenges. But . . . yeah, maybe don't tell Baz that either. I think he wants us all to be cut-throat competitors."

"Or hot to trot," Dan said, and gave his bubbling laugh again, though this time it had a surprisingly dirty edge. "He's probably filming us right now, with some caption about our growing bond."

"Jesus!" I looked around, surprised. "You don't really think that, do you?"

Dan shrugged.

"Maybe. Maybe not. But there's a camera up there." He pointed to a neat little white box mounted below the guard rail on the deck above. I hadn't even noticed it before he'd said, but now I couldn't tear my eyes away from it, from its little black eye, impassively reflecting the sparkle of the waves. Was it true? Were we being filmed right now?

I shivered, and resisted the childish urge to stick two fingers up at the camera, then turned my back to it, looking out to sea again.

"Well," Dan said, stretching his arms behind his back as though working out kinks in his muscles, "I don't know about you, but I'm going to make sure I'm packed. It doesn't look like we'll be much longer, and I want to make sure I'm first off the boat to get dibs on the best villa. Nice to meet you, Lyla."

"Nice to meet you too," I said, and watched as he made his way, a little unsteadily, along the deck towards the door that led to the cabins. I had been intending to follow, begin the work of getting our stuff together, but instead I turned back to the horizon, watching the island, Ever After Island, edging closer. It was almost hypnotic—the blue of the sea, the blue of the sky, the little slip of white sand in between, moving in time with the rise and fall of the boat.

Just a minute more, I told myself. Just a minute more alone, just me and the horizon.

Well, and the cameras.

02/22—09:37 a.m.

Oh God, please, please, Dieu, why isn't anyone coming. We have no idea what to do. The boat has gone, they have took our phones, and all we have got is this fucking radio that personne doesn't know how to work—please, please answer us. People are dying—people are dead. Oh Dieu, we will all be dead soon if someone doesn't come. Someone has to be monitoring this channel. No, tais-toi, Joel, I will not turn this off. I fucking will not. I don't give a shit about the battery. What good will the battery make when we are all dead?

CHAPTER 7

"HO. LEE. SHIT."

Nico had stepped off the boat onto the white sand, taken off his shoes, and was standing on the beach, scrunching his toes into the silky white grains with a look so blissed out, I wished I had a camera. Unfortunately, every single one of my devices, from my phone to my work laptop, was in Baz's personal safe on board the *Over Easy*, so I had to hope that the camera crew currently circling the group was capturing his reaction.

Behind us was the yacht, moored about a hundred yards offshore, the little dinghy we'd actually crossed to the island in, and beyond both were miles and miles of sparkling blue sea, given an eerie iridescence by the sun flickering off the white sand. Ahead of us was Ever After Island—a slip of land only a few miles long, but large enough for what looked like a small forest, filled with what I could already see were palm trees, tall shrubby plants hung with comically large bunches of short stubby bananas, and many more flowers, trees, and plants that I didn't recognize. I wasn't sure whether the island would be big enough to support animals—but I could hear the sound of birds filtering through the trees, and high above Nico's head a butterfly swooped past, its wings seeming too comically large and slow to keep itself aloft. It looked . . . well, it looked exactly like the photos Baz had sent through. Only better. So much better.

"Wow," I said. "Just . . . wow."

"Tell Nico how you're feeling, Lyla?" a producer said, stepping towards me, and I saw that a fluffy mic had swung in front of me, just above my head.

"Oh!" I was instantly taken aback, unsure how to react, and glanced at the gaping black hole of the camera lens and then back at the producer. What I was actually feeling was . . . ruffled. Our arrival in paradise had been somewhat marred by full bag and body searches for communication devices before we were allowed to disembark. I was fairly sure I wasn't the only person still bristling from the indignity of an intimate pat down and a crew member rummaging through my underwear; the others were just hiding it better than me. "I mean . . . great. Relieved to be off the boat."

"Can you tell Nico about that? And don't look at the lens, honey, if we want you to talk direct to camera we'll pull you out for an otto."

"An otto?" I wasn't sure if I'd heard the word right.

"An O-T-O—a one-to-one interview. But don't worry about that, honey, just talk to Nico. Pretend I'm not here." I could tell the producer was becoming a little testy at my failure to understand what was required of me, but it was quite hard to pretend the crew weren't there with the huge black camera looming in my face, and the boom mic waving overhead. Behind me I could see Bayer and Angel vamping it up for the cameras—Angel squealing and spinning around with her hair fanning out like the petals of a flower, Bayer scooping her up, grinning, and kissing her as she wrapped her long legs around him. Only ten minutes ago Bayer had been tantrumming about having his bags searched; now they looked like something out of a movie. I could see precisely how the scene was going to go down with viewers, the heart-eyes emojis, the tweets about what a cute couple they were. Farther over, Santana and Dan were wandering hand in hand across the wet sand. Dan had his shirt off and his trousers rolled up, Santana's high heels were trailing from her free hand. They looked like the kind of soft-focus aspirational poster your co-worker would have pinned up in their cubical to help get them through the working day. Maybe with the slogan *happiness is . . . your hand in mine* or something equally sappy in a flowing font.

Every single one of them was providing an object lesson in what the camera wanted—and what I was completely failing to provide.

"Um . . . wow, Nico, isn't this great?" I said at last.

Nico swung round. He had undone a couple of buttons on his loose white linen shirt, showing his tanned chest, and just the right amount of chest hair—no Burt Reynolds–style chest wig, more Poldark's scything scene. Whatever he'd been doing in the gym recently was working; I could see his abs through the shirt.

"It's paradise," he said seriously, and I could tell that although he was looking at me, he was speaking for the camera. "And the only thing that makes it better is that I'm here with you. You're all I've ever wanted, Lil." And then he came over, took my face between his hands in a way he had never done before, a way, I realized suddenly, that people did in the movies, and kissed me passionately, full on the lips.

For a minute I had no idea what to do. I knew that I was standing stiffly, my lips immobile under Nico's, but I was also aware that the producer was hovering just behind my shoulder, that the camera was almost certainly zooming closer, and that this pose, with Nico theatrically clasping my head instead of putting his arms around me in his usual affectionate way, was strangely awkward. The whole scene felt completely and utterly fake, and I realized with a sudden shock, that I wasn't just kissing my boyfriend—I was kissing a professional actor, and he was performing for the camera.

When we broke apart I resisted the urge to blink and wipe my mouth. Instead, mostly to give myself an excuse to walk away from the camera, I took Nico's hand, shamelessly copying Dan and

Santana, pulled off my sandals, and began to walk along the shore, the gentle surf lapping at my ankles. I had been expecting the sea to be a refreshing change from the humidity in the air, but the water was surprisingly warm—almost blood temperature.

"It's like a bath!" I said to Nico in surprise, and then, "Oh wow, look, a fish!"

"It's the sea, Lyla," Nico said with a laugh, but then he saw what I was pointing at—a tiny minnow barely longer than my finger, with stark black and white stripes, darting through the turquoise water. As we watched, fascinated, a little shoal of bright orange fish followed it, shockingly vivid against the blue water.

We watched, mesmerized for a few minutes, and then Nico pointed to a little path leading into the forest.

"Where do you think that leads? Maybe the villas?"

"Let's find out," I said, with a smile that I was conscious was as much for the camera crew following a few steps behind as for Nico himself. As we crossed the beach and made our way into the trees, I could see the shape of one . . . two . . . no, three low-slung villas, white walls gleaming through the lush greenery.

"Which one do you think is ours?" I said aloud.

"God, I don't know, they're all incredible," Nico said, and then gave a stagey gasp as we rounded a clump of trees and saw in the distance, stretching out across the water, the honeymoon villa I'd seen online—the one on stilts above the turquoise ocean. "Holy fuck! Look at that one!"

"Please don't swear!" the producer said from behind us in an irritated tone. "We're aiming for a PG-13 audience. I can't use the footage if you swear."

"Oh my days!" Nico said obediently, with just the same amount of awed shock in his voice as the first time round. "Lyla, look at that!"

"That can't be ours," I said, not trying to keep the envy out of my voice.

I let Nico's hand drop and went up to the first little villa we were passing, nestled in a clearing between palm trees like a little jungle oasis. On the door was tacked a piece of paper.

Santana and Dan, the note said. *Welcome to Forest Retreat.*

"This is Dan and Santana's," I called over my shoulder to Nico. "Let's find ours!"

He nodded, grabbed my hand, and we ran down the little pebbled path between the trees, the camera man loping in our wake. As I pushed aside the flowers and palm fronds blocking our path, I wondered how he managed to keep the footage steady—wouldn't it be jolting all over the place? But I didn't have time to wonder for long, because Nico had spotted another villa, this one at the top of a little outcrop above the sea.

He was first to it, peering at the note.

"'Bayer and Angel,'" he read aloud. "'Welcome to Ocean Bluff.' Okay, this isn't ours. Keep hunting, Lyla!"

I grinned and nodded. I was getting into this now, almost forgetting the camera crew behind me and the producer jogging in their wake. I followed Nico along the shore towards another villa, this one practically on the beach itself.

"'Conor and Zana,'" I read out. "'Welcome to Paradise Cove.'"

We were almost at the honeymoon villa now, and I stepped onto the jetty that joined it to the mainland, feeling the planks shift a little beneath my feet as the waves slapped at the wooden struts. It couldn't, it *couldn't* be ours, could it?

But as I drew closer, I could see that it wasn't. I couldn't quite read the note on the door, but it was of a different format to the letters pinned on the other villas, shorter, with no address at the top. Sure enough, when I stepped off the jetty and onto the veranda, I could see the pinned card didn't have anyone's name on it. *Ever After Villa,* it read. Nothing else. It must be some kind of reward villa. Maybe you got to have dinner here if you aced one of the challenges. Or perhaps it was where Baz was staying.

The producer was hovering as I retraced my steps back to the beach to break the news to Nico that no, we weren't staying in the over-water villa, but thinking of Baz had made me wonder something else.

"Where are the crew staying?"

"On the boat," the producer said. "Most of them anyway. When the resort is finished there'll be a full staff accommodation block on the eastern side of the island, but unfortunately that hasn't been built yet. There's only a few temporary amenity huts put up by the construction company."

"So there won't be any crew here in the evenings?" I asked, a little doubtfully.

The producer shook her head.

"No. There's a radio in case of emergencies, and we'll have a couple of staff members staying in the amenity huts, just in case. But we just don't have the facilities to house the majority of the crew. Most of the out-of-hours filming's going to be done by remote."

"Remote?"

The producer frowned.

"Didn't your agent explain all this? The villas are all fitted out with cameras. Not in the bathrooms, obviously, so if you want to change or anything, you go in there—though don't worry, we won't be showing any nudity regardless. Like I said, Baz is aiming for a PG-13 rating, though if everyone keeps swearing, that might be wishful thinking." She rolled her eyes. "But otherwise . . . assume you're being filmed twenty-four seven."

"I'm sorry, *what*?"

"It was all in the contract, honey," the producer said. She looked a little defensive.

I turned to look at Nico.

"Did you know about this? Cameras in all the rooms?"

"Lil," Nico said. He had that voice on, the *calm down, Lyla, don't be so uptight* voice that's guaranteed to make me lose my shit. "Have you ever *seen* a reality TV show? This is how they work. They want unguarded moments."

"Unguarded moments? Is that the new term for people shagging?"

The camera man took a step forward, swung the lens towards me. I gritted my teeth, resisting the urge to tell him to fuck off. At least if I did, they wouldn't be able to use the footage. Unless they bleeped it, of course. And then how would it be edited? Probably me reading the note saying that the water villa wasn't for us, then cut to me throwing a hissy fit at Nico. *Did you know about this?* Then, *And you can fuck off as well* to the camera man.

Week one: Lyla is promoted from *boffin* to *diva bitch.*

I remembered Conor's words on the boat—*every show* needs *a villain.* With a temper tantrum like that, I'd be putting myself forward for the role fair and square. The question was, did I mind? In some ways it might work out better for Nico—when I was eliminated, he'd look a lot more sympathetic pairing up with other people if I'd been edited into a complete cow.

But Conor's words kept coming back to me—*every show needs a villain.* And I didn't watch much reality TV, but I did know one thing: the villains were hardly ever eliminated, at least not until the final showdown. They needed that grit in the oyster to make the show interesting. I had no idea how the challenges were going to work, but one thing I was absolutely certain of—they could be rigged. And if I made myself too interesting, they were never going to let me go.

I forced myself to smile sweetly.

"You're right. I was being naive. Of course they'll want to get as much footage as they can. Come on. Let's find our villa."

And then I turned and stomped off up the beach, trying not to let the anger show in the set of my spine too clearly.

*   *   *

I HAD CALMED down a little by the time we found our villa—just a little bit back from the beach and surrounded by a cluster of palm trees. *Nico and Lyla, welcome to Palm Tree Rest* read the note on the door. There was no ocean view, just a sliver of sea between the trunks, but personally, I was happy to have the extra shade—though maybe not the extra mosquitoes, I thought, as one buzzed past my nose and I flapped at it reflexively.

In all the haste of disembarking, I'd forgotten to put on any deet, and now I wondered what mosquitoes carried here. Probably not malaria, if this island had the same risk profile as Indonesia, but possibly dengue. I hadn't managed to get a good look at the mosquito that had buzzed past my face, but the fact that it was out in the day meant it was most likely *Aedes Aegypti*, the kind that carries dengue and chikungunya, not *Anopheles*, which is responsible for malaria.

Part of me was intrigued. Although I'd spent years studying mosquito-borne illnesses, I'd never actually had dengue, or chikungunya. Perhaps now was my chance. And the first time you got dengue, it wasn't usually much of an issue. It was reinfection with a different serotype that was the big risk factor for hemorrhagic fever. But on the other hand . . . I made a mental note to get the deet out of my luggage as soon as we were allowed and to remind Nico to do the same.

While I was pondering mosquitoes, Nico had opened the door into the villa and begun exploring.

"Ho— I mean wow, Lyla, come and have a look!" I heard from inside, and now I followed him over the threshold, making sure to brush the sand off my bare feet on the hessian entrance mat.

Inside was a square room, just one, but more than big enough for two people—all white walls and dark shining wood, with a huge four-poster bed at the center, hung with nets that rippled in the breeze. Through an open doorway I could see a bathroom almost as big as the bedroom, complete with double sink, giant stone bath, and a rainforest shower the size of our kitchen at home.

It was clearly all brand-spanking-new—the overriding smell was of wood oil and fresh paint, in spite of the stiff breeze coming through the open windows, and I could see some of the windows still had suction cup marks on them, where the construction workers had maneuvered them into place. Still, we weren't the first guests. As I stared upwards, where the raftered ceiling soared to a point, I saw a tiny gecko run for the shadows with a flick of its tail, and I smiled. Not everyone would welcome a little lizard friend in their room, but I was happy for him to deal with the mosquitoes.

"This is beautiful," I said sincerely to Nico, and he grabbed me by the waist and swung me around, whispering *I love you* into my hair. I never liked it when Nico did his twirling-around act—it made me feel off-balance, and kind of like he was flexing the undeniable fact that he was bigger and stronger than me, and could pick me up if he wanted, no matter how much I didn't want him to. But this time I pressed my face into his neck and let him, knowing it was his way of trying to make up for our simmering nonargument on the beach.

When he set me down, I stood for a moment, regaining my balance with one hand on the bedpost—and there it was; a little white box in the corner of the room, with a single unblinking dark eye, overlooking every inch of the place, and most particularly the bed. I felt the smile fade from my face, but the truth was, Nico was right. This *was* the reality of reality TV. I had signed up for this, even if I hadn't fully understood what I was letting myself in for at the time.

"Knock knock!" came a voice from the door, and I swung round to see Camille standing there, smiling and holding a big bunch of tropical flowers. She held them out, and for a moment I hesitated.

"Are those . . . for me?"

Camille nodded.

"A little welcome gift for our Perfect Couple stars! Can I just—" She stopped for a moment, her hand pressed to the earpiece wedged into her ear, nodding. "Blast . . . it looks like there's a problem with this one as well. One second."

She pulled a chair over to the corner of the room where the camera was situated and climbed onto it, peering up into the black empty lens, wiggling something at the rear of the camera.

"Is that better?" she said into her mic. Nico and I couldn't hear the answer, but apparently it wasn't what she'd wanted, as her face fell. "Well, there's nothing we can do now, we'll have to get the spares when we do the helicopter run tonight. Or do you think it's a software issue?"

There was a pause, the person on the other end of the earpiece evidently talking.

"Yes, so that's Forest Retreat." Camille was ticking them off on her fingers, though the other person couldn't see the action. "Palm Tree Rest, Island Dream, and the west cabana camera." Another pause. "No, that one's okay; I used the spare to replace it and it seemed to be fine when I left." Another pause. "I've not checked there yet, I'm still at Palm Tree. I'll go there next, but do you want me to bring this camera back to the boat, or leave it up?"

More speech we couldn't hear, but apparently the answer was leave it up, because Camille climbed down without removing the camera, her expression annoyed.

"There's a problem with the sound in some of the villas, unfortunately, so we might have to send someone over to do filming in person tonight. It'll depend how it goes with the task this evening. The cameras are filming okay, but the mics aren't picking up any speech. We'll get it fixed tomorrow, but in the meantime, please try not to say anything too interesting!"

"We can guarantee that," Nico said with a laugh. "Don't forget, Lyla's a scientist, so unless you're into viruses . . . *Joke*," he added, poking me in the ribs as I made a mock offended face. Camille's rather tense expression broke into a reluctant smile.

"I'm sure you're both *very* interesting, Nico. Now, we'll give you a few minutes to freshen up, and then we'd love to see you in the cabana for some brunch."

"Where's that?" Nico asked, and Camille pointed out the back of the villa, the opposite direction to the beach.

"Just over there, through the trees. It's a kind of communal area where the boys and girls eat and hang out and so on."

Boys and girls? It seemed a strangely twee term for a group with an average age pushing thirty, but before I could ask, Nico spoke.

"Great, I'm starving."

Camille smiled back.

"Good. But be warned—there'll be some games to play too. See you there!"

Nico and I waited, as her shape disappeared between the trees, and then he turned to me.

"So? I mean—this is everything we were promised, isn't it?"

I nodded. It was true; the island really *had* lived up to the pictures Baz had sent, I couldn't deny it.

"Yes, you're right. It's just as beautiful as the photos. I just—"

Nico rolled his eyes.

"You just what? For God's sake, Lyla. We're in literal paradise. Are you never satisfied?"

"I *am* satisfied," I protested. "It's just—it's not finished. Doesn't that bother you? You can literally still smell the paint, and half the facilities aren't even built yet."

"So? I can't imagine Baz would have got this place for free once it was up and running and taking millionaire guests every week. And we're the first people who get to enjoy it—isn't that something to celebrate?"

"It's not the paint, Nico, it's more the fact that we're acting as guinea pigs for this place. If there *are* any issues with the infrastructure, we're going to be the ones finding out. What happens if the generator gives out? Or the desalination plant breaks down?"

"Desally what?" Nico looked blank.

"The water, Nico! They have to get it from somewhere. They're hardly going to be piping it thousands of miles from the mainland, so they must be desalinating seawater—reverse osmosis, I'd guess, which is a pretty technical process. I mean, they can't even get the cameras working properly." I gestured at the box on the wall. "What if something that actually matters goes—"

"Then I imagine they'll call in an engineer from the mainland," Nico broke in impatiently. "This is what telly's *like*, Lyla. You're the scientist, so I'm not going to argue with you about reverse whatever it was, but this is *my* professional area and I'm telling you, this is totally normal. You don't get it because you only see the front of everything when you watch a show—you don't see the unfinished woodwork behind set and the costumes held together with glue and staples. We're backstage at the theater, honey—this is what it looks like."

"Don't call me honey," I snapped.

"It's a term of endearment," Nico retorted, but I knew it wasn't, not really. When Nico was feeling affectionate, he called me Lil and told me he loved me. *Honey* was reserved for something else—the moments when he felt I was putting him down and he wanted to hit back.

For a long moment we stood, glaring at each other, and then Nico's face softened.

"Look," he said, moving across to me and putting his hands on my shoulders. "Lil, I get it. This is weird for you, being in my world. But this *is* my world, so could you please just trust me that I know what I'm talking about? Because I *do* know TV, and I'm telling you, this is a hell of a lot more fancy than most of the sets I've been on, and I think we're pretty lucky to be here. But more to the point, we *are* here. And like it or not, there's no going back. So you might as well stop fussing about the details and enjoy the ride, because there's nothing else you can do."

His words were meant to be reassuring. And as he put his arms around me and hugged me close, I knew he wanted me to say that they were—that I was just stressed about my own work and taking it out on him.

But the truth was, I felt the exact opposite of reassured. Because he was right—everything he'd said was completely correct: we *were* here. And there was no going back. And there was nothing either of us could do about it.

02/23—09:54 a.m.

Hello, if anyone can hear us, please, please, send urgent help. My name is Lyla Santiago. I'm marooned along with six other survivors on an island about fourteen hours by motorboat, south or southwest of Jakarta. Our boat was swept away by the storm, along with the rest of our party. We have very limited food and water and are in urgent need of medical assistance. Three people have already died. I repeat, this is an SOS call. If anyone is monitoring this channel, please send help. We have no idea how long we can last. We will make the same call this time tomorrow. Over.

CHAPTER 8

THE CABANA TURNED out to be a kind of open-air bar / dining area overlooking the tip of the island. It was shaded by a roof made of palm fronds and set back from the beach on a little promontory, slightly higher than the rest of the island, and as we made our way through the trees, I could hear the voices of the other contestants rising above the sound of the waves and see the occasional flash of a dress or a colorful shirt as we converged on the meeting point.

I snuck a covert look at Nico as we walked, trying to measure both of us up against the other contestants. Nico was wearing ripped jeans and a very sheer white shirt, only held by a couple of buttons, and his hair was tousled by the breeze in a way that was definitely working, though I had seen the ten minutes of swearing and tweaking that those artless curls entailed. I had wanted to wear jeans as well, but Nico had talked me out of it, telling me that all the other girls would be in dresses—and in the end I had caved and worn a loose turquoise handkerchief dress that showed the straps of my new pink bikini, deliberately little makeup, and hair that was supposed to look tousled and beach-dried. I knew in my heart that I couldn't hope to compete with the level of hair and makeup skills I had seen at the meet and greet. I would have to try to make a virtue out of my low-maintenance, girl-next-door charms.

In other words, I realized as we came out of the trees into a sun-drenched clearing, exactly how Baz had originally characterized me. Was I really so easy to predict? The thought was not entirely pleasant, but I didn't have time to dwell on it because we were at the cabana—the camera crew in the corner were pointing their lenses our way—and Dan and Santana were standing up to greet us.

Dan was still shirtless, but his admittedly impressive torso was totally eclipsed by Santana, who was wearing what looked like a one-piece bathing suit that showcased her lush cleavage to a truly impressive degree. They were both at one end of a long table, spread with a mouth-watering array of cakes, pastries, and what looked like some kind of ricey porridge, all of which made my stomach rumble in a way that reminded me forcibly of the fact that I'd skipped breakfast.

"Lyla!" Santana called as we made our way up the steps, trying not to look at the camera crew hovering in the corner. "And Nico! So great to finally meet you!"

She came out from behind the table, and I saw that what I'd taken for a bathing suit was actually the fitted top part of a stunning maxi dress in tropical colors that set off her deep tan and revealed something I hadn't noticed before on her upper arm—it looked like a little white pill box stuck onto the skin, but I was pretty sure I knew what it was. My cousin had had one growing up. It was a glucose monitor, the kind worn by diabetics.

She moved across to embrace us both in a flurry of silky hair and air-kisses, and close-up, I noticed that she was even more unbelievably pretty than I had first thought, with lashes longer than I had ever seen, and skin like something out of a moisturizer commercial, all bare and glowing. My own amateur makeup job in the villa bathroom suddenly felt more than a little inadequate.

"Nico," Dan said, clapping him on the back in a very manly way. "Good to meet you, mate! And Lyla." He gave me a little wink. "I feel like we're old friends now."

"Coucou, chéris" came from down the steps, and we turned to see Angel making her way through the trees in a diaphanous, ankle-length white dress, the lace trim just trailing on the forest floor in spite of her height. Behind her was Bayer, muscles positively bulging out of a shirt with the sleeves rolled up to a tightness that looked like they were about to give his biceps a tourniquet.

"All right," he said as they mounted the steps, nodding around the group in a way that came across reserved, bordering on suspicious. The thought crossed my mind that he was the one who'd made the fuss about his Apple watch—when, judging by the implant on her arm, Santana had a much better reason for not wanting to give up her tech—and that maybe *he* was going to be the villain of the show. In spite of his looks, he had a kind of muscle-bound bullish quality that wasn't entirely attractive. I thought he might easily be the kind of person to snap in an argument and throw the first punch.

Within a few minutes, Romi, Joel, Conor, and Zana had arrived too—and so had Camille, who was looking a mixture of nervous, stressed, and excited.

When we were all seated around the big table, looking enviously at the food but not quite daring to touch it, Camille stood up.

"Okay, so the presenting format of this show, I'm not sure if you know, will be voice-over. We're going to have a *very* exciting celebrity presenter, but for contractual reasons I can't reveal who it is—"

"That means they haven't actually signed anyone," Dan whispered in my ear, and I suppressed a laugh. "They're hoping for Neil Patrick Harris but they're probably going to end up with that permatanned guy from the shopping channel."

"—and for logistical reasons it's just easier if they record their commentary to be dubbed on afterwards—"

"Again, haven't signed anyone," Dan whispered.

"Shh!" I hissed back sternly, and he made a mock contrite face and folded his hands.

"—so what's going to happen is I'm going to read off the challenges, the crew will film your reaction shots, and we'll overlay my voice with the voice of the mystery presenter in edits. For that reason, please try not to look at me when I'm reading out the tasks. We want it to sound like there's a disembodied voice and to really maintain the idea that you're alone on this secluded island. To make it easier, I'm going to stand out of eyeline." She indicated a bamboo screen standing in the corner of the cabana, and then moved across to it, shuffling a stack of cue cards in her hands.

"Okay, everyone ready?"

There were murmurs from around the table and Camille cleared her throat.

"Welcome to Ever After Island, contestants! Here we'll be finding out who among you is truly the perfect couple—and who are Mr. and mismatched." There was a pause and then she stuck her head out from behind the screen. "Kim, I don't love that pun, I'm not sure if Baz approved it, but we might tweak in edits, okay? I think something about kissing frogs would be better. So, guys"—she turned to us—"just bear in mind the final voice-over might not be exactly the same, but we'll make it work in the editing suite." She cleared her throat again and continued, "For this first challenge we'll be running a Mr. and Mrs.—with a difference. You'll each be assigned a tell-all questionnaire to fill out about everything from your favorite dessert to your deepest and darkest secrets."

There was a distinctly stagey gasp from Angel, and glancing around the table I realized that the other islanders were vamping up their reaction shots in a way that I totally wasn't. There were varying expressions of shock, surprise, and laughing trepidation. Nico was looking around the circle, wide-eyed. Romi, Joel's partner, had her hands clasped in a pantomime of terror, and Bayer was blowing a kiss at Angel with a very macho display of self-confidence. Only Conor was leaning back in his seat, looking truly relaxed, though beside him Zana looked anything but—she was gripping the edge of the table so hard that her knuckles were white. Glancing across at the crew, I saw that one of the cameras was pointing my way, and I tried hastily to adjust my face to something that wouldn't look completely gormless on-screen—a kind of intrigued surprise—and then realized Camille was still speaking, and that I probably needed to listen to what she was saying.

"—end of the day, you'll be asked for the answers . . . and we'll find out the truth about how well you all know your partners. Who was their childhood crush? What's their worst habit? To truly love someone, you have to know them through and through, flaws and all. So let's find out: Who's really the *one* perfect couple?"

There was a brief pause, and then she emerged from behind the screen and said, "Was that okay, Kim? Do we need any more reactions?"

"I don't think so." Kim was staring down at the screen in front of her, apparently scrolling through the various camera angles. "We've got plenty of angles, and we can always patch it together with other footage if we need to fill time."

"Okay, you're good to eat, guys," Camille said. "I'll be coming around with the questionnaires in just a minute. In the meantime, fill your boots, because we won't be stopping again until dinner."

There was a moment's silence, and then Joel stood up and reached for the coffee, and it was like a signal had been given, and everyone began to dig in.

I was extremely hungry, I realized, as I began loading my plate and filling up my cup, but when I sat down and finally took a bite of a jam-filled croissant, I found the food wasn't quite as good as it looked. It had clearly been shipped in, ready-made, and the pastries and Danishes in particular had the slightly plastic quality of long-life food. The fruit salad was obviously out of a tin, which seemed nuts on an island covered in coconuts and bananas, and the bread had a spookily soft crumbly texture that was more like cake. The best thing was the rice porridge, which Santana told me was called congee.

"Dan and I positively *lived* off this in Thailand," she said between mouthfuls. "Absolute heaven, total comfort food."

Across from me, Angel was picking disdainfully over the pastries.

"Carbs, carbs, it is all carbohydrates," she said a little disgustedly. "Where is the protein? Where are the nuts and fresh fruit? I cannot drink this." She flicked a long, manicured nail at a big jug of orange juice that looked like it had last seen an orange quite a while ago. "It is basically Orangina minus the gas." She pronounced it *gaz* with a z.

"Chill, babe." Bayer, beside her, was shoveling down a raspberry Danish and gulping at a tall mug of black coffee. "God, this coffee's shit. Wish I'd brought my Nespresso."

"Hi!" Romi was saying to some of the crew, who were paying her absolutely no attention and were busy taking action shots of Santana booping Dan on the nose with a tinned cherry. "Hi! Could I get a soft-scrambled egg? Ideally two."

"Hon." Joel pulled at her arm. "Romi, let's leave it. I don't think they've got time to be making food right now."

Only Zana wasn't really eating anything. She had a plate of food in front of her, filled up by Conor, I'd noticed, but she was picking at it without any evident enjoyment, pulling the blueberries one by one out of an oily-looking muffin. Beside her, Conor glanced at her plate and put a hand on her knee as if silently encouraging her to eat something, but she only pushed the plate away. Yikes. I'd been at an all-girls school and seen my fair share of eating disorders, and this was ringing all my alarm bells. I glanced across at Nico, to see if he had noticed too, but he was busy chowing down a chocolate croissant, and when I caught his eye, he only blew me a kiss, checking to see that the film crew had caught it.

We were finishing up when Camille came back with a set of envelopes, each with one person's name on it.

"Right," she said busily, distributing the envelopes. "Here are the rules. You're going to be split up from your partners—boys stay here in the cabana, girls go to the Ever After Villa. You can chat, but do *not* reveal too much about your answers. We want to save that for later."

"So wait," Romi said, her brow furrowed. "I don't get it. Am I answering for me, or Joel?"

"For you," Camille said patiently. "The other part of the Mr. and Mrs. will come later. Ready girls?"

It was a long time since I'd heard someone seriously address a group of women my age as "girls," but nevertheless, we all stood, Romi still looking a little puzzled, and followed Camille down the steps.

The island was a maze, I realized, as the five of us followed Camille along a twisting little sandy path. The routes zigzagged through the trees in a way that contrived to make the forest feel much larger and denser than it really was. Tip to tip, the island was quite long, at least a couple of miles, judging by what I'd seen from the boat. But now that we were actually on it, I realized there was no way it could be more than ten minutes from side to side. Nico and I had walked from the boat, which was moored up on what must be . . . I glanced overhead, trying to get my bearings, and deduced from the position of the sun that the boat must be on the east or northeast side of the island. The villas were mostly clustered along the western shore, facing the coral lagoon, and it had taken us only a few minutes to go from one side to the other. But the paths were deliberately constructed in a way to make each part of the island feel as secluded as possible. I also realized that I had yet to see any of what must surely be the island's infrastructure. There had to be a desalination plant somewhere, as I'd said to Nico, and presumably some kind of electrical generator, whether motor-powered or solar. Plus, of course, the construction huts the producer had mentioned. But none of them were apparent from this part of the island.

Just as I was beginning to think that Camille had gotten us lost, and we were walking in circles, we popped out onto the beach, in front of the Ever After Villa.

"So, ladies," Camille said, waving a hand at the floating gangway leading out to the villa. "Make yourselves comfortable! I'll be back in a couple of hours to collect your questionnaires."

Zana, Romi, Angel, Santana, and I glanced at each other, and then across at the veranda of a villa where a crew member was standing with a tray of brimming champagne flutes. A tempting array of bean bags, hammocks, and loungers was scattered around the deck. There was a moment's silence, and then Angel stalked onto the gangway, grabbed a glass, and draped herself into the most comfortable-looking chair—a kind of wicker throne strewn with kilims, cushions, and throws.

"Hell yeah!" Romi said. She tossed her platinum-blond hair over one shoulder and crossed the walkway with surprising speed, given the height of her platform sandals, then flung herself into a striped hammock with a little whoop. Santana gave me a grin and a shrug, kicked off her heels, and stepped onto the gangway too.

Only Zana and I were left, and I realized, as I turned to her, that we'd barely exchanged a word.

"Ready?" I said with a smile. Her eyes were huge and light brown, fringed with lashes that, together with her willowy limbs, gave her the look of a startled baby fawn.

"As I'll ever be, I guess. After you."

"No, after you." I held out a hand. She was the youngest person here, I'd realized, and I felt a sudden rush of protectiveness. Bobbing her head with a kind of nervous acceptance, she stepped onto the platform, closing her eyes as she did.

"Are you okay?" I asked curiously, and she shook her head.

"I'm . . . I'm just . . . I'm quite scared of water. Not swimming pools, I'm fine in those. I'm even okay on big boats, if I don't have to see the sea too much—but that trip across from the yacht in the dinghy was horrible."

"So, it's not that you can't swim?"

Zana shook her head.

"No, it's not that. I'm actually a pretty good swimmer. It's something about the depth of the sea. I always think—" She stopped, swallowing convulsively, the muscles in her slender throat working under the pale skin.

"Yes?"

"I always think there might be something down there, waiting. In the darkness. Waiting to . . . grab me."

On the face of it, it was stupid. A child's fear—*a monster under the bed, something in the water.* Images of rubber sharks or giant squid. But something about her face, or maybe her voice, low and full of dread, made me shiver involuntarily. Then I forced a smile.

"The good thing about this water is it's so clear, you can see the bottom. Look, nothing there at all."

I pointed down at the clear turquoise depths, and she leaned over, forcing herself to look, and then smiled. But the expression was clearly fake, a pretense of reassurance that she very evidently didn't feel, and when we got across the gangway to the veranda, I noticed that she took a seat as far away as possible from the water's edge and downed her champagne like someone throwing back medicine.

The others had already pulled out their questionnaires, and after a moment watching Zana, trying to make out if she was okay, and whether we should ask to move back to the island, I took out my own envelope and began reading.

The questions were fairly standard, and I started to fill them in, pressing the pencil awkwardly against my knees.

Name: *Lyla Santiago*

Star sign: *Pisces*

What do you think that says about you?

Huh, that was a poser. I was definitely *not* a believer in astrology.

"Hey, Angel, can I ask you something?"

"If you wish," she said, not looking up.

"Do you know anything about star signs? What kind of person are you if you're a Pisces?

That made Angel put down her pencil and look at me over the top of her oversized sunglasses, her dark eyes narrowed in a frown.

"Tu rigoles?" And then, as I looked at her blankly, "Are you joking me?"

"Um . . . no. I'm not. I mean, I'm not really into that kind of—" I stopped. *That kind of woo* was what I'd been going to say, but it struck me that the word might come over a little needlessly offensive. "K-kind of thing," I finished instead.

Angel rolled her eyes a little but said, as if talking to someone very stupid, "Pisces women are typically highly spiritual. They make excellent romantic partners because they are very intuitive, very in touch to their partner's emotional needs."

Another huh. I hoped I was a good girlfriend, but *spiritual* and *intuitive* weren't honestly words I would have chosen to describe myself. Perhaps Angel could see the blankness in my face, because she added, "However, they can also be very analytic."

"Okay," I said slowly. "Thanks." And then, more to be polite than anything else, "What's your star sign?"

"I am a Virgo." She pronounced the word with a rolling *rrr* that made me smile, and she raised one eyebrow. "Are you laughing at me?"

"No! I'm sorry, not at all. I just— I loved your pronunciation of Virgo."

"Oh God, yeah," Romi chimed in, chewing the end of her pencil. "Your accent is so lush."

"Thank you," Angel said. She looked a little mollified as she threw her hair back over one shoulder, preening a little as she did, and then took another sip of champagne.

I am both intuitive and analytical, I wrote in the box, and then carried on.

"Childhood crush," was next. That was a tough one. I hadn't honestly *had* any childhood crushes, not the kind I thought they meant anyway. I'd never been the kind of kid to moon over Justin Timberlake or Ricky Martin. Of course, there had been boys at school that I'd liked. I'd had a huge crush on my neighbor, a boy two years older than me called Oliver Dixon, for one long painful summer that had had me mowing the lawn more times in one month than I'd done in my life since. But I definitely hadn't mentioned his name to Nico, and I wasn't sure I wanted to advertise my teenage yearnings on national TV if we were forced to read out our answers. His parents still lived next door to mine.

In the end I thought about the number of times I'd watched *Point Break* as an impressionable teen and wrote down Keanu Reeves. He looked vaguely similar to Nico, and I still would, even though he was a silver fox these days.

"Ideal night in?" was the next question. I wrote down *Paneer cheera curry with lemon rice, a big glass of red, and a really good drama series.* Then, thinking that sounded a bit me-me-me, I added, *and someone to snuggle up with to watch it.* Although in all honesty, Nico wasn't really the best telly-watching companion since he had a pathological inability to pay attention for more than five minutes, so I spent more time explaining the plot than watching myself.

"Ideal night out?" came next, and that took a bit of thought. Nico was the social one in our relationship. He was out three or four nights every week. I often had to work late or start early, ruled by the demands of cell lines and when I could book time on the various machines I needed to process samples. And to be honest, I wasn't that social at the best of times. In truth, my ideal night out was something pretty close to my ideal night in—a good meal somewhere not too shouty, with someone who could hold an interesting conversation. But that made me sound so middle-aged I thought I might get kicked off the program.

In the end, though, I couldn't think of anything that sounded better. An evening at the theater sounded hopelessly wanky. A night out clubbing was just . . . well, it was untrue. I hadn't been to a club since I was about twenty-five. Camping, board gaming, pub crawls . . . none of that was me. And I assumed the whole point of these answers was to test them on Nico. There was no way he'd say I liked any of those things. In the end I wrote down the truth and just tried to make it sound as romantic as possible: *A delicious meal in the company of someone I really care about, long chats between courses, something interesting to discuss. Maybe we share a pudding, then a taxi home and curl up in bed.* Cliché, but the alternative was a flat lie, and I didn't think that would help anyone, least of all Nico.

The next one, however, made me do a double take. Biggest secret.

My first reaction was to think that I didn't *have* any secrets— certainly not from Nico. My life was so boring there wasn't much to conceal. But then, completely unbidden, a thought popped into my head, one I most definitely hadn't admitted to Nico, and maybe hadn't even admitted to myself until that moment: *I can't see myself with Nico in five years' time.*

Fuck. Was that true?

As I turned the discovery over in my mind, I realized that it had been gnawing at the edges of my subconscious ever since Baz had asked the question and forced me to face up to something that, until recently, I hadn't dwelled on much: the future. Now, I tried to imagine us living in suburbia, Nico knuckling down to a nine-to-five to pay for a mortgage, maybe even nursery fees . . . and I couldn't. I just couldn't. I could see *me* there, all too easily. It was what I really wanted. But Nico? There was no way I could make him fit in that picture.

The realization made me feel a little sick, but there was nothing I could do about it now. It was a question for me and Nico to thresh out when we got home—and it definitely wasn't something I could admit on the form. Which meant I needed something else. What?

I didn't really want to come here. I only said yes because it made Nico happy.

I blinked. Where had this sudden, inconvenient attack of self-analysis come from?

Beside me, Angel and Romi were scribbling away, Santana was actually giggling as she filled out one of the fields. Only Zana looked as paralyzed as I felt, staring out at the water with panicked dark eyes.

I forced my gaze away from her, back down at the form. What could I put? What on earth would pass muster as my biggest secret, yet was something I was prepared to have read out on national television, hell, maybe *inter*national television if Baz got his way? I racked my brain. Gross habits? Nothing Nico didn't know about. Illegal addictions? Didn't have any. Childhood idiocies? Maaaybe that could work . . .

Until I was twelve, I thought pregnancy was a disease you caught from being around pregnant women, I wrote at last.

It was slightly pathetic as far as "biggest secrets" went, but I certainly wasn't giving them any of my actual secrets. They were secret for a reason. Still, it felt like it needed something else, something a little more embarrassing to justify the header.

Sometimes, I still hold my breath when I pass pregnant women on the street, I added, and then immediately regretted it. It was actually true—although only in a kind of silly, reflexive way, the way as an adult you might avoid the cracks in the pavement like you did as a child, but not because you seriously thought anything might happen. But it was a bit too near the knuckle, given my first thought. The truth was, the more I thought about it, the more I realized that I was beginning to want a baby—but not with Nico. And that was a problem. But there was no rubber on the pencil, so I couldn't erase the second sentence. I'd just have to hope they didn't press me on it.

Sighing, I moved on.

The rest of the questions were less tricky. Favorite film (*The God-father*), pet hate (people who stand on the left of the escalator on the

Underground), thing I dislike most about myself (the way I judge people), significant ex (my uni boyfriend Jon who broke my heart), and a bunch of others that didn't give me more than a few minutes' pause, though I did run aground on the last one: Which male contestant *other* than your boyfriend, would you want to be stuck on a desert island with? After a few moments of pondering, I put down Joel, mainly because I felt like Nico would find him the least threatening option.

When I finally set down the form and picked up my glass, Angel, Romi, and Santana were chatting and laughing, and only Zana was still holding her pencil, with that same look of paralyzed anxiety on her face.

"Which one are you stuck on?" I asked at last, feeling sorry for her, and she jumped and looked around. I noticed one of the crew had refilled her glass, and it struck me that they were probably trying to get us, if not drunk, at least sufficiently uninhibited to reveal stuff we wouldn't normally be prepared to say on camera.

"Oh God, you startled me." She picked up the glass and nervously knocked back another gulp. "Nothing in particular, it's just . . ."

"It's just what?"

"I keep thinking . . . he's going to read them, isn't he?"

"Baz? I'd assume so. I wouldn't put anything too private."

"No, I meant—" She broke off, looking almost scared. Her big eyes were wide as Bambi's.

I frowned.

"Zana, who are you talking about? Wait— Do you mean . . . Conor?"

"He's going to have to guess the answers," she whispered. I suppressed my smile and tried to look sympathetic. I could remember exactly what it was like being twenty-two and in a relationship with someone you truly cared about. I couldn't imagine the agony of having to fill out a questionnaire like this for my first serious boyfriend, listing my grossest habits and biggest secrets. But surely it wasn't worth this look of absolute terror?

"You don't have to put down the real answers," I said comfortingly.

"I'm definitely not prepared to have my biggest secrets read out on TV, so I just put some guff about stupid stuff I believed when I was a little girl."

"I know," she said. "But I'm just— I keep thinking, this isn't just about me—it's about Conor. What if I embarrass him, or let him down?"

"Zana, he loves you," I said. I took one of her hands. It was ice-cold. "He's not really going to care if you pick your nose or whatever. But if you're worried, just don't put that."

"What if I put something wrong?" She was looking at me, her eyes wide and desperate, and I found my initial amusement turning to slight irritation. No doubt she and Conor were in the honeymoon phase, but honestly, this was a bit overdramatic.

"There're no wrong answers," I said, trying to sound reassuring. "Look . . ." I turned my head sideways to look at her answers. The worst habit line was missing. "Okay . . . so . . . I don't know . . . forgetting to brush your teeth? Spending too much on lattes?"

"Oh." Her face cleared and she looked relieved. "That's such a good one. Thank you."

"What did you put for biggest secret?" I asked, and then remembered we weren't supposed to compare answers. "Sorry, no, scrap that. I forgot we're not supposed to ask."

"It's okay," Zana said with a tremulous smile. She nodded at the sea. "You already know it."

"That you're scared of water?" I'd lowered my voice, and now she nodded again, jerkily this time, as though her nerves were wired a little too tight.

"Heyyyyy ladies," I heard over my shoulder and, turning, I saw one of the assistants—not Camille—stalking across the gangway. "How are you getting on? Ready to reveal all to the cameras?"

The only response was a gale of giggles from Santana and Romi, who had apparently been making hay with the champagne while I helped Zana with her form. Angel rolled her eyes.

"I must fix my makeup," she said a little haughtily. "The humidity here is very bad for my skin."

"Oh God, mine too!" Romi exclaimed. There was a short, good-natured fight as the others crowded into the little bathroom of the villa, Santana dabbing at dewy skin that frankly didn't need any help, and Zana fussing anxiously over a stray eyelash that wouldn't stick down—I hadn't even realized they were false, unlike Romi's huge sparrow wings. I hovered in the back, unsure what to do. I hadn't brought any of my makeup with me—not even a lip gloss, a fact that now seemed monumentally naive.

"Are you okay?" Santana asked over her shoulder, seeing me standing there. "Do you want a corner of the mirror? I'm basically done.

I shrugged.

"I didn't think to bring anything."

"God, help yourself," Santana said. She peered into her bag. "I'm not sure my foundation would do, we're not quite the same coloring, but you're welcome to my lip gloss. Masacara?"

In the end, I borrowed a swipe of transluscent powder to take the shine off my nose, and then stood back and watched Romi frantically retouching her eyebrows, and Zana fixing and refixing the errant lashes, looking more stressed by the minute.

"Okay!" came a voice from behind us as Zana finally breathed a sigh of relief and put her eyelash glue back in her handbag. "Everyone ready for your OTO?"

Like the producer earlier she pronounced it "otto," but everyone seemed to know what she meant, and only nodded.

"Who wants to go first?"

CHAPTER 9

THE OTO ROOM turned out to be a little sound-proof booth set up in one of the staff cabins, which were sited in the least glamourous part of the island, where the lush landscaping and palm frond roofs gave way to concrete paving and corrugated iron. It had clearly been used as a temporary sleeping area for the workmen—I could see folding beds stacked against one wall—but now it had been converted into a kind of makeshift interview room, with a wicker chair at one end, draped with embroidered throws and cushions, and opposite a row of chairs for the crew. The contestant end looked glamorous, but it was hot as hell inside the cabin, and I could smell the sweat of the camera crew and the people who'd been interviewed before me. The crew had clearly been stuck inside for hours and were visibly wilting.

Thankfully, when it came to my turn, the interviewer didn't press me on the pregnant women thing. In fact, there was very little interviewing as such at all. It was mostly a case of reading my own answers straight to camera, and then guessing Nico's.

One thing that Nico and I hadn't had a chance to discuss was how to play this and how early I should start trying to flunk the challenges. In the end, after a moment's quandary, I answered straight down the line, doing my honest best to predict what I thought Nico would have said. Partly, I didn't know how they were scoring this, and, if we were being marked as a couple, I didn't want to accidentally sabotage Nico's position and risk *him* being sent home early too. Partly, I would have to drop out at some point, and fairly soon, but I didn't really want to do it on the first night. I'd come all this way and the thought of getting straight back on the boat wasn't enticing. There was plenty of time to intentionally mess up when we knew how the scoring worked.

It was a relief when we were finally done and I could escape back out into the comparative fresh air, but that didn't mean the filming was over. Instead, we went back to the Ever After Villa to do some background footage of us chatting—"Talk about your boys, ladies!"— as well as reshoots of each of us writing, wearing appropriately thoughtful or nostalgic expressions on our faces.

The sun was almost setting by the time we were back at the cabana where the men—or boys, as the production team kept referring to them—sat grinning at the far side of the table. They had clearly been drinking as much as we had, and a production assistant hastily swept a stack of empty beer bottles off the table as we sat down.

I was starving and had been hoping for another spread like brunch—I could have murdered one of the plastic brioches by this time—but it seemed that wasn't to be. Instead, someone distributed more beer and wine—the last thing I felt like at the moment—and Camille stepped up to the head of the table.

"Okay, so this will be another voice-over section, so you can react to what I'm saying—in fact, please do, we want lots of nice reaction shots—but try to keep it nonverbal, okay, because we'll be dubbing over with the mystery presenter's voice. Okay?" We all nodded, and Camille pulled out her script and began to read, a broad smile on her face. "So, couples. You've spent the afternoon looking deep into your own hearts and trying to guess the secrets of your partner's. Now it's time to see how well you did. How well do you *really* know the person you came here with? Do you know the inner workings of their heart—or is it a closed book to you? Or could it be that your perfect match is on the island . . . but arrived here with someone else? It's time to find out."

She rustled through some sheets and then said, "Okay, so at this point there will be a montage of everyone answering the questions to camera, intercut with their partner guessing the responses. We won't be showing all of them obviously, just the funniest or most moving or whatever. We haven't settled on the final lineup, but in the meantime, here's a rough cut of some of the best."

She pressed something on a remote control on the desk, and a screen above the bar lit up with what I guessed was the logo for the show, a stylized desert island in the shape of a heart. After a short countdown, Conor's face appeared. He was sitting on the wicker chair, speaking directly to the camera, and looking thoughtful.

"My perfect night out . . . I'd have to say . . . taking Zana somewhere truly stunning, maybe the restaurant at the top of the Eiffel Tower, or a gondola in Venice. We'd drink champagne . . . I'd feed her her favorite dessert—chocolate-dipped strawberries—and then we'd walk home hand in hand and kiss under the stars. As for hers?" He blushed, his tanned face looking almost embarrassed for a moment. "I— God, I don't want to sound hopelessly big-headed but . . . I think she'd say a night at my place. I know that's not really a night out, but she just loves spending time together."

The camera cut to Zana, staring into the lens with her huge brown eyes.

"Conor? Oh, I think he'd say . . . a dinner somewhere sophisticated and exotic—a restaurant in Paris, maybe, or the Maldives. Fine wine, good food. We'd toast each other and then walk home—he loves to walk at night, he loves the stars. As for me . . ." She looked down at her lap, twisting her fingers. "The truth is, I'm more of a simple stay-at-home type. I'd be happy anywhere Conor was happy, that's the honest truth." Then a shy little smile flickered across her face. "Though I wouldn't say no to a chocolate-dipped strawberry."

Camille paused the screen and turned back to the group, a big smile on her face.

"I don't know about you guys, but I'm giving that . . . ten out of ten! Right?"

There was a wave of assent, rather half-hearted from the other contestants, and some laughter and clapping. Conor put his arm around Zana, squeezing her hard, as Camille hit play again.

We went through all of them. There were some incredibly lucky hits (I scored a bullseye guessing that Nico's perfect vacation would be Las Vegas, which was a total shot in the dark, and another when I said that his biggest secret was that he used fake tan, I'd guessed correctly that he wouldn't mind admitting that). There were also some comically bad misses. Angel had said, understandably, that her worst habit was smoking, whereas Bayer had said that it was clipping her toenails in the shower and leaving the shards, which caused her to shoot daggers at him.

I also knew perfectly well what Dan's biggest secret was, because he'd told me—it was the fact that he had a boyfriend. I could see from the panic in his eyes as he answered that question that he knew Santana would be skirting around it and wasn't sure how best to handle the uncertainty. In the end he said that his biggest secret was that when he was little he'd wanted to be a cage fighter when he grew up. Santana on the other hand guessed that his biggest secret was that he couldn't tell the time on a clock with hands. That provoked a gale of laughter—the secret as well as the mismatch between the two—though it was fairly sympathetic. Dan, however, looked like he'd had a sense of humor bypass, and I could understand why.

"What?" Santana mouthed across at the table at him. "I'm sorry!"

"It was one time! I can tell the fucking time!" Dan said irritably, prompting a throat-cutting motion from one of the producers, reminding us about swearing.

But the biggest surprise—to me, at least—was how many things Nico got wrong about me. I wasn't sure if they were picking out comically bad examples, but I didn't see them screen a single right answer from him. He said that my childhood crush was Harry Styles, whose career didn't even launch until I was in my twenties. He said that my biggest secret was that I was afraid of mice—which I'm not and have never been. He said that my perfect night out would be a pub curry and a pint with friends, which, okay, I enjoy a curry as much as the next person but it's not exactly my dream night out, and I don't drink pints. It was just bad shot after bad shot. I couldn't believe this was the person I'd shared nearly two and a half years of my life with. Had he been paying any attention at all? Nico had ended up on the other side of the table from me, between Dan and Bayer, and as the clips unfolded, I tried to catch his eye, see what he was making of it all, but his gaze was fixed the screen, laughing along with the others, as if it was hilarious that he seemed to know nothing about his own girlfriend.

At the end of the reel, Camille clicked off the screen and turned back to the group. The sun was properly setting, fairy lights had winked on around the edges of the cabana, and I could see that everyone was very tired, very hungry, and very drunk. Tempers were, if not fraying, at least wearing a little thin. Dan looked like he was still seething over the telling-the-time thing. Bayer, who had made several stupid mistakes with Angel, including revealing that her biggest secret was that she'd had a boob job, looked sulky. In the camera lights I could see moths and mosquitoes beginning to gather. I swiped as something settled on my arm and was glad I'd remembered to put on repellent beneath my bronzer.

"And now . . ." Camille said, "the moment of truth. Which couple truly knows each other through and through, and which couple are a hopeless mystery to each other? And finally . . ." She paused dramatically. "Which couple are *really* the most compatible on the island?"

There was a long pause. I could hear crickets in the trees, and far off a bird screamed, or maybe a monkey, I wasn't sure.

"The person who got the highest score on their partner's answers was . . ." There was a long pause, Camille dragging the tension out until I could tell everyone around the table wanted to scream. "Lyla!"

There was an audible gasp from around the table, maybe because they'd just watched Nico fuck up response after response. Nico looked positively smug.

"Congratulations, Lyla! You truly know your partner through and through; his heart is an open book to you."

I had no idea what to do. I could tell the cameras were zooming in on my face and I could only blink and say, "Oh, um, thank you." And then, almost as an afterthought, "I love you, Nico!"

"Love you too, babe!" he called from the other side of the table and made a heart shape with his hands.

"But!" Camille was still speaking, and the table quickly hushed, hanging on her words. "The person who scored the lowest on their partner's responses was . . ." There was another long pause, even longer than the one before. This time Camille really dragged it out. I heard a groan from across the table, and saw Bayer drop his head to the table-top and bang it on the surface in what looked like real frustration.

"Was . . ." Camille repeated, and then, finally she put us out of our misery. "Nico."

There was another set of gasps from around the table, and I realized that one had come from me. I knew Nico had done badly, but the worst out of *everyone*? We'd been together a little over two *years*. Clearly *I* had been paying attention at some point during that time, long enough to salt away enough information for a bunch of lucky guesses, anyway.

And what did this mean for the show? Was Nico—

But then my stomach seemed to drop. No. Absolutely not. There was no way Nico could be . . . going home? *My* results had to count for something, didn't they?

"Nico," Camille was saying, and now she looked compassionate and, something else, something close to a little nervous, I thought. "Nico . . . I'm so sorry."

"What?" Nico said, interrupting.

"You're going home."

"*What?*" He looked from me to Camille, his expression genuinely confused. "But—you can't. I've only just got here."

"I'm sorry, Nico," Camille said again. I could see the cameras zooming unforgivingly in on Nico's face. "It's time to go."

"I'm—no," Nico said flatly. He gave a little laugh, as if this might all be a huge gotcha. "I mean, no. I'm not going." He folded his arms as if to prove his point. "What about all the stuff I got right? You have to give me another chance."

"I'm sorry, Nico," Camille repeated. She glanced at the camera crew and nodded, and one of them, a big guy with powerful shoulders, put down the fluffy boom mic he was holding and moved forward.

"Is this real?" Nico asked, this time with a tinge of real outrage creeping into his voice. "Are you seriously kicking me off the show?"

I felt a sense of panic grip me. This was not the plan. This was never the plan!

"Nico?" I said blankly, and he turned to face me.

"You *stupid* cow!"

I recoiled.

"I'm sorry, what?"

"Honestly, what the fuck were those answers! A paneer what the whatever it was fuck? How was I supposed to guess that? And Keanu Reeves? He's old enough to be my dad!"

"Paneer cheera is what I *always* get!" I felt my temper flare, not helped by Camille making *stop swearing* gestures behind Nico's head. I didn't need reminding that this was all on camera. "Every single time! It's not my fault if you always leave me to order. And

Harry Styles? Seriously? How could he have been my childhood crush?"

"You sabotaged me," Nico said. His face was suddenly ugly. "You did this deliberately. What game are you playing?"

"What the actual *fuck*." I knew Camille was signaling, and I didn't care. The more I swore, the less likely they were to use this footage of my relationship imploding. "Are you serious? I don't care about your stupid little—" *Fuck fuck, no.* I had enough self-control to back-pedal from what I'd been about to say, which was *stupid little reality TV fantasy*. Whether or not Nico went, I would still be stuck here for another week. Insulting the show in front of people who were presumably happy to be on it wouldn't go down well. "S-supposed games," I finished, stumbling over the words as I tried to recover. "I'm not playing anything. I tried to say things I thought you'd guess. It's not my fault if you guessed wrong."

It's not my fault if you haven't paid attention to anything I said the entire time we've been together, was what I really wanted to say, but that felt like I would be crossing a line. Whatever he'd just said to me, I wasn't ready to dump my live-in boyfriend on national TV.

I remembered Joel's words on the boat. *If they succeed in breaking one of the couples up . . . it's going to be car crash TV. A real long-term relationship ripping apart on-screen.*

And now that car crash was Nico . . . and me.

"You've humiliated me," I heard from Nico, but two crew members were leading him away. He was still shouting over his shoulder. "You set me up. This wasn't what was supposed to happen. This wasn't what we agreed!"

And then his voice faded between the trees, and he was gone.

There was a long, stunned silence. The thing that kept rattling around my mind, absurdly, was how upset my mum was going to be when I told her what had happened. She *loved* Nico. He was the son she'd never had—handsome, charming, a little bit cheeky. But for myself, I felt . . . nothing. Only numb. Was I in shock?

Angel silently slid a bottle of wine across the table to me, and I forced a smile and filled my glass, knocking it back with a hand that was still shaking.

"Well . . ." Dan drawled, leaning back in his seat. "At least you didn't accuse him of not being able to tell the time."

There was a sudden gale of laughter, the nervous, explosive laughter of people with pent-up emotion, relieved to channel it into humor rather than anger.

"I'm glad you've forgiven me, darling," Santana said. She moved round the table to thread her arm around him, poking him in the ribs, and he snorted and tickled her back. I wondered in that moment whether the producers could possibly be fooled. They were so obviously more like brother and sister than girlfriend and boyfriend, with their physical, bantering antagonism. Was this going to be the next big reveal—Dan's boyfriend coming on with folded arms to denounce Dan as a traitor? It would certainly make good TV.

I refilled my glass and was shakily downing another gulp, when Camille came back out of the darkness. Presumably she'd finished escorting the raging Nico back to the ship.

"Right, gosh, well that was dramatic." She gave a little laugh, but it was slightly nervous. I wondered how much experience she had on this type of show. "Are you okay, Lyla?"

I shook my head. I honestly wasn't. This had blown everything out of the water. All my plans. All Nico's dreams. No one was going to be offering him any fantasy boyfriend roles on the back of that performance. And it had also put me firmly on the map as far as the TV series went. I'd been hoping to slip in and out of the series before anyone much remembered me. There wasn't much chance of that now, after that scene.

"Are you ready for your OTO? We'd love to get a few thoughts from you about Nico's departure."

"Oh God." I put down my glass. "Seriously? Now? I think I've just been dumped, live on TV, or near enough. Could I not have a drink first?"

"Um . . ." Camille looked over her shoulder and one of the other producers beckoned her over. They had a whispered conference, and then Camille came back.

"Okay, sure. In fact, there's one other bit of business we probably ought to do before we do the OTOs anyway, so let's get that out of the way and you can have a moment to collect yourself, Lyla. And then we can do the one-to-one sessions while everyone eats. Does that sound okay? I think everyone needs some food."

There were nods of assent from around the table, and someone muttered something about being fucking starving. I was fairly sure I wasn't the only one with a sour champagne headache setting in.

"Okay, so the last bit of filming is the big reveal," Camille was saying, and I saw some puzzled frowns, people shooting glances at their partners across the table. I didn't *have* a partner anymore, so I didn't have anyone to share my puzzlement with. But surely that had to be it. There couldn't be any more big reveals—could there?

Camille was pulling out her script again, and standing just behind the camera she began to read.

"Making up and breaking up is all part of finding the one true love, the person you're really meant to be with. For Lyla, it looks like that *wasn't* Nico. But on Ever After Island, breaking up doesn't mean you have to be alone. As the highest scorer, Lyla gets to spend the night in the Ever After Villa."

I blinked, remembering the picture-perfect water villa perched on stilts over the turquoise sea. Okay, well, every cloud, I guessed, although it would have been more fun to be there with Nico, not recently single, and presumably about to depart from the show myself, unless I could make a strategic alliance with one of the other soon-to-be-singletons, which I didn't particularly want to do.

"The twist?" Camille said, quizzically, and then answered her own question with dramatic emphasis. "She *won't* be there alone. The Ever After Gods have compared the islanders' secret answers, sprinkled on a little Perfect Couple magic, and the person whose answers most closely corresponded with Lyla's was . . ."

I felt my eyes go wide. What. The. Fuck.

"Joel."

There was a moment of utter silence. You could have heard a pine needle drop.

Then, "I'm sorry, *what*?"

It was Romi, her voice shrill with wine and shock.

"Joel," Camille said, "you'll be spending the night in the Ever After Villa with Lyla, to find out if the two of you are *really* the perfect match for each other. Romi, you'll be spending the night alone at Island Dream. Everyone else, you'll have one week to look deep into your hearts, to figure out if the person you're coupled up with is *really* your perfect match—and if not, to seek out a new coupling in time for the first Ever After Ceremony this time next week."

She closed the script, and then said, "And that's when we'll go to credits. I should say, you won't necessarily have a week before the first Ever After Ceremony, the week refers to the viewer's week, not yours. We're playing the schedule by ear, but it'll be at least a couple of days, as we have to get some of the other challenges out the way first."

"Hang on," Romi said icily. "You, what's your name—"

"Camille," Camille said without rancor.

"Camilla, yes, look, I'm sorry, but my boyfriend is not spending the night with some slag—" She turned to me. "No offense—"

"None taken," I murmured, trying not to let the hysterical laugh that was threatening to erupt, bubble out.

"—in some shag-pad villa. That was all for the cameras, right?"

"I'm afraid not," Camille said apologetically. "They do actually have to sleep there. I mean, obviously no one has to do anything they don't want to—"

"I should fucking hope not!" Bayer growled into his beer.

"—but that's the format. The winner of each task and their perfect match—and that's decided by a different format each time—will spend the night together in the Ever After Villa, and after that, the two contestants can decide whether or not to return to their former partners or make a new couple."

"Well, the *format*," Romi spat, "can go fuck itself right in the hole."

"Romi—" Joel said. He had stood up and was leaning across the table towards her. Romi rounded on him.

"Did you put her up to this?"

"What? No! Who?"

"*Her.*" She jerked her head at me. "I saw the two of you plotting together on the boat. Did you give her your answers?"

"No! Of course not. How would I even know to do that? We had no idea what the task would be."

"Well, if you wanted to humiliate me—congratulations, you've succeeded."

"Romi!" Joel was scarlet with mortification. "First, could we *please* not do this here—" He made a small, almost involuntary gesture towards the ranks of camera operators spaced around the cabana. "Second, why the hell would I want to humiliate you?"

"You've never got over me and Dean. Even though I *told* you I was drunk and it was a mistake. Even though I said sorry like a thousand times. Are you ever going to stop holding him over my head?"

A muscle twitched in Joel's jaw and there was a short, charged silence in which the only sound was the palm trees rustling in the wind coming off the sea.

"You're the only person mentioning his name right now," he said at last, very evenly.

"Well, he's not doing it," Romi announced, turning to Camille. "He's not going to that villa. Are you, Joel?"

"That is enough." A deep voice came from the back of the room, and my first clue as to who'd spoken was the fact that the whole crew seemed to stiffen and stand to attention. A small group of producers and assistants parted like the Red Sea and Baz came through, his face dark as thunder. "You—" He pointed to Romi. "I've heard enough from you. If you don't like the rules, you can get off the island. Now."

Romi opened her mouth to speak, and then shut it again.

"And you"—he pointed to Joel—"and you"—jabbing a finger at me—"will be sleeping in the Ever After Villa tonight, end of. What you do there is between the two of you, but you'll abide by the rules or fuck off. Got it?"

"Got it," Joel murmured. He shot an apologetic look at Romi, whose face was scarlet with a mixture of wine, sun, and the effort of not biting back at Baz.

"Now wind this shit show up and get the crew across to the water villa to do the Ever After sequences," Baz snapped. "I want the whole crew back on the boat by nine p.m. to go over today's footage."

"Do you want to leave Phil and Jen here to go over the—" Camille began, but Baz raised his voice.

"I said the whole crew. This is an all-hands meeting. Capiche?"

"Yes, Baz," Camille whispered, and "Yes, boss," came filtering back from the few other crew members who dared open their mouths. And then Baz turned on his heel, with Camille hurrying after him, and left, the camera crew following in his wake like a flock of little ducklings trailing after their mama.

After they'd gone, nobody said anything for a long moment. The fairy lights strung round the cabana were swaying in the wind, casting shadows that lurched drunkenly back and forth with each gust. It was Romi who broke the silence.

"Shit show is right. I mean, he said it. Where's the fucking welfare team? Where's the psychologist? I *know* how this stuff ought to run, and this show is a joke. Maybe I *will* walk."

"What do you mean?" Santana asked. She was frowning, and looked pale and sweaty, a sharp contrast to her dewy glow from earlier. Now she drew out a boxy blue monitor and pressed something. "God, I need to get some food inside me. My bloods are really low. Has anyone got anything sweet?"

"That!" Romi said, pointing at the glucose monitor stuck to Santana's upper arm. "That's *exactly* what I mean. Where's the medics keeping an eye on us? Where are the psychological interviews to make sure none of us are off our fucking nut? I've tried out for a bunch of these things and none of them have been run like this. We should have had evaluations and access to a trained counselor. You can't just stick people in front of a camera and wash your hands—not anymore. They're running this like it's 1999."

Angel had stood up and walked across to a corner of the cabana, where the debris from lunch had been stacked up, and now she came back with a banana, more or less intact apart from a bruised stem.

"Here," she said to Santana. "Is this okay for your sugar?"

"I mean . . ." Santana took the fruit and looked at it a little dubiously. "Something like juice or gummy bears would be better but . . . yeah, it'll do for the moment—at least until I can get to my glucose tablets, or they feed us." She pulled off the peel, stuffed a piece in her mouth, and said, through a mouthful of fruit, "So . . . do you think this is shady? I thought it was supposed to be big budget. Isn't it Real TV's flagship show?"

"I do think they're cutting corners," Dan said. He looked a little worried. "I wasn't sure at first, but Romi's right about the psychological stuff. A friend did *Love Island*, and this absolutely isn't how it's supposed to work. There's supposed to be welfare teams and so on."

I frowned. Now Dan said it, I recalled there had been mention of a welfare team in the booklets Camille handed out. But where were they?

"And the crew is weirdly small," Dan was continuing. "From what John told me, they've normally got dozens and dozens of people working on this stuff. But Baz seems to be stretched bloody thin. I mean, they're relying on all these remote cameras that aren't even working properly."

"Don't you think it's a little weird that there's no staff outside the production crew?" Santana said through a mouthful of banana. "I thought there'd be, you know, maids and chefs and cleaners. But it seems to be just us and the TV crew. I do accept that the resort isn't up and running yet, but shouldn't Baz have brought those people in temporarily?"

"I'm not convinced they've sold it," I said. My voice was quiet, and Bayer turned to me, his eyebrow raised so that the ring glinted in the glow from the string lights.

"*What* did you say?"

"I said, I don't think they've sold the show," I repeated more loudly. The others turned to look at me, their expressions ranging from skeptical to perplexed. "Something Baz said in our interview, about everyday contestants like me and . . ." I looked around the circle, trying to assess who wouldn't mind being described as *everyday*. ". . . and, um, Joel, being what would sell it to the networks. Ari—that's Nico's agent—he made it sound like a done deal, but I haven't seen a single bit of evidence that Real TV is actually on board. Have you?"

There was a quiet murmur from around the table as everyone assessed this idea. Dan spoke first.

"It would fit with there being no presenter. I mean, they're not going to get a big name for a show that hasn't sold . . . are they?"

"And it'd make sense of why the budget is so tight," Santana said slowly. "If Baz is doing this out of his own pocket, hoping to sell it on spec. Shit, do you think it's true?"

"If it *is* true, I will fucking kill him," Conor said. His voice was low but full of menace, and turning to him, I realized it was the first time he had spoken. He looked extremely contained, but in the way a bomb might—a sealed package full of volatile material. "I'll strangle Baz with my bare hands, and then I'll fly back to the UK and do the same to my agent. If they've dragged me halfway around the world to some show that hasn't even sold to a network—"

He broke off. Zana's eyes were fixed on him and she was biting her lips, looking almost as pale as Santana.

"Look, I *have* to get some food," Santana said at last into the strained silence. "Or I'm going to go hypo. Does anyone want to come down to the staff quarters with me to see what we can fix up? They must have some kind of supplies—and presumably there's a kitchen."

The others nodded with varying degrees of resignation and exhaustion, and then began making their way down the pebbled path towards the staff area.

As they did, almost unconsciously, they paired off, two by two, into their original couples, leaving me trailing in their wake, a lone singleton. It felt . . . I don't know. Symbolic, maybe. *Was* I single now? Had Nico and I just broken up? I wondered what he was doing, whether he was having some kind of debrief on board the *Over Easy* right now, spewing his resentment to the camera. Or maybe he was sitting in his cabin, head in hands, as shell-shocked as me, wondering how it had all unraveled so fast. He had spent longer on the flight from the UK than he had on Ever After Island. If he caught a flight out tomorrow, which was the fifteenth, he could be back at his barista job by Monday—the whole thing like a distant dream. Except that when he woke up, I wouldn't be there.

As I walked down the path in the wake of the others, I realized something: if tomorrow was the fifteenth, today must be Valentine's Day. No one else had mentioned it, perhaps because we were all disoriented by the time zone changes and endless flights, and perhaps too because when the show aired it would seem weird to have contestants celebrating something that had happened months ago.

But today was the fourteenth of February—and the anniversary of the day Nico and I had made out at my friend's Valentine's Day Massacre party. If our relationship *had* just ended, live on camera, and I still wasn't sure if that was the case, then maybe it was oddly fitting that we had stumbled from one horror show to another. Because, no matter how you spun it, this *was* a horror show—or at least a pretty far cry from what either of us had intended. And now I was alone on a tiny island, thousands of miles from home, wondering what on earth I'd let myself in for. I supposed I was about to find out.

02/24—07:47 p.m.

Listen to me, if anyone is listening to this, you need to get here now. Now, do you understand me? Because this is not a game. It's not a joke. This is life or death, and we are stuck on this fucking island with a murderer. We are— Shit.

Hello—hello? Hello?

Fuck, it's dead.

PART TWO

THE STORM

My name is Zana Robertson. Today is Monday, 26 February. At least I think that's right. My head aches. It's hard to remember.

What follows are the pages of a diary I've been keeping since the storm. I don't know why—I've never written a diary before. I told myself that it was because I was frightened of losing track of the days. But I think it was more than that.

Maybe it was so that if we were found, I'd have some kind of record of what happened, some way of remembering that this totally unreal experience was actually real.

Or maybe it was the opposite. Maybe I began to write this because even in those first early days I knew . . . we might not be found. The boat might not come back. Or not until it was too late.

It's taken me a long time to face that possibility. And even now, there's a voice in the back of my head that insists that we will be found. We HAVE to be found. Someone must be out there looking for us. Someone knows what happened. We just have to hold on.

But we are almost two weeks in now. The water is starting to run low, and there is no boat in sight, and I have to admit . . . I have to admit, this could be it. This could be how it ends.

So maybe that's why I started writing this. Because I want people to know how hard we tried, how long we fought, how tenaciously we took care of each other. If you've found this, if it's too late . . . just know that we tried. We really, really tried.

CHAPTER 10

"ARE YOU OKAY?"

Joel spoke the words into the pitch-black, and I rolled over, facing him across the wide expanse of bed. In spite of the uncurtained windows, the room was incredibly dark. Clouds had covered the sky, blocking out the moon and stars, and the Ever After Villa faced out to sea, so we couldn't even see the shapes of the other villas. The only illumination was the unblinking red LED of the camera mounted in the corner of the room, and the faint reflection of the lights from the island, bouncing back at us from the sea. In their dim glow, I couldn't see Joel's expression, or even really his face, just the outline of his body beneath the white sheets. He was huddled as far away from my side of the bed as it was possible to get—quite far, given I had done the same.

"Yes, I'm okay," I said. "I just can't sleep."

"Me either. I think it's the wind."

It had picked up after the camera crew had left, and now it wailed through the palm trees with a long, low urgency, making it hard to sleep. The sea had roughened too, and I could hear it slap-slap-slapping against the veranda with a kind of contained violence. Presumably this was the storm the crew member had mentioned back on the mainland. Clearly it had arrived ahead of schedule.

"Do you think this place is safe?" Joel asked now, and I shrugged one shoulder, forgetting he couldn't see me.

"It must be reasonably robust, or it'd blow away every time they had a monsoon. Wait, do they have monsoons here?"

There was a silence as Joel tried to figure this out.

"I don't know," he said at last. "Isn't the monsoon to do with landmass? They don't have it in the Maldives, I know that."

"Well, regardless," I whispered, "I'm sure they've had storms before, so the fact that this place is still here is reassuring."

I heard, more than saw, Joel nod—heard the movement of his beard against the pillow, though even as I said the words it occurred to me, we didn't actually know how long this villa had been standing. Maybe it had never weathered a storm. Still, there *must* be building codes. Mustn't there? Joel spoke again, and I dragged my mind back to the present.

"Are you okay about Nico? It must have been a shock. I know it's not—you know. Not what you planned."

"No." That was putting it mildly. I sighed and turned my pillow to the cool side, willing myself to relax, but I was too keyed up.

After Santana had fixed us up a rudimentary picnic from leftovers she'd found in the staff quarters, Joel and I had been dragged off to the one-to-one booth for interviews, and then to the Ever After Villa, which had, horrifyingly, been dressed up as a romantic honeymoon suite, complete with a heart in scattered rose petals on the bed, a champagne bucket full of ice, and two white fluffy robes. There was only one bed, and Camille shook her head when I asked about the possibility of getting some kind of blow-up mattress.

"I'm sorry, Lyla, there's nothing of that kind on the island, and as you can see, getting a regular mattress across the jetty wouldn't be easy. Plus it wouldn't look great on camera. But I'm sure this one is big enough for two. You can always build a pillow wall!"

In the end, after Joel and I had changed into the robes and done a series of mortifying champagne toasts to each other, followed by shots of us leaning side by side on the veranda fence, staring up at what was supposed to be the moon, but was by now nothing but clouds, the crew had relented and let us go—although more, I suspected, because it was five to nine and Camille was getting increasingly antsy about Baz's injunction to be back on the *Over Easy* before nine o'clock.

Before they'd left, I had managed to get the basics of what would be happening to Nico.

He was back on the ship, being filmed and debriefed right now, and then, as soon as the rest of the crew rejoined the boat, they would set sail overnight for an island about six hours away with a helicopter pad, where he'd be picked up and flown back to Jakarta for return to the UK.

The *Over Easy* would turn around and return here in time for another day's filming. That was why Baz had been so insistent about the 9 p.m. cutoff—there was a very narrow window for them to get to the helicopter site and back in time for breakfast.

After the crew had left, Joel and I had had a polite but ultimately futile argument about who would take the floor, lots of *but I insist* and *no don't be silly, I prefer a hard surface.*

In the end though, sense had prevailed and we'd agreed to sleep at the far sides of the very large bed, which was honestly farther away from each other than if one of us *had* been on the floor. We agreed though, not to tell Romi.

"If she asks, I slept in the bath," Joel said firmly, and I nodded. It was only afterwards, when I was changing into an old T-shirt for bed, that I looked up and clocked the impassive black lens of the camera mounted in the corner of the room. I had no idea what footage they'd be using—hopefully not me scrabbling to unhook my bra—but it would most definitely not show Joel sleeping in the bathroom. It might be better for Joel to tell the truth, given it was going to come out anyway. That said, I wasn't convinced he and Romi were going to survive this experience. Not just the Ever After Villa—I didn't flatter myself that my fatal allure had the power to break up long-standing relationships—but the whole thing. The TV show, the exposure if it aired . . . all of it.

Now, two hours later, I was lying awake in the dark, listening to the wind and wondering whether Nico too was lying awake in a cabin on the *Over Easy*. Maybe he hadn't even gone to bed. Maybe he was busy pouring out a stream of bile to some exhausted camera crew. Or maybe he'd drunk himself into a stupor and was snoring his head off.

"What did you put on your answers, then?" Joel whispered, and I sighed.

"Pretty much exactly the same as you, going by the snippets they broadcast. I mean, our ideal nights out were virtually identical, and I picked *The Godfather* as my favorite film too. And for the place I'd love to go but have never been, I put Venice."

"Same. What did you put for your favorite book?"

"*Rebecca*. What about you?"

"I put *Remains of the Day*," Joel said. "Romi put *Fifty Shades of Grey*." He sighed, and above the sound of the wind, I could hear him rubbing his hand unhappily over his face as if trying to rub away the reality of the day. "I know. Says it all, doesn't it?"

"Joel, why *are* you together?" I asked, without thinking, and then wished I'd bitten my tongue. "I'm sorry, that was— I didn't mean it like that; it's just that the two of you—you're not . . ."

"What?"

"Not a very obvious couple, I guess?" As soon as the words came out of my mouth, I regretted them. I had tried to phrase it as neutrally as I could, but I could tell that Joel was nettled. His voice, when he spoke, sounded defensive.

"I could say the same about you and Nico."

I shrugged. I wanted to argue, but he had a point, one the last few days had made painfully obvious. There was a silence, and then Joel spoke, his voice very low, as though he were trying to make sure it didn't get picked up by any hidden microphones.

"I don't honestly know anymore. We've been together for years—we met backpacking in Goa after uni, and somehow being far from home . . . maybe it felt like we had more in common than we did. But since then . . . we've just got more and more different. She doesn't like any of my friends. I try, but to be honest, I'm not really interested in any of hers. I'm sporty, she's not. I'm a saver, she's a splurger. We watch completely different programs. When we met in Goa we were both these grubby, cheapskate students in flip-flops and ripped T-shirts, and since then she's got more and more high-maintenance, while I'm only marginally more scrubbed up than I was in Anjula Beach. But it's more than that. We just don't spend any *time* together anymore. And somehow now we're here . . ."

He trailed off. I thought of Nico and me, the nights I spent at the lab, listening to my podcasts as I pipetted and aliquotted my samples, Nico off at some bar. The way he was extrovert, I was introvert. He was instinctive, I was analytical. He lived life in the moment, I was a planner. And the way we had rubbed along for the best part of two-and-a-half years, our mutual attraction papering over the cracks . . . until Ever After Island had turned them into a chasm.

"I know what you mean," I said at last, a little unhappily, and suddenly I wished I'd never brought up this topic in the first place. "Well, we'd better get some sleep, I guess. Good night, Joel."

"Good night, Lyla," he said, and then turned over, and within a few minutes I heard the sound of faint snores.

It took me longer to drop off, made uneasy by the weather and, perhaps, by our conversation. But I was finally drifting into sleep when there was a particularly loud roar from the wind and a huge wave came up and over the jetty, slapping into the windows of the villa. I heard the glass creak with the impact, and when I sat up, I could see drops of water glinting on the polished floor where the wave had forced its way under the frame.

Leaning over, I flicked the light switch beside the bed. Nothing happened. I flicked it back—stupidly. I'm not sure why that would have worked. Still nothing. Then I scrambled out of bed, feeling for the fluffy robe I'd left draped over the foot, and went to the master switch beside the veranda, toggling it back and forth. Nothing. Nothing. The power must be out. I felt suddenly, deeply uneasy.

Joel was asleep, or seemed to be. In the darkness I could just make out his shape, sprawled against the white sheets.

"Joel," I whispered. "Joel, are you awake?"

"Wha?" he mumbled, throwing out an arm.

"The power's out. I'm getting a bit worried about this storm. I'm going to see if I can find anyone, see if there's anywhere else we can sleep."

"'Kay," Joel muttered. I wrapped the robe more tightly around myself, picked up the sandals I'd been wearing earlier today, and opened the door onto the veranda.

As I stepped out onto the jetty, the strength of the wind hit me—literally. It buffeted me like a physical thing, sending me staggering back against the wall of the villa. Dimly, I could see the gangway stretching across to the beach, but now it was swimming with water, each wave overtopping the decking as it peaked. The fairy lights strung along its length were dark, and if it hadn't been for the rope balustrade sticking up out of the water, I wouldn't even have been completely sure where the central section was. Now I felt an echo of Zana's earlier terror as I stepped gingerly onto the slick planks, the waves splashing at my calves as they crested. As I crossed, I could feel the gangway creaking beneath my feet, but the struts were solid and unmoving, so I had no real fear of it giving way, and the shape of the island made a natural harbor, sheltering the villa and its jetty from the full force of the waves. Still, I was relieved when my feet touched the sand at the far side. I pulled on the sandals and made my way up the beach and into the woods, heading for what I remembered as being the route to the staff quarters.

In the shadows of the trees, the night was even darker—clearly the Ever After Villa wasn't the only place to have lost power—and I had to keep my hands outstretched in front of me to prevent myself from stumbling face-first into a palm tree. Luckily the pebbled path felt distinctively nubbly under the thin soles of my sandals, which stopped me wandering off course, and when it forked, I was able to remember roughly the right direction. As I walked, I could feel the wind tugging at my robe, my hair whipping at my face, and hear the far-off crashing of the waves, punctuated by the screams of the birds in the trees. I tried to imagine what it would be like to be an animal on a night like this. Were they scared? Or exhilarated? Maybe they were used to it.

Rain had started to fall in fat, sporadic drops by the time the pebbles under my feet changed to hard concrete slabs, and I came out into a clearing surrounded by the distinctive huddle of the small, metal-roofed staff huts, quite different from the roomy villas dotted around the rest of the island. The huts were dismayingly dark, and silent, but I knocked on first one, then another, and when there was no answer, I began opening doors.

The first turned out to be the one-to-one booth—I hadn't recognized it in the darkness—and was empty apart from the wicker throne and the camera, standing there silent and unpowered. In the second hut was what seemed to be a rather sparsely utilitarian kitchen, all stainless steel and the scent of bleach. I could hear the drumming of the rain on the corrugated iron roof as I stood there, screwing up my eyes and trying to make out shapes in the darkness.

"Hello?" I called out, but there was no answer, and I turned to leave.

Either the wind had picked up, or it was much stronger on this side of the island, but as I closed the door of the kitchen hut, the wind ripped it from my fingers, slamming it against the frame with a force that would have taken off a finger if I'd still been holding the doorjamb.

As I made my way across the courtyard to the last two huts, I found I was crouching, trying to make my body a smaller target for the wind and the rain that was now beginning to spit quite hard, but even so, as I came close to the third hut, a piece of something—a branch from a palm tree, maybe—came whistling through the darkness and struck me across the cheek with shocking force, making me cry out and fall to my knees.

I knelt there, gasping, and then after a moment put my hand up to explore my face. There was a cut across my cheekbone, and I could tell the flesh around it was beginning to swell. I was going to feel that in the morning—and I had no idea how a bruise like that would look on camera. I definitely hadn't brought any makeup heavy duty enough to cover it up, though maybe the production team would have something. Still, there was no time to worry about that now—the rain was coming down with shocking force, and I just needed to get out of this storm.

When I stepped inside the third shack, I almost stumbled again. I'd been bracing so hard against the driving wind and rain that its absence seemed shocking. This hut seemed to be some kind of break room for the crew. There was a makeshift table with a kettle and a number of mismatched chairs, and up against the far wall were two bunkbeds. Both were empty, but the bottom one looked like someone had been sleeping there—there were sheets thrown back, and the pillow was dented, but when I put my hand to the mattress, it was cold. Whoever it was could have left hours ago.

In the dim light I could see notes scattered around, an empty packet of Oreos, and someone's sunglasses, but nothing I could use. Perhaps a mobile phone would have been too much to hope for, but a laptop didn't seem unreasonable. Whatever they'd had though, they'd clearly taken it with them when they went to the *Over Easy*.

There was only one shack left now, and I didn't hold out much hope for crew members. It was by far the smallest, smaller even than the OTO booth—and from the outside it looked more like storage than a sleeping area. Still, though, there might be a phone in there. Surely there had to be *something* on the island.

When I stepped inside it took a moment for my eyes to adjust to the darkness, and when they did, I could just make out it was full of equipment. I could see what looked like more cameras, a bank of what might have been sound or mixing decks and . . . I peered into the darkness. There, in the corner, was a green LED, its glow reflecting off a fluffy boom mic propped up against it. Did this place still have power?

Just in case, I felt for the light switch, and flipped it hopefully, but nothing happened. Instead, I groped my way across the room to the LED, banging my shin painfully on a chair. As I got closer, peering into the darkness, I recognized the device it was attached to. It was a radio, *the* radio in fact, the one the producer had mentioned earlier in the day, and which I'd totally forgotten. Was it working? If the LED was lit, it had to be, surely?

I began to feel my way across its surface, trying to make out the controls. There was a rubbery black receiver attached by a coiling black wire, like a telephone, and when I ran my fingers over the surface of the radio itself I could feel a gridded speaker and a bunch of buttons. When I pressed one at random, an orange digital display lit up with a brightness that made my eyes hurt after the pitch-black of the shed, showing a bunch of numbers and symbols that made no sense to me.

I felt a surge of relief, swiftly tempered by the realization that I had no idea how to work the thing. After some thought, I decided that if the radio had been used to communicate with the *Over Easy* earlier that day—which seemed likely—it was probably best not to change the channel, since that was the one the boat was most likely to be monitoring. When I picked up the receiver, however, nothing happened.

"Hello?" I said into it, in case it was voice activated, but there was no answering burst of static, only the steady drumming of the rain on the tin roof. I twisted the knob on the radio itself and there was a screech of static, so I turned it hastily back, and then remembered something from watching films—you had to press and release a button on the receiver when you wanted to transmit. Sure enough, when I ran my fingers over the mouthpiece, I found there was a button on the side, and when I pressed it, I heard an answering crackle from the speaker.

"Hello," I said cautiously. "Hello? I'm not sure how this thing works, but this is Lyla, to the *Over Easy*." Then I remembered the film I'd seen and added, "over," and released the button.

There was a crackle as I did, but although I waited, no answering voice came over the speaker. I pressed the receiver again.

"Hello, is anyone receiving this? This is Lyla to the *Over Easy*, please come in. Over."

Again, I let go and waited, but I could hear nothing apart from the quiet hiss of static from the radio and the drumming rain, and the scream of the wind outside the shack.

"*Over Easy*, can you hear me?" I could tell my voice was getting desperate, but I didn't try to hide it. This was beyond frustrating. Maybe I was doing something wrong—but what was the point in *having* a radio if no one monitored it? I spoke again. "The wind is really picking up and I'm getting seriously concerned. Is there any kind of storm shelter on the island?"

I let go of the button and waited again, this time with dwindling hope. If the *Over Easy* was out there, they were either too far away to hear the transmission, or they weren't monitoring their radio channels. Both options were worrying.

I was just groping for the receiver again when something struck the side of the hut with a bang like a firework, and a force that made the whole thing shudder to its foundations. The shock made me jump almost out of my skin, and I stood there, my heart thudding, and then reached out to touch the side of the hut where it had been hit. The entire wall was bowed in, and I could feel that in places the corrugated iron had cracked. The rear wall of the hut had been hit by something very big and very heavy. If it had collided with the other wall—the one with the window—it wouldn't have been stopped by metal sheeting, it would have shot through the glass and most likely brained me. As it was, it felt uncomfortably close to luck that the sheeting had withstood the blow.

I made up my mind. It wasn't safe here. This side of the island was much more exposed than the villa side. I would go back, tell Joel what was happening, and then make my way to Palm Tree Rest, the villa Nico and I had been allocated on the first night. I doubted it would be locked—evidently the staff quarters weren't— but if it was, well, then, I'd just break in. If Joel wanted to come— fine. If he wanted to return to Romi—also fine. I no longer gave a shit about the rules. I was just hoping we'd all be in one piece in the morning.

I picked up the receiver. I would make one last attempt before I left, and that was it.

"*Over Easy*, if you're receiving this, please come in, this is urgent," I said, speaking rapidly now. "The storm is getting really bad and I think we might need to evacuate. Just now—"

But I never got to finish the sentence. As I said the words, something huge and dark and shaped like a cannonball came flying through the window of the hut with a deafening crash. Glass flew everywhere, and the object landed with a sickening crunch on the mixing desk, crushing the bank of instruments to smithereens, along with the sturdy table beneath.

I found I was still holding the radio receiver, gasping like a fish. I think I was saying something like, "Oh God! Oh God!"

If I had been standing just ten centimeters to my left, I would have been dead—my chest crushed into the same pulp as the table and mixing desk.

As it was, I could feel cuts from the glass all over the parts of my arms and chest not protected by the robe, and the warm drops of blood beginning to trickle down my skin, mixed with the driving rain now coming through the smashed window, along with the wind.

For a moment I couldn't move. I just stood there, gasping and shaking, unable to compute how close I had come just now to dying.

Then I let the receiver drop from my hand and ran.

CHAPTER 11

"JOEL!" I COULD hardly get the word out. I had run all the way from the staff quarters, through the maze of paths, trusting to luck more than instinct as to which way to go. Now I was standing, soaked and shivering at the foot of the bed, the blood running down my arms and mixing with the rain and sea spray still clinging to my skin. My robe was wet and blood-stained, and still glittering with broken glass, my chest was heaving, and I was shaking with the adrenaline of my near miss. "*Joel!*"

I was shouting, but it was still an effort to make my voice heard above the noise of the wind and the sea. How on earth was he sleeping through this? Another huge wave came crashing over the veranda, rattling the windows in their frames, and I made up my mind. This was not safe. Soon we wouldn't be able to cross the gangway. I was going, *now*, whether Joel wanted to come or not.

I was groping my way to Joel's side of the bed, ready to slap him awake if I had to, when something, some sixth sense, or maybe a sound, slightly different from the regular roar of the waves, made me pause and turn around. Another wave, even larger than its predecessors, was heaving itself up and out of the gray sea. As I braced myself, it came crashing over the veranda balustrade and once more smashed into the French windows.

Only this time, the windows didn't hold. The force of the water snapped the flimsy catch, the windows burst inwards, and a drenching gush of seawater came flooding into the room, soaking me and sending me staggering me backwards.

For a moment I simply stood there, gasping and holding on to one of the four-poster's poles, listening to Joel scrambling up and out of bed.

"Jesus Christ!" he was yelping. "What the fuck!"

"We've got to get out of here," I said. My teeth were chattering. "It's not safe."

"Out of this villa, or off the island?" Joel was scrabbling around for his glasses. Now he slotted them over his ears and stared at me.

"I mean—both, but I tried radioing the *Over Easy*, there's no one there."

"There's a radio?" He looked confused, and I waved my hand. No time to explain. We needed to get out of here.

"It doesn't matter, I'll show you later. Come on, we have to get out."

Joel nodded, and we made our way cautiously out onto the veranda.

Outside, the force of the wind was terrifying, and the waves were sucking so hard at the base of the villa that I could see the long struts buried in the sand, far below the low-tide mark. Then, as the breakers came rushing back in, the whole structure was sent awash, water flooding in through the open French windows and tossing around the veranda chairs and throw cushions like toys.

Joel looked doubtfully at the gangway, barely visible in the driving rain, and flooded by several feet every time a wave came in.

"You crossed that?"

"Yes, but the sea wasn't as high when I did it before."

I was hesitating now. In the trough of each wave I could see that the gangway was still there, and the balustrade was still poking up out of the water, providing some measure of security, but the force of the waves crashing over the top every few minutes was giving me pause. This wouldn't be a case of dashing across with the water at my ankles, the way it had been an hour ago. This would be a case of hanging on for dear life, and if one of us slipped, it wouldn't end well.

"Should we hold hands?" Joel asked. "In case one of us slips?" He pushed his glasses up his nose, looking nervous. There was rain running down his face. I nodded.

"Probably a good idea. One hand on the balustrade, one hand for each other. Okay?"

"Okay," Joel said. He pushed at his glasses again and held out his hand. When I took it, his hand was bony and surprisingly strong, his grip hard. It felt comfortingly secure. "Shall I go first?"

I shrugged. I didn't think it would make much difference.

"Okay, but let's be as quick as we can."

Joel nodded, took a deep breath as he waited for the trough of a wave, and then as the sea pulled out, revealing the wooden planks, he set foot on the gangway.

He had only taken a couple of steps when the wave came back and hit him. It flung him against the rope balustrade with a force that cracked one of the wooden supports, and in an instant, faster than I can possibly describe, he was being pulled out to sea, hanging on for dear life to the balustrade rope with one hand, and my wrist with the other.

I think I screamed. I know I grabbed hold of one of the veranda posts with my free hand. The pull of the wave, trying to tear Joel away from me and suck him into the sea, was impossibly strong. I could hear Joel yelling over the roar of the wind, feel his fingers desperately digging into my wrist, and I could see the far end of the balustrade rope trailing out to sea, totally untethered. There was nothing holding Joel, apart from the end of the rope fastened to the villa, and my grip.

"Hang on!" I yelled. I got one arm wound around the veranda post and shut my eyes with the effort of holding Joel's weight.

Above the noise of the wind and waves, I could hear Joel screaming something. He was half submerged, choking on seawater. And then the force of the waves changed direction, tossing him back towards shore, and I pulled with all my might, yanking him towards me. This was our only chance. I couldn't hold on against another buffet like that.

"Now, Joel!" I shouted, and in a desperate, scrambling rush, he let go of the rope, just as the sea twisted it from the last remaining balustrade post, and I grabbed hold of him and pulled him back up onto the veranda.

He was shaking and soaked from head to foot. Miraculously his glasses were still on, though I doubted he could see much. My arm felt like it had been twisted almost from its socket, and I was fairly sure I'd pulled something in my back—but that was the least of my worries at the moment. As we stood, gasping and holding on to the veranda posts, the wave sucked back out, and we saw that half of the walkway had gone, the planks ripped from their posts. We were stranded.

"Oh my God," Joel said at last. He was still panting and shaking with cold. He pushed his wet fringe back from his face, his teeth chattering. "You s-saved my life."

"Maybe." I was still staring at the place where they gangway had been. "But I don't know how much good that's going to do either of us. We're stuck."

Joel turned, and we both looked at the long, wild stretch of water between us and the rest of the island, now completely uninterrupted by any signs of the walkway except when the waves pulled out to their farthest extent, and the bare struts were faintly visible, sticking out of the sand.

We were still standing there, gazing at the island, only a few dozen yards away, though it might as well have been a mile of shark-infested water, when there was a far-off sound, like a crash of thunder, and then another.

"What was that?" I asked.

"Thunder?"

"I don't think so." I shook my head doubtfully. "I didn't see any lightning."

"Must have been a palm tree blowing down," Joel said. He had wiped his glasses and was now staring into the darkness, trying to make out the shape of the island through the rain. "Fuck, I hope Romi's okay. Our villa was right in among the trees."

"That's maybe safer?" I said doubtfully. "I mean, I guess the trees will protect each other to an extent? I'd imagine it's the outlying palms that are the most vulnerable."

"I hope you're right." We were both still standing there, staring into the rain-drenched night, when another enormous wave broke over the side of the veranda and crashed into us, sending me staggering backwards, and bringing me to a fresh realization of our position.

"Look," I said, making up my mind, "we need to get inside. There's no way we can get to the island now, we'll just have to hope we can ride out the storm."

Joel nodded, and together we went back inside the villa, bolted the French doors, and did our best to push the heavy bed up against them to reinforce them. Then we turned to look at each other—dripping and shivering with cold. All our bags were back on the mainland, and the clothes we'd worn the night before were damp with spray, but they were better than our soaked robes. We changed hastily, teeth chattering, and climbed into the still-damp bed to wait out what promised to be one of the worst nights of my life. How long the storm would last, I had no idea—nor did I know whether the villa could take the increasing violence of the waves.

I only knew that we had no choice but to sit it out, wait, and hope.

It was as I wrapped the damp sheet around myself, as some scant protection from the cold, that it occurred to me to wonder how Nico was faring. Was he lying belowdecks, green with sea sickness, the big yacht scudding before the wind? Or had they made it to the rendez-vous before the storm broke, and he was sitting it out in some concrete airstrip, waiting for the wind to die down so his helicopter ride would come and collect him? I didn't know. I could only pray that he was safe—and that we both made it to morning.

CHAPTER 12

I DON'T KNOW when I fell asleep, but it must have been some time shortly before dawn, because I opened bleary eyes to find pink rays of sunshine illuminating the ceiling, and Joel leaning over me, gently shaking my shoulder.

"Lyla?" he was whispering. "Lyla, are you awake?"

"I am now," I said a little grumpily. I had no idea how many hours sleep I'd managed, but it couldn't have been more than two or three. As I struggled upright, raking the hair out of my eyes, I saw that the wind had dropped, the clouds had broken, and apart from the fact that there was seawater all over the floor and the patio furniture had all been swept away, the Ever After Villa was miraculously unharmed. We'd made it.

"I'm sorry," Joel said penitently, "I didn't want to wake you, but I didn't want to just disappear without telling you."

"Disappear?" I rubbed my face, feeling the grittiness of sleep—or maybe dried seawater—on my cheeks, and the welt from where the branch had hit me the night before. "Where are you going?"

"I need to go check on Romi," Joel said. His expression was worried. "She'll have been all alone in her villa in that storm, and she's probably losing her mind about me. I need to make sure she's okay."

"I'm so sorry, of course you do." I sat up properly, swung my legs out of bed onto the damp boards, and looked out at the stretch of water between us and the island. The storm seemed to have passed, but the sea was still a far cry from the clear, tranquil blue it had been when we arrived. It was cloudy gray with stirred up silt, and the huge breakers were still crashing into the shore. The formerly pristine white beach was strewn with debris—broken furniture, branches, coconuts, and brittle chunks of coral flung up from the depths. More than that, the whole shape of the beach itself had changed—a deep channel had been scoured out of the far end of the curve by the surf, while sand had been flung far up, either side, into dunes that hadn't existed last night. If I squinted, I could make out, even from here, some of the damage that the storm had wrought on the island itself. Dozens of trees had come down, and between the trunks of the remaining ones I could see the white glint of villas that had been previously hidden by forest. As I watched, a huge tumbleweed of something pale and straw-colored cartwheeled across the beach—but it was too large and too irregularly shaped to be an actual tumbleweed. It took me a few minutes to recognize it for what it was—the roof of one of the villas, or at least a good chunk of one. I felt a shiver of apprehension run through me.

"How are we going to get across?" I asked now. Joel bit his lip.

"I've been watching the surf and I *think* I can swim for it."

"Christ." I looked out at the crashing breakers. "Are you sure? It's pretty rough."

"I think so. The jetty's basically gone—and it's probably more unsafe to go wading around all those submerged posts, anyway. Easy way to break a leg. And there's a rip, but it's going down the far side." He pointed at a deceptively smooth streak of water coming off the northern edge of the beach, following the path of the scoured-out channel. "I mean, it's rough, but I'm a fairly strong swimmer, and I'm used to surf. I think I'll be okay."

"And what about sharks?" Even as I said the words they sounded faintly ridiculous, but this *was* the Indian Ocean. It wasn't a hyperbolic question to ask. But Joel was shaking his head.

"I asked one of the producers yesterday. He said the big ones can't get inside the reef. They stick to the deep water. I'll be all right, I promise."

I nodded and, pulling the heavy bed away from the French doors, I opened them a few inches and squeezed through. Outside, the surf felt, if anything, more intimidating, but the wind was blowing onshore and I had no reason to disbelieve Joel about the riptide. Joel had followed me, and together we stood shading our eyes and gazing at the shore.

"Are you a surfer, then?" I asked. Joel shrugged. A figure had appeared in the far distance, stumbling along the beach, but I couldn't see who.

"Not anymore, really, but I guess you could say I was. I grew up in Cornwall. We were always messing around in the sea. You learn the basics."

"So how do we do this?" I said. The figure had disappeared into the trees.

"We?" Joel raised an eyebrow, and I shrugged.

"Look, I'm not staying here by myself. I've never surfed, but I did get my silver swimming badge."

"Okay," Joel said mildly. "If you're sure. Do you want me to go first? Just in case?"

I thought for a moment, and then nodded. There wasn't really much benefit in us swimming together. If anything, we were less likely to notice the other getting into trouble. Joel was already stripping off his clothes.

"So the thing to do," he said, as he pulled his T-shirt over his head, "is kind of body surf on the waves as far as possible. It's not as easy without a board, but the energy of the wave will do the hard work, particularly with an onshore wind. And if you find yourself in a rip, don't try to swim against it, that's a fast way to drown. Swim sideways if you can, get out of its pull, or if you can't, just hang tight and wait for it to exhaust itself. Though that might be a gamble if it carries you out beyond the reef."

I nodded. Joel was down to his pants, and now he took off his glasses, looking blankly around.

"Shit. What do I do with these? I can't wear them, they'll get washed away."

"Um . . ." I had a sudden idea, and going back into the villa, I rummaged in the bathroom and came back with my washbag, a simple drawstring bag made of waterproof material. It was the only thing I'd brought across to the water villa, aside from my pajamas. I dumped out my shampoo and deodorant and handed it to Joel.

"Will this do?" I asked. "It's strong, and you could tie the straps to your wrist." Joel nodded, tied it tightly around his arm with a double knot, and then shrugged.

"Well, wish me luck."

"Good luck," I said. My heart was in my throat as he stepped closer to the edge of the veranda, where the waves were buffeting with a force I could feel shaking the decking. He stood for a moment, inhaling deeply, and then poised himself and dived, with a surprising grace, into the surf.

For a long time, he didn't surface, and I found I was counting under my breath, watching for his head to come up between the waves. *Thirteen elephants . . . fourteen elephants . . .* when I got to twenty-two elephants, I was beginning to get seriously worried. Had he got caught in some underwater current not visible from the surface?

But then, just when I was beginning to debate if I should wait a little longer, or strip off my own clothes and jump in, and whether that would do any good at all or just result in both of us getting swept out to sea, his head came up between the waves, much farther away than I would have expected, and he caught a wave, and let himself be carried almost halfway to shore.

When he finally scrambled up the beach on his hands and knees, I felt like applauding. But then he turned and waved, and I realized it was my turn.

The thought gave me a jolt. What I'd told Joel was true, I *couldn't* stay here all day, and I did have my silver medallion. But it was a long time since I'd done any serious swimming, and what I had done had been pretty much exclusively in swimming pools. Also, the dress I was wearing was woefully unsuitable.

"Just a sec!" I yelled across to Joel, though I wasn't sure if he'd be able to hear me above the sound of the surf. I turned my back and began pulling the diaphanous maxi dress over my head. Once it was off, I stood for a moment at the edge of the veranda, feeling strangely vulnerable in my bra and knickers, and trying to summon up my courage. Then, knowing that my nerve would fail me if I waited any longer, I jumped, with considerably less grace than Joel, into the waves.

The first thing that shocked me was that it was *very* cold. Much, *much* colder than the baby waves I'd paddled in with Nico yesterday, when we first arrived. Colder even than last night, when I'd waded across the jetty to the island. Evidently, the storm had stirred up water from the deep, untouched parts of the sea, the part where even the tropical sun rarely reached. With unpleasant images in my head of giant squid and those weird eyeless fish with glowing antenna, I took a deep breath, and began to strike out for shore.

The second thing I realized, and it didn't take me very long, was that Joel had been sensible to dive under the waves for as long as he had, and that he'd made the swim look far easier than it really was. Swimming in the impact zone, where the waves were beginning to break, was incredibly tiring, and surfing a wave without a board was much harder than Joel had made it seem. Twice I managed to catch the momentum of a cresting wave, only to be forced under when it broke, coming up gasping and disoriented, being sucked back out to sea.

I swam . . . and I swam . . . for what felt like a terrifying, insurmountable amount of time. Every time I thought I was getting out of the break zone, another huge wave would crash over my head and its backdraft would pull me back into deep water. My arms were screaming with tiredness, and I was blue with cold, but at last I felt my knees crack into something rough—a piece of coral, probably, and when I put my hands down to try to fend off whatever it was, I realized I was in shallow water.

When I scrambled the last few feet to shore, my knees were skinned and bleeding, and I was shaking with a mix of exhaustion and cold, but Joel was standing there, cheering, and ready to help me to my feet.

"Are you okay?" he said, almost before I'd shaken the water out of my ears. "Can you walk?"

"Yes," I gasped. I understood his anxiety—he wanted to get inland, check on Romi.

"Are you sure? I can leave you here if you're tired, but—"

"I understand," I said. My chest was still heaving, but I was recovering the power of speech. "Go. I'll catch up."

Joel nodded, then jogged up the path into the trees. I stood for a moment, catching my breath, then straightened up to follow.

I had barely made my way off the beach and into the trees, when there was a crashing sound from the undergrowth, and a wild-eyed Dan came bursting out from between two banana trees. He was shirtless and covered in dried blood.

"What the fuck!" I blurted out, and he grabbed me like a drowning man gripping a piece of driftwood.

"Lyla! You're okay! Jesus Christ, you're okay, thank God you're okay. We were sure you'd be dead, out there on the water."

"We're fine," I said. "The jetty got swept away, but the villa was okay. But Dan—what's happened?"

"It's Santa." His voice broke. "She's— Oh fuck, Lyla, I know you're not a real doctor, but you work in medicine, don't you?"

"No!" I was getting really alarmed now. "Dan, no, I work on viruses. It's not the same— What's happened to her?"

"She went out, into the storm, to try to get help. She got hit by something—metal sheeting, I think. I got her back to the villa, but she's badly hurt."

"Oh fuck." I felt sick to my stomach. I had no idea what to do, but I also had a strong suspicion that totally unqualified as I was, I might still be the most knowledgeable person here. At least my work had given me a solid understanding of pathogen control and microbial reproduction. And I'd got my First Aid badge as a Girl Guide. Good thing it was only twenty years out of date.

"Oh my God," I heard through the trees. It was Joel, his voice a cry of total horror. "Oh my God, Romi. Romi!"

"Hold that thought," I said to Dan. "I'm sorry, I *will* come with you, just—"

"Romi!" I heard from up ahead. Joel's voice was a scream of desperation. "Romi, Romi! Talk to me!"

Dan shot me a look, and we both ran up the path in the direction of Joel's cries.

When we came out into the clearing, what we saw made me skid to a halt and my stomach lurch even more sickeningly than it had done hearing about Santana.

In the middle of the clearing was a little villa, the only one Nico and I hadn't stumbled over yesterday, though it was a carbon copy of the other four land villas. Or rather, it would have been. But sometime during the night, a huge palm tree had fallen clear across it, smashing the roof like an eggshell and crushing the walls to the ground. I could see broken glass scattered across the clearing, shards of polished wood, throw cushions flung into the undergrowth by the force of the impact.

Apart from Joel's sobbing there was total, absolute silence. It didn't seem possible that anyone could have survived.

"Maybe she wasn't in there," Dan whispered, clearly running through the same thought process as I was. But I'd seen a foot with rose-pink nail polish sticking out from beneath one of the broken chunks of roof, and now I turned away, breathing hard through my nose and trying not to lose it.

"Romi." Joel had seen the foot too, and he ran forward, tugging at the palm-frond roof. I forced my frozen limbs to move. However unlikely it was, if Romi was alive under there, I had to help Joel get her out. Together, the three of us all heaving at the debris, we cleared away enough to make out Romi's body. But it *was* her body. She was very clearly dead—and it must have been nearly instant. While her head and legs were almost untouched, her torso was crushed between the trunk of the palm tree and the mahogany bedframe, crushed in a way that even a child could have told you was not compatible with life. There was surprisingly little blood—but her eyes were open, staring sightlessly up at the blue sky, and the pupils were dilated to darkness.

"Romi." Joel was sobbing, brokenly. He knelt beside her, brushing the palm fronds off her face. There was a fly on her forehead, and a trail of ants moving across her body to the blood, and he swatted them angrily away.

"Oh my God, Joel, I'm so sorry," I whispered. He gave a groan that sounded like someone was twisting a knife in his side.

"I should have been here."

"You couldn't have done anything," Dan said quietly. "Nobody could. You'd just have died too. I'm so sorry, mate."

"I could have woken her up," Joel sobbed. "I could have told her to get out."

"Mate, we tried," Dan said. "Me and Santa. We tried to get out and it—it didn't end well." He glanced at me, and I knew what he was trying to say. We needed to get back to Santana.

"Joel," I said gently. "Joel, listen to me, Santana's hurt. Will you be okay here for a few minutes if I go and see what I can do?"

Joel shook his head uncomprehendingly, but I wasn't sure if he was really listening to me, or just brokenly trying to refute the reality of what was in front of him.

"Joel, listen, I have to go and try to help Santana," I said, "but I'll be back, okay? I *will* come back, so just stay here, all right?"

"All right," he whispered, but I had no idea if he was just echoing back my own words, or if he'd really taken in what I'd just said.

"Come on," I said to Dan. "Show me where she is, and I'll see what I can do."

Dan nodded, and I followed him away from the wreckage of Joel's villa and into the trees.

DAN AND SANTANA'S villa was another hut, like Joel and Romi's that was buried deep in the trees, but theirs had been luckier. Several trees had come down, including one right across the path, but none had hit it, and the roof was still intact. Whoever had lost the huge chunk of roof that I had seen scudding along the beach this morning, it wasn't them.

Inside, though, it was a mess. Santana was lying on a pile of pillows against the headboard of the big double bed, her face gray and sweating, and her hair plastered to her forehead. There was blood all over the sheets, and when I arrived, she gave a ghastly rictus smile.

"Hey Doc."

"I'm not a doctor," I said, shaking my head, but I could tell she was joking. "Are you okay?"

"Never better, darling," she said with an effort. "Just this little old . . . thing." With a convulsive jerk she pulled back the bloody, wadded sheet covering part of her leg, and I saw that her thigh had been ripped open, a six-inch bloody gaping wound all down the outside.

"Oh Jesus," I said involuntarily, and Santana gave a sickly grin.

"You're politer than me. I used the f-word when I saw it. A lot."

"Oh shit, Santana. This is bad."

"Right? Lucky me!" She was panting in little shallow gasps.

"What can we do?" Dan asked. He was shifting his weight nervously from one foot to the other like an expectant dad in a hospital waiting room, only with a much lower prospect of a happy outcome. "I tried to put pressure on it. Isn't that what you're supposed to do?"

"You did right," I said, though in truth I didn't really have any idea, but I was pretty sure that pressure would be the correct thing in the short-term. Whatever he'd done, it seemed to have stopped the worst of the bleeding. It had slowed to a trickle, but when I knelt at the side of the bed and looked more closely at the wound, I could see dirt and pieces of rust adhering to the sheet, and more stuck to the raw flesh. I pressed my lips together. *This* was why I had never wanted to be an actual doctor. And now here I was, stuck with pretending to be one.

"Okay." I was thinking hard. Given it seemed like Santana wasn't bleeding out, infection control was going to be the next most crucial thing. It was a long time since I'd properly studied microbiology, but I dimly remembered that some forms of sepsis could set in very fast, possibly even before the *Over Easy* could get back here to rescue us, and definitely before anyone could airlift Santana to a hospital. It was crucial to stop the wound getting infected. Which meant washing— ideally pressure washing, though I didn't want to do any additional damage—and covering. "Okay, we need to clean this wound. Any idea when you last had a tetanus shot?"

"Did we have one to come here?" Santana asked Dan.

Dan looked blank.

"God, I honestly don't remember, we got so many jabs. Was that one of the ones on the list?"

I was racking my brain, trying to remember tetanus vaccine protocols, and the lengthy health forms Nico and I had filled out for the show. I had been up to date on everything—one of the less exciting perks of working in a lab is they're pretty rigorous about requiring employees to be vaccinated against any pathogens they might come into contact within the course of their work. Nico had required a few boosters, and I had a vague recollection tetanus had been one of them.

"I'm fairly sure that tetanus was on there," I said. "And from what I can remember, tetanus vaccines take effect pretty fast—in fact you can have them postexposure, so you're probably fine."

That was one thing off my mind. There was only sepsis left, and without antibiotics, that was in the lap of the gods. I looked around the room, trying to see if what I needed was here. The answer seemed to be no: the small minibar fridge in the corner of the room was empty apart from a bottle of wine, and a stack of what I guessed must be Santana's spare insulin, in little boxes.

"I'll be back," I said to Santana, shutting the fridge. She nodded, but Dan looked alarmed.

"Where are you going?"

"I need to get supplies. Clean water for one, and bandages if they've got any." I had no idea if the bathroom taps were working, but even if they were, bottled water would be safer, and I was fairly sure I remembered seeing some in the staff kitchen. "I'll be back, I swear."

And with Dan looking mournfully after me, I ran down the pebbled path and into the forest.

IT TOOK MUCH longer getting to the staff area than it had last night, in spite of the fact that it was now daylight and I could see my way. Partly because I didn't know the way from this part of the island and kept getting turned around by the layout of the paths, but partly because so many trees were down, and I kept having to stop and scramble over them or force my way through the undergrowth—not easy in just my underwear.

By the time I made it to the huddle of huts, I was scratched and bruised from forcing my way through bushes and climbing over the rough trunks of fallen palms. I was so busy looking down at my bleeding shins and wondering if I should have detoured past the villa where my clothes were, that I almost didn't notice the huts until I was upon them.

Or rather, the hut. Because there was only one left, and even that one was barely standing.

The one-to-one booth and the rec room had both simply gone—there was nothing left apart from the rectangular concrete foundation slabs and, far across the clearing, the wicker chair wedged into the leaves of a banana tree, like some surreal fruit.

The kitchen had lost two walls and part of the roof. The remaining walls and roof section had folded in on itself, like a cardboard box that someone had stamped on. All around the clearing were scattered boxes of food, exploded bags of snacks, and big square bottles of water—the five-liter kind. And in the center, a small patch of rust red that had soaked into the sand, and which I didn't remember from the previous day.

As I stood there, looking at the devastation, a bright green snake leisurely unwound itself from the shade of a box of cookies and slithered unhurriedly across the clearing. I watched it go, fighting back my revulsion, and then forced my attention back to the one hut that was still standing—the radio shack. Part of the roof had been ripped off, and the huge hole in the window, where the coconut had come barrelling through, looked even more shocking than it had last night—but it was still there. I didn't recall seeing a first aid kit in there, but if it had been stored in one of the other huts, it was probably long gone, so I hurried across the clearing, pushing thoughts of the green snake out of my head, and opened the door.

Inside, everything was covered in splinters of glass and wood from the shattered window, but the radio was still there, and the LED was still gleaming in the dim light. Although I was conscious that Santana and Dan were waiting for me, I picked it up and pressed the button on the receiver.

"Hello?" I said, experimentally. "Hello? Is anyone out there?"

I let go, and just as last night, there was a brief crackle, but no response. I sighed. Fuck. Maybe people were listening but not coming in because they didn't recognize me. What were you supposed to say in these situations? Mayday? Or was that only for ships? At this point I didn't really care.

I pressed the button again.

"This is an emergency Mayday call. We are stranded on an island in the Indian Ocean after the storm last night." Well no shit, anyone listening would be in the Indian Ocean, so that wasn't exactly very helpful. I tried to think how to describe our position more accurately. "I don't have any coordinates, but we flew into Jakarta and sailed southwest on a yacht called *Over Easy*. The yacht is gone and we have no idea what's happened to it." What else. Something to make them realize our plight maybe? I had no idea if the others were still alive, but it seemed likely that Santana and Romi weren't the only casualties after last night. "Several of our group are seriously injured and need medical help. I don't know how long the battery on this radio will last, but if anyone can hear me, please send help. I repeat, this is an emergency Mayday call for medical assistance."

I let the button go. Again it crackled, and again, nothing else happened.

"Can anyone hear me?" I said, fighting to keep the desperation out of my voice. I wanted to scream down the receiver—*get the fuck out here, people are dying!* But screaming wouldn't bring help any faster, and losing control now would be the worst thing I could do. All my life I had been the logical, analytical person in any group, the one who didn't shriek at the sight of a maggot in her apple, who didn't cry when my professor told me my paper wasn't up to scratch. Even as a little girl I'd been the person who carried the daddy longlegs out of the room when my mum was standing on the sofa with her hands over her hair, holding the fluttering thing gently in my cupped hands and telling myself, *it's fine, it's just a crane fly,* tipula paludosa, *they don't bite or sting and they don't have any transmissible diseases.* No. I was the person who kept it together and sorted everything the fuck out. That was my role. That was *who I was.* And I was not about to lose it now. "Can anyone help? Over?"

I waited. Nothing. *Nothing.* Fuck.

Knowing I couldn't afford to play around with it any longer, I let the receiver drop, and with a last look around the cabin, I went back out into the glare of the sun, which was beginning to feel even hotter than yesterday, in spite of the vestiges of the storm winds, still blowing off the sea.

There was no first aid kit in the kitchen, or not that I could find, but I picked up one of the big water bottles, the package of Oreos that had split, and were attracting a small crowd of excited ants, a roll of janitorial paper—the blue kind that's used for drying your hands in industrial kitchens—and, almost as an afterthought, a roll of duct tape that I tripped over on my way out of the hut. It wasn't exactly perfect, but it would do to tape the wound shut until we could get Santana to an actual doctor.

I was almost across the clearing when something attracted my attention. It was the sound of buzzing flies, coming from a thicket of bushes. There was something ominous about the noise, and I was half afraid of what I might find, but I stepped off the path, towards the sound, pushing aside the leaves as I went.

The hum was getting louder, but it wasn't until I pushed aside the last frond of banana leaves that I saw what was making it—and when I did, I dropped what I was carrying, and covered my nose and mouth, my shocked cry escaping through my fingers.

There was a body lying under the bushes, the flies already swarming, and the face was one that I recognized, though I didn't know the woman's name. It was one of the producers from the day before, and her head had been cracked like an egg. There was blood everywhere. She had evidently stumbled through the bushes before collapsing and bleeding out.

So there *had* been a staff member left on the island, just as Camille had promised. I shut my eyes, counting to ten in my head, trying not to give way to the panic and revulsion that was pulsing through me. Instead, I tried to piece together what had happened. She'd been hit by some flying object, maybe a coconut, that much was obvious. But had she been dead before I even arrived at the radio hut? Or had she been stumbling through the storm in the opposite direction, even as I was trying to find her?

It was impossible to know, but thinking back to the rumpled bed and cold mattress I guessed that she'd probably been the first casualty of the storm—dead before I even left the water villa. Perhaps she'd been trying to make it to the radio shack and had been hit by some storm debris, then had stumbled blindly through the clearing and into the undergrowth to die.

I opened my eyes, forced myself to look at her face one more time, making sure that she was really dead, and then I turned. There was nothing I could do for her. It was the living who needed help now, and I had to get back.

*   *   *

BACK AT THE villa, I found Santana lying with her eyes closed and looking even worse, blue-lipped and with her hair stuck to her sweating forehead.

"Thank fuck," Dan said as soon as I pulled open the door. "What took you so long?"

"I came as fast as I could," I said. I let the water thud to the floor, followed by the kitchen paper. The face of the dead producer kept flashing in front of my eyes, but now wasn't the time to bring it up. We had enough to deal with here. "Do you have anything sharp, Dan?"

"Sharp?" Dan looked blank.

"I've got some spare syringes," Santana said. Her voice was croaky and faint, but she opened her eyes and propped herself on her elbow. Then her gaze alighted on the cookies I was holding. "Oh my God, Oreos, can I have some? My blood sugar is really low."

"Of course." I pushed them over to her, cursing the fact that I hadn't looked for soda or anything faster-acting. "I think a syringe will be too small, I was thinking more like a ballpoint pen, or a pocketknife."

"I've got a pen," Dan volunteered. Digging in his pocket, he brought out a metal-tipped Biro with a fine point. I nodded.

"Okay, well when you've got a bit of sugar in your system, come through to the bathroom, Santana, and we'll make a start. I warn you, it's going to hurt."

"I'm ready," Santana said through a mouthful of crumbs. She swallowed, with an effort. "And it hurts like a bastard now, so I doubt you'll make it any worse." She hauled herself upright with a sickly smile and followed me into the bathroom.

Once inside, I made her sit in the shower stall—sit because I was worried about her slipping if the pain got too bad—and stick out her wounded leg. Then I stabbed the tip of the ball point pen into the bottom corner of the big water carrier, aimed the thin jet at the long wound running down Santana's thigh, and squeezed as hard as I could.

It wasn't perfect—a proper squeezy bottle would have been better, but at least this was sterile, and it came out with surprising force, blasting away the fragments of rust and dirt sticking to the wound. The jet was so strong in fact that for a moment I stopped squeezing, worried that I was going to disturb the clotted blood and set the wound gushing again, but when the water had drained away, it didn't seem to be bleeding any more than it was before I started.

Santana spoke, her voice ragged.

"For Christ sake, keep going, I want to get this over with."

I nodded and squeezed again, and this time she groaned as the jet hit her thigh, but she didn't move, only bowed her head with her teeth gritted against the pain. I kept sluicing, watching as the pieces of metal and clots of blood disappeared down the drain, until the water ran clear with only a pinkish hint of blood. At last the pressure began to fail, and I stuck the bottle upside down in the sink to save the rest of the water, and helped Santana stand up.

The towels in the bathroom were still clean, and between us, Dan and I dabbed gently at the uncut part of Santana's leg until her skin was as dry as we could make it. Then, I unwound the catering paper until we got to an untouched part of the roll, tore off a long strip, and wadded it into a makeshift dressing. Pressing the sides of the wound together, I laid the blue wad on top, protecting the broken section of skin, and then taped the whole thing up with duct tape, trying to keep the pressure up as I did, to give the wound the best chance of knitting.

When I was finished, I sat back and examined my handiwork. I had no idea if what I'd done was right, but it would at least stop dirt from getting in the cut, and it would probably do until help arrived.

Santana was sweating worse than she had been when we started, but she looked less gray, and she gave me a watery smile.

"Thanks. You're amazing, Doc."

"For the last time, I'm not a fucking doctor," I said, but I was grinning too—more out of relief that it was done, and I hadn't nicked an artery or anything. "Look, will you be okay? I should go and check on the others—and then I have to get back to Joel."

"Joel?" Santana was hobbling back to the bed, and now she sank into the pillows with a barely disguised sigh of relief. "What happened to him?"

"Not him." I glanced at Dan, unsure how to say this. "Romi. She— I mean . . . she's—"

"She's dead, Santa," Dan said. He said it, not casually, but without preamble, and I realized that it was the only way. There was no way to soften this news, no way to make it less than what it was—a horrific, inescapable truth.

Santana gave a gasp like she'd been punched.

"You're kidding? How?"

"A massive tree came down over their villa," I said. "She was crushed. I don't think she would have known anything. And . . ." I swallowed, hesitating, but it was probably better to get this all over with at once. "And that's not all. I found the body of one of the crew— one of the producers, I don't know her name. She's down by the staff quarters. She's—" I stopped, there was no point in inflicting what I'd seen on the others. "Well, she's dead. Very dead."

"Oh God." Santana shut her eyes. Her lips were moving, but I couldn't make out what she was saying, whether it was a prayer or just some kind of denial of the situation we were in. "Go," she said aloud at last. "You should go, and Dan, go with her."

"Santa—" he began, but she broke in.

"Go! I'm fine. There's probably others who need you a lot more. I've got the rest of the cookies, and water." She gestured at the quarter-full bottle upturned in the sink. "So go. Do what you need to do."

I nodded.

"Okay. We'll be back soon. I promise."

It was what I had said to Joel. I just hoped we weren't going to find anything worse.

Today is Thursday, 15 February, and I have decided to write a diary—my head is so full of everything that's happened since the storm last night, and I needed some way to make sense of it all.

We are all reeling—from the storm, which seems to have blown our boat off course, but also from the terrible shock of poor Romi's death—she was killed when a palm tree came down on her villa, crushing it to bits.

It's hit all of us, but Joel the worst. He's destroyed. He found her early this morning, and I will never forget his cries. Conor was trying to persuade him to come away so he and Bayer could pull the debris off Romi's body. I remember him cradling Joel and saying over and over, "I've got you, brother. I've got you."

The only comfort is that Lyla says she didn't suffer, that it must have been instant. And there is a kind of comfort in that, although I don't think poor Joel is ready to see it yet.

Romi wasn't the only casualty from the storm. One of the producers was killed—we don't even know her name. Santana was hit by some flying metal and got a horrible gash in her leg.

And Bayer's shoulder was dislocated—but Conor managed to pull it back into place. I keep replaying the sound it made inside my head, that sickening crack. I thought I might throw up. Bayer went green with pain, but he looked better afterwards. He'll have to keep it strapped up, but thank God Conor knew what to do. I have no idea how he knew all of that.

Eight of us. Just eight. And two injured. It feels more vital than ever that we take care of each other until the boat gets back for us. How long will it take to get here? Two days? Not more, surely.

We can do this. I know we can. We just have to stay strong.

CHAPTER 13

IT TOOK US some time to persuade Joel to leave Romi, but at last we convinced him there was nothing more he could do, and together the three of us made our way back through the forest, towards the beach. We passed Palm Tree Rest, which was miraculously unharmed, and I ducked inside and grabbed a top and some jeans, as well as some sunblock—the sun was beginning to blaze fiercely overhead and I could tell I was beginning to burn. Then we pressed on.

We found the others—Bayer, Angel, Conor, and Zana—huddled up at the cabana. Amazingly they were all more or less okay, though Bayer looked like he was in pain, and had his hand to his shoulder. All four of them looked round as we came up the steps to the cabana, and their faces broke into varying shades of surprise and thankfulness.

"Grâce à Dieu," Angel said. She had twisted her braids up into a top knot and was kneeling by Bayer's side, trying to examine his arm. Now she stood up, undisguised relief on her face. "You are alive! But where is Santana? And Rosie?"

"Santana's hurt her leg," I said. "And Romi—" I stopped, swallowed, looked at Joel, unsure what to say.

"Romi's dead." Joel's voice cracked. "A massive tree fell on our villa in the night. She was killed straightaway."

"Oh my God!" Zana's hand flew to her mouth, and I saw there were tears standing in her eyes. Bayer shook his head and sucked in his breath.

"Joel, brother, I am so sorry," Conor said. He put out his hand and touched Joel on the shoulder, but Joel flinched away. He was standing, his face averted to one side, his eyes refusing to meet anyone else's. Of course I didn't have any idea of how he felt, not really. But as the hours passed, I found I was becoming more and more worried about Nico. I had no idea what time it was, but the sun was high in the sky, and the *Over Easy* should have been back here ages ago, going by its original schedule. Even allowing for some lost time spent sheltering in the harbor, I was beginning to get concerned that we'd seen nothing, not even a shape on the horizon. What if the storm we'd experienced hadn't been the worst of it? What if the *Over Easy* had . . .

But no. I refused to think about that.

"One of the producers is dead too," Dan said. His boyish, friendly face looked like he had aged ten years since yesterday, drawn into tense lines. "Lyla found her down by the staff quarters."

"Putain, what happened?" Angel asked.

"I don't know," I said wearily. Everything that had happened since Joel and I woke up was beginning to catch up with me, and I felt strange and shaky. I sat on the bench beside her. "Hit by something in the storm, I'd guess. The staff huts are basically destroyed."

"Staff huts ain't the only ones," Bayer said with a grimace. "Our villa's fucked. Storm took off half the roof."

"Shit, that was yours?" I thought of the huge chunk of palm fronds I had seen cartwheeling down the beach. Angel nodded.

"It was impossible to stay. We ran—but a tree came down and hit Bayer's shoulder."

"I think it's dislocated," Bayer said. His teeth were gritted, the muscles in his jaw standing out. "Happened once before, in a football game."

"Do you want me to try to put it back in?" Conor said. He stood up.

"I really don't think that's a good idea—" I said, at the same time as Bayer said, "D'you know how?"

"I've seen it done," Conor said. "When I was out climbing. Guy fell and dislocated his shoulder, and another guy pulled it straight." He shrugged and then looked at me. "What do you think, Doc?"

"For the last fucking time," I said, more wearily than annoyed, "I'm not a doctor. I just want to make that really, really clear. If you've seen it done, you're more of an expert than me. But I know the general advice is let the professionals do it if you possibly can—you can do more damage if you trap something or rip a tendon."

Dan made a heaving face, and Conor shrugged.

"That's all true. But there's risks in leaving it untreated . . . I guess it depends how long we reckon the professionals will take to find us."

A silence fell around the table as we all contemplated that question. Then Bayer spoke.

"Fuck it, do it."

"You sure, man?" Conor asked. Bayer nodded.

"Yeah, I'm sure. Look at that sea." He gestured out towards the wild waves still racing in from the deep ocean. "Who knows when they'll be able to get back to us. And I'm useless like this."

"You're not useless," Angel said stiffly, but Bayer stood up.

"This is a survival situation, babe, and I've got one working arm."

"Hey." I put out a hand. "Hey, I don't think we're exactly Swiss Family Robinson yet. The boat's a few hours late—"

"A few hours late?" Bayer said. "Woman, did you see the sea last night?"

Woman? I gritted my teeth, forced my voice to stay calm.

"Yes, I saw the sea. I was out in it, in that water villa, remember?"

"He's not wrong," Joel said. His voice was flat, and we all fell silent at the sound of it. "And we've got no idea if we had the worst of it, or if it was even worse over on the other islands."

There was a long pause. I could see everyone looking at each other wondering . . . A real tropical hurricane, one that devastated miles of coastline . . . how long would it take help to arrive?

"They'd have forecasted it, wouldn't they?" Dan said uncertainly. He pushed his bleached fringe out of his eyes, frowning. "I mean . . . they've got hurricane forecasts down to a pretty fine art."

"There *was* a storm forecast," I said a little reluctantly. "I heard some of the crew members talking about it. They asked if they could speak to Baz. But they said it wasn't due for another couple of days."

"Look, can we just quit jabbering," Bayer said impatiently. "The point is, we don't *know.* We don't know if the boat's coming back, we don't know when we'll be able to get to a hospital, and I'm fucked if I'm walking around with my arm like a dead fucking fish nailed to my side, not to mention it hurts like a bastard." He was telling the truth about that. There were beads of sweat on his forehead, in spite of the stiff poststorm breeze still whipping through the cabana.

"Okay," Conor said, flexing his fingers. "If you're sure, then let's get on with it. You'd better take off your shirt and lie down."

We all watched as Bayer maneuvered awkwardly out of his T-shirt, showing an expanse of olive-tanned skin covered in black-ink tribal tattoos. They reminded me of the fake tattoos we had given each other with Sharpies in maths, when I was a teenager—meaningless interlocking swirls that covered his chest and arms, and seemed designed mainly to show how hard he was to endure so many needles. Once he was out of the shirt, he lowered himself gingerly to the ground, with Angel's wrap under his head.

"Don't sue me if I fuck up your shoulder, bro," Conor said.

"I won't," Bayer said. He gave a sickly grin. "What do I do now?"

"Just try to relax. I'm going to take your arm . . ." He picked up Bayer's limp, swollen arm. ". . . and I'm just going to pull very slowly and steadily, and I'll be as gentle as I can, but it's going to hurt."

"I can take it," Bayer said, but there was something slightly unconvincing about his voice, and I saw that he'd shut his eyes. "Do it, man."

Conor sat down beside him and braced one foot against Bayer's rib cage. Then he began to pull.

For a second nothing happened. Then Bayer began to cry out, a long groan of pain that rose with a few seconds to an uncontrolled shriek of agony. For a second he writhed, clearly trying to wrench his arm out of Conor's iron grasp. Then, just when I was on the point of jumping up to intervene and shout at Conor to stop, there was a horrible, squelching *thunk*, not a pop, something duller and deeper, and Conor let go of Bayer's arm and stood up from the ground, dusting down his shorts.

"There you go. Good work, man."

I looked up at him, unable to be anything but slightly impressed. In his shoes I would have been as rattled and sweating as Bayer, who was lying on the ground writhing and panting with pain, his right hand clutched to his left shoulder. But Conor looked entirely self-possessed.

"I'm sorry," he said sympathetically, "that probably hurt like a bitch. Apparently, it's worse on people with a lot of muscle. You should splint it up or something, make sure it doesn't slip out again."

"Christ, man," Bayer was groaning, "you nearly ripped my bloody arm off." He was still rolling on the floor, holding his arm. Angel knelt beside him in the dust and helped him sit up. Bayer was pale and covered in sweat, but his shoulder was back in place, and as he groped his way upright, supporting himself on the table with his right hand, I saw his left arm was moving more easily.

"I have some painkillers in the villa," Angel said. "If they have not blown away."

"I'll go," I said. "Our villa—" I stopped, mentally correcting myself. *My* villa. "It's fine, anyway. No storm damage, I mean, and I've definitely got some paracetamol. Or maybe ibuprofen, but if you've got internal bleeding, you don't want anything that thins the blood. How's the bruising?"

"It hurts like a motherfucker, if that's what you mean," he said a little sulkily, and I nodded.

"Yeah, I mean, it will. And Conor's right about the sling. I'll see if I can find a scarf or something."

"So your villa's okay?" Conor said now, and I nodded. Conor was looking thoughtful.

"The ones that are still standing . . . that's Dan and Santana's and yours, right?"

"And the water villa," I said. "But the jetty's gone, so you have to swim out. What about the others?"

"Well, Joel and Romi's is gone," Conor said, ticking them off his fingers. "Bayer and Angel's has lost the roof. And mine, all the windows got smashed in the storm. None of them are really habitable, at least in the short-term. We need to make sure everyone has somewhere to sleep tonight—and that probably means moving the mattresses around the huts. And then—"

He stopped.

"And then?" I prompted.

"And then . . . then we need to dig the graves."

There was a sudden, bleak silence. It was as if, for a moment, we had almost forgotten the reality of what had happened last night—caught up in the practicalities of Bayer's arm, and where to sleep. For a moment it had felt almost as if the night had been a bad dream—just another reality TV scenario, a team game we had to work together to overcome, using all our skills to add to the prize pot.

And then Joel let out a choking sob, and suddenly it was all real again.

And it was very far from a game.

Two days since we saw the Over Easy, *and I think we are all starting to get seriously worried, though everyone is trying to keep it together in front of the others.*

By day we're keeping ourselves busy—catching fish, trying to patch up the villas. Santana's leg is looking better, and that's something at least. But the question we are all asking in secret is the same one: What do we do if it doesn't come back for us?

No one has had the courage to say it out loud yet. I think we all know that once we voice the suspicion, it will become real. I haven't even told Conor my fears, but I can see them in his eyes, and I know he is doing the same—trying to stay strong for me.

But the question is there, beneath the surface, eating away, and it's worst at night when it becomes unignorable. What will we do if it doesn't come?

CHAPTER 14

WE HAD ALMOST finished our makeshift dinner of curling sandwiches, cheese, and charcuterie from the fast-warming fridge, the shadows were lengthening, the mosquitos were whining, and the sun was beginning to set, flaming, into the peach-colored sea, when Conor brought the subject up again.

"Guys, I think it's time."

"Time for what?" It was Santana who spoke. With Dan's help she had limped down the path from the villa to the cabana, and was looking surprisingly okay, though I kept glancing nervously at her thigh. I don't know what I was looking for exactly—signs of infection, perhaps, though what that looked like, I couldn't have said. Now I remembered that she hadn't been at the discussion earlier.

"Time to . . . to bury them," I said, with a glance at Joel, who had his head in his hands. He had barely touched his food.

"But . . . surely we can't?" Santana looked puzzled. "Should we leave the bodies for . . . I don't know. The police or something?"

"This ain't a crime scene, woman," Bayer said angrily. The pain in his shoulder was evidently nagging at his nerves, and he had been snapping and growling at everyone. Even terrified, Bambi-eyed little Zana had been called a stupid cunt when she knocked his bad shoulder accidentally, handing him a sandwich. Conor had said nothing, but I had seen the muscles in his jaw move as he gritted his teeth to stop himself from replying. Now Bayer had been drinking—beer was one of the few liquids we had other than water—and I could see he was spoiling for a fight.

"It's not a crime scene," Santana said spiritedly, "but they're both unnatural deaths and I'm assuming that means they'll have to be autopsied."

"For Christ's sake!" Joel broke out, as if he couldn't bear to hear it anymore. I thought that for a brief moment this afternoon he had managed almost to forget about what had happened to Romi, kid himself that she was on the boat back with Nico and the others. Now it was coming horribly back to him.

"I'm sorry," Conor said. There was sympathy in his voice, but also firmness. "And you're right, Santana, but we can't just leave the bodies there. That's not dignified, and more to the point, it's not safe."

"What do you mean, it is not safe?" It was Angel who asked, looking up from where she was lying, stretched out on the cabana banquette. In the setting sun, she looked unbelievably and incongruously beautiful, her long bronzed limbs glinting in the deepening red-gold rays, and if you looked away from Santana's leg and Bayer's arm, you could almost believe this scene was a still from a holiday brochure. *Tropical Paradise. Happy ever after.*

"I mean, we don't want to attract predators or disease."

Joel got up and left the table. I could see him pacing about at the far end of the cabana. Conor lowered his voice and spoke to the rest of us, trying to keep quiet enough that Joel wouldn't hear what he was saying.

"Between the insects, the birds, and the heat, if the boat doesn't come soon, there won't be much left of either of them to autopsy, and this island isn't big enough for us to ignore a rotting corpse." Angel made a grossed-out face, but Conor ignored her and carried on. "They'll both be in a better state if we bury them somewhere now, with dignity. We can show the authorities where they are when they find us, if it comes to that point."

"I think Conor's right," I spoke up reluctantly, trying to keep my voice quiet enough that Joel wouldn't hear it. "We can't just leave them. And I kind of think . . ." I swallowed, looked up the terrace at where Joel was standing, his silhouette dark against the evening sky. "I think maybe it would help Joel come to terms with it."

WE BURIED THEM on the edge of the beach at sunset, the producer first, and then Romi after, pulling her shrouded body gently out of Joel's hands, as if he couldn't bear to let her go, and lowering her into the hole with as much dignity as we could manage.

The sun was just dipping beneath the horizon, and the bats were beginning to swoop low across the peach-colored sky, as Joel threw the first handfuls of sand onto her body. Zana, Santana, and I had done our best with both women, wrapping them in all the bed sheets we could spare, rolling them around and around to try to protect them from the elements as much as possible. The sand on the island was soft, and even without proper shovels, it had not taken Joel, Dan, and Conor long to dig two shafts deep enough for graves.

Now we all stood around in the dying light, as Joel wept, and each of us tried to think what to say. Somehow with the producer it had been easier; she was a complete stranger to all of us, and though we all felt a terrible compassion for her lonely death, without a name, it was hard to make what had happened to her seem real.

But with Joel standing there, his face streaked with dirt and tears, it was impossible to forget that a flesh-and-blood person lay at the bottom of Romi's grave—someone who had been vibrant and alive and loved only twelve hours ago.

In the end it was Santana who spoke, clearing her throat and stepping forward, looking down unflinchingly at the body.

"I didn't know you well, Romi, but I wish I'd known you better. I could tell you were a person who loved life, and I am so sorry that your time here was cut short so cruelly."

There was a moment's silence, and then Dan stepped forward.

"Romi, you lit up the room in the short time I had to know you, and I'll always remember your smile. Rest in peace."

Angel said a short poem in French, at least I assumed it was a poem, and then took a shell she had picked up from the beach and tossed it into the grave.

Bayer and Zana both said a few words. Then it was my turn.

"I'm so sorry, Romi." The words seemed to stick in my throat. I was trying to keep my mind on Romi, but the pictures in my head were all of Nico—of the *Over Easy*, drifting down through deep water, Nico sobbing as he clawed at the little porthole window in his cabin as it filled with water. "What happened . . . it was so unfair. I wish this hadn't happened to any of us. I wish you'd had longer. I wish I'd known you better. I wish none of this was happening."

My throat was closing up, and I knew I was on the verge of tears that had nothing really to do with Romi, and everything to do with Nico, and our own plight here on this fucking island. Why had we come? For fame? For some dream of unearned stardom? What a price we were all paying for that.

I was just wondering what to do, what else to say, when Conor stepped forward. He squeezed my hand briefly, then let go.

"Rest in peace, Romi," he said, his voice low. "You'll never be forgotten by any of us."

"Goodbye, Romi," Joel said. His voice was thick with tears. "I'm sorry. I'm so sorry for all of this. I'm sorry I wasn't a better boyfriend, I'm sorry I couldn't stop this. I love you—"

His voice cracked, and then he pushed an armful of the piled-up sand onto her body and fell to his knees, weeping bitterly.

It was Santana who led him away, while Bayer, Dan, and Conor filled in the grave. Zana had made two little crosses out of driftwood and scratched Romi's name onto one. Now she laid them over the gently rounded graves, and I saw a single tear slide down her face.

"I don't know why I'm crying," she said, very low, not to me so much as to herself. "I hardly knew them."

But I knew why she was crying. It was the same reason I was. She was crying for Romi, yes, and for the nameless woman lying beside her in the sand. But she was crying for the rest of us too.

CHAPTER 15

"LOOK, I THINK we need to organize ourselves."

It was Conor who spoke. We were sitting around the cabana in the early morning cool, listening to the chatter of the birds and the screech of the parrots, and finishing off a breakfast scrounged from the broken boxes down at the staff quarters. We'd had to throw the sandwiches away, but there were croissants, tinned fruit salad, and brioche. I was getting incredibly tired of brioche, and it had only been two days.

"What do you mean?" Dan looked up from his bowl, where he was scooping up the last of the fruit salad with a chunk of muffin. "Organize ourselves for what? Local elections?"

Bayer laughed, but Conor ignored him.

"We need to know what we're up against. We don't know how long we'll be here—" He raised his hand as a protest erupted, voices exclaiming that it couldn't possibly be *that* long. "I know, I know, but look, we're already on day three since the boat left. I think we have to hope for the best, plan for the worst. And the worst-case scenario is, we're stuck here for a while. So that's what we have to plan for, even if we hope it doesn't happen. We need to know how much water we've got, how much food, whether we've got any means of contacting the mainland. Maybe someone's left a mobile phone in one of the shacks."

I raised my hand, and then felt annoyed with my own subservience, put it down, and spoke.

"There's a radio."

Conor raised an eyebrow.

"Does it work?"

"It seems to. Though who knows how long the battery will last. But I already tried to broadcast on it; no one came in."

"Okay, well, let's finish up here and then head over to the staff quarters and see what's what. You can show us how the radio works, and then afterwards we can make a proper inventory, see what we're dealing with. Bayer, are you okay to help?"

Bayer nodded. His arm was black with bruising under the tattoos, but he was moving it all right.

"Santana, you'd better stay here, keep an eye on things."

"Are you sure?" Santana looked a mixture of relieved and disappointed. "I *can* walk, you know."

"I know, but the last thing we need is you opening up that wound. Lyla did a pretty amazing job, all things considered, but let's not push our luck."

Further nods. I stood up, feeling the aching muscles in my back and arms stretch. I had been more tense than I knew, clenching my fists against some unspoken dread.

Hope for the best . . . plan for the worst. The question was . . . how bad could it get? And the answer, I was beginning to fear, might be pretty bad.

WHAT WE WERE dealing with, it turned out, was a lot and also . . . not a lot. We had bottled water, a couple of hundred liters at a rough count, though we'd already drunk a good twenty or thirty liters—a worrying amount in just two days. There was also toilet paper and some basic cleaning supplies. And we had some food, though not a great deal. Everything perishable had gone off in the sultry heat—the sandwiches curling into ant-infested mounds, the cheese and cold cuts so rancid that Angel gagged when she opened the refrigerator door and swung it quickly shut again.

What we were left with was dry goods and tins. Which meant chips and pretzels, cookies, and a stack of boxes full of the everlasting pastries and long-life brioche. There was precious little in the way of anything fresh, aside from the tinned fruit salad. We also had a small amount of beer and wine—though not much; evidently, Baz hadn't trusted us enough to leave most of the alcohol on the island—and the radio.

On the minus side, there were no first aid supplies beyond what we'd each brought with us, and the island's infrastructure looked damaged beyond what any of us could possibly repair. Down near the waterline Conor had discovered a smashed-up hut filled with tanks and equipment that looked worryingly like the remains of a desalination plant, and the power was still out. We had no idea how electricity to the island had been supplied before the storm—if there had been solar panels, we couldn't see them now, and an underwater cable seemed unlikely, given how far we were from the nearest big island. Regardless, there was a strong smell of diesel wafting across the staff quarters, and down by the wrecked desalination plant you could see a small lake of iridescent oil spreading over the surface of the waves. If the desalination shed had housed the backup generator, it was no longer much of a backup.

The animals had already started to pick over the broken boxes, so under Conor's instruction, we packed up the remainder of the food and carted it to the cabana.

"Who died and made him fucking king," Bayer grumbled as he and I started our second trek through the forest, holding armfuls of plastic-wrapped food—chips and cakes and the kind of additive-laden cookies I'd never been allowed as a child. I said nothing. I couldn't blame Conor for taking charge—somebody had to, and everything he'd suggested was sensible. We did need to make an inventory of food and get it away from being pecked at by birds or nibbled by rats. But I also couldn't blame Bayer for being angry. We were all exhausted. It was swelteringly hot, I could feel my back burning through the thin cotton of my shirt and the sweat trickling down between my breasts, and I knew Bayer's arm must be killing him. And more than that—Conor was making us face up to something that none of us wanted to admit: the possibility that the *Over Easy* wasn't coming to rescue us any time soon.

It was Angel who forced the issue, with a tantrum down at the ruins of the staff quarters when Conor ordered a third trip up to the cabana.

"Why are we doing this?" she shouted. "The boat *has* to come back eventually, and then personally je fous le camp aussi vite que possible."

"And what if it doesn't?" Conor asked pleasantly.

"The boat *has* to come back," Angel repeated, stubbornly. "But I am not carrying one more package of fucking food. And you are not the boss of this island to tell me!"

"If you want to eat it, you'll carry it," Conor said. His tone was flat, and on the surface his voice sounded fairly matter-of-fact, but there was a menace underneath that made the group fall into silence. Bayer stepped forward.

"Don't talk to my woman like that," he growled. Conor turned to him and smiled, but it was a completely mirthless smile, one that didn't reach his extraordinary pale eyes.

"So she should benefit from everyone else's hard work while she does nothing?"

"Santana is," Bayer said. He was squaring up to Conor, the muscles in his shoulders and neck standing out.

"Santana's got a six-inch gash in her leg, you moron," I snapped.

As soon as the words left my mouth I regretted them. They were true, and there was no reason why Angel couldn't pull her weight like the rest of us, but I knew that deep down, that wasn't why she was refusing—it wasn't laziness, it was a terror at what this level of preparation meant, a refusal to look that possibility in the eye.

Bayer wasn't interested in psychoanalysis though.

"What did you call me?" he snarled.

"Hey!" It was Joel who stepped forward, hands outstretched. "Mate, calm down. Look"—he glanced at Conor—"maybe we should have a break, get some food into everyone, and then finish up in the afternoon when it's less hot?"

Conor looked up at the sky, as if calculating the time, and then shrugged and nodded.

"Okay. That's not a bad idea."

"And before we go, shall we try to figure out this radio?" Joel said. Conor nodded again.

"Where did you say it was, Lyla?"

"In that shack over there." I pointed, and we moved across, a little ragged group, hot and bad-tempered, to take another look.

Inside the hut it was dark, and almost cool after the blaze of the sun outside. The radio was still sitting there, the LED still glowing green, and when I picked up the receiver, the display lit up just like before. This time I noticed there were wires coming out the back, leading to something that looked a lot like a car battery.

"Has anyone used one of these before?" I asked. Heads were shaken all round, and I felt my heart sink a little. "Me neither. I basically guessed before. But look, this"—I twisted the knob that made the static flare and reduce—"seems to be some kind of volume control, and you press this button here on the receiver to transmit. But this"—I pointed to another knob—"I think is to change the channel. The problem is, I've got no idea what channel we should be using. I left it on the preset one because I thought that was the one the *Over Easy* would be monitoring, but if they're not in the area, maybe we should be using a Mayday channel."

"Which is?" Angel asked a little snippily. I raised my shoulders a little defensively.

"I have no idea. That's the problem."

There was a long pause.

"Look," Joel said at last, "I think the only thing we can do is just try as many as possible. Flick through the channels and repeat the message each time with as much information as we can. Do you agree?"

"I mean . . . yes," I said reluctantly, "except that it's battery-powered and we have no idea how much charge is left." I pointed at the chunky orange battery sitting under the table, the wires from the radio coiled around the terminals. "So we're going to have to strike a balance between broadcasting as widely as possible now, and saving some charge in case . . ."

In case we needed it in the days and weeks to come, was the unspoken message, but I didn't want to say it. If the storm had been a bad one, maybe even still circulating along the coast of Indonesia, it was perfectly possible that all the boats and fishing vessels were tied up in port, safely waiting it out. We might have a better chance of passing traffic in a few days. But if we'd used up all the battery before that, we'd have shot ourselves in the foot.

"You're both right," Conor said at last, decisively. "Joel, you stay here and broadcast a Mayday call on half a dozen different frequencies, see if you can get any response. If you can, write down what the frequencies were. And then if that doesn't work, we turn off the radio to conserve power and try again tomorrow. Lyla, did you scroll through to see if you could hear anything?"

"Um . . . no," I said, a little shamefacedly. As soon as Conor had said the words, it seemed like such an obvious step. Of course, if there were a channel people were already using, it made sense to put a call out on that one. "No, I didn't think of that."

"Well, it's probably a good idea to do that first, see if we can pick anything up. If we can't, just pick some frequencies you can remember, Joel, and we'll try different ones tomorrow."

"Okay," Joel said. He picked up the receiver and began turning the dial, listening intently as the static ebbed and rose.

"The rest of us will take one more set of supplies up to the cabana, and then we'll break for lunch."

Joel nodded. He had run through the full spectrum of the dial now, and as we walked away from the hut to pick up a last set of supplies, I could hear him beginning to broadcast.

"Hello, my name is Joel Richards, this is . . . God, I'm not sure. Maybe our third Mayday call? Please, if you can hear us, send urgent help. We're stranded on an island about twenty hours southwest of Indonesia. Twenty hours by boat that is—we came here by boat."

His voice was getting fainter as I picked up a box of tinned tuna salad and added some vacuum-packed croissants on top.

"There are people here with serious injuries. . . ." I heard, as I walked away from the clearing, up the path to the cabana. "If anyone can hear me, please respond or send help. We don't know how long they will last."

Today is 17 February—three days since the storm, and I think the gravity of the situation we are in has begun to sink in. Something must have happened to the boat—which is a terrifying thought.

Yesterday we had a group meeting and totted up all of our water and food supplies. Bayer worked out that we have just over two hundred litres of water, plus some liquid from the tins, and whatever we can forage from coconuts and so on. It's not a lot. Even if we restrict ourselves to a liter a day—which Lyla says is barely what you need to survive in heat like this—we're talking eight liters a day between all of us, which is about a twenty-five-day supply. Less than a month.

Today was the first day we tried the new allocation, and God it was hard. Breakfast was fine, but by the evening I was so thirsty, I couldn't think of anything apart from water. I was fantasizing about it, about taking big glugs from a jug, or standing in a shower and letting it pour down my body. We had agreed to dole out the evening allocation when the sun hit this tall palm to the west of the island, but as we watched it inch over the forest I nearly cracked and begged for my allowance early. I think if it hadn't been for Conor I would have—but he talked me through it. We played this game—I closed my eyes and imagined myself walking through the rooms of my childhood house, describing each one to him. It felt so incredibly real. And when I opened my eyes, I realized that the sun was almost setting, touching the tip of the palm tree.

I nearly ran to the cabana. I have never been so glad to see anyone in my life as Bayer handing out the cups of water.

I am dreading how much harder it's going to get. But I can't think about that yet. Someone will come. Someone has to come.

CHAPTER 16

WHEN I AWOKE the next day, it was to a sense of complete disorientation, followed by a wash of dread.

The disorientation was from the realization that I was not in my own bed, or even in *a* bed, but once again lying on a mattress on the floor of Forest Retreat, surrounded by the snores of Joel, Dan, and Santana.

The wash of dread was when I realized another twenty-four hours had gone by, and there was no producer banging on the door of the villa demanding to know if we were okay, no Camille panting up the path from the bay. And with every hour that passed, it seemed more likely that something terrible had happened to both the *Over Easy* . . . and Nico.

I wasn't sure how early it was, but the thought had chased away all sleep, so I got up, pulled on my shoes, and then let myself quietly out of the villa, closing the door behind me.

The first thing I did was walk to the far shore of the island, where the boat had anchored that first day, in the faint hope that it might be, if not there, at least a shape in the far distance, coming closer. But there was nothing at all—not so much as a fishing boat on the horizon—just uninterrupted blue as far as the eye could see and, high above, a single contrail of a jet marring the scorchingly blue sky.

I felt all the hope drain out of me.

"Watching the horizon too, huh?" came a voice from behind me, and I swung around to see Conor standing there, bare chested. He had his hand up, shading his eyes, and the movement made the eagle wings stretch and ripple across his torso, like a bird about to take flight.

"God, you startled me."

"Sorry. I had the same . . . well, I don't want to say hope, because I'm not sure I really believed there would be anything there, but I had to check."

"What are we going to do, Conor?" I blurted out. I was surprised at the desperation in my own voice. I'd been working so hard to keep the terror in check, keep focusing on the practicalities of solving each obstacle as it arose—but that pitiless blue was somehow worse than anything I'd imagined. Blue—just blue as far as the eye could see. Not a boat, not an island, not even a piece of driftwood. "If the boat doesn't come, I mean? What the fuck do we do?"

Conor shrugged.

"We . . . survive, I guess. That's all we can do. Someone is going to come looking eventually. They must know where we were heading."

"You think?"

"They must do. Baz hired this island off someone. There has to be a production company back in the UK. When they don't hear any-thing, *someone* will check in, follow the breadcrumbs."

"And how long will that take? Especially if the storm was as bad or worse on the mainland. They may not have the local resources to be out looking for a parcel of idiot reality TV show contestants."

"I don't know," Conor said quietly. "Obviously I hope this hur-ricane wasn't too destructive, but if it wasn't a big deal on the other islands . . . well, put it this way, I'm almost more worried about that possibility."

"What do you mean?" I was puzzled. "You're worried the storm *wasn't* bad enough? That doesn't make sense."

"I mean, if the storm was a big deal, it'll have made the news in the UK. People will want to know we're okay, and when they can't contact Baz, they'll start to get worried. Family members will start making a fuss. Contacting Real TV. But if it was just a local thing . . ."

"Shit." Suddenly my hands felt cold, in spite of the rising heat of the day. "If no one in the UK knows what happened, they may not know to send out searches."

"Exactly. I mean . . . how long was filming supposed to last? Six weeks? Eight? And we told everyone not to expect to hear from us while we were on the island. If they don't hear from us for a couple of months, do you think they'll be concerned? Or will they just think we made it to the winning pair?"

"I think my boss would be," I said slowly. "Concerned, I mean. I only took two weeks off." But even as I said the words, I wondered . . . would he? Or would he just think I'd become despondent about my job and jacked it in? And even if he *was* concerned, would he know whom to contact? Had I told him anything about the production? He might ring my mum, I supposed. She was down as next of kin on the university pension database. She knew about the show, and about my plan to bail out early, but she also knew that it was supposed to last up to ten weeks. What if she assumed I'd changed my mind and decided to stay on? I thought of the brief WhatsApp message I'd sent before giving up my phone, saying I'd be out of contact for a few weeks, and not to worry if she didn't hear from me. That now seemed monumentally stupid.

"Surely Baz must be checking in with someone?" I said at last. "He's got to be sending footage home, don't you think?"

"I don't know," Conor said simply. "I have no idea."

"You knew him though, right?" I asked, though I realized even as I said the words that I had slipped into the past tense, a past tense that I wasn't yet ready to apply to Nico.

"Baz?" For the first time, Conor's gaze shifted away from my face, towards the horizon. In the harsh light his pupils had contracted to pinpricks, and his eyes looked almost pure ice gray. It was so extremely obvious that I'd been talking about Baz that the question seemed incongruous, like a way of giving himself time to think about his reply. "I mean . . . yeah, kind of. We had . . . people in common, I guess. But that's not much to hang our survival on."

Our survival. The two words hung in the air, pushing out all other considerations. No one had set it out so starkly until now—but it was true, that's what we were talking about. Our life or death, everything or nothing, last-roll-of-the-dice survival.

And below all of that was the unspoken truth that if the boat didn't come, then Nico was probably already dead.

I pushed my hands through my salt-tangled hair as if I could push that thought out of my head.

"How long do you think we can last?" I said instead, as much to distract myself from thoughts of Nico as anything else. Conor shrugged.

"It depends what we can scavenge from the island," he said at last. "Bananas. Coconuts. Fish. Maybe bats, if we can catch them. Have you seen those fruitbats hanging in the trees at night? They're huge— easily the size of a rabbit."

Bats. Even the idea gave me a jolt of revulsion, but I knew on some level, he might be right.

"We've got a ton of food though," I said, trying not to sound like I was arguing back. "I mean, there's boxes and boxes of brioche and croissant, and all those tins. I know it's not exactly gourmet cuisine, but . . ."

"There's eight of us," Conor said rather flatly. "Eight. So even if we limit ourselves to a couple of pieces of carb and a tin of something per day, that's still well over a hundred bagels or whatever per week. I did a rough count, and we're talking . . . a few weeks. If that."

I felt the color drain from my face. When he put it like that . . . our predicament was stark. I hadn't counted either, but I doubted there were more than a couple of hundred muffins and Danish, and probably less than that of tins. And two Danish a day didn't feel like much to survive on. The question of what happened when we ran out of food was something I didn't want to think about. But Conor was still speaking.

"I'm actually more worried about the water. You're supposed to have a minimum of two liters a day or thereabouts, but let's say we can keep it to one. Which won't be fun in this heat, but it'll probably keep us alive. That's eight liters for all of us, just under two of those big water bottles per day. And I don't think we've got more than about forty of those. We drank at least three yesterday, maybe four. So we're talking . . ."

"About three weeks," I finished. There was a hollow sensation in my stomach. I thought of the liters of water I'd poured down the drain when sluicing Santana's leg and felt more than a little sick. "Unless we can get the desalination plant going."

Conor shook his head.

"Did you look at it? It was missing great big chunks of stuff that must have been washed out to sea. I don't think even an engineer could get that working. But we should set up water butts and stuff, in case it rains."

We both looked up at the cloudless sky. There didn't seem to be much to say. I swallowed. I felt suddenly very thirsty.

BACK UP AT the cabana, the others had woken up and had been busy making breakfast. There was a little driftwood fire smoldering in the sand just off the corner of the decking, and Dan and Santana were drinking cups of something that looked and smelled a lot like black coffee. Angel was picking at a tin of fruit salad, and Bayer had unscrewed the lid of one of the water bottles and was chugging directly from the neck, water running down his chin. Joel was nibbling a brioche. On the far side of the clearing a bird was sitting in a tree, balefully nibbling on a brioche it must have stolen when no one was looking. Only Zana wasn't eating or drinking.

"Look, I found coffee!" Santana called as we came closer, holding up her cup. "You want some?"

"Put that down," Conor said flatly. Santana set down her coffee cup.

"I *beg* your pardon?"

"Not you, him." He nodded at Bayer, who lowered the water bottle with menacing slowness.

"*What* did you say?" His voice was full of a pent-up aggression that made me pause in my ascent of the steps, but Conor didn't blink. He walked up to the table and sat, his demeanor calm.

"Look, we should have talked about this last night, but we need to start rationing our supplies. Particularly water. Lyla and I were just down at the cove. There's no sign of the boat, and we have to assume we might be in this for the long haul."

"What do you mean, particularly water?" Angel raised one eyebrow. "We have liters and liters of water. We spent all day hauling the stupid stuff up from the staff quarters."

"We actually don't have that much," I said, a little diffidently. I sat down beside Joel. "Conor and I were just running through the maths and . . . he's right. We're going to need about eight liters a day just to survive. At that rate, we'll be through the water in two or three weeks."

"Sorry, but eight liters is ridiculous," Santana said with a smile. "Even the biggest hydration freak wouldn't drink that much. We don't need to wash with bottled water, we can use the sea for that."

"Not eight liters a person," Conor spelled it out. "Eight liters for *all* of us. A liter each. Per day."

"What?" Dan looked confused. "But—that's not enough to survive? Not in this heat."

"Unless it rains, it'll have to be. I went all over this island and there's no water supply."

"We could dig a well?" Santana said uncertainly. Conor shook his head.

"We're basically a big sand bar in the middle of the ocean. Any well is just going to be seawater, and we've got plenty of that already."

"Fuck." Bayer banged the big bottle down on the table so hard the water splashed and spattered the surface. Everybody winced. I caught Joel staring at the droplets, watching as they evaporated from the hot surface of the wood.

"We've got the tins of fruit salad," Conor was saying. "They have a fair amount of liquid we can use to pad out the water. But no more coffee." He nodded at Santana and Dan's cups. "It wastes too much in the grounds."

"But wait," Santana said, "two or three weeks, the boat *has* to be back by then, doesn't it?"

I exchanged a glance with Conor.

"I think . . ." He was speaking slowly, and for the first time I got the impression he wasn't sure how to put into words what he wanted to say. "I think if the boat were coming . . . it would have been here by now."

There was an instant hubbub of protest and disbelief, and Conor raised his voice, speaking above the others.

"I'm sorry, I know it's not what anyone wants to hear, but wherever they were going, they were supposed to be there and back in twelve hours. It's been more than thirty-six since they left, and the sea's been calm as a pond for twenty-four hours of that. Even if you give them a generous stretch of extra time for getting blown off course, if they were coming, they would have been here already."

"What if the boat's damaged?" Santana said. "They might have had to stop for repairs."

"Then why haven't they sent help?"

"Maybe everyone's busy! Or maybe they've run out of fuel and they're floating somewhere waiting for people to come find them. Or maybe—"

"Maybe, maybe, maybe," Conor broke in impatiently. "There's a ton of possible explanations, but none of them are certain enough to gamble our survival on." Survival. It was the same word he'd used down at the beach, and it gave me the same jolt hearing it for the second time. "We have to act like they *won't* be coming, otherwise we could be sitting here in a week's time looking at a row of empty bottles."

"But what's the long-term plan?" It was Zana's voice, so unexpected that we all, all of us turned to look at her. She was sitting at the corner of the table, and she looked, if anything, even thinner and more fragile than she had the night before, a kind of desperation and fear in her eyes that made me flinch to see it. "I mean, what you're saying, it makes sense. But what difference does it make if we're sitting here in a week, looking at the empty bottles, or in three weeks? We're still screwed either way."

"It gives us more time," Conor said. He moved to the other end of the table and took one of her hands in his. "In three weeks, anything could happen. A fishing boat could come past. Someone in the UK could figure out what's wrong and charter a helicopter. It could *rain.*"

There was a long, long silence. Then Joel ran his hands through his hair, so it stood up, stiff and tangled with salt.

"Fuck. I hope you're right. I really, really hope you're right."

Today is Wednesday, the 21st—exactly one week since the storm. When I woke up this morning and the boat still wasn't there, I felt . . . I don't know. Something close to despair. A week. Even if the boat had broken down, surely, surely they would have raised the alarm by now. Something terrible must have happened.

If I think about it too much, I feel like I might go mad. The only thing that's keeping me sane is the fact that I'm here with Conor. He's so calm, so strong, even in a situation like this. And he's practical too. He was the one who thought of rounding up all the food and water from the staff quarters and figuring out how long we could ration it out to survive.

I'm writing this in the water villa—that's where we're living now, me and Conor. It's not ideal, the jetty is very rickety, but there were only three villas left standing after the storm—ours, Lyla's, and the water villa, so we didn't have much choice. In some ways it would have made more sense for me and Conor to stay in our original villa, but Bayer's shoulder was dislocated in the storm, and since then he hasn't been doing so well.

We had a private chat, Conor and I, and he asked whether I'd be prepared to offer Bayer and Angel our villa—give the two of them some space and give Bayer some peace and quiet to recuperate. I'm not so keen on water, but I agreed that it wouldn't be safe for Bayer to try to make it out here every night. If he fell in, I don't know if he could swim with his bad shoulder.

So in spite of my misgivings, I told Conor to go for it—to tell Bayer and Angel to take Palm Tree Rest. And you know what, I'm glad I did. The water villa—it's beautiful. And somehow, out here, surrounded by the waves, I'm not so scared anymore. But the real reason I said yes was for Conor. He makes me want to be a better person. God, I love him so much.

CHAPTER 17

OVER THE NEXT few days, we fell into an uneasy rhythm. In the mornings we gathered at the cabana for breakfast, then someone, usually me or Joel, would make our way back to the staff quarters to try the radio. The rest of the day we would spend fishing, exploring the island and then, as the heat grew more unbearable, everyone would retreat for the afternoon to the shade of the villas, playing cards, sleeping, and trying to ignore our growing thirst—waiting impatiently for the sun to touch the leaves of what we'd started to call the Water Palm on the tip of the island, when Conor doled out the evening ration.

Conor, Zana, Angel, and Bayer seemed at first to have established themselves in Palm Tree Rest, the villa Nico and I were to have had, but after the altercation between Conor and Bayer over breakfast, it quickly became apparent that that wasn't going to be an arrangement that could stick, long-term.

I had half been expecting that one couple would make a move to begin renovating one of the wrecked villas—probably Bayer, as he seemed most unhappy with the current arrangement, and in fact had twice spent the night in the ruined Ocean Bluff, sleeping under the stars. But what actually happened was something quite different—something none of us had predicted.

We didn't notice it until we gathered at the cabana for supper one evening, and then it was Santana who spotted it. She was leaning over the railing of the cabana, looking out at the sunset, beyond the beach, when she gave an exclamation.

"Wait, who's been rebuilding the jetty?"

"That would be me," Conor said with a grin. "Cave man tools—a rock and scavenged nails—but it worked. Kind of."

We all crowded to the wall and looked over, and I saw that Santana was right—someone, presumably Conor, had scoured the beach for the washed-up sections of decking, and had fastened the pieces back onto the upright struts that had survived the storm. It wasn't remotely perfect—there were some very large gaps, and the planks were broken and uneven. And the rope handrail was long gone, along with the lights strung along it. But you could once again make your way out to the water villa without swimming.

"Zana and I will be sleeping there," Conor said. He turned to Bayer and gave a little nod. "You can have Palm Tree Rest."

"Oh I *can*, can I?" Bayer said sourly. He had plainly found some beer and had been drinking—we had been able to smell the beer coming off his breath the moment we sat down at the table with him, and Dan and I had had a whispered discussion about whether beer had been factored into the liquid allowance, and if not, how to raise it, before deciding now probably wasn't the time.

"Bayer . . ." Angel said placatingly. She put one hand on his leg, and Bayer growled and turned away.

I was looking at Zana, who was sitting at the far end of the table, her hand in Conor's. She looked pale and miserable, and I couldn't help recalling the visceral terror she had displayed at getting over to the water villa first time round. How was she going to manage on a rickety, jerry-built gangway?

"How do you feel about that, Zana?" I asked, and she flinched.

"Fine." Her voice was monotone, and so faint I could hardly hear it. She sounded almost comically unfine, in fact. I glanced curiously at Conor, to see what he made of all this, but there was no response from him. Yet he couldn't be unaware of Zana's phobia of water, could he?

"More cheerfully," Dan said, with an effort at bringing the mood of the group back, "look what Lyla and I found this afternoon."

He reached below the table and came up with a hand of bananas, plus three ripe and two unripe coconuts. We had tried the bananas in the forest and found they were smaller, starchier, and less sweet than the ones in the supermarket back home, with enormous black seeds you had to spit out, but they'd been tasty enough to eat, and beggars couldn't afford to be choosers. The coconuts, we'd found on the ground. There were dozens of them lying around the forest, and when I found the first one I'd been jubilant—thinking that our water troubles were over—but Dan had shaken them, listening for the sound of sloshing, and had shaken his head. They were too ripe. If we wanted coconut water we needed the green unripe ones, which were, frustratingly, mostly still in the trees, tantalizingly high above our heads.

While Dan and I divided up the bananas, and Joel and Angel puzzled over how to break open the coconuts, Conor began measuring out the water. We'd agreed half a liter each morning and evening, but it turned out that in this heat, half a liter wasn't a lot to get you through to supper, and now I found myself watching him greedily as he poured each person's allowance into a tin can marked up for the purpose, and then decanted carefully into a mug. When he set mine down in front of me, I had to fight the urge to pick it up at once and down the lot—but I didn't want to. I wanted to save it.

Bayer, on the other hand, put down the bagel he was chewing and gulped the whole lot, wiping his mouth, and then bit into his banana. He made a face.

"Gross." He spat a handful of seeds onto the ground. "Tastes like shit."

I exchanged a glance with Dan. *Thanks* seemed like a more appropriate response given Bayer hadn't brought anything to the table, but I could tell that neither of us were in a hurry to provoke him. He seemed to be spoiling for a fight.

The silence was broken by a cheer from Joel, and Angel standing, triumphantly holding up the coconut, which now had two small holes in the top, where they'd managed to pound a nail through the eyes.

"Et voilà! Coconut water!"

"Hold out your cups," Joel said. He was grinning.

We all did, and Angel carefully drained a little of the liquid into each cup. It was cloudy and mixed with bits of shell and hair, but none of us cared about that—none of us, that is, other than Bayer, who pushed his cup away roughly as Angel poured the coconut water in.

"That's disgusting. You've just poured a load of crap into my water."

"It is not *crap*," Angel said impatiently, rolling the *r* sarcastically on the last word. "It's perfectly clean coconut hairs."

"You drink it, then." Bayer shoved the cup towards her, almost tipping it as he did. Angel raised one eyebrow.

"Seriously?"

"Seriously." Bayer's voice was truculent. "I don't want this now you've filled it with dirt."

Angel shrugged, picked up Bayer's cup, and drained it.

I was expecting Bayer to make a fuss, say that he'd been joking, maybe even take Angel's water from her. The idea of lasting all night without any more water wasn't pleasant. But he did none of those. Instead, he pulled the big five-liter water bottle towards him, the one Conor had set down after carefully measuring out our rations, unscrewed the top, and took a long gulp.

For a moment there was absolute silence. We all just stared at Bayer, unsure what to do. Then, almost involuntarily, I found my eyes going to Conor.

"Put. That. Down." Conor said very quietly. The words dropped like stones into the silence.

Bayer put the bottle down and grinned, widely. There had been almost a liter left in the bottom. Now there was barely half a cup.

"Sure," he said.

"Listen to me." Conor's voice was calm, but deadly, and it made a shiver run down my spine. "I am giving you three strikes, Bayer, and you've had two of them. But if you try something like that again, you're out."

"Out?" Bayer gave a guffawing laugh. "I don't know if you've noticed, mate, but there is no *out*. There's nowhere to fucking go."

Conor had stood up, towering over Bayer, and now Bayer stood up too, putting them nose to nose. The air crackled with testosterone, and beside me I heard Joel swallow nervously.

"Guys—" he tried, but neither of the other two men even acknowledged him.

"You think you could take me?" Bayer was asking. Conor just shrugged.

"I can hold my own."

Bayer laughed, scoffingly, as if he doubted that, but looking at the two of them, I wasn't so sure. True, Bayer was the more muscled, he must have had a good stone on Conor, and he looked like he wouldn't mind fighting dirty. But he also had the beefed-up bulk of someone who's spent a long time pumping iron, but not much time on cardio—and his dislocated left shoulder definitely wouldn't help. Conor, on the other hand, looked *fit*. There wasn't an ounce of fat on him, and his muscles were hard, with tendons like whipcords. And there was something in his stance that told me this wasn't the first time he'd been in this situation—and that he wasn't scared.

I swallowed too, my throat suddenly dry in spite of the coconut water.

"Bayer," Angel said now, standing up. "Bayer, stop being a dickhead. Conor, look, Bayer should not have done that, he knows this, but it was one time. He will respect the ration from now. Won't you?" She glared at Bayer. "*Won't you.*"

"Respect has to be earned," Bayer said, his lip curling. But he turned away from Conor's pale, unflinching gaze and began walking into the night. "Come on, babe."

Angel gave a look back at the group as if to say, *what can I do?* Then she followed Bayer into the gathering darkness.

There was an audible exhalation of breath from around the circle, and a feeling like a balloon had been pricked with a slow puncture, a dissipating tension. Conor flexed his fingers and shoulders, and I heard his neck crack. Maybe he had been more tense than he had been letting on.

"I'm sorry about that," he said. Santana shook her head.

"It's okay. Someone had to say something."

Dan nodded.

"Yeah, I'm glad you put a line in the sand. Fuck knows, I wasn't about to fight him, but we couldn't let him keep getting away with flouting the rules, could we. Right? I'm not wrong, am I?" He glanced around the circle, looking for agreement, and I found myself nodding, though I didn't like the *them and us* mentality that was developing. Every reality TV show I'd ever watched, there was the pack, and the outsiders. And both could be a dangerous place to find yourself.

I remembered Conor's words on the boat—*every show needs a villain.* And I remembered, too, Joel saying, *these things have a formula . . . there's always the alpha males, the ones who're duking it out for the prize . . .*

We were falling into the reality TV tropes I'd seen play out on-screen. And the implications of that unsettled me in a way I couldn't quite articulate. Because the stakes here were so much higher than a trophy or a cash prize. The stakes here were life and death.

"I'm going to bed," I said at last, standing up and draining the last of the coconut water in my cup. Somewhere over the course of the evening, a raging headache had set in, maybe thanks to the heat and dehydration, or perhaps triggered by the argument between Bayer and Conor.

"I'll come too," Santana said, and Dan nodded.

"Coming, Joel?"

"I'll follow up," Joel said. "Give Conor and Zana a hand clearing up." I nodded.

"Thanks, Joel. Will you guys be okay?"

"We'll be fine," Conor said. "Won't we, Zana?"

"Yes," Zana said, almost inaudibly. I bit my lip. I had to say something.

"Zana, listen, are you *sure* you'll be okay getting out to the water villa? Because if you're not—"

"She'll be fine," Conor said reassuringly. "Won't you, Zana?"

"I was asking *Zana*," I said, unable to prevent a note of irritation from creeping into my voice. Conor smiled and put up his hands.

"You're right. Rude of me. Zana?"

"I'm fine," Zana said, echoing Conor's words. But she didn't look it. She looked deathly pale. I turned and looked at Santana, trying to communicate my unease, but Santana was frowning down at her diabetes monitor, fiddling with something on the display.

"Dan?" I said at last, but he only shrugged.

"I'm bushed. Are you coming or not?"

I felt a wave of powerlessness sweep over me. But what could I do? If Zana was determined not to admit her fears in front of Conor, how could I bring them up?

"Okay," I said. "Good night, all."

And then I turned and followed Dan and Santana into the darkness.

It's now more than a week since any of us have had a shower, or washed our face in fresh water, or drunk as much as we wanted to slake our thirst—and honestly, right now, I would give my kidney for a cold Coke brimming with ice, or a huge pitcher of fresh lemonade, misted with condensation. I lie awake at night and dream about water—in my dreams I'm gulping it down; it's running over my face.

I'm not the only one suffering. I know the others must have found it just as hard, maybe even harder—particularly the men who have more body mass, and probably by rights ought to get more water, though we agreed we'd share it out equally. I tried to persuade Conor to take some of my fruit at least, but he wouldn't. We help each other to keep strong. It's amazing what you can survive when you have people telling you that they have faith in you, that you <u>can</u> get through it.

If I get through this . . . God . . . if we get rescued, I swear I will never take water for granted again.

CHAPTER 18

"PUTAIN! ELLE EST où, la bouffe?"

It was Angel, standing in the middle of the cabana, shrieking the words at a volume that made the birds in the trees dotted around the clearing screech and take to the wing, rising up in an indignant flock to circle and resettle.

I sighed, rubbed the sleep out of my eyes, and climbed the steps.

"I don't speak French, Angel."

"The food! The fucking food!" she shouted in my face. "Where is it? And the water, too."

I looked around, blinking. The sun had only just risen and the shadows were long, making confusing shapes out of the tables and chairs, but even so, I could see Angel was right. The big stack of boxes and bottles over by the end of the cabana had gone. There was nothing there. Just the marks of footprints.

"Okay, look, don't panic." I tried to think. "There must be an explanation. It was there when we went to bed last night."

Joel was coming up the steps behind me, yawning and stretching, and now I turned.

"Joel? Do you know anything about this?"

"About what?"

"About the fucking food and water!" Angel screeched. "Which has *gone*, if you would wake up. Putain de merde, I am on this island with fucking idiots."

"These fucking idiots are right here, Angel," I said a little irritably. My headache from yesterday had not gone, and I had spent the last few hours fiercely looking forward to a cool cup of water. Now my mouth was dry and my head was throbbing with every dramatic shriek Angel uttered. More than that, there was a coiling sense of dread in the pit of my stomach. Where had our supplies gone? Had someone moved them? But if so, why?

"What's going on?" The voice was Dan's, and I turned and saw him coming through the trees. He looked tired and worried.

"It's the water," I said shortly. "And the food. It's gone."

"Fuck." Dan looked stricken. "I was coming to get something for Santa. Her bloods have gone very low overnight."

"Shit. Is it her leg?" I asked. Dan shook his head.

"I don't think so. The cut seems to be healing, but she's having trouble getting her insulin right in this heat. I know we're rationing the food, but that doesn't count for something like this, surely?"

"I mean—" I waved a hand at the empty space where the boxes should have been. "I would have said not. But extra nothing is still nothing."

"Where is the fucking food?" Angel yelled.

"What food?" came from the far side of the clearing, together with, "I have it," from behind us.

We all swung around in different directions, trying to identify the voices.

Bayer was coming up the path from Palm Tree Rest, his face like thunder. Conor, calm and collected, was walking up behind us from the beach, with a bottle of water and a box of muffins in either hand.

"I have it," Conor repeated equably. He held up the box. "Don't worry."

"You?" Angel stalked down the steps towards him, her hands on her hips. She looked like a haughty queen. "*You* have the food? Where is the rest of it?"

"It's safe, don't worry. But rats had started to go for some of the packaging, and in view of that, and your boyfriend's elastic attitudes towards rations, I felt it would be safer over at the water villa."

"I'm sorry, *you* felt?" I said at the same time as Bayer growled, "You have got to be fucking kidding me," and Dan said, "Wait, you *took* our food?"

Angel seemed to have lost the power of speech. Only Joel looked unshocked. In fact, he looked more than unshocked. He looked . . . shifty.

"Joel." I swung round on him. "Did you know about this?"

"I—" He opened his mouth, closed it, and then tried again. "I mean, he's not wrong. We were going to lose half of it to rats. The water villa is a much safer place to store it."

"Then we *discuss* that." I could feel my blood pressure rising. "You don't just wait until we go to bed and make a unilateral decision."

"We're discussing it now," Conor said. He smiled, but I didn't smile back.

"There is fucking nothing to discuss," Bayer said furiously. The veins in his neck and forehead were standing out, and I could see one big vein running down from his jaw that was throbbing visibly. "Nobody died and made you king of this island, you fucking prick. Give me back my share or I will *end* you."

He said the last words with a barely contained ferocity that sounded like he meant it literally. I think if he could have killed Conor in that moment, he would have done it.

But Conor didn't back down. He didn't even move. He simply set the water bottle down on the path and folded his arms.

"I'll give you your share when you prove you can be trusted," he said. Then he smiled. I think it was the smile that did it—at that, Bayer snapped.

He rushed at Conor with his head down, like a bull, and slammed into him with a force that I felt in my knees. Conor folded with the impact, and the two of them crashed onto the path, grappling like pro wrestlers, rolling this way and that on the sand. Angel was shrieking again. Dan was shouting, "Stop it! Just fucking stop it, the two of you!"

Conor had pulled himself upright, and now he was backing away from Bayer, towards the cabana steps, but Bayer rushed him again and they both fell to the ground again, their bodies thumping against the wooden stairs in a way that made the whole cabana shake. For a few minutes there was nothing but confusion, their bodies rolling this way and that, first Conor uppermost, then Bayer, then Conor again. And then, somehow, Bayer was on top, straddling Conor. He pulled back his fist and punched Conor square in the face. Blood sprayed everywhere, spattering across the sand, and then Conor twisted out of Bayer's grip and was on top of him, straddling him like a bull. He was hitting Bayer again and again in the head, Bayer's skull bouncing off the steps with every blow.

"Stop it!" Angel was screaming. "Stop it, you're killing him!"

And then suddenly . . . suddenly I knew she was right. Bayer was no longer fighting back. In fact, Conor had him by the front of his T-shirt with one hand, hitting him with the other, and Bayer's body was flopping like a rag doll with every one of Conor's punches.

"Conor!" I shouted. "Conor, for God's sake, *stop*, stop right now!"

For a minute I wasn't sure that Conor had heard me. And then, with what looked like a supreme effort, he got ahold of himself and let Bayer's shirt go.

Bayer fell back onto the steps with an audible thud, and Conor stood up and staggered over to the bushes, spitting blood out of his mouth.

Angel rushed across to Bayer, and I followed.

"Bayer," she was crying, kneeling beside him. "Bayer, are you okay? Wake up! Fuck, Lyla, *help* me, he won't wake up."

"Bayer?" I crouched beside her, touching his cheek. There was no reaction. In fact, no sign of life at all that I could see. The blood in his nostrils wasn't bubbling, and I couldn't detect any trace of breathing, though it was hard to hear anything above Angel's stifled sobs.

"Bayer." I slapped his cheek very gently and then pulled back an eyelid. My stomach turned uneasily. Beneath, the pupil of his hazel eye was dilated to a glassy, uniform black—and it didn't contract as the light hit it. I pressed a hand over one ear and put the other to his chest but could hear nothing above the sound of Angel weeping. "Angel, I'm sorry, could you be a little quieter?" I felt horrible asking her, but it was impossible to hear anything with her gulping next to my other ear.

"Angel," Dan said softly. "Angel, come and sit over here with me for a second. Just a second, okay?"

He led her a few feet away, and I put my ear back to Bayer's chest, right over his heart, and held my breath, the better to hear.

There was nothing. No familiar thump and whoosh. No gurgle of lungs struggling to breathe as they filled up with blood.

I felt my own heart begin to beat faster, so fast in fact that I could hear it pounding in my ears, making it harder to be sure that it wasn't Bayer's. Instead, I sat up and put my fingers to Bayer's neck, over the big vein that ran down from below his jaw, the vein I had seen pulsing with anger just a few minutes before.

There was nothing there.

I felt a sickness rise up inside me.

"Joel," I called. "Joel, can you come here for a second?"

Joel came hurrying over, his face anxious, and I pulled him down next to me and said very quietly, "Joel, I think . . . I think Bayer is dead."

He went white.

"You're kidding me?"

"I wish I was. Can you hear anything?"

Joel pressed his ear to Bayer's chest, closing his eyes. There was a long, long silence, broken only by the sound of Angel's quiet sobs from the other side of the cabana, and Conor hawking and spitting blood into the sand. When Joel raised his head, there was a fear in his eyes that hadn't been there a few minutes before and, very gently, he shook his head. I felt my stomach drop.

Angel must have sensed something about our interaction, because now she stood up, her expression wary.

"Bayer? Lyla, is he okay?"

"Angel, I—" I stopped. How the fuck did you say this?

"Is he okay?" she demanded, more forcefully, stalking across the decking towards us. I stood too.

"Angel, he's— I think . . . I think Bayer is dead."

Her scream echoed around the clearing, sending the birds shooting up into the clear blue sky with alarm, and the fruit bats shifting uneasily on their branches.

Conor had turned and was looking at us, perplexed. It seemed like he hadn't heard what I'd said—and perhaps he hadn't, with his ears still ringing from the fight. The front of his T-shirt was running with blood, and he was pinching the bridge of his nose as if trying to stem the flow.

"Angel?" he asked, as if confused. "What happened?"

"You fucking monster!"

She ran at him, slapping and hitting and screaming. Conor didn't try to fight back or restrain her, just fell back, his arms up, protecting his face, and it was Joel and I who had to run to try to hold Angel back, prevent her from scratching out Conor's eyes. When we finally had her, she was panting and weeping, and Conor's face was adorned with several long scratches in addition to his bloody nose.

"Tu es un monstre!" she was sobbing. "You have killed him. You killed him."

"It was an accident," Joel said helplessly. "Angel, please, I'm so sorry, but it was an accident."

Angel yanked herself out of our grip.

"Leave me alone. Leave me fucking alone. I am going to get us out of here. I am going to *leave*."

And then she turned and ran, away from the cabana, down the path to the staff quarters and, presumably, the radio.

The rest of us looked at each other, our expressions silently reflecting the unfathomable horror of what had just happened. Bayer was dead. *Dead*. I didn't think I was the only person having trouble processing the realization. Dan looked like he was going to throw up. Zana was sitting on the edge of the cabana steps next to a bleeding Conor, and her face was completely colorless. I thought she might be going into shock.

"You'd better go with Angel," I said to Joel, who was standing at the end of the path, looking at the clump of trees where Angel had disappeared. "Show her how it works." *Keep an eye on her* was the unspoken message. There was a sick feeling in my stomach, and I was having unpleasant mental images of Angel stomping on the radio receiver in a rage if she couldn't get through to someone. Joel nodded, turned, and walked after her, and then I turned back to Bayer's body, wondering how the hell it had come to this.

WE BURIED BAYER at sunset, and I'd expected that Angel would be weeping, but she wasn't. It was as if she had cried out all her tears, and now she simply stood, stone-faced, as the rest of us threw handfuls of sand onto his sheet-shrouded body in what was fast becoming a sickly familiar ritual.

I knew from Joel that the radio call had come to nothing, as had all the others, and that it had taken him a long time to persuade her to put down the handset and conserve the battery.

For the rest of the day she had simply lain in the villa, her face to the wall, refusing to talk to anyone or gather coconuts, or do any of the other tasks that we had divided up to try to eke out the rations—fishing, picking fruit, and rigging up a crude rainwater collection system over in the staff quarters.

Now, as the day drew to a close, we trailed back from Bayer's grave to the cabana, where Joel was already stirring up the fire, and I found that in spite of my grief about Bayer and my worries about Angel, my stomach was growling at the prospect of something that wasn't tinned.

"I'm so hungry," Santana said as she limped up the path towards the cabana, and I nodded.

"Me too."

We were approaching the steps and I found myself slowing, almost as if I were reluctant to tread on them. This was where Conor and Bayer had fought. This was where Bayer had broken Conor's nose, and where Conor had hit him so hard Bayer had collapsed. This was where Bayer had died. You could still see the marks of the scuffle in the sand, see the blood in the bushes where Conor had tried to staunch his streaming nose. I hadn't been back here since it had happened, neither had Angel. And now, somehow, we were all going to be expected to sit around, pretending nothing had happened.

Perhaps Santana had noticed my steps faltering, because she said, "Are you okay?"

I shook my head. Of course, she hadn't been here at breakfast.

"I—I'm fine. It's just—" I put out a hand, gesturing to the steps. "That's where it happened. The fight."

"God, I'm so sorry. I didn't know. Were you there? It must have been awful. Did he hit his head?"

I flinched. Her words had brought back the *smack, smack* of Bayer's head cracking against the step as Conor hit him. I didn't know what to say. Yes, he had hit his head. But somehow that didn't do justice to how it had unfolded, to Conor's quiet, calculated violence. All I knew was that I wasn't ready to talk about it. Luckily Dan's footsteps, coming up the path behind us, gave me an excuse to change the subject.

"How are you feeling? Dan said you were having trouble with your pump."

"A lot better. It's just hard to get the dosing right in this heat. It affects how fast your body processes the insulin."

Something had occurred to me, with her remark about the heat, and I asked, "Isn't insulin supposed to be refrigerated? How long will it last?"

Santana shrugged, but not in a kind of *don't know, don't care* way, more, helplessly, like someone who doesn't know the answer and has no way of finding out.

"I have no idea. It's supposed to last about a year if it's sealed, but that's at fridge temperatures. I'm keeping it in the fridge anyway, just because it's cooler than the rest of the villa, but it's bound to be degrading. I don't think it'll go toxic or anything, I think it'll just be less effective, but who knows what that means. I guess I just have to cross my fingers and use extra if I need to."

"And how much did you bring?"

"About three months' worth. I always overpack. But that's three months under normal conditions." She didn't say what we were both clearly thinking—that this wasn't in any way normal.

"And what happens—" I stopped, trying to think how to put this, but there didn't seem to be a tactful way to do it. "What happens if you run out?"

"I die," Santana said simply. "Within about thirty-six hours. So I have to hope the boat comes before then, don't I?" There was a long silence, broken only by the spit and crackle of the driftwood fire as Joel turned the octopus he'd laid across the embers. Then Santana gave a brittle laugh. "On that note, I wonder if Conor will let me have a beer?"

"Grub's nearly done," Joel called, as the others came into view, and Santana and I moved across to the table, where Joel had begun putting chunks of barbecued octopus onto plates, along with the now depressingly stale bagels and croissants. Angel picked up the largest portion, but she didn't move to sit down. Instead she turned wordlessly away, presumably intending on taking her portion back towards her villa.

I opened my mouth, intending to say something—to ask if she was all right perhaps, though that seemed hopelessly facile—of course she wasn't all right. Her boyfriend had *died*, this morning, not ten feet from where we were eating now.

But Conor's voice forestalled me.

"Put that back."

"I am sorry, *what*?" Angel said. She stopped in her tracks and looked back, one eyebrow raised in haughty distain. She was staring at Conor like he was something she had scraped off her shoe.

"You heard me." Conor moved closer. Not for the first time I noticed how tall he was—he had a good six inches on Angel, who was tall herself, and now, without apparently even trying, he exuded a kind of physical menace as he stood over her, forcing her to look up at him. "Put that back. You didn't contribute a thing today; you don't get first pick of the food."

"Conor," Joel said uneasily. "Come on, mate."

"What? This is a collective. We all contribute, we all eat."

"Conor, her boyfriend *died* this morning," Santana said. *At your hand*, was the unspoken coda, though it hardly needed stating.

It was too fresh for anyone to have forgotten. "Give her a break maybe?"

"I am giving her a break," Conor said calmly. "I'm letting her eat. In spite of the fact that she's done nothing all day. But this"—he gestured to the size of the portion—"is taking the piss. I'm not letting her take the piss."

"You're *letting* her eat?" I couldn't stop the words coming out, incredulously. Conor turned to me. His pale eyes were ice-cold.

"Yes. Do you have a problem with that?"

"Conor—" The voice was quiet, but it made us all stop, more in surprise than anything. It was Zana. She moved across to where he was standing, uncomfortably close to Angel, and put a hand on his arm. "Conor, maybe . . . just this once?"

Conor said nothing. His face was impassive, but I had the sudden disquieting impression that he was holding his emotions in check, and only barely.

Then he turned and smiled, but there was nothing about the smile that gave off warmth. It was the coldest, most frightening expression I'd ever seen.

"You're right. Just this once. Go ahead, Angel."

"Fuck you," Angel said. She pushed past him, back to the table, and slammed the plate down, flicking her fingers at it with a contemptuous gesture. "I don't want your—" She stopped, searching for the English word, and then with a noise that was more expressive than any sentence, she gave a snort of fury and stormed off into the night.

There was a collective exhalation of breath, and we all picked up our plates.

"Should someone go after her?" Dan said, a little uneasily. "I don't like to think of her all alone in that villa."

"Leave her," Conor said. Dan looked across at me and Santana, then shrugged and sat down, and began picking at the fast-cooling octopus.

"This is really good," Conor said. His voice was almost cheerful, as if he was making an effort to smooth over the altercation that had almost just happened. "Bravo, Joel."

"Thanks," Joel mumbled, and we all chorused our thanks, and then began to eat. But the shift from overt tension to faux cheerfulness was unnerving, and I knew I wasn't the only person whose appetite had disappeared.

Gradually though, as the food hit stomachs, and Conor passed around bottles of beer from the fast-dwindling stash, people began to relax. Dan was asking Joel about the octopus he had caught, and some fish he had seen over by the edge of the reef. Joel was drawing a map in sand on the decking and marking up other places he thought would be worth trying.

"I'm impressed," Santana whispered under cover of the conversation. I looked up from trying to cut my octopus.

"By Zana?"

"Yeah. She stood up for herself! Go Zana."

I nodded. But I was looking at Zana, who was sitting, staring miserably over at Angel's empty plate, without even touching her own food. Her face looked stricken, as if she was wondering what she had done. And I found myself wondering what her outburst might be about to cost her.

Bayer is dead. Oh my God, Bayer is DEAD. I'm sobbing as I write this. It doesn't seem real.

Part of what makes it so hard to accept is that it was so sudden. He hadn't been looking great the last day or two, his arm was very swollen, and he kept complaining of a headache. We tried to persuade him to have a bit of extra water allocation, or at least to drink more coconut juice, but he kept refusing—he said it wouldn't be fair on the rest of us.

But then this morning, as we were all heading up to breakfast, talking about the day, he got halfway up the steps to the cabana and just stopped, kind of swaying back and forth. He took a step up, then another—and then he crashed out full-length.

His head hit the stair with the most awful sound I've ever heard— a kind of crunching crack. Angel just screamed. We knew it was bad straightaway, because there was blood, it spattered all over the steps. We all ran over to try to help him up—and that's when we realized he was dead. Just . . . dead. He wasn't breathing, and we couldn't feel his heart. Lyla pulled back his lids and his eyes were black and unresponsive to light. And just like that, he was gone. His life snuffed out.

I keep running over what happened in my head, trying to figure out what we did wrong, how we could have saved him. Was it heatstroke? Did he need more water than the rest of us? Or was it something to do with his shoulder, some kind of clot maybe, that broke away and travelled to his brain?

Lyla says we'll never know, that there's no point in torturing ourselves. Conor is broken by it—Bayer was probably the person he was closest to on the island, after me. He shut himself in the water villa, and I know he was crying, although when I came to find him he pretended he was okay.

Our only hope now is the radio—poor Angel spent the rest of the day down there, trying to find a ship, trying to find a signal. I know she blames herself, thinks that if she'd managed to make contact earlier, someone could have saved Bayer.

Please, God, let someone find us. We are seven people now. Just seven. How long can we hold on?

CHAPTER 19

"GOD I'M THIRSTY."

It was Dan who spoke into the darkness of the villa where the four of us were lying, sweating, and staring at the shadowed rafters. I heard a sigh from Santana as she rolled over in bed.

"Me too. I've had a dehydration headache ever since we started rationing the water. But until it rains, I'm not sure what else we can do."

"Being in charge of our own supply would help." Dan's voice was resentful, and I knew why. The long gap between breakfast and supper had been particularly hard today, and I'd seen Dan down by the sea, rinsing his mouth out with seawater more than once, though I wasn't sure the harshly salted tropical water would do much to slake anyone's thirst. The idea of a small gulp of fresh water, even one that had to come out of our supper allowance, had been almost unbearably tempting.

"If we're not careful, we're all going to end up like Zana," Dan said.

"I'm sorry, what?" Joel said. He sounded puzzled. "What the hell has Zana got to do with anything? And what do you mean, end up like her?"

"I mean . . . he's pretty controlling," Santana said. "Don't you think? And not just over her."

There was a long silence. No one had discussed Conor's increasing autocracy, and the decreasing willingness of the group to stand up to him. It wasn't just his grip over the food and water. It wasn't just the brutal efficiency with which he had taken out Bayer. It was everything. In the beginning I think we'd all been grateful for his willingness to take charge, set the rules, make us all feel safe, but day by day, inch by inch, Conor had slowly eased himself more and more into a position of control. Now, somehow, we had found ourselves in a situation where he was dictating not only how much we ate and drank, but when, and even if. His remark to Angel, that he was *letting* her eat, had been an admission of something that none of us had wanted to face up to—but now Conor had put it into words, and I felt a cold, chill certainty coalesce in the pit of my stomach. Zana was not okay. None of us were. And we were too scared to challenge him.

"She's frightened of him," I said. It felt like a realization, but as I said the words, I knew that it wasn't, not really. It was an admission of something I'd suspected almost since the first day on the island.

"*What?*" Joel sounded nonplussed. "How do you make that out? I've never seen them exchange a cross word."

"You've never seen them exchange a cross word because she never stands up to him," Santana said tartly. I nodded.

"That argument tonight, about Angel's food—that was literally the first time I've seen her push back at anything—even though she's terrified of that bloody water villa. And she's a completely different person when she's not around him. I spent all day trying to rig up a rain catcher with her, and it was like being with another girl."

"What do you mean?" Joel asked.

"It's like . . ." I struggled to put it into words. "Well, for one thing, she's got a personality when she's not looking over her shoulder and worrying about what he's thinking. She'll argue back, she'll make her point. She had this genius idea about sinking the bottles into the sand to minimize evaporation. But when she's around him . . ." I trailed off.

"When she's around him, she seems scared," Santana finished my sentence for me, and I nodded, though I knew no one could see me in the darkness. On his mattress on the other side of the double bed, I could hear Joel shifting uncomfortably, as if he didn't know what to say.

"I should have known from the start," Dan said bitterly. "It was all right there in his videos. But he seemed so nice in person."

"Videos?" I was puzzled. "You mean his YouTube channel? How did you manage to access that without a phone?"

"He was on the list they posted round to everyone's houses." Dan said. "The first thing I did when we got the info pack was google everyone on it. He's . . . well, he's quite a piece of work."

I frowned. What info pack? But Dan was still speaking, sounding like he was trying to marshall his thoughts.

"He's . . . he's one of those *I'm just asking the question* guys, you know? The kind it's really hard to pin down, because they never actually say the racist stuff themselves, they're just like, *hey, thought experiment here, but what if racism wasn't so bad?* He'll have someone incredibly shitty on his channel and he'll be like *well, now, I'm not endorsing Andrew Tate, obviously, but I am interested in his point of view on . . .* and the end result is that you find you've sat through twenty minutes of some men's-rights nut not being challenged about his views, because Conor's just quote, unquote *asking questions.*"

"Yeah, but . . ." Joel sounded like he was struggling. "I have to say, I've seen some of his stuff—"

"Wait, you've *seen* it?" I don't know why, but the news shocked me. Then I remembered Joel's words to Conor on the boat, the day we met. *I know who you are of course.* At the time I'd assumed he'd simply come across him in the press. Now, the remark had a very different slant. "Are you one of his subscribers?"

"I'm not a Co-bro if that's what you mean," Joel said a little defensively, and Dan burst out laughing.

"Co-bro? Is that what his fans call themselves?"

Joel carried on, doggedly, as though Dan hadn't interrupted.

"In fact, if you want to know the truth, I came across him because he had a run-in with Romi. So I'm hardly some kind of uncritical admirer."

"*What?*" This was all getting more and more confusing. "I'm sorry, did Romi *know* him?"

"No, but he called her out on his channel. She was absolutely furious about it. He did this whole segment on beauty influencers and body image, and he called out a load of TikTokers he felt had damaging messages. Romi wasn't the target, but she was one of the channels he quoted. Anyway, she was mad as hell, but when I watched it . . ." He shrugged helplessly. "Honestly . . . I thought he had a point. Some of the stuff she says—" He swallowed painfully, and I saw him correct himself. "*Said*, was . . . kind of toxic, when you really thought about it."

"Let me guess," Santana's voice was unimpressed, "all the toxic people he called out were young women, yes? And his 10.4 million followers probably descended on their feeds and made their lives miserable? So much for standing up for women. If it looks like a misogynist and barks like a misogynist—"

"Can we not just go by what he's actually *said*?" Joel broke in. He sounded like he was becoming frustrated. "Okay, he's had the odd controversial guest on, and okay, his followers don't always behave perfectly. But unless you can point me to where *he's* said or done something wrong, this feels a bit guilt by association."

"Look, you've clearly watched his channel more than me," Dan said. His voice was placating, though beneath it he didn't sound convinced by Joel's point. "So I'll take your word on that. But for someone who claims he's not a racist, homophobic piece of shit, he sure attracts a lot of racist, homophobic piece-of-shit followers." Joel made an unhappy noise, and Dan waved his hand, dismissing the point of

Conor's YouTube. "Let's put that aside though—I wasn't even talking about YouTube originally. It was the food and water situation I wanted to discuss. Is no one else bloody uncomfortable about all this?"

"Yes," Santana and I both said, at the same time as Joel said, "But it makes sense."

"What makes sense?" Santana demanded. "Him hoarding all the supplies over at his villa? How does that make sense, Joel? Help me understand, because at the moment, all I'm seeing is *some animals are more equal than others.*"

"What?" Dan sounded puzzled, and Santana made an impatient noise. "*Animal Farm,* Dan. We were in a tutorial together at uni. Did you pay *any* attention that year? But regardless, it *doesn't* make sense, Joel, and you know it. All that stuff about rats getting at the food was just an excuse."

"How was it an excuse?" Joel said. His voice had risen and he sounded more than a little aggrieved. I guessed he was feeling got at by implication, because of the way he'd fallen into trying to defend Conor's YouTube channel, and now his complicity in helping to move the food. "He wasn't making that up. I saw it—there'd been rats at the cardboard boxes, and there were trails of ants all over the place. None of that's a problem out at the water villa."

"So what's the excuse with the water? I can't see rats getting at the water."

"The *reason,*" Joel said, his tone irritable now, "is because some people didn't seem able to stick to their rations. What if we came down and found Bayer had drunk the whole lot?"

"First, Bayer is *dead*, Joel. Do I need to remind you? At Conor's hands, no less. Second, you give everyone their own allocation!" Santana's voice was rising too. "You don't take a unilateral decision to hold everyone's water hostage."

"And then what?" Joel said. He had sat up in bed, plainly too annoyed to lie down, and I could see his shape silhouetted against the night sky, his shoulders visibly tense even in outline. "When the water started to run out? What if someone decided they deserved a bit more and felt like they'd take it by force? No. You give it to the strongest, most trustworthy person and put them in charge of making sure it's doled out fairly."

There was a long silence. Then Dan spelled out what everyone, apart from Joel, was apparently thinking.

"The problem is, mate, we *don't* trust him. And to your point about rations, we have no idea if he's sticking to his allowance out there, because we have no idea what's going on. No, I'm sorry, the longer we let this go on, the harder it's going to be to challenge it. I'm going to say something tomorrow."

"Dan . . ." Santana sounded worried. "Do you think that's wise?"

"I'm not going to be a dick," Dan said. "I'm just going to calmly point out that this isn't a fair way of organizing anything. And if everyone backs me up, I don't see that he can kick off about it. So will you?"

"Are you talking to me?" Joel asked.

"I'm talking to everyone. Will you back me up if I talk to him tomorrow, yes or no?"

"Yes," Santana said. "But I wish you wouldn't."

"I'll back you up," I said. "But Dan, *please* tread carefully on this. The last thing we need to do is set up some kind of feud. Things are bad enough."

"Like I said," Dan said. "I'm not going to be a dick about this. I'm just going to point out that this is a democracy, and we didn't agree to this. And what about you, Joel?"

"I just think—" Joel said, and then stopped. He didn't sound convinced. At all. He sounded defeated, and like he'd had enough of arguing Conor's corner, but he didn't sound convinced.

"Go on," Dan said, but not goadingly, like he genuinely wanted to know. "You can say it."

"I just think . . . look, I think you're hanging a lot on his girlfriend being a bit shy and some commenters on YouTube being twats. I feel like you've written the guy off based on—what? Nothing. Conjecture. Some video you didn't like. And none of that has anything to do with his actions here, does it?"

"No," Dan said. His voice, in the darkness, was persuasive. "No, it doesn't. And look, I take your point. If this was a court of law and we were on a jury, I'm not saying I'd convict him on this evidence of being a dickhead wifebeater. But like you say, none of that's relevant. All I'm asking him for is the water back, and a discussion, going forward, on how we handle things. Okay? That's it. No one reasonable could possibly object."

Joel didn't reply, but I saw, silhouetted against the moonlit forest, his head nod slowly, and then he slid back to lie down.

But as I rolled onto my side to wait for morning, I couldn't help but wonder, exactly how reasonable *was* Conor? Either way, we were going to find out. I just hoped we could live with the answer.

CHAPTER 20

BREAKFAST WAS A tense affair, with Joel, Santana, and me all waiting on tenterhooks to see if Dan followed through on his promise to say something to Conor. He said nothing as Conor doled the water out, and nothing again as we passed around chunks of tinned papaya, increasingly unripe bananas, and the everlasting pastries, now starting to taste distinctly off.

But as Conor stood and stretched, and Zana began picking up the plates and gathering banana peelings into a pile to be tipped into the sea, Dan coughed.

"Um . . . listen, before we all disappear, could I ask a question?"

"Yes, where *is* Angel?" Conor said, looking around, and then down the table where her plate stood untouched, with the beaker of water next to it. "Is she okay?"

It was a good question, and for a moment the realization distracted me from what Dan was about to say, but Dan was plainly not to be diverted.

"Actually, that wasn't what I was going to say," he said. "Conor, listen, we had a bit of a chat last night—"

I winced internally, wishing he hadn't said that. That was the exact thing I'd wanted to avoid—a *them and us* situation arising from the suggestion that we were ganging up against Conor. But maybe it was inevitable.

"And?" Conor said, raising one eyebrow.

"And . . . we understand the need to protect the food from animals and from, um—" I could see he'd been about to say *Bayer*, and then thought better of speaking ill of the dead. "Well, all that. But, um . . . we'd like to have a chat about the best way to handle the rations going forward."

"Right," Conor said. He folded his arms and tipped his chair back.

"Well . . . I think . . ." Dan looked around the circle, seeking backup, and I saw Santana nodding vigorously. "I mean . . . we'd all feel more comfortable if we had our own individual rations of food and water."

"Yeah, that's not going to work," Conor said dismissively. "Zana, sweetheart, could you go down and check on Angel, make sure she's okay?"

Zana nodded and turned, and I saw Dan take a deep breath and clench his fists against the arm of his chair. I prayed he would be able to stick to the plan and hang on to his temper.

"Conor, listen, this is a democracy, and I think we're all agreed—"

"Who said this is a democracy?" Conor said pleasantly. I heard Santana's intake of breath, and saw a muscle twitch in Dan's jaw.

"I'm *sorry*?" he said. Conor shrugged.

"You heard me. No one said this was a democracy. I certainly didn't."

"So are you saying you *won't* give us back the water?"

"Dan, bro." Conor put out a hand to Dan's shoulder, but Dan flinched violently away. "Listen, it's safest out at the water villa. It won't get eaten by pests or pinched in the night, and we all know where the buck stops if there's any question over fairness."

"With you?" Dan said. I could tell his temper was at snapping point. "Is that what you're saying? The buck stops with you?"

"Yes," Conor said simply. "That's what I'm saying."

"Conor." Santana's voice was pitched half an octave higher than usual, and I could tell her teeth were gritted with the effort of not giving way to her anger. "This is bullshit. You have absolutely no right to do this."

"Sure. So what do you propose to do about it?" Conor said. He sounded almost . . . interested.

"Lyla? Joel?" Santana turned to us. "Do you have anything to say?"

I shut my eyes. This was going down *exactly* as I had feared. A rift was developing that would be very hard to mend, and our food and drink were on the opposite side of that rift. But I had no choice but to speak up.

"Conor," I said, trying to keep my voice measured. "Look, I get why you're doing this, and I agree there's a lot of merit to the idea of keeping all the food and drink in a secure location, but I think everyone just feels really uncomfortable about the idea that you're in control of every single aspect of that. No shade on you—we'd feel uncomfortable if *any* one person had total oversight over all the food and drink. Why not keep the food out at your villa, and divide the water up so everyone has their own ration?"

"That's not going to happen," Conor said calmly. I felt my temper rise, and across the table I saw Dan stand up, and Santana grab his hand and force him back down.

"You don't think that's a good idea?" I asked instead, keeping my voice level. Conor shook his head.

"It's too risky. What happens if someone loses their self-control and drinks all their water? Are we really going to sit around and watch them die of thirst for three weeks? No. So we'd end up feeling pressurized into sharing, and then everyone suffers. And that's without even going into the most likely scenario—that someone steals someone else's allowance or takes it by force."

Like you did, I thought. The hypocrisy was overwhelming.

"I just—" I began, but Dan had lost patience. He pulled his arm out of Santana's restraining grip and stood up.

"Conor, mate, sorry but this is BS. And we're not going to stand for it."

"Is that so?" Conor said.

"No," Dan said firmly. "And look, I didn't want to put it like this, but there's four of us, and two of you. So . . . you do the maths."

"Oh, I have," Conor said pleasantly. He smiled, stood up, stretched for all the world like he didn't have a care, and then clicked his neck. "Now, I'm going fishing. Anyone want to join me?"

"Did you hear what I just said?" Dan demanded belligerently. He had walked around the table and was squaring up to Conor like he was about to punch him.

"Dan," I said. "Dan, *please.*"

For all Dan's bravado, seeing the two of them practically nose to nose made it abundantly clear that there was no contest. Dan was impressively sculpted, with a torso like a boy-band member, but Conor had four inches and several dozen pounds on him, and more to the point, he *looked* like he knew how to fight. His muscles were of a different quality—lean and hard, like someone who hadn't just worked out, but had actually *worked.* I remembered the cold efficiency with which he'd taken care of Bayer, remembered the smack, smack of fist into face, and I felt a shiver run down my spine, in spite of the heat.

"*Dan,*" I said, more urgently.

But Conor was smiling down at Dan and looked very far from snapping.

"I did hear what you said," he said pleasantly. "And now I'm going fishing."

"No," Dan said. "No. You're not. Joel?"

He turned to look at Joel, who looked like he wanted to melt through the floor.

"Dan," he said, very quietly, "I don't think this is the right way to handle this."

"Oh, fuck *you*," Dan said. I had the strong impression he was trying not to cry, though I had no idea whether it was tears of anger or betrayal that he was holding back. He turned back to Conor and stabbed his finger towards him. "And fuck you too. Watch your back, *mate*."

Then he stalked off into the trees.

There was a long silence, and then, from the opposite direction, we heard the sound of a long, slow hand clap.

We all turned, and Angel was standing in the clearing in a long white dress that billowed in the sea breeze.

"Bravo, Dan," she said, but she was looking at Conor as she said the words. "Someone has finally to stand up to the murderer."

Conor smiled, showing all his white teeth. Santana put her head in her hands. Joel looked like he was about to burst into tears himself. Suddenly I couldn't take it any longer. It wasn't just the atmosphere in the cabana, it wasn't even just the fact that Conor was now nakedly holding our water hostage and not even pretending to the contrary. It was everything. The fact that I was trapped on this island with a group of people preparing to tear each other apart. The fact that Nico was very likely dead. The fact that with every day that passed, our situation was getting more and more desperate.

"I'm going to the radio shack," I said. Joel opened his mouth to say something, but I held up my hand, trying to signal with that one gesture that no, I didn't want company, I didn't want his advice, I didn't want anyone. I just wanted ten minutes to myself, nursing the fantasy that someone out there was going to pick up our Mayday call.

Because someone, *somewhere* had to be looking for us. Didn't they?

I couldn't sleep last night. I was so thirsty, but it was more than that—I kept running over all the what-ifs everyone has been so carefully staving off, trying not to think about. What if the boat doesn't come? How long will our water last? What if Santana runs out of insulin? I was trying not to cry, but the tears came in the end, and woke Conor up, and . . . God, he was amazing. He just held me, and sang to me, hour after hour, all our favourite songs and some I'd never heard before. And the whole time he was telling me that it was going to be okay—it was all going to be okay, we just had to stay strong, look after each other, hang in there until help arrives.

And eventually, some time before dawn, I drifted off to sleep with him holding me. I don't know if he slept himself.

Conor's arms are the only place I feel safe now—the only place I feel as if nothing can harm me—but even that makes me feel scared. Because what if something happens to him? I feel like he's the only thing on this island keeping me from falling apart.

It's not just me. Everyone's tempers are fracturing. This morning, at breakfast, Dan broke down and demanded more water—and when everyone banded together to tell him he couldn't have it, that we were all as thirsty as he was, he stormed off. We haven't seen him all day. We're all just praying he's okay.

The truth is, it's just . . . it's just getting to us, in a way it didn't before.

CHAPTER 21

"**HE IS A** psychopath, of course." Angel said the word *psychopath* matter-of-factly, but it was somehow the *of course* that had the most chilling effect. The casual acceptance of something I hadn't even begun to consider. "Or perhaps a sociopath. The difference is probably academic in this situation. But then, he is a Gemini. They are notorious serial killers. The duplicity comes naturally to them."

Santana and I looked at each other, and then back out to sea, where Joel and Conor were fishing in the shallow reef just off the water villa.

Dan was nowhere to be seen, and hadn't been seen for hours, not since the fight at breakfast. He hadn't even drunk his morning water allocation, which was now sitting, covered with a leaf, up at the cabana, and I could only hope that he had taken something with him to drill coconuts, otherwise he'd be dangerously dehydrated by the time he reappeared.

Angel, Santana, and I had spent the day on the little headland that had been the site of Angel and Bayer's villa, Ocean Bluff, before it had been destroyed in the storm. It had been Angel's suggestion to use the palm frond roof and timber from the broken villa to build a bonfire, ready to light if a ship came past.

"Will they realize it's a distress signal though?" Santana had asked, doubtfully. "What if they just think it's holidaymakers having a beach barbecue?"

Angel had shrugged.

"It is possible of course. But what can we do? We have to try."

And I saw her point of view. It was a long shot, but it was better than doing nothing, and the radio display was getting increasingly faint, which made me suspect the battery was dying.

It had taken us most of the day to round up the pieces of roof that had blown across the beach and dry them on the sun-scorched rocks, but now we were tired, sunburnt, and had a huge pile of hopefully highly flammable material weighted down by rocks and timbers to stop it from blowing away. Angel straightened up from placing the last beam, stretched, and looked across to the water villa, where you could just make out Zana sitting on the deck, pulling apart one of her shirts to make something—fishing line, I guessed.

"I am going to ask her to come and join us," she said now. "It isn't good, to have her isolated like that, and it's time we ate. Hoy!" She called across to Joel, who was wading intently through the reef, staring down into the water with a sharpened piece of bamboo in one hand. "Hoy! Joel! Did you catch anything? We want to eat!"

"I don't know if she'll come," I said. "She's terrified of water. She only crosses the gangway when Conor makes her."

"See?" Angel said, shrugging. "What kind of man deliberately puts his woman through that? I will tell you. A psychopath."

Down on the shore, Joel was holding up a stick with three long fish skewered on it. He waved it triumphantly.

"I'm going up to the cabana," Santana said. "Start the fire for supper."

"I'll meet you there in a sec," I said. "I need to use the bathroom."

The toilets were the one part of the island infrastructure that was still working—possibly temporarily, we weren't sure, but as long as they were operational, I was going to make the most of a proper loo.

There was no water to flush, but pouring a bucket of seawater into the pan did the job fine, and seawater was the one thing we had in abundance. Presumably somewhere on the island was a septic tank that would eventually fill up—but I suspected if we weren't rescued before then, we'd have bigger problems to worry about. Water, for a start. And Santana's insulin.

When I entered the villa something seemed odd, and it took me a minute to realize what it was—the door, which we usually kept carefully shut to help keep out snakes and mosquitoes, was standing open. I frowned. Had Dan come back?

"Dan?" I called as I entered the villa, but there was no one there, just the flick of a gecko's tail as it disappeared into the rafters.

Feeling a little puzzled, I peed, washed my hands in the bucket of seawater standing in the shower tray, and then made my way back to the cabana.

Santana was there alone, crouching over a little fire of driftwood, blowing on the embers. She looked up when she saw me.

"Hey. Angel's lighter's getting *really* low, you know. Do you think we should reserve it, in case a ship comes?"

"To light the beacon, you mean?" I thought about it. "I guess so . . . but I suppose the lighter fluid won't last forever so there's probably no point in hoarding it indefinitely. I take your point though—it's going to run out either way. What can we use instead?"

"Joel's glasses?" Santana said, and then laughed. "Bit *Lord of the Flies*, I know. Or does anyone know how to do that stick-rubbing thing?"

Down on the beach I could see Angel had crossed to the water villa and was crouching down, talking to Zana.

"Do *you* think she's being abused?" I said to Santana, who sighed and stood up.

"I don't know. I only know . . ." She stopped, and I looked at her, puzzled.

"What?"

"Well, look, I didn't say anything because it seemed weird but . . . I knew his ex."

"Whose? Conor's?" I was puzzled. Santana nodded.

"I was at school with her—she was in the year below me. She was seventeen when they got together. He was twenty-four, which at the time sounded quite glamorous, but looking back . . . I mean, it's border-line creepy if you ask me. Seven years is a lot when you're seventeen."

I nodded. I could see that. Seventeen-year-olds aren't even adults—they can't legally drink, they can't vote, they can't buy ciga-rettes. Twenty-four-year-olds are in a different world.

"What was he like back then?" I asked. Santana shrugged.

"That's the thing—I never met him. I just heard about him from Cally. It was Conor says this, Conor says that. You'd have thought he could walk on water."

"So how did you join the dots?" I asked, wondering where this was going. There was something about Santana's tone I didn't like. "I mean, there's a lot of Conors. Are you sure it's the same guy?"

"When we got the information for the show, I realized I knew his name. I asked around, and one of Cally's sisters confirmed it was him. And she also told me what had happened to Cally."

"Which was?" I asked, a little puzzled by her reluctance to get to the point.

"She's dead," Santana said flatly. She paused and swallowed, but I didn't get the impression she was holding out on me, more that she was trying to gear herself up for how to say something upsetting. "She—she committed suicide. Two days after her nineteenth birth-day. Two days after he left her."

"Oh my God, Santana, that's awful."

"I know. Nineteen, Lyla. *Nineteen.*"

"*Fuck.*" I tried to process what that meant. "Why didn't you say something?"

"Say what?" Santana said unhappily. She turned back to the fire, poking at it with a little stick, though it didn't really need tending. She seemed more to be avoiding my gaze. "Oh, you don't know me, but I went to school with your ex who killed herself? It's not really something to bring up over dinner, is it."

"No." I ran my hands through my salt-stiffened hair. "No, God, no I can see that. But do you think—" I stopped, unsure where I was going with my train of thought. Santana waited for me to continue, and then when I didn't, she finished the question for me.

"Do I think she killed herself because he was an abusive piece of shit? I have no idea. I honestly haven't got a clue. He could have been a model boyfriend whose girlfriend tragically couldn't deal with their breakup. But at the very least it shows a pattern, doesn't it? A pattern of picking emotionally fragile younger women and making them very, very dependent on him."

I looked out to sea, where Angel had taken hold of Zana's arm and was coaxing her, plank by plank across the fragile jetty.

And I couldn't deny Santana was right.

AFTER SUPPER, WE washed the plates down at the shore, kneeling on the rocks at what was fast becoming the dishwashing station. It was just us girls—though of course we weren't girls, any of us, any more than the men on the island were boys. We were adult men and women. But somehow, without meaning to, I had fallen into the Perfect Couple lingo. *The Girls, the Boys, the Lads, the Islanders.* We were still falling into teams, playing the parts assigned to us by the production company. Sometimes it was hard to remember that Bayer and Romi were dead—not just eliminated from the competition like Nico. But then . . . as I stared out at the vast, empty ocean, turning orange in the setting sun, I forced myself to admit it: there was every chance that Nico was dead too.

Joel and Conor were up at the cabana, talking earnestly about something. Joel had sketched out a map of the island in sand on the tabletop and was pointing at the various bays. Conor was nodding. Watching the two of them together made me feel uneasy in a way that I couldn't explain. I shouldn't *want* Conor and Zana to be isolated from the rest of us. Having such deep divisions among the islanders wasn't good for anyone, particularly given Conor still had all the food and water held hostage out at the water villa.

But seeing Joel acting so pally with the man who had—no two ways about it—stolen our supplies and been responsible for Bayer's death, was somehow deeply unsettling. Didn't he *care*? Dan did. In fact, he still hadn't returned, and that was another thing keeping me on edge. Here we were, looking like something out of a travel brochure, four bikini-clad girls, tanned, beautiful, kneeling in the surf and silhouetted against the most stunning sunset I had ever seen—and yet all I could think about was the darkness beneath the picture, the rifts pulling our little community apart.

"Angel," I said now, as she rinsed out the last cup and wiped it carefully on a towel. "I really don't like thinking of you all alone down at Palm Tree Rest. Are you sure you don't want to bring your mattress up to our villa? There's room, isn't there?" I looked at Santana, and she nodded vigorously.

"Yes! Absolutely. Plenty of room."

Angel was looking thoughtful.

"I must admit," she said at last, "I did not enjoy last night. It's not that I'm afraid of being alone, you understand. But . . ."

She didn't finish. She didn't have to. We all knew what she meant. It was at night that the thousands of miles of empty ocean stretched out the longest, and the fears came crowding hardest: What if we're never rescued? What if the water runs out? What if we die here, like Romi, like Bayer, like the poor woman whose name we didn't even know, lying in an unmarked grave?

Having someone else's snoring to distract you from those what-ifs
... well, even just the presence of another warm body was immensely
comforting.

"What about you, Zana?" Santana asked. "You know, if Angel is
moving in with us, you and Conor wouldn't have to stay in that water
villa. You could take back Palm Tree Rest."

But Zana was shaking her head, and I knew the answer before
she spoke: Conor would never allow it. He would never abandon
the food and water, no matter what it cost Zana, who was already
looking sick with nerves at the prospect of making the crossing to
the water villa.

Truth to tell, I wouldn't have fancied it much myself—and I had
no fear of water. Down here at the water's edge, you could see all too
clearly how rickety Conor's makeshift jetty was—just salvaged planks
and pieces of driftwood cobbled together with nails bashed in using a
rock. I had seen Zana and Angel cross it earlier, watched them totter
from one piece of wood to another, Zana's hand gripping Angel's like
it was the only thing keeping her from death. It was barely functional,
let alone safe, and for someone with a fear of water it would be a
nightmare.

"Zana, he can't *make* you stay there," Santana said now. She took
Zana's hand, opening her mouth to say something else, but as she
gripped Zana's wrist, not roughly, but firmly, Zana winced and pulled
it back.

All three of us—me, Santana, and Angel—looked down at Zana's
hand. She had balled it up and now she plunged it in the water, scrubbing the last of the dishes with unnecessary energy.

It was too late though. We had all seen it. A small, distinct black
bruise on the inside of her wrist, as if someone had pinched her there,
very hard.

"Zana—" Santana began, and then stopped, as if at a loss for what
to say. She glanced at the two of us as if urging us to step in, but Angel

didn't meet her look. She was staring, stricken, at Zana's wrist, her face as pale as if she had seen a ghost.

"Are you okay?" I asked at last. It was pitifully inadequate. It wasn't what I wanted to say. *Is he hurting you?* was what I wanted to ask.

"I'm fine," Zana said. She stood up, holding the plates to her chest as if to protect herself from our collective gaze. "I mean, as fine as anyone can be in this situation. And I don't need to move. I'm very—" She swallowed, as if the lie was hard to say. "Very happy. At the water villa. *We're* very happy. It's beautiful."

But her voice wasn't remotely convincing, and as she turned and began walking back up the beach to Conor and Joel, I could hear the plates she was carrying chinking together, as though her hands were trembling.

THE SUN WAS fully set, the island in rustling moonlit darkness as we made our way along the pebbled path from Palm Tree Rest, Angel's blankets slung over my arm, her clothes and washbag in her own. Santana was up ahead, holding Dan's water and food from supper. He still hadn't returned.

We were rounding a turn in the path, the route made strange and unpredictable by the sharp moonshadows crisscrossing the ground, when there was a sound in the bushes up ahead, and a figure appeared, silhouetted against the trees, dark against dark.

"Joel?" I said uncertainly, but the shape wasn't right. It was a man, but not Joel; it was someone stockier, more muscled.

"Dan?" Santana was peering into the shadows, and then she gave a kind of choke of relief and ran forward. "Dan! You absolute fucker. Where have you *been?* I was going out of my mind."

"I'm fine," Dan said, but he didn't sound fine. His voice was rough and croaky. "Is that water mine? I'm so thirsty."

"Yes, it's yours. And so's the food. It's your ration from supper.

Hey, don't down it like that. You'll make yourself sick." Dan had tipped the canister up to his lips and was gulping the water like a man who hadn't drunk a drop since breakfast—which he probably hadn't. "Where the hell were you?"

"Up the other end of the island. Where's Conor?" Dan's voice was still hoarse. I exchanged an uneasy look with Santana.

"He's still at the cabana," Santana said at last. "Talking with Joel and Zana."

Although that was not strictly accurate. Zana hadn't said a word since we washed up the dishes, and when we had left the three of them, she had been sitting, staring out at the water villa like someone sentenced to execution staring at the gallows.

"I don't like it," Dan said. "I don't like it at all. He's taking his side. Did you hear him last night? He wouldn't listen to my point at all. Just kept defending Conor."

I realized, with a sinking feeling, that he was talking about Joel.

"Dan, that's not fair," I began, but Dan was in no mood to listen.

"What's not *fair*," he spat, "is that fucker hoarding all our food and water, and Joel backing him up. If he'd taken our side . . ."

Ugh. There it was. *Our side. Them and us.* The rifts were becoming irreparable.

"I don't think he was trying to take anyone's side," I said desperately. "He was trying to be fair to everyone. Look"—as I saw Dan was about to explode again—"I take your point, I do. And I'm not saying I disagree. I feel bloody uncomfortable about the whole thing—about Conor, about Zana, about the food—everything. But we have to live with each other for the foreseeable future. We can't afford to tear this island in half."

"May I remind you," Angel said stiffly, her accent as French as I had ever heard, "that Conor *killed* my boyfriend? Fuck his stupid YouTube videos. He is a murderer."

I shut my eyes, gritted my teeth. It was true—and I couldn't deny it to Angel's face. Conor had killed Bayer. There was no two ways about it. But murderer felt like a stretch. Because it was *also* true that Bayer had picked the fight, and Bayer had swung first. In a court of law . . . well, I would have put even odds on Conor getting off on self-defense. But we weren't in a court of law. We were a long way from any kind of justice at all. And we had all stood by and watched Conor beat a man to death.

"Look, there's nothing we can do about it tonight," Santana said. "And as far as we know, Joel is still sleeping here, so please, let's try not to pick another fight when he gets here. Our issue is with Conor, not Joel. And definitely not Zana."

Angel nodded. Dan merely looked mutinous.

We were almost at the clearing for the villa and Santana said, with the air of trying to change the subject, "Enough of that anyway. Angel, where do you want to sleep? Do you want the bed with me?"

"Don't you and Dan want the bed?" Angel asked, looking puzzled, and I realized—she still didn't know. Dan gave a laugh, a slightly bitter one.

"Haven't you heard? I bat for the other team. No one was supposed to know, but I don't suppose it matters now. Gay or straight, we'll all be dead before the boat gets here."

"Dan—" Santana broke in, and he turned to her.

"What? It's true. There's no point in kidding ourselves. If we were going to be rescued, we would have been by now. The boat isn't coming. It's probably at the bottom of the Indian Ocean, and no one knows we're here."

"Dan, we've been here for—" I stopped, realizing I wasn't sure, and mentally counted. "Nine . . . ten days, maybe? That's all. We have enough water for at least two or three more weeks. Nearly a month. A lot could happen in a month. I mean, what about the septic tank? Presumably someone has to come past to empty it. Or to service the desalination plant. *Someone* will come. I'm sure of it. We just have to hang in there."

We had reached the villa now, and Santana opened the door. It was dark inside of course, as it had been every night since the storm, but there was a full moon illuminating the clearing, and Santana waved a hand around the room, from my mattress wedged in the corner next to the bathroom, to the big double bed she had been sharing with Dan, to Joel's mattress on the far side, next to the veranda.

"Here we are. Home sweet home. If you want your own space, we could probably fit a third mattress at the foot of the bed, or if you don't fancy dragging a king-size all the way from Palm Tree Rest, I could kick Dan out and you could double up with me."

"Or me," I volunteered. "I don't need a double all to myself."

"I will share with Lyla for tonight," Angel said decisively. "I'm sure Dan doesn't want to share with Joel."

We all exchanged glances. It was a good point, although the subtext was . . . unless Joel didn't come back. Maybe he was Team Conor now.

"Okay," Santana said. "And then tomorrow we can figure out if there's space for a third mattress."

We all nodded, and Santana began moving belongings around to give Angel and me a little more space. She was just pushing the little fridge farther back against the wall, when she stopped.

"Huh. That's weird."

"What's weird?" I asked, but Santana didn't answer. She had dropped to her knees and was peering inside the little fridge. Then she yanked it out from the wall and put both hands inside, feeling around. When she stood up, I could see, even in the moonlight, her face was pale and stricken.

"Dan, Lyla, did either of you touch my insulin?"

"Your insulin?" I was puzzled. "No, of course not."

"Me either," Dan said. "How come?"

"Because it's . . . it's not there." I could tell she was trying to stay calm, but there was a tremble in her voice that belied her level tone.

"It's not *there*?" Dan sprang across the room, picking the fridge up and tilting it as if he didn't believe Santana, but of course she was right—all that fell out was a metal shelf. Dan swore and threw the fridge down, causing Angel to wince, and Santana to protest.

"Dan, for fuck's sake, there's no need to smash the place up. There must be some explanation. It's no use to anyone but me."

"But why would anyone move it?" Angel asked. She was frowning. "Who would mess with another's medication? It seems very strange."

"It's him." Dan's expression was murderous. "Conor. It's fucking him. This is his way of getting back at me for this morning—by punishing Santana."

There was silence from the rest of us as we tried to make sense of this possibility, and he swung round to face first me, then Angel, then finally Santana.

"It's *him*. Admit it! It's the only thing that makes sense."

Angel folded her arms and gave a very Gallic shrug.

"I am in accord with you, Dan. There is only one psychopath on the island, and it is him."

"When I came back earlier, before dinner," I said slowly. "The door was open. I thought it must have blown open, but that must have been whoever took it."

"Fuck *whoever*, it's fucking *him*," Dan yelled. There was a vein standing out on his forehead. "I'm going to confront him."

"Dan, no," Santana said urgently. "Listen to me, my pump is full, I have at least three days before I need to start worrying, maybe more. Let's take tonight to figure out—"

"I'm taking nothing." Dan was shaking with rage. "I'm going down to confront him."

"Dan, *please*!" Santana said, but Dan was already heading towards the door. "Dan!"

She ran after him, grabbing for his hand.

"Santana, stop it." Dan's voice was hard. "This is between me and him—"

"It's my fucking insulin!"

"This isn't about the insulin. The insulin is just one more way for him to control all of us, and I'm not having it."

"We don't *know* it's him," Santana said desperately. "Dan, please. Dan!"

But Dan shook her hand off and headed out into the night.

Santana burst into tears. Angel went to comfort her, and I stood, uncertainly, looking from the weeping Santana to the track leading into the dark forest where Dan had disappeared. Fuck. *Fuck.* This was all going so wrong. And where was Joel?

The question had hardly occurred to me, when I saw a shape moving through the trees. My first idea was that it was Dan, having second thoughts, and I felt a rush of relief, but as the shape moved closer I saw it was Joel. I ran out to him.

"Joel, did you see Dan?"

"Dan? No. How come?"

"Fuck. He—he's gone to confront Conor. He thinks Conor has Santana's insulin."

"*What?*" Joel looked more confused than anything.

"Her insulin. It's gone missing. Dan thinks Conor took it as retaliation for their argument this morning. He's gone down to have it out with Conor. We need to go after him—stop him."

But Joel was looking uncomfortable.

"I—look, I mean, I don't know if that's such a good idea. Dan's pretty pissed off with me—I'm not sure me popping up to tell him to chill out would really help."

"Well, what do we do? We can't sit here and wait for him to come back with a smashed face."

"No, you're right. Shit." Joel ran his hand through his hair. "So what do we do? The thing is, if I interfere, that's not likely to calm him down. Maybe we should just let him say his piece—get it off his chest."

"That didn't exactly work out for Bayer," I said shortly. My pulse was hammering, my mouth was dry, and I felt light-headed—a mix of fear for Dan and exhaustion from the day's work. I was fairly sure we were all chronically dehydrated now and had been for days. What that was doing to our stretched nerves, I had no idea.

"Hey," Joel said sharply. He looked at me in the moonlight, frowning. "Bayer *punched* Conor, remember? He swung first. If Dan doesn't assault anyone, I'm sure he'll be fine."

But I was remembering Dan's voice, shaking with rage as he stormed off into the night. And I couldn't be sure he wouldn't let his anger get the better of him, as Bayer had.

"I'm going to go down," I said, making up my mind. "If nothing else—"

If nothing else, my presence might hold both Conor and Dan back from doing anything stupid, was what I was thinking, though that had hardly helped with Bayer.

"If nothing else?" Joel asked.

"Nothing. Just—just look after Santa. I'll be back. Hopefully soon."

Joel nodded, and I headed off into the dark.

IN THE CLEARING the moon had seemed astonishingly, almost preternaturally bright. But as I entered the forest, the palm trees and banana bushes blocked out most of the sky, letting only flickers of white light through in a confusing crosshatch of moonlight and shadow that was more disorienting than complete darkness. I found I was feeling my way, more than seeing, and it was a relief when I noticed a break in the trees and groped my way out of the thick cover onto the moonlit beach.

I had come out farther down the beach than I had meant to—I must have taken a wrong turn in the darkness—and now as I walked slowly along the sand I strained my ears to listen for any disagreement coming from the water villa, but I could hear nothing, just the rhythmic shush of the waves.

When I got to the jetty, I had to stop and steel myself for what was coming. The makeshift, gappy planks were bad enough by daylight, but now, in the shifting unreliable moonlight, they looked positively lethal.

"Conor?" I called across the wide stretch of water, but there was no sound from the villa. No door cracked open. No head appeared on the veranda. I took a deep breath and set foot on the first plank. It shifted and creaked, but held, and I stepped to the next.

As a journey, it wasn't quite as terrifying as when Joel and I had swum across the roaring, wind-tossed stretch of water in the aftermath of the storm, principally because this time, if I fell in, I was fairly sure I could just swim back to land. But all the same, the idea of falling into the dark water, likely full of submerged pikes and broken debris from the storm-wrecked jetty, was not enticing, and I held my breath as I stepped from rocking plank to creaking pile, feeling the splinters and mismatched fastenings beneath my bare feet, never sure if the next step would be the one that drove a nail deep into my heel, or sent me falling into the black waves beneath.

I was shaking by the time I reached the water villa, wondering how Zana could bring herself to make the journey every morning. She must be terrified, every single time. Maybe once you'd done it a few times it felt better, but I had no fear of water, and the thought of making the same journey back was if anything worse, now I knew how slippery and bendy the jerry-rigged planks really were.

But there was no point in dwelling on that. I was here to find Dan, and for the moment at least, I was safely on the solid surface of the veranda. Stepping forward, I banged firmly on the glass door of the water villa.

For a long moment nothing happened. I banged again, and then cupped my hands around my face, peering into the darkness inside. Nothing was moving, and I felt a twinge of anxiety. Then I saw a shape rise from the bed, and a figure—it looked like a man—swing something white around his middle. He came over to the door, opened it, and I saw Conor standing there, his hair wet and tousled, a towel wrapped around his hips.

"Lyla?" He sounded genuinely confused. "Is everything okay?"

"I came to ask you the same thing." My fears about Dan were ebbing away and being replaced with a very different kind of anxiety. "Have you seen Dan?"

"Dan? No. Why?"

"Because—" I stopped. Should I come out with it? *Because he was marching over here to accuse you of stealing Santana's insulin.*

No. That wasn't why I was here. I was here for Dan, to make sure he was okay. We could figure out the insulin tomorrow. Tonight was about making sure Dan and Conor didn't come to blows.

"He was coming here," I said instead. "To talk to you."

"I haven't seen him." Conor looked puzzled. "I was asleep, as you can see." He waved a hand at the interior of the villa, where I could just make out Zana sitting up in bed, the sheets clutched to her bare chest.

"Is everything okay?" she said. "Who is it?"

"It's me, Lyla. Listen, are you telling me Dan *didn't* come here?"

"He's never set foot here," Conor said. "I swear it." He looked as bemused as I felt. "Did he actually say he was coming out here?"

"More or less." I had turned away from the water villa, and was scanning the beach, feeling more and more worried by the second. "Where the hell could he be?"

"Maybe he changed his mind and turned back. The jetty isn't for the faint-hearted at night."

"Maybe." I bit my lip, trying to figure out what to do. It was true the jetty had looked terrifying in the darkness. And it was also true that I hadn't come the most direct route down to the beach. Had Dan and I crossed in the forest? Maybe he was back at the villa right now, wondering where I was. I half turned, ready to cross back to the island, and then paused and said, "Listen, if Dan does turn up here—"

I stopped. What could I say?

"Yes?"

"Tell him . . ." I racked my brain for something, anything, that would deflect Dan's intent to have it out with Conor. "Tell him I was here, and that Santana needs him back at the villa, okay?" It was the only thing I could think of, the only thing that might stop Dan in his tracks, if he thought Santana was in trouble.

"I'll tell him," Conor said. He watched me as I made my way back to the jetty and stepped cautiously onto the first plank. It rocked, alarmingly, and I froze, waiting for it to stabilize. "Will you be okay? Getting across, I mean?"

"Yes, I'll be fine," I said a little tersely. I didn't want to waste any more time. I wanted to get back, find Dan, and make sure he was okay. Still, I felt Conor's eyes on me as I crossed plank by plank, listening as they creaked and groaned under my weight, and he didn't move until I set foot onto the sand. Then, with a wave of one arm, he turned and headed back into the water villa, and I trudged up the beach towards home.

CHAPTER 22

"NO, WHAT THE fuck are you talking about? Of course he's not here." Santana's face was white and strained in the moonlight, and I bit back what I wanted to retort, which was to please not swear at me, I was the person who'd been doing my best to track him down. "I'm sorry," she said, as if reading my thoughts. "I'm sorry, I shouldn't have sworn at you. I'm just—what the hell is he doing, pissing around in the forest? First he disappears all day—now this."

"The main thing is, he thought better of going to the water jetty," I said, trying to keep hold of the positives. "So he's not having it out with Conor. Anything's better than that."

"You're right . . . I guess." Santana sounded unhappy. "I just—what a fucking idiot though."

She walked to the door, opened it, and yelled out into the night, "Dan! Daaaaan! Where are you?"

There was no response, just the shushing of wind in the trees and the sound of the sea.

"Dan?" Again, nothing.

"Daniel!" It was Angel, her voice a yell of irritation that sent the birds cawing in angry sympathy. "Get back here, you stupid espèce de merde. We want to go to bed!"

We all waited. It wasn't the approach I would have taken, but I had to admit, if anything was likely to bring him storming back out of the trees, it was that—if only to tell Angel to shove it. But as the forest died back into silence, no footsteps sounded from the dark. No answering irritated voice called back, asking who was calling who a piece of shit.

Nothing. Just . . . nothing.

At last Joel cleared his throat.

"Look . . . I mean . . . there's nothing we can do until morning. Even if we wanted to go after him, we'd never find him in the dark. Shall we just go to bed?"

There was a long silence. Then Santana let out a breath that shuddered, as if she was very close to tears.

"Okay. I don't want to, but I don't know what else we can do. You're right, we won't find him in this. Oh, Dan, what the fuck are you doing?"

Her voice wobbled on the last word, and I put my arm around her. It occurred to me that she and Dan were the last couple left on the island, aside from Conor and Zana. Everyone else had lost their other half. But until tonight, Santana had always had Dan in her corner. And now he seemed to have disappeared too.

"I'm sure he's fine," I said, trying to imbue my words with a confidence I didn't really feel. "He was at the other end of the island before, wasn't he? He's probably gone back there to cool off."

"Why though?" Santana said. Her voice sounded tight, as if she was trying not to give way to the tears I could hear hovering at the edges of her words. "Why wouldn't he come back here? Did he get lost?"

I shrugged. Unlikely though it seemed, it wasn't impossible. The island wasn't big, but at night the twisting paths and dense trees made the paths disorienting.

"I don't know. But the island isn't that big—if he wants to come back, he'll find his way eventually. If not, well, worst-case scenario is he spends a night in the open."

Getting bitten by God knows what, was the subtext, but I didn't voice those doubts. The slim green snake I had seen on the first day kept floating through my head. I had no idea whether it was poisonous or not, but I didn't want to find out.

"Lyla's right," Joel put in, though he sounded uneasy. "We can't do any good sitting up worrying like this. He could be safely tucked up at Palm Tree Rest, for all we know. Let's get some sleep, and we can be up at first light to look for him."

There was a long silence, and then Santana said, in a defeated-sounding voice, "Okay." It was only one word, but her voice wobbled.

"Yeah?" I squeezed her shoulders again, more tightly, and felt her nod her head. "Come on then, let's get to bed. Ten to one, Dan will be lying beside you in the morning, snoring his head off."

"Yeah," Santana said. "I hope you're right."

But I wasn't.

WHEN I AWOKE the next day, it was to the sound of Santana pacing back and forth on the veranda, her footsteps making the wooden boards shake, and I knew before I opened my eyes that something was wrong.

I could smell my own sweat, feel the dry cracking of my lips, and the salty itching of skin that hadn't seen fresh water for over a week, and I felt a sudden visceral longing for a shower—for the warm water running down my body, splashing over my face—but I pushed that thought aside, hauled myself to my feet, and went out to where Santana was still pacing, staring sightlessly out into the forest.

"I take it—" I said, and then realized my throat was dry as dust and my voice barely audible. I coughed, tried to moisten my lips, and tried again. "I take it Dan's not back?"

Santana's head had whipped around at the sound of my cough, but at the sight of me she seemed to deflate. Now she shook her head.

"No." Her voice was as croaky as mine. "I've gone over all the accessible parts of the island—the staff quarters, the empty villas, the cabana—nothing. I'm really worried, Lyla. What if something's happened to him?"

I bit my lip. What I wanted to say was that if something had happened to him, he was probably fucked. But then, that increasingly seeming like it was true for all of us—the only question was how fast.

"Good morning," we heard from behind us, and both Santana and I turned to see Angel standing there, stretching to the sky. She looked improbably coiffed, her hair wrapped up in a headscarf that gave her face the look of a queen: all sculpted cheekbones and tilted eyes.

"Angel. How did you sleep?"

"Okay. It was good to have company." Her face was somber. "Have you heard from Dan?"

Santana shook her head. There were tears brimming at the corners of her eyes, and I thought perhaps she didn't trust herself to speak.

"I'm really scared," she said at last. "Wh-what if he went after Conor and something happened?"

"I really don't think he did, Santa." I put my hand on her arm. "I went out there last night, and he looked genuinely like he'd been asleep."

"Did you ask him about the insulin?" Santana asked, and I shook my head.

"No, I thought about it—but I didn't want to start something in the middle of the night while we were still looking for Dan."

"But also . . ." Angel said, and then stopped.

"But also?" I prompted.

"But also . . . well, I have been thinking about the insulin. It was here, yes? In the villa?"

Santana nodded.

"If Lyla is right and the person who took the insulin was also the person who left open the villa door, evidently it must have been taken after breakfast and before supper. Correct?"

I looked at Santana and we both nodded. I wasn't quite sure where Angel was going with this. But Angel spread her hands, a look of pantomime astonishment on her face that we were being so stupid.

"Mais, dis donc, it could not have been Conor. He was on the beach all day, no? We would have seen him from the place where we were building the bonfire."

I frowned. My brain felt like it was running at half speed—a mixture of lack of sleep and dehydration, I suspected, but I forced myself to think back to the day before—and from what I could recall, Angel was right. Angel, Santana, and I had been up on the headland all day, watching the sea, and we would have seen Conor if he'd headed into the forest. Santana was frowning too.

"I . . . I'm trying to remember but . . . look, he *must* have gone somewhere. He must have taken a piss or something, surely? Was he really in the water all day?"

"He went into the water villa," Angel said. Her voice was patient as if she was speaking to small but stupid children. "Two times. But he did not go into the forest. I would have noticed. I do not trust that man. I keep my eye upon him." She wisely tapped at the corner of her eye, and then folded her arms, as if that proved her point.

"You're right," I said slowly. "As far as it goes. But it depends if I'm right about the door. It might be unconnected. What if he took it yesterday?"

"Before Dan argued with him about the water?" Angel was looking skeptical, but Santana was shaking her head.

"No, not possible. I refilled my pump yesterday morning, straight after breakfast. All the vials were there then. It must have been taken some time after we went up to the headland to build the bonfire. And

Conor was already fishing by the time we got there." Angel opened her mouth to speak, but Santana was warming to her theme, "But *also*, and this is maybe more to the point, how would Conor have known it was there? He's never been in our villa as far as I know—was anything else moved, Lyla?"

I shrugged.

"Not that I could see. It didn't look like any of our bags had been searched."

"Right. So, whoever took it, went straight for the insulin. Like they *knew* where it was."

There was a sudden, ugly silence, and our eyes, all of them, turned to Joel's sleeping form, sprawled out across his mattress, as if drawn by magnets.

"No," Santana whispered. "No. He wouldn't."

"He and Conor are very close," Angel said thoughtfully. "He helped him take the food, after all. They are . . . what's the English expression for friends like pigs?"

"Friends like pigs?" Santana looked at her blankly.

"Yes, ils sont copains comme cochons. Very good friends. Thick like thieves, that is the expression!"

"Thick *as* thieves," Santana corrected, and Angel rolled her eyes. I couldn't blame her. Her English was about a hundred times better than my French—or presumably Santana's.

"Who's thick as thieves?" Joel's sleepy voice came from behind us, and we all jumped guiltily. My eyes met Santana's, wondering what to say. She opened her mouth, and then closed it again, and I knew she was wondering the same thing I was: Should we ask him directly whether he had taken the insulin? But at the same time, this was *Joel*—Joel, who had slept side by side with us for days now. Joel, who had wept over Romi and hugged us and listened as we cried out in the night with bad dreams.

He had denied knowing anything about the insulin last night,

and to ask him directly now was to say to his face, more or less, that
we suspected him of lying.

More to the point, if Joel really *had* taken Santana's insulin, presumably to give to Conor, we were highly unlikely to get it back for
the asking.

"We were just talking about English expressions," Angel said at
last. She shot me and Santana a look, as though inviting us to back
her up. I felt a coldness around my heart. She didn't trust Joel. And
the worst thing was . . . I wasn't sure I did either now. Because her
logic made sense. Someone had taken that insulin, and I couldn't see
how it could have been Conor. Which meant someone on the island
had betrayed us.

Dan is back. Thank God. We were all so worried about him. He just appeared out of the forest while we were all fishing and swimming and apologized to the group for worrying everyone and for losing his shit over the water. Then he drank down the whole allocation we'd saved up for him while he was away.

We told him we understood—of course we did. Poor Dan. None of us blame him. It's hard. I could be the next person to lose it—or Lyla. Or even Conor, though that's hard to imagine.

We all hugged him, and Conor said, "Don't do that again, okay, mate? It'd break our hearts to—"

He stopped, but we all knew what he was going to say. To lose another person, after Romi and Bayer.

Dan didn't say anything, he just nodded. But I could see he'd been crying. I hope he's okay.

CHAPTER 23

THE FOUR OF us spent the rest of the day looking for Dan, spreading out across the island, calling his name, but as far as we could make out, he wasn't there.

It was impossible to be sure, of course. At the villa end of the island the forest was relatively manicured, punctuated by paths and little artificial clearings. But at the far end it was wilder and much more untouched, and it was impossible to penetrate some of the thickets without a machete and protective clothing. None of us wanted to hack our way through untouched forest in shorts and flip-flops—who knew what snakes and spiders might be waiting for us.

It was hard to believe that Dan could be in there though. And even if he was, surely he would have called out when he heard us. One thing seemed certain, if he *was* on the island, he didn't want to be found.

When sunset came, we trailed back to the cabana, Santana limping a little now, though her leg was much better than it had been, and she was no longer wearing my makeshift bandage. We drank the meager ration of water and stared at the pile of breads and croissants in the center of the table. There was mold on one, I saw. We had stripped all the bananas that were even remotely ripe days ago, and we had all been so focused on looking for Dan that no one had had time to fish today. We were down to stale pastries and the last few tins of fruit salad. Santana simply sat, staring at the plate in front of her, and then she put her head in her hands and burst into tears.

We all clustered around, trying our best to comfort her, but it was Zana who knelt in front of her, putting her hands either side of her face, speaking to her directly, who managed to calm her.

"Hey," she kept saying. "Hey, Santana, hold on, okay? Just hold on. It's going to be okay."

"You don't know that," Santana said. She looked up at the sky, turning a deep indigo now, spattered with stars that were brighter and more beautiful than anything I'd ever seen in London. Her eyes were huge and full of tears. "You have no idea if that's true. We're going to die here."

"We still have the radio," Zana said. "And Lyla's right about the septic tank and the services on the island, someone is *bound* to come past eventually, they have to, we just have to hold out until they come."

But Angel had given a start at the word *radio*.

"We didn't radio today," she said. "With everything about Dan— I am going down to the shack to try."

"Good idea," Conor said. "I'm going down to the shore. I have this theory boats might be easier to spot at night, with their lights. And they'd see our beacon better too if we tried to signal."

Angel nodded and set off for the radio shack, while Zana and I tried to persuade Santana to eat something. Only Joel did nothing. He was sitting with his head in his hands, looking more despondent than I had seen him since Romi died.

Santana had stopped crying and had managed to swallow some croissant, with the moldy parts picked off, and eat some chunks of coconut, when we heard Angel coming back up the path from the shack. I don't know how, but just the sound of her footsteps was ominous, and I looked up to see her face was set and grim as she came towards the fire.

"What is it?" I asked.

"It is dead." Angel's voice was flat.

"What?"

"The radio. The fucking radio. The battery is dead!"

"Are you sure?" Joel asked, and Angel turned on him savagely.

"Sure? Of course I'm sure, you idiot. Yesterday there was a light, today there is not! And yes, I checked the connection, but we all knew the battery wouldn't last forever."

"Shit." Santana had lost all color again. "Is there nothing we can do? Can't we—I don't know. You know when your torch runs out and you put the batteries in your armpit to warm them up. Can't we . . . can't we warm up the battery?"

"We could try again tomorrow at midday," I said wearily. "When the sun's on the shack. But I don't know if that's how those big car batteries work. They're lead acid, aren't they?"

"They could be radioactive," Angel said. Her voice was stony. "And it would not change the facts. The thing is dead, and even if we manage to get a trickle of charge from it tomorrow, it will be dead after that. We are all completely screwed."

"Look—" Joel said, at the same time as we all heard a shout from the beach.

"Hey! Hey, come here, come quick."

We stopped, frozen in the actions we'd been performing, like children playing statues. It was Conor's voice, but he didn't sound excited, as if he'd seen a ship. He sounded . . . afraid.

"Can someone please come!" Conor yelled again.

And then, as if released by his words, we all jolted into action and began running down the path towards the beach, as fast as we could in the thick velvet dark.

I could see Angel's pale dress fluttering in front of me and hear Joel panting at the rear. It took only a few moments, and then we broke out into the moonlight and saw Conor standing far up on the shore, a dark shape at his feet.

"What is it?" Zana called. She had pulled off her Birkenstocks and was running through the sand with surprising speed. "Have you found something?"

"Has something washed up?" Joel asked. But Conor didn't say anything, he just stood there, staring down at the thing at his feet.

It was Santana who saw it first, and even then I didn't understand the scream that ripped out of the throat, the way she gathered up her skirts and began to run haltingly down the beach towards where Conor was standing.

And then, I knew, and I was running too, falling to my knees in the surf beside the thing that had been Dan.

He had been badly torn up—whether by sharks, or just by the action of the coral, I wasn't sure. His face was unrecognizable, but the clothes were his, from the Bermuda shorts to the thin red string tied around one wrist. One arm was flung beseechingly out on the sand, while the other was curled into his body, as if protecting himself from a blow. Most heartbreaking of all—where his shirt had been ripped I could see a very small tattoo, just above his hip. Mickey Mouse—the matching companion to Santana's Minnie.

It was that simple little thing that undid me, and I put my hand over my mouth, holding back the sob that threatened to erupt. Santana had lost it entirely—she was kneeling over him, holding his out-stretched hand, weeping in violent, choking gasps, until Zana led her gently away to try to comfort her.

Joel, Conor, Angel, and I dragged the body up the beach. There was nothing to do except begin the now familiar macabre ritual of digging a grave in the clearing beside the others. We couldn't leave him out here overnight for the birds to continue what the fish had started.

When the hole was deep enough, the four of us each took a limb, ready to lower the body into the makeshift grave. Conor and Angel were holding his ankles, Joel his left arm, and I his right.

We were slowly lowering him into the grave, trying for something more respectful than simply dropping him, when my grip on his wrist gave, his hand slipping through mine, and I clutched at his fingers, breaking the rigor mortis. The joints gave with a horrible crunching noise, but I managed to grab hold of his hand, and as I did, I felt something in it, something hard and round and smooth against my palm, as if Dan were passing it to me. A pebble, maybe. Or a fragment of the rocks he'd slipped from.

It was only when Dan's body was stretched out below us, covered with a sheet, that I looked down at what I was now holding. At first I didn't recognize it, and when I did, I didn't understand it. It was more on instinct than by calculation that I slipped it quickly into the pocket of my shorts, hiding it from view.

All through the makeshift ceremony, the object gnawed at my mind, whispering questions beneath the sound of Santana's tearing sobs. What did it mean, this thing that Dan had been holding on to so desperately as his body was swept out to sea?

It didn't make sense. None of it made sense. The question was, what should I do now?

CHAPTER 24

NONE OF US could sleep. Santana was lying in the bed that had been hers and Dan's, weeping slowly but steadily into the pillow, a low, tearing moan of grief.

Angel was lying behind her, stroking her back in a soft rhythm, whispering soft words in a French none of us could understand, but which were no less comforting for that.

Joel, I could see was standing outside the villa, leaning on the veranda rail, staring out into the darkness.

And I was lying there, fully awake, feeling the small, hard presence of the object I had found in Dan's hand, now gripped in my own.

At last, worn out by Santana's grief, I got up and went outside to join Joel, shutting the door gently behind myself as I did.

Outside I could hear the whine of the mosquitoes and, farther away, the sound of the surf breaking against the coral. Once it had been soothing; now it was a horrible reminder of Dan's death.

Maybe it was because I hadn't known Bayer as long, or maybe it was because he had been the one to attack Conor, but somehow, Bayer's death hadn't hit me the way Dan's had. It had almost felt unreal—just another contestant eliminated from the reality of our lives.

Standing there in the clearing tonight though, with the four crosses white in the moonlight, I had been forced to understand something—we *were* being eliminated—all of us. And by someone who was determined to win this game at any cost. But the prize was no longer fame and money. It was survival.

"Are you okay?" Joel asked as I came over to join him, and I shook my head.

"Not really. You?"

"No. I knew I wouldn't be able to sleep."

"Me neither."

There was a long silence, and then I said, with the feeling that I was about to step off a precipice, "Joel, listen. I found something."

I had no idea whether I was about to make a terrible, terrible mistake. I only knew that if I didn't talk to someone about this, I would go mad—and Joel, for all his ties to Conor, had been kind to me from the very beginning.

"You found something?" Joel turned to me in the moonlight, frowning, and I could tell that he was trying to parse my tone, trying to figure out whether this something was good news or bad, and how he should react.

I nodded, feeling the trepidation ballooning inside me like a sickness. And then I put my hand in my pocket and held it out—the object Dan had been holding in his grip when he washed up on the beach. A vial of Santana's insulin.

For a moment Joel peered at it as if he didn't understand what he was looking at. Then he made a sound like he'd been punched in the gut, and I knew he had recognized it, and that he knew what he was looking at.

"That's—that's—" He stopped. All the color had drained from his face. I finished the sentence for him.

"Santana's insulin. Yes. It was in Dan's hand. I found it when we were lowering him into the grave."

"And what—" He stopped again, as if completely lost for words.

"What does it mean? I don't know. I don't think Dan took it, if that's what you mean. His outrage last night was real. Which means . . ."

I stopped speaking, let the silence stretch, waiting for Joel to put two and two together and understand what I was saying. If Dan hadn't taken the vial, then someone must have given it to him, or put it in his hand.

"Is there something you want to tell me, Joel?"

"No," he said reflexively, but he looked sick. Very sick.

"Joel, you can talk to me," I said, keeping my voice low. But Joel shook his head. He wouldn't look at me. He was staring out into the forest as though he was urgently searching for something in the darkness.

"Joel?" I said, and he shook his head.

"Lyla, just— Can you just . . . leave me alone for a bit, okay? I need to think."

"Okay," I said. I turned, opened the veranda door, and slipped inside. Angel was still crooning in French to Santana, who was lying with her head in Angel's lap, her eyes closed, her face still stained with tears.

The room smelled of sweat, and up in the rafters I heard the scuttle of a gecko, and the whine of a mosquito zipping past my ear. I slid onto my mattress and pulled the thin sheet up over my shoulders. Then I closed my eyes and waited for Joel to decide which side he wanted to be on.

WHEN I OPENED my eyes, it was morning, the sun was streaming in through the thin cheesecloth curtains . . . and Joel's mattress was empty. I sat up and my gaze went automatically to the door, checking if he was still standing, leaning on the veranda rail, but he wasn't there. He wasn't in the villa clearing. He wasn't in the bathroom. He wasn't anywhere.

Angel and Santana were still asleep, and I got up, quietly pulled on a T-shirt and flip-flops, and headed out into the forest.

The morning was quiet, and it was early enough that the fierce heat of the day hadn't yet set in, but I could feel the skin on my nose protesting already when I walked through the sunny clearings. We had started to ration the sun cream along with everything else, trying to cover up when we could, rather than slather on the factor fifty as we had at first.

Now, as I came out into the sunny glare of the cabana, two things hit me. The first was the full force of the morning sun. The second was the fact that Joel wasn't there.

The uneasy feeling was mounting in my gut as I walked down through the forest to the beach and scanned it. Nothing. No one. Just the marks of our feet from the night before; the long, sickening scrape of sand where we'd tugged and carried Dan's body up the beach; the smooth stretch below the waterline.

In the distance I could see the water villa. The curtains were closed and there was no one on the veranda. Unless Joel had spent the night with Conor and Zana, which seemed unlikely, he wasn't there.

Next, I checked the other villas. First Palm Tree Rest, where Bayer and Angel had been sleeping until Angel moved into Forest Retreat with the rest of us. No sign of anyone.

Then up to Ocean Bluff, which was more of a skeleton than a villa since we'd stripped it to provide materials for the bonfire. I wouldn't have been surprised to find Joel up there, staring at the horizon, looking out for ships, but there was no one there, and no sign of any movement since yesterday. Everything was exactly as we'd left it before Dan's death.

Then, with trepidation, I made my way back into the forest, to Island Dream, the villa where Joel and Romi had spent their first day—the villa Romi had been sleeping in when she died.

I don't know why, but I felt a kind of superstition about going back there. I hadn't visited it since the first day after the storm, when we'd retrieved Romi's body from the rubble and then later, that same day, when we'd rescued Joel's belongings. Now it had a strange, haunted air, quite different from the other damaged villa. Had Joel gone back there to try to figure out what Romi would have wanted him to do, to try to connect with the person he had been before all this had started?

The answer, when I got there, seemed to be no. The villa was silent and empty, as far as I could make out—just a long brown snake sunning itself on the caved-in roof. At the sound of my footsteps, it uncoiled itself unhurriedly and slithered across the clearing, its strong muscular body writhing sinuously across the shattered palm fronds.

I watched it go, feeling my pulse quicken a little in spite of the logical side of my brain telling me I had little to fear. You're ten times more likely to die from a mosquito than a snake, a stat I had trotted out many times over the course of my career. But the human brain is bad at evaluating risk, and worse at assessing the true dangers all around us—and I was no exception to that. The scientist in me couldn't override the little atavistic pulse of adrenaline I experienced as I watched the snake disappear into the bush.

And as I looked around the empty clearing, I realized, it wasn't just the snake. I had been bad at assessing danger since the day I set foot on Ever After Island. I had trusted the wrong people, made the wrong decisions. I had let my instincts override the evidence in front of me.

If I had learned one thing from my job, it was to accept the truth, no matter how much I wished things might be different. I had a sharp flashback to that day, just a few weeks ago, though it felt like a lifetime, when Nico had told me about One Perfect Couple and I had sat there, distracted, half listening to him talk, but really watching the graph of my results fill out on my laptop. The whole time he was speaking, I'd been willing the dots to make a different pattern, the nice, neat correlation I'd been hoping to see. But they didn't.

I could have tried to ignore the data. I could have massaged my results, or quietly erased a couple of points to make the pattern I wished was there look more persuasive.

But I hadn't. I had looked at the information in front of me and accepted what it meant, because that was my job. Because my sole, overriding duty as a scientist was to face up to reality.

And now I had to do the same thing here. I had to look at the facts—and face up to what was happening on Ever After Island. I had to find out the truth.

Dan is dead. I can't believe it. Another accident—it just goes to show how fragile our lives are out here, how powerless we are when something goes wrong.

And it was such a beautiful day. We were all down at the sea, laughing, swimming, playing in the waves . . . for a moment I think we'd almost all forgotten the reality of our situation. We were just seven young people, hanging out, having . . . a kind of fun, really.

We were throwing around a makeshift ball we'd made out of one of the big empty water bottles, and Dan had swum far out, ready to catch it—and then suddenly, he was really, really far out.

Angel called to him to come back, and he seemed to hear, and he turned, and began striking out for shore—but he wasn't coming any closer. He was swimming and swimming, frantically, towards us, but his shape was getting smaller and smaller. I couldn't understand it. And then Joel suddenly said, "He's caught in the rip— He's in the rip."

He began yelling and shouting, "Swim sideways! Don't swim against the current, swim along the shore!" but I don't know whether Dan could hear. He was so far out, and the wind had picked up. The waves were starting to break over his head.

Conor began to strip off, and Joel said, "No, let me, I'm a stronger swimmer," and pulled off his T-shirt. He dived into the water, but we could see, even before he had gone more than a few metres, that it was hopeless. And then Dan disappeared.

Joel's head surfaced above the water, checking his direction, and he stopped.

"Where is he?" he called back to shore. "I can't see him. Point me to where he is?"

But Dan was gone, so far out to sea that we couldn't even be sure when we lost sight of him.

Joel was beside himself. So is Santana, of course, she's absolutely destroyed, but Joel—I think Joel felt responsible. Like he should have noticed earlier, though of course we tried to tell him that wasn't the case.

"I should have told him about the rip," he kept saying. "I should have warned him."

We have lost another person. I keep saying it, aloud, trying to make it real. We've lost another person—lovely Dan, who was always laughing and joking and trying to make everyone else feel better.

We have lost him.

CHAPTER 25

"LOOK, I NEED to talk to you."

We were down at the beach waiting for Conor and Zana to wake up and bring us the morning water ration, but for once, thirsty as I was, I wasn't counting down the seconds until Conor came across the jetty, water bottle in hand. Because I wanted to speak to Angel and Santana before he got here.

"To me? Or Angel?" Santana turned to me, her face listless and incurious. She was like a different person since Dan's death, as if all the vitality and laughter had drained out of her.

"To both of you." I dug in my pocket and held out the vial of insulin I had found in Dan's hand. "I found this yesterday."

Angel peered at the tiny bottle, her face uncomprehending, but Santana's gasp was instant, and she snatched the insulin out of my hand.

"*What?* Where did you find this?"

"In Dan's hand. I think . . ." I swallowed. "I think he was holding it when he died."

"That is your insulin?" Angel asked, comprehension dawning. She took a long sucking breath between pursed lips, and then seemed to realize what this meant—or could mean. "Wait, are you saying *Dan* was the thief?"

"Bullshit!" Santana cried, at the same time as I said, "I don't think so, no."

"But if he had the insulin—" Angel began, but Santana cut her off.

"No. No, I don't believe it. It's bullshit, Dan would never. He would never! He knows what that means to me. It was Conor. It was Conor punishing him for standing up to him. I know it was!"

"It wasn't Conor," Angel said patiently. "We have been through this, Santana."

"I'm pretty sure it was Joel," I said. "I showed him the vial last night—"

"You did *what?*" interjected Angel, but I kept going, doggedly, speaking over her.

"—and his reaction was really off. He looked guilty as hell. But he also looked . . . stricken. In a way I didn't completely understand. But I think I do now."

"What do you mean?" Santana cried. "And more to the point, where's the rest of my bloody insulin? That vial is half-full." She pointed at the little bottle in my hand, which had a pinprick in its lid.

I took a deep breath, marshalling all the clarity I could. The sequence of events had seemed so clear when I was running through them up at the villa, but now I was doubting my own logic. It made sense though. I *knew* it made sense. I just had to convey it to Angel and Santana.

"I think Joel took the insulin and gave it to Conor. I don't know why. Probably Conor asked him to steal it because he knew we'd suspect him and would be on our guard if he started sniffing around our villa. Maybe he came up with some argument about Dan being a loose cannon, and it being safer for everyone to have a hold over him. Or maybe he just straight-up bribed Joel with some water. I don't know about you, but there's not a lot I wouldn't do for an extra liter right now."

"I wouldn't fucking steal someone's medication," Santana growled, but I saw Angel run her tongue unconsciously over her cracked lips, and I thought she knew what I meant, and was honest enough to know that we might all have been tempted, with the right ask.

"But how did it end up in Dan's hand?" Angel asked. "Are you saying it was . . . comment on dit, mise-en-scène—staged? That Conor put it there when he found the body?"

"I don't think so," I said, shaking my head. "Dan had rigor mortis. His hand was completely clamped around the bottle. No, I think Dan *did* go and see Conor the other night."

"But you said Conor and Zana were alone?" Santana objected. "You said you would have seen Dan coming back."

"I think I was wrong. I think Dan went out to the water villa, and he got hold of a vial somehow. I don't know how—maybe he found it, or maybe Conor offered it to him, to try to placate him, and it backfired. Either way, I think they ended up fighting and Conor drowned him, and then pushed his body into the riptide to be carried out to sea. It was just his bad luck that the currents carried it back—with the insulin."

"You cannot know any of that," Angel said skeptically, and I shook my head.

"No, I can't. But going on what little data we do have, it's the only way I can make sense of Dan holding the insulin the moment he died. He *must* have taken it from whoever killed him—and we know that wasn't Joel. Joel was in the villa with us all night. And there's something else. Conor's hair was wet when I went out to the water villa that night."

"Wet?" Santana said blankly. "What do you mean?"

"I mean, wet. Like he'd had a shower. He was wearing a towel as well. Now, it's possible he went for a last-minute swim before bed to cool down. . . ."

"But it's far more likely he got wet drowning Dan," Santana said. Her voice cracked. "Oh, darling Dan, you stupid fucker. I begged him. I begged him not to go out there."

"I know," I said quietly. Angel put her arm around Santana's shoulders and she wept, dry, racking sobs. "You didn't do anything wrong."

"So we confront him?" Angel said now, her voice fierce. "We get Joel to confess what he did, the little worm, and then we confront the psychopath?"

"Well . . ." I said reluctantly. "That's the other thing I'm worried about. I asked Joel about it last night."

"And?"

"And he looked . . . sucker punched. More shocked than I would have expected. I didn't accuse him in so many words, but it was pretty clear what I was saying. But I don't think that was what shocked him. I mean, he knew what he'd done—he must have known that there was a chance we'd put two and two together. No, I think he was shocked because when I told him Dan had been holding a vial of insulin, he realized what I did—that if Dan was holding the bottle when he died, that meant he did see Conor the other night. And it probably meant that Conor had murdered him."

"So he is forced to reckon with the true nature of his psycho friend. And now he is gone to have some midlife crisis moment in the forest?" Angel said scornfully. Her voice was full of disgust. I shrugged.

"I mean . . . it's possible. And it's what I hope."

"It's what you hope?" Santana looked up. Her eyes were red with unshed tears.

"It's what I hope because the alternative is worse." The problem was, it was also more plausible. I didn't think Joel was the type to go hang out in the jungle with the snakes.

"What are you saying?" Santana looked taken aback. "Are you saying Joel's gone over to Conor's side?"

I shook my head. Though I didn't want to say it aloud, the truth was, Joel had already *been* on Conor's side, we just hadn't realized it. But that wasn't what I'd meant.

"The alternative is . . . Joel didn't want to believe what I was suggesting. Didn't want to believe that the man he'd put his trust in had murdered someone in cold blood. The alternative is, he went to confront Conor. And Conor killed him, too."

There was a long, long silence. Three pairs of eyes turned to the water villa. And then we saw the door crack open, and Conor begin to walk across the jetty.

I stood up, off the sand. My heart was pounding.

Conor had killed Dan, I was sure of that. And it seemed increasingly likely with every moment that Joel didn't appear that he'd killed Joel too.

Which meant, we were on an island with a murderer. A murderer who was viciously strong and who, increasingly, appeared to be without a conscience. The question was, what should we do about it? We had less than five minutes to decide.

Santana and Angel were clearly going through the same thought process. As Conor began to pick his way across the planks, Santana turned to us, her eyes wide and panicked.

"What are we going to do? Should we say something?"

"Dieu." Angel spat the word out like a curse. "As if this situation could not get worse. No, we should not say anything. The man is a psychopath. Do you want him to kill us too?"

"But we have to get back my insulin! How can we do that without confronting him about Dan? About Joel?"

"You think if the man stole your insulin and murdered your boyfriend he will give it back upon request?" Angel demanded. I resisted the urge to put my hands over my ears, shut out their bickering while I tried to think. Because the truth was, it *wasn't* bickering. This was a life-or-death decision, and Conor was almost at the beach.

"How many days' insulin do you have?" I asked Santana. "Here, I mean—not counting the vials Conor's got."

Santana blinked.

"Fuck. I don't know. Two, maybe three in my pump. Maybe five days in the vial you found. But I don't know if it's usable—it could have got seawater in it."

"Look"—I made a rapid decision—"let's not burn any bridges now. If we say something we can't take back . . . that might not end well." Conor was on the sand. I was speaking quickly now, my voice low. "We have to make him *want* to give back the insulin. We have to make it easy for him. If we tie him having the insulin to an accusation that he murdered Dan and Joel . . . do you see what I'm saying? He'll never be able to admit that he has it. We need to find a way of getting the insulin back that lets him maintain plausible deniability."

"Okay," Santana said, but her face was pale, and I wasn't sure she was convinced by my argument. "So . . . we ask where Joel is?"

"Yes. We stick to facts. We ask where Joel is and we ask—"

But Conor was almost up to the group, and now I realized something else. He wasn't carrying the water.

"Hi, Conor," I said as he approached. He smiled, pleasantly enough, and I saw that his lips weren't dry and chapped like the rest of us, but full and moist.

"Good morning, ladies. Where's Joel?"

"We were just about to ask you that." I tried to keep my voice even—anxious, but not overly so. "He left the villa last night. Did he come to see you?"

"No." Conor was either truly concerned or doing a very good acting job. He looked genuinely surprised and more than a little alarmed. "What time did he leave?"

"Midnight, maybe? We haven't seen him since."

"Well, I'm afraid I know what you do." Conor spread his hands. "Nothing."

"Well, now that we agree on that." Angel's voice was full of a contempt she wasn't bothering to hide. "Perhaps we could have our water?"

"Ah." Conor put his hands behind his back, linking his fingers and stretching so that his joints clicked, and the powerful muscles in his shoulders bunched. "Well, yes. There's a problem."

"A *problem*?" Angel's voice could have taken the nonstick off a pan. The rolled *r* in *problem* sounded like a tiger with its temper barely under control. "There is a *problem*?"

"Yes, it's February twenty-fifth, by my reckoning. Which means we've been here just over ten days."

"And?"

"And we've got through almost half the water. We have to face facts, in another ten days, we could be looking at single-digit liters."

"But wait—" I put out a hand. "There were eight of us when we calculated the water ration. There's only six now." Maybe five if Joel was gone, though I wasn't ready to say that out loud. "That gives us an extra twenty-five percent leeway."

"Okay, then." Conor spoke impatiently. "An extra twelve days. What does it matter? The point is, we're running out of water. We're all going to have to work a bit harder for our liquid allowance."

"What does that mean?" Santana looked at him through narrowed eyes. I saw that her shoulders were peeling viciously where the sun had caught them yesterday.

"It means that in order to qualify for liquid allowance, everyone is going to have to bring two green coconuts to the table each morning."

"What?" It was Angel who exploded with the question we were all suppressing. "C'est quoi, ces conneries? You know perfectly that there are no green coconuts left. We searched all the island for them—all the fallen are dry."

"Then you'll have to climb the trees," Conor said pleasantly.

"Climb the trees? Are you insane? We climbed everything possible. The ones left are forty meters high!"

"Or knock the coconuts down. I don't care how you do it—that's your business. But if you don't contribute, you don't drink."

"And what about you?" Santana demanded. "Where are your coconuts?"

"I'll be fishing. Assuming you want to eat."

"Conor, look," I put in, trying to keep the desperation out of my voice. My throat was suddenly very dry—drier even than it had been a few minutes ago. I swallowed painfully. "We take your point—we need to find other sources of liquid. But give us our allowance now, and we can go out and figure out how to get the coconuts down."

"I don't think so," Conor said. "I find most people work better with a little bit of incentivization."

"Conor . . ." The soft voice came from behind him, and we all turned, surprised to see Zana padding along the beach. She looked pale and even thinner than when she had first come to the island, but there was a kind of resolve about her. "Conor . . . I think Lyla has a point."

"Oh you do, do you?" Conor said. His voice was mild, but there was a kind of underlying menace in it. Zana took a step back, and then seemed to catch herself and stood up taller, nodding.

"Yes, I do. Give everyone their water now, and they can earn the supper allowance."

"Come here," Conor said with a smile. He held out his hand. Zana looked puzzled, but she put her hand in his, and he drew her closer. For a moment I thought he was bringing her in for a hug and remembered the way Zana had stood up for Angel over the food, after Bayer's death, and the way Conor had backed down. But then, Zana began to squirm, and then she gave a cry, and then a full-on whimper of pain. At first I didn't understand, and then I realized she was trying to pull her hand away from Conor. I looked down, and I saw that Conor had her hand in his and was digging his nail into the white half-moon at the base of Zana's thumbnail, so hard that she was literally buckling at the knees with pain.

I had a sharp, agonizing flashback to a time when I had been pinning up the hem of Nico's trousers for an alteration and he had taken a step back and trodden, in his dress shoes, on the flat of my thumbnail. He hadn't stamped hard, just shifted his weight, but it had all rested on exactly the place where Conor was pressing into Zana's nail. It had been—no exaggeration—one of the most painful things I had ever experienced. I had screamed, and Nico had startled, fallen off the stool, and afterwards he had accused me of being a drama queen. "There's not even a mark!" he'd said, although that wasn't totally true. Later on a faint purplish bruise had spread across the base of my nail.

But the white-hot pain of it had stayed with me ever since, and now the thought of Conor doing that to Zana deliberately, holding her while she twisted and tried to get away, while her knees gave way with the pain . . .

"What the fuck are you doing?" I yelled, and Conor let go of Zana's hand and turned around on me, and for a moment his cold calm was gone, and his face was full of an anger that made me step back.

"Holding my girlfriend's hand, what are *you* doing?" he snarled.

"You were hurting her." My heart was thudding, and my hand was drawn back, although to do what, I could not have said. I didn't think my punch would do more than irritate Conor.

"She's fine," Conor ground out. "Aren't you?"

But Zana was curled over, cradling her hand, and didn't answer.

"Get back to the villa," he said now, but I moved to stand in between them, and now I found Angel and Santana were there too, side by side with me.

"Leave her alone," Angel said. She said the words very quietly, but each one was spat out like something poisonous. For a long moment Conor stood there, towering over Angel, the muscles in his shoulders standing out like a bull about to charge—and then he smiled.

"I'll be fishing. If you need me, Zana. And remember . . . two coconuts each, ladies. *If* you want to drink."

"Oh, we'll remember," Angel said. Her voice was shaking with rage. Conor turned on his heel with a little wave and walked back to the water villa, presumably to get his fishing spear. Beside me, I heard Santana's shaky exhalation of breath, and I realized that I was trembling, my muscles quivering like someone who's tried to hold a yoga pose too long.

It wasn't just fear of Conor—though that was part of it. It had been fear of what Angel might do, and how Conor might retaliate. We couldn't lose another person. We couldn't. I found I was holding Angel's wrist, as if I could somehow hold her back from going after Conor, and I let go and gave a shaky laugh.

"Wow. Okay. Zana, are you all right?"

"I'm fine," she said, but her voice was wobbling as if she was trying to hold back tears. "He—he isn't normally like that."

"Nor was my last boyfriend," Angel said bitterly. "Until the first time he was. And then the second time. And then every time he drank or his team lost or he had a bad day at work."

"You were in an abusive relationship?" I asked, taken aback. I don't know why I was surprised—except that Angel was so extraordinarily beautiful, it seemed as though she would be untouchable, would have the pick of only the best and kindest men. I knew that was ridiculous, that abusers often went for the trophy girlfriend, and then ground them down. Perhaps half the triumph was in slashing down the tallest poppy. But Angel—she was *so* beautiful.

So very take-no-shit and zero tolerance. Maybe I was just starting to understand why.

"For two years," Angel said matter-of-factly. "It is part of the reason why I left France. He was very convincing, even some of my friends picked him when we split up. He was very good at leaving no marks."

It took me a moment to understand what she was saying, and then I did a full-body shudder in spite of the heat of the day. I remembered the way she had stared down at the mark on Zana's wrist, as if she was seeing a ghost from her own past—and now I understood why.

"He won't stop, you know," she said to Zana in a conversational tone. "It will only get worse."

Zana shook her head.

"It's not like that. *He's* not like that."

Angel said nothing. She only smiled, but not mockingly, or patronizingly. She looked sad, as if she knew exactly where Zana was at—and where she would end up.

"Well . . ." Santana said after a long, awkward pause. "Those coconuts aren't going to get themselves. And I don't know about you, but I'm bloody thirsty. Shall we make a start? Or should we look for Joel first?"

Angel and I exchanged a look over Zana's head, and I knew what we were both thinking: either Joel was hiding of his own accord, in which case, frankly, fuck him for leaving the four of us to deal with Conor alone. Or something had happened to him. Probably at Conor's hands. In which case no search was going to change anything.

"I feel . . ." Angel said, delicately, "that perhaps the coconuts are our priority, non? We are all very thirsty. If Joel is hiding, well, he will return when he is ready. And if he's not . . ."

There was a long pause.

"If he's not, then we can keep an eye out for him while we look for coconuts," I said, trying for brisk optimism, but I wasn't sure I hit the mark.

Zana nodded, and then slowly, Santana did too, but there was a sorrow in her face that made me think that she knew what Angel and I had been trying not to say. Then the four of us stood up and began walking up the beach towards the forest.

CHAPTER 26

WE ALREADY KNEW from our exploration of the island that the majority of the palm trees were close to the villas. Although there were trees and even palms in the wilder, scrubbier part of the island, they were mostly a kind that none of us recognized, without much in the way of fruit. Certainly nothing filled with the water we desperately needed.

The coconut palms were clearly imports—planted when the southern tip of the island was landscaped for the villas, and there weren't that many of them. We had already eaten the windfalls and stripped off the low-hanging fruit. A few days ago, Angel had even picked the unripe nuts from the tree that had crashed into Romi and Joel's villa, though it had felt like a kind of violation, watching her pick her way through the rubble, just yards from where Romi's body had lain.

"What?" she had said when she saw me hanging back. "It is not like we can bring her back." And I had shrugged but seen her point. We hadn't told Joel where his portion had come from.

With all the easy fruit gone, we were left with only two options: throwing or climbing.

Initially, we tried to knock them down. Santana went first, with a startlingly hard, accurate rock that pinged off the coconut she hit and ricocheted into the forest. The coconut wobbled tantalizingly but didn't fall. For the next half hour we all tried different trees and techniques— large rocks, small ones, sticks and pebbles, even shaking the trunk, though that felt risky given you'd be standing right underneath when the coconut fell—and the end result was three green coconuts that sloshed when we shook them, and one slightly riper one that didn't seem to have any water in it. Better than nothing—but not the eight Conor had demanded, to release our water.

We were all beginning to droop with the heat, and as we stood in a clearing, panting and considering our next move, I found my eyes straying to the sliver of beach visible through the forest. There, knee-deep in the azure sea, was Conor, peering intently down at something in the water. Presumably he was fishing, but at the same time I couldn't help noticing that in spite of being the tallest and strongest of any of us, he'd awarded himself the job that involved strolling around in the cool sea, while the four women were standing in the burning sun, staring at coconuts that might as well be on the moon for all we could get to them.

I was still watching him, feeling the dryness of the sand between my toes and thinking longingly of tonight's water ration, when Zana spoke.

"I'm going to climb that one." She pointed at a sloping palm leaning back from the villa, as if stretching towards the sea.

"Are you mad?" Angel said it matter-of-factly. "It is far too high. If you fall, you will be killed."

"They're *all* far too high," Zana pointed out, reasonably. "That's the point; that's why they still have their fruit. And I don't think I'd be killed. Look, there's a lot of bushes and greenery underneath to break my fall."

"Okay, but if you fall, you will break your leg," Angel said with a shrug. "Which is the same thing, as we have no medical assistance and you will be dead from gangrene in ten days."

"We'll *all* be dead in ten days if we don't get more water," Zana retorted.

"Unless it rains," Santana put in, but the silence that greeted her remark showed how likely we all thought that was. We hadn't seen a cloud in the sky since the Valentine's Day storm.

Still though, I thought I knew what was behind Zana's determination to get the coconuts, and it wasn't just our need for more water, pressing though that was. She was desperate, maybe even more desperate than the rest of us, for everyone to meet Conor's target. If we turned up with eight coconuts . . . well, no one had to find out if he was willing to carry through with his threat and leave us without water. We were already operating at the limits of hydration—mouths permanently dry, lips cracked, constant headaches and dizziness. I didn't think it would take much to tip any of us into collapse.

Zana didn't want to find out how far Conor was willing to go. And she was prepared to put her own life at risk to avoid testing him.

"Look..." She had taken off her T-shirt and was standing in her bikini top, holding up the T-shirt, looking up at the tree as if measuring something out. "I saw someone do this on TikTok once. I really think it will work." She was twisting up the T-shirt into a rope as she spoke.

"Zana—" Santana began, but Zana had already stepped up to the tree.

"Lyla, can I borrow your shirt?"

I nodded and pulled it over my head, and Zana laid it carefully on the sandy ground and began to brush off her feet, removing all the sand and debris. When her feet were completely clean, she tied the two ends of the T-shirt rope together, and stepped into the ring she'd made, twisting the material around her soles and ankles.

"I hope this will work." She looked up at the tree anxiously. "The video I saw was using a rope, but this can't be that different, right?"

"Zana, you don't have to do—" I began, but Zana didn't let me finish.

"I do." The set of her shoulders was pure determination. "We have to drink."

"Should we— Should we stand underneath?" Santana said a little helplessly. She looked around at me and Angel as though seeking answers. "Try to catch her?"

"Dieu, non!" Angel said, her voice almost comically horrified, at the same time as Zana said, "No. You might get hit by a coconut. And if I fall, better for me to fall on sand or bushes than on you."

"Zana, wait," I said. "Look, we can get a mattress from the other villa. Just—please, ten minutes."

But Zana shook her head. She stepped forward to the tree, wrapped her arms around it, and gave a great leap, hoisting her legs up towards her waist and using her feet to push the makeshift T-shirt brace against the tree trunk.

For a moment I didn't think it was going to work. I could see her feet slipping, sliding down the smooth trunk, and it looked like it was only going to be a matter of seconds before she couldn't hold on any longer and her arms gave way too. But then, miraculously, the material seemed to catch on the bark. As I watched, Zana dug in her toes, and held her position, braced against the twisted T-shirt rope.

She gave a kind of incredulous laugh, straightened, and hugged the tree farther up the trunk, and then repeated.

It was working. Unbelievably, it was working. Beside me Santana gave a whoop, half-terrified, half full of glee.

"Go Zana!" Angel shouted. And she *was* going, in a series of awkward, almost bunny hops up the trunk of the tree. It was strange and ungainly, but it was as if every jump gave her more confidence that she could do this, that she could reach the top. As she got higher and higher, I found my palms were sweating with moisture I could ill afford to lose, and my heart was thumping. She was past the point where a fall would mean bruises, and well into the height that could mean broken bones or worse.

"You can do it!" Santana yelled, and Zana gave a choking laugh.

"I'm okay! I'm doing it!"

"You're incredible!" I called. She was almost at the top now, reaching out for one of the branches to try to pull herself up the last few feet—but no sooner had she hooked her arm over it, than I realized something. It was browned and desiccated, and I could see it was cracking as she began to put her weight on it.

"Zana!" I shouted. "Don't—"

But it was too late. There was a tearing crack, and the whole branch fell, whistling to the ground where it landed with a crash that sent the birds and bats scattering through the trees. Zana gave a terrified cry and grabbed hold of the trunk. Her feet had slid several feet down the tree, but somehow, miraculously, she'd managed to halt her fall. There was a long, tense silence as she clung there. I could see her arms shaking.

"Zana?" Santana called. "Are you okay?"

"I'm—I'm okay." Her voice was trembling. "I'm fine." She reached up, cautiously this time, and repeated the bunny hop. "I'm okay." Her voice was steadier now. One more hop, and she was back at the canopy again. This time she reached up, testing the branches one by one, before grabbing hold of a green one, and hooking her arm over it. "I'm here. I can just . . ." She was leaning out, precariously, reaching for one of the green coconuts closest to her. She managed to twist it . . . twist it . . . and then it fell with a thump to the sand below.

We all let out slightly hysterical whoops and shrieks.

"Fuck yeah!" Angel shouted. "You are a goddess, Zana!"

Another coconut. We had six now, counting the overripe one. Then another. Seven.

We were all cheering, and Zana was reaching out at full stretch for the last coconut in the bunch when she stopped, staring at something in the distance.

"Zana?" I called up, but she didn't answer, only hung there, frozen, looking over the top of the forest towards the sea and frowning against the sun. "Zana? Are you okay?"

And then, suddenly, she was slithering down, fast enough to take the skin off her palms, yelling something that I couldn't make out.

"What? What are you saying?" Angel cried plaintively. "Please enunciate!"

"It's a ship!" Zana shouted. She almost fell the last six feet, crashing to the sandy ground with her feet still tangled in her torn-up T-shirt. "I saw a ship."

It took a minute for all of us to understand, and then Santana let out a shriek like a steam engine.

"Fuck! The beacon!"

We dropped everything and began running towards the beach, only for Angel to remember halfway that her lighter was up at the cabana. She doubled back, and the rest of us ran on, ripping pages out of a copy of *The Woman in Cabin 10* that Santana had snatched up as we ran past our villa.

We were panting and out of breath by the time we reached the ruins of Ocean Bluff and the beacon we'd made. I saw that Zana's feet were bleeding from her hasty descent down the tree. Santana began stuffing the torn pages into the center of the beacon, her hands shaking.

"Where's Angel?" she yelled, and I looked back down at the beach, shading my eyes against the glare of the sun. No Angel, but Conor was there, still knee-deep in the ocean in front of the water villa, his fishing spear in his hand. He was looking up at us, frowning.

"There's a ship!" I yelled down to him, stabbing my finger towards the misty shape, far out to sea. "There's a ship, help us get the beacon lit!"

He didn't respond, but then I saw Angel appear from the forest, waving a lighter, running through the dunes towards us. She crested the little hill and then dropped to her knees in front of the beacon and began frantically clicking at the lighter.

"Light. Light! Allume-toi, espèce de merde!" she was begging it. And then, suddenly, the lighter flared into life, and she was holding it out to the paperback pages Santana had scattered across the debris. First one caught . . . and then another . . . and then the whole mass was burning, the flames licking at the straw roof that was beginning to sullenly smoke.

We all began waving our arms, shrieking even though it was impossible that the ship would hear us. It was almost at the horizon, and I wasn't even sure if we would have been able to make it out, if Zana hadn't spotted it from her forest perch.

"Come on!" Santana was yelling. "Come on you, fucking piece of shit, turn around. Turn around!"

The bonfire was really smoking now. A great plume of white smoke was rising into the still air. It seemed impossible that the ship wouldn't spot it.

Down below on the beach, Conor was standing, looking out to sea, shading his eyes, but he wasn't dancing and screaming like the four of us on the headland. He was standing stock-still, staring intently at the horizon as if trying to make out what the ship was doing.

"It's turning," Santana said, her voice pleading, breathless. "Is it? It's turning, I really think it's turning."

But as we watched, it became increasingly clear that it wasn't. It wasn't turning. It was continuing along the horizon, until at last it disappeared completely.

PART THREE

THE
RECKONING

CHAPTER 27

"FUCK." IT WAS Santana who kept moaning it. She was on her knees beside the now-roaring beacon, her sunburnt face turned to the sky, and now she screamed it to the endless blue as if to God himself. "*FUUUUUUUUCK!*"

"It didn't turn." Zana was still staring out at the blank horizon as if she couldn't believe it. "It didn't see us."

"Look," I said, trying to hold on to the shreds of the positivity we'd all felt a few moments ago. "Look, this ship didn't see us—but the point is, there *was* a ship. That probably means fishermen are getting out and about after the storm. This might even be a shipping route, for all we know. It's only a matter of time before another ship comes past."

"Yes, but how *much* time?" Santana said desperately, rounding on me. "How much time, Lyla? We'll be dead in a few weeks. If Conor doesn't give me my fucking insulin, I'll be dead in a few *days*. We don't *have* time."

"Santana!" Angel hissed, flicking her eyes at Zana, and I remembered that we had agreed not to talk about this today—agreed not to antagonize Conor by forcing him to admit he'd stolen the insulin.

But the mention of Conor's name had made me realize something. What *about* Conor? Why hadn't he come running up the beach to help us light the bonfire? Why had he just stood there, staring at the horizon? Didn't he *want* to be rescued?

The question nagged at me all the rest of the day, long after we had pulled ourselves out of the slough of despond caused by the ship and forced ourselves to stand side by side with Conor as he grilled fish over the barbecue with the last vestiges of Angel's lighter.

It lasted all through supper, though I didn't have the courage to bring up the question then. It continued as we took our water allowance from Conor, and then watched Zana screwing up her courage to cross the rickety bridge to the water villa, Conor holding her wrist in a grip that no longer looked protective, but simply controlling.

It continued to nag at me as Santana, Angel, and I traipsed up the hill in the growing darkness, and the fact of Joel's absence settled around us like a cloud.

We were sitting around in the fast-darkening villa, the ever-present thirst creeping gradually back, and chewing on the flesh of the green coconuts to try to keep it at bay, when I realized that I couldn't keep it to myself any longer. I had to say something.

I swallowed and cleared my throat.

"Today . . . when we saw the ship . . ."

"Don't remind me." Santana put her head in her hands. "God, that was one of the worst moments of my life."

"Do you think it will come back?" Angel asked. I shrugged.

"I hope so. But listen, that's not what I was going to say. Did either of you think Conor's behavior was . . . odd?"

"Odd?" Angel sat back, picking a piece of coconut out of her teeth. "Psychopathic is the word I would have chosen, personally. Controlling. Highly dangerous. But if you prefer odd . . ."

"I meant about the ship. Why didn't he try to light the beacon? Why didn't he do anything?"

"Huh." Santana crossed her legs, wincing a little as the scab over her wound tugged, and sat up, frowning. "You're right. That *was* odd. He didn't do anything at all. It was almost like . . ."

"Almost like he didn't want it to see us," I finished. "Yeah. That's what I mean. Odd. And worrying."

"But he *must* want to be rescued," Santana said. She looked puzzled. "He may be dangerous, he may even be a killer, but he's not suicidal. He doesn't want to die any more than we do. Isn't that what all of this has been about—making sure he's going to come out on top in all of this? Making sure that *he's* got all the food and water and supplies he needs to survive, and fuck the rest of us? Why go through all of that if he didn't want to be rescued?"

"But why be rescued if you're going to face prosecution for murder," I said. There was a long silence while Santana and Angel grappled with this question. I could almost feel their brains ticking as they weighed up the pros and cons of what I was suggesting.

"What are you saying," Angel said at last. It wasn't really a question. At least, she didn't phrase it as one. There was no upward interrogative tick to her voice, just a flat statement. "Because for sure he wants for him and Zana to be rescued."

"I think he wants him and Zana to be rescued, yes." My stomach twisted, and not just because all I'd had today was Conor's fish and underripe coconut. The brioche had finally become too moldy to be eaten, and we had only a handful of cookies left. "I'm just not sure he wants us to make it as well. It would be a lot more convenient for him—" I stopped. I couldn't say the words aloud, but I didn't have to. Santana said them for me.

"It would be a lot more convenient for him if we all died too. Shit. I think you're right."

There was a long silence. Then Angel spoke, saying words that neither Santana nor I were ready to admit.

"So we must kill him, before he kills us. It has come to that."

"We're not killing anyone," I said automatically. "Right, Santana?" But Santana said nothing. She was looking at the empty fridge, the fridge that had once held her insulin, and hugging her knees.

"Lyla, chérie," Angel said, and now her face was compassionate, "listen to me. Perhaps you have never lived with a man like Conor. But I have. And I know this to be true, if it is him or you, he will choose himself every time. And he has killed before. He killed my boyfriend. He killed him in cold blood, in front of witnesses. And I think we both know that he killed Dan, and probably Joel, no? So how long do you think he would hesitate before killing you and me? He would do it right here in the villa; he would strangle us one after another, and there would be nothing we could do."

"He can't though," I said, more confidently than I felt. "That's the thing. I've been thinking about this, and he's not going to kill us here. He's been careful about that."

"What do you mean?" Santana said, puzzled.

I took a deep breath and I pointed up at the unblinking black eye in the corner of the room—at the camera.

It took Angel and Santana a minute for them to realize what I was pointing at, and a minute longer to realize what I was saying. But then Santana frowned.

"The cameras? But Lyla—they can't possibly still be working. There's no electricity."

"They're battery-powered. And I have no idea where the footage is stored or for how long. Have you?"

"If it's on a central drive there would be no record . . ." Angel said slowly. "Because the Wi-Fi is not working. But if it's stored on the camera itself . . . that, I agree, could be a risk for him. But he could destroy the cameras, Lyla."

I shook my head.

"Can you imagine if someone took down every camera on the island, only to be found as the only person alive two weeks later? It would be practically a smoking gun, no matter what explanation he gave. No. He can't afford to do that. All he can do is make sure that everything that happens—every threat, every suspicious death—they all happen off camera. I'm pretty sure that everyone who's died, it's been either in the forest, or down at the beach. There are no cameras there."

"What about the fight with Bayer?" Angel asked. "That was up at the cabana, and there are two cameras there."

"Yes. One at each end of the main table. But Bayer wasn't killed up there, he was killed on the steps, and there's no coverage there. I'm not saying that was premeditated—" I said quickly, in answer to Angel's skeptical look. "I think it was pure luck. But I think it made Conor realize he had a narrow escape, and he's been careful ever since."

"But our conversations," Santana said. "All of our suspicions about him. The discussion about him stealing my insulin. They'll all be recorded. Okay, it's not murder—but it's bloody incriminating for Conor. It'd be more than enough to throw suspicion on him if we all disappeared."

"Not if the microphones aren't working," I said. Santana looked blank for a moment, and then realization dawned in her eyes.

"Fuck. I'd completely forgotten that whole thing with the sound. They never replaced the cameras, did they?"

"No." I racked my brain, trying to think back to that first day and what Camille had said about the dodgy cameras. "I know mine and Nico's was out. And she definitely mentioned one of the cabana cameras, and at least one other villa."

"Ours was out," Santana said. She looked resigned. "I remember that Camille girl coming round to try to fix it. Fuck." She kicked angrily at the foot of the bed and then swiped at a mosquito whining past her. "Fuck, fuck, *fuck*. Why does everything keep stacking against us? How can he keep having all the luck?"

"He cannot," Angel said. She said it calmly, but there was a grimness to her tone that I didn't like. "Lyla, these broken microphones, they work two ways. Yes, they make it easier for him to kill us. But they will make it also easier for us to kill him."

"We are not killing him," I said through gritted teeth.

"We may not have a choice," Angel said. "Are you prepared to sit there and let Santana die without insulin?"

"That won't happen," I said. "There's three of us and only one of him—"

"Two, counting Zana," Angel broke in, but I plowed on.

"And if it gets to that stage, we will *make* him give us the insulin."

"What do you mean?" It was full dark now, the quick tropical dusk that turned the sky from milky lemon to deep night in just a few minutes, so I couldn't see Santana's face, but her voice was curious. "What do you mean, the missing mics will make it easier for us to kill him?"

I clenched my fists. I didn't like that *will*. Not *would* but *will*.

"Because if he dies, they will have to prove motive," Angel said calmly. "And without the microphones, we will not have one."

"We are not killing him," I said. I lay down on my mattress, pulling the thin sheet up to protect myself from the mosquitoes. "It's not going to come to that. It won't."

But as I lay there, staring into the darkness, a picture came into my head that was not entirely comforting.

It was Conor, standing on the beach, shading his eyes as he looked at the boat with an expression on his face that was not relief.

It was calculation.

And it took me a long time to fall asleep.

CHAPTER 28

"**WHERE IS ZANA?**" Santana was standing, her hands on her hips, facing up to Conor. Her sarong was bunched up around her waist, and from where I was standing I could see the livid red scar where she'd been slashed in the storm. It should have made me feel better in a way, proof of my first aid ingenuity, and of the human body's power to survive and heal itself, but it didn't. The scar was proof of one other thing: how long we had been on this island. Long enough for a cut like that to heal over and scar. And that was increasingly terrifying. How long had it been? Two weeks? Three? All I knew was that I was starting to lose track of time, that things like baths or flushing toilets or hot meals were starting to feel like a distant memory—and that Conor still hadn't given us our water for today. Now he was standing in front of us with empty hands and an infuriatingly calm expression on his face.

"That's none of your business," he said. "She's fine."

"Yes, it's my fucking business!" Santana shouted. "And I don't believe you!"

She tried to push past Conor to the gangway out to the water villa, but Conor held her back easily with one hand, and I made up my mind. We weren't going to get past him, so I would go around.

I pulled off my T-shirt, dropped it onto the sand, and waded quietly into the sea behind Conor's back, breaking into long strokes as soon as the water was halfway up my body.

Conor was so busy arguing with Santana, I was halfway to the water villa before he realized what was happening. I heard the splash as he dived in after me, glanced behind me, and felt my pulse quicken as I saw his dark shape moving through the blinding turquoise water.

"Zana!" I yelled, pushing the wet hair out of my eyes, and I saw a silhouette move in front of the windows of the water villa. "Zana!"

I glanced over my shoulder again. Conor was head down, scything through the water with an easy powerful stroke. I broke out into a crawl, but Conor was faster and more powerful, and as he came up beside me, I felt his hand close on my shoulder, pushing me down into the water.

For a second, I honestly thought he was going to drown me. The sea closed over my head, my nostrils filled with brine, and I thought, this is it. He's going to kill me like he killed Dan, like he probably killed Joel. Only he's going to do it right here in front of everyone. But then, just as I was beginning to thrash with panic, I felt a hand in my hair, and he dragged me up and out of the water.

"Let go of me!" I snarled as soon as my face broke the surface, and I twisted myself out of his grip. Conor laughed, derisively.

"I was saving your life, Lyla. Maybe you shouldn't go out of your depth if you can't swim."

He was panting, treading water, and there was a cut on his eyebrow where I must have caught him as I struck out in panic.

"I can swim fine." I coughed and spat water. "Leave me alone. Where's Zana? Santana and I aren't going anywhere until we know she's okay."

There was a pause, Conor clearly calculating something, and then he seemed to sigh and make up his mind.

"Zana . . ." he called. "Zana, come out. Apparently, Lyla's going to spend all day in the sea unless she sees you."

There was another movement behind the windows of the water villa, and then the pane slid slowly back, and Zana stepped out onto the veranda.

I gasped, so hard I nearly swallowed seawater again, and had to cough and choke.

Zana had a black eye. A very spectacular one that bloomed halfway down the side of her face. Someone had hit her. Very hard.

From the beach, I heard Santana's gasp too, a few moments after mine, as she made out what I'd been able to see immediately.

"Get back here!" she called to me. "Lyla, get back to the beach. Now. And Zana, come here."

But Zana was shaking her head. I stayed, treading water, keeping a wary distance between myself and Conor.

"She's fine," Conor called. "Aren't you, Zana? She just slipped on the jetty last night, hit her face."

But it didn't look like a cut from falling. It looked like a punch, from a man's fist. And from the way she was clutching her dressing gown around herself, I was pretty sure it wasn't the only bruise.

This was the price Zana had paid for siding with us yesterday, for helping us source the coconuts, and for lighting the bonfire.

"Lyla!" Santana barked, furious with anxiety. "Get back here, *now*."

I hesitated. My instinct was to go to Zana, check she was okay, but there wasn't much I could do, treading water mid-ocean with Conor beside me. I certainly couldn't pull myself up onto the jetty. It was too high above the waterline, and I was too weak from dehydration.

"Zana," Santana was calling. "Zana, come over to the mainland. Tell us what happened."

"I told you what happened," Conor's voice was flat, hard, as cold as his extraordinary pale-gray eyes. "She slipped. Didn't you, Zana?"

Zana nodded, tremulously, and then she turned and disappeared into the water villa. I trod water, staring after her for a while, and then, realizing there was nothing more I could do, I turned and swam back to the shore, feeling Conor's eyes boring into my back with every stroke.

SANTANA AND I arrived back at Forest Retreat hot, thirsty and very angry, to find Angel hacking at a green coconut. She looked up as we came into the clearing, and her face fell.

"Where is the water?"

"We didn't get it." I flopped onto the sand beside her. The adrenaline of the encounter with Conor was wearing off, and I felt sick and dizzy. "We didn't get a chance even to discuss it."

I lay back, feeling my pulse pound in my throat, while Santana filled Angel in on what had happened.

As I could have predicted, she exploded, throwing down the coconut and jumping up to pace the clearing.

"And you still tell me we shouldn't kill him?" she demanded to me. I shut my eyes, feeling the saltwater stinging at my corneas. The sight of Zana's bruised, battered face floated in front of my eyes. I didn't know anymore.

"I have maybe two days left of insulin in my pump," Santana said softly. "And whatever I can scrounge from that vial, and after that I'm pretty sure he's going to let me die. You said it yourself, Lyla. He doesn't want us to survive. He can't afford us to go public about what he's done."

"So what do we do?" I sat up, ran my hands through my salt-stiffened hair. It felt like we weren't playing at survival anymore. It felt like this was really it. Him or us. But maybe Conor had known that from the very beginning. "Because I can't kill someone in cold blood, Santa. I can't. Maybe in self-defense, but—"

"This *is* self-defense," Angel broke in angrily. She was over on the far side of the clearing, and her eyes were fierce. She looked like an avenging angel, the kind with a flaming sword. But she had only a piece of bamboo she was slashing at the undergrowth with. Slash. Slash. "It is him or us, Lyla." Slash. "Stop kidding yourself." Slash. "He has been in this to win, from day one. It has just taken the rest of us longer to understand the rules of his game."

"So what are you proposing?" I snapped. "Bludgeon him to death with a piece of bamboo? Drown him, like he did Dan?"

"I don't know," Angel said. She hit bad-temperedly at the under-growth again, and this time there was a sudden commotion in the leaves. Angel jumped back, and we all saw a big brown snake rear up from its nest. For a minute it looked like it was poised to strike, and Angel gave a little shriek. And then it slithered away, into the forest, with shocking speed.

Angel had her hand pressed to her chest. She looked pale, and there was a clammy prickle of sweat on her upper lip.

"Grâce à Dieu. Do you think it was poison?"

"God knows." Santana didn't look afraid, more curious.

"Perhaps that is what we should do," Angel said. She was looking a little better, recovering from the shock of the snake. "Poison him, and pretend it was a snake."

"I'm sorry." I spread my hands, incredulous. "Am I hallucinating here? You are officially off your rocker."

"Poison is a good idea . . ." Santana said thoughtfully, as if I hadn't spoken. "We're not likely to be able to overpower him physically. He was stronger than any of us before this started, and I'm pretty sure he's not been sticking to the rations he's been giving us."

I thought back to Conor's face, close to mine in the sea, and I had to agree. He was sunburnt and mosquito-bitten like the rest of us—but he didn't have that sunken, dehydrated look I was begin-ning to recognize in Angel and Santana, and which I could feel in my own dry and cracking skin and parched lips. But Santana was still speaking.

"We'd have to be careful what we used. It would have to be something organic, something that didn't show up as suspicious on a post-mortem."

"I have sleeping pills," Angel said. She looked like she was considering all the options. "They are still in my washbag. But I don't think I have enough to kill him. I don't know what is the fatal dose. And I am sure they could be detected after death."

I was sitting back, watching and listening, and suddenly I was overcome by a strange feeling of detachment. Maybe it was the surreal tone of the conversation, Angel's matter-of-fact voice as she discussed killing a man like getting a stain out of a favorite top. Maybe it was the dehydration getting the better of me, but the whole situation no longer seemed entirely real.

I felt like I was outside my body, watching the whole scenario— comparing the gaunt, desperate women crouching in a circle on the ground with the fashionable, polished creatures who had first set foot on the island two, three weeks ago. It wasn't just our chapped lips and torn clothes, it was everything. Santana's extensions had begun to fall out, giving her strawberry blonde hair a strange lopsided quality. Angel's acrylic nails had long since broken, and now she had a mix of jagged edges, and one long nail remaining on her little finger. And me . . . what had happened to me? I had never had their beauty, their sheen, but I had been at least neat and healthy. Now there were cuts on my legs that wouldn't heal, blisters where the salt had chapped my skin, my shoulders were raw with sunburn, and I tasted blood every time I licked my lips.

The scientist in me wondered what this was doing to my body. Presumably my skin was cracking because my body was pulling water back from my nonessential organs to safeguard my brain, my heart, my kidneys. But that couldn't last forever. We were operating at a water deficit, I knew that. Every day we lost a little more and drank a little less. Every day our mouths were drier, our urine darker, our lips more ragged.

And every day the scientist in me shrank a little more. I no longer cared about my career. I had barely thought about Professor Bianchi since we got here. I was only one thing now: a survivor. Like Angel. Like Santana.

Like Conor.

"I have an idea," Santana said, her voice dragging me back to the present. We had fallen silent, exhausted by the building heat, even in the dry shade of the clearing, and now I came to with a jerk and opened eyes that were scratchy with salt. "About Conor. I have an idea." She sat up straighter, pushing matted hair back from her face. "The insulin. The vial of insulin. It's poison, if you take too much of it. If a healthy person was injected with that whole bottle . . . I'm pretty sure it would kill them within a few minutes. And . . . I don't know if it would be detectable on a postmortem. Would it?" There was a pause. "Lyla, do you think it would be detectable?"

I started, and realized she was talking to me.

"God, I don't know. I mean . . ." I racked my brains, trying to remember everything I had learned about insulin in molecular biology. It felt like a terrifyingly long time ago. And a world away from where we were now. "You probably know more about this than me, Santana, but from what I can remember, synthetic insulin is biologically identical to human insulin. It's the exact same chemical structure. So it's not like . . ." I tried to think of an example. "It's not like heroin or alcohol, something that would show up on a tox screen. Insulin in the blood . . . it's not going to be remarkable. You're *meant* to have insulin. You're just not meant to have that much."

"So would it be detectable?"

I shook my head.

"I honestly don't know. Maybe, if a really good pathologist had a hunch, and it hadn't broken down too much? I don't know how stable it would be in a dead body." Then I realized what I was saying. What I was doing. I was collaborating in a murder. "But Santana—"

"It is our best chance," Angel said. There was steel in her tone.

"There's just one problem," Santana said in a low voice. "Well, more than one actually. I mean, we'd have to get it into him, and without it being picked up on the cameras." She nodded towards the villa, where the camera still sat, pointing out across the room. "But the big problem as far as I'm concerned is that that's the last of my insulin supply. If Conor's hidden the rest of the insulin—and he's not an idiot, I highly doubt he's left it lying around his villa—and I use up the vial to kill him . . . I'll have days left. Maybe hours."

"We don't *know* he took it," I said. I felt desperate. "What if we're wrong? What if he didn't take it after all? What if we're killing an innocent man?"

"It is true that Joel is missing . . ." Angel sounded thoughtful. "It would be a terrible irony if we killed Conor and then found out that Joel was alive and had had the insulin all along."

"Angel, Lyla, focus," Santana said. She leaned forward, her hands flat on the hot sand. Her face was fierce. "Look at the facts. He killed Bayer. He stole our water. He is beating up Zana. And if Joel is missing, then he's missing with no water on an island with no water supply, so he's dying or dead. None of that is speculation. It's all true. Undeniably true. Conor will kill us if we don't kill him first."

"This is true," Angel said. "I agree. He must be killed." She sounded matter-of-fact. I couldn't believe it had come to this.

"I just—" I began, but Santana stood up. There was something terrible in her face, a kind of anger so deep, I knew that for her at least there was no going back.

"Lyla, listen to me. I am dead in two days if we don't get that insulin. Dead. Do you understand that? It's him or me. So choose. Choose right now. Because you won't get a second chance."

There was a long, long silence.

"I choose you," I said. But all I felt was a terrible foreboding.

CHAPTER 29

FOR THE REST of the day, we searched for coconuts to slake what was fast becoming an unbearable thirst and discussed how to tackle Conor.

It wasn't the injection itself that was the problem—Santana had plenty of spare syringes and she'd explained that she didn't need to find a vein—insulin was delivered by injecting it directly into fatty tissue like the stomach or thigh. That would take only seconds to do, and once it was in, the insulin itself was the fast-acting kind that would take effect within ten minutes.

The problem was how to get close enough to Conor to deliver it.

"We could put sleeping tablets into a coconut," Angel said thoughtfully as we watched Santana trying to copy Zana's coconut-harvesting technique, climbing up the trunk with her sarong wound around her feet. For the second time, barely halfway up the trunk, she lost her grip, landing with a crash in the undergrowth. A single coconut plopped after her, shaken loose by her fall. It was something, at least.

"Are you hurt?" I asked, and she shook her head with a rueful smile.

"Just bruised my arse, which luckily is fairly padded. How did Zana make it look so easy?"

With the one that had just fallen out of the three, we now had three coconuts. Three short of the two-per-person quota Conor had demanded yesterday in exchange for the water, and that was assuming we could hold off drinking them until evening.

"I don't know," I said tiredly. My head was throbbing like a bastard, but I knew that I didn't have it any worse than Angel or Santana. All I could think about was water. I shook the coconut that had just fallen off the tree, listening to the tantalizing sloshing inside.

"I say we grind the pills," Angel said, keeping doggedly to the topic, "and put the powder into the hole at the top. Any residue would be hard to taste, Conor would probably think it was just pieces of shell."

"But isn't it too much of a risk?" Santana demanded. She sat back on her heels and pushed her hair back from her face. Her cheeks were bright red and the skin on her nose and the backs of her shoulders was peeling horribly. "The pills would be detectable at postmortem."

"So we feed him to the sharks," Angel said with a shrug. "Or we claim that he was sleeping badly and I lent him the pills. If it is not sufficient for a lethal dose, it would be hard to prove he didn't take it himself."

I shook my head wearily.

"Zana's never going to go along with that. You know she won't. She knows full well Conor is sleeping fine and certainly isn't going to be accepting drugs from any of us."

"There's three of us," Santana pointed out. "If we club together and say that yes, we saw Conor asking Angel for the pills . . . I mean, that's three against one, right?"

"Yes, but that one is a pretty compelling one, especially if (a) she's his girlfriend, and (b) Conor is *dead*," I said, trying to keep my tone even.

"So what do you propose?" Angel asked. Her voice was acerbic. "You have pointed out many problems, Lyla, but I don't hear many solutions."

I shut my eyes. She was right.

"Okay. Okay, I'm sorry. So what's the plan, then? We give Conor the drugged coconut, then wait until he's asleep and creep into the water villa? What if Zana wakes up?"

"We hope she doesn't?" Santana offered. "I mean, I don't know what the alternative is. We could drug her too, but that would make her really smell a rat."

"Or . . . maybe not?" Angel said. She looked like she was thinking hard. "What if we *all* wake up the next day and say that we feel terrible and could not wake up. It could be some toxin in the food, or the fish, no? And then if Conor is dead . . ." She shrugged.

We were all silent, thinking over her plan. It didn't seem ridiculous.

"What about the camera?" Santana asked at last. "In their villa, I mean. It'll see us break in."

"I've been thinking about that," I said. In fact, I'd been thinking about it since early that morning, since we'd seen Zana hovering at the window of the water villa. "I think Conor may have taken it down."

"How do you know?" Angel asked. I shook my head.

"I don't know for sure, but I stayed there, don't forget. I remember where the camera was, and I'm pretty certain that when Zana opened the window earlier today, the camera wasn't there. And I'm not even sure it was there when I went out a few days ago to look for Dan." I'd been trying to cast my mind back, picture the villa as I'd seen it that night, Conor standing there with the towel around his waist, Zana sitting up in bed, an anxious ghost in the darkness. I couldn't be sure, but I couldn't remember seeing the now-familiar white block on the wall to the left of the bed. And I was almost certain it hadn't been there this morning. It was hard to remember, because my focus had been on Zana, and in keeping my own head above water, but the more I thought about it, the more I thought it hadn't been there. "I think Conor took it down," I said. "Because he didn't want anyone seeing what he was doing out there."

"What he *is* doing," Santana said. Her mouth was twisted, as if the words tasted rotten. "To Zana."

There was a long, long silence.

Then Angel spoke, and this time her voice was hard.

"So. It is agreed, yes? We put half the sleeping pills in a coconut for Conor, and half for Zana. Yes?"

"How many have you got?" Santana asked. "We don't want to kill Zana by accident."

"I have six tablets," Angel said. "I use them only for jetlag, but one is enough for me to sleep like a baby. So three . . . ?" She shrugged.

"And what's the toxic dose?" I said.

"I have literally no idea." Angel's voice was tart. "It is not something I have had any desire to research. But the tablet I have is not the strongest type. My doctor said she would prefer to start me on the lowest dose. So, I imagine three will not be a problem."

"Give Zana two," Santana said. "And give Conor the rest. He's twice her size anyway, and there's a good chance some of it will get left in the coconut."

Angel nodded soberly. I did not. There was an uneasy feeling in my stomach, which had been building all day, ever since Santana's suggestion of using the insulin to kill Conor. Were we really going to do this? Were we really going to poison someone in cold blood, and live with that for the rest of our lives?

"Listen," I said. "I think we owe it to ourselves to try one last time. There has to be a way of resolving this that doesn't involve killing Conor. What if we drug him and use the opportunity to take back the water and search his villa for the insulin?

But Santana was already shaking her head. Angel had crossed her arms.

"And what if he wakes up?" she asked. "What if the insulin is not there? Or what if we successfully kidnap the water—but then he wakes up the next day and beats us to death in order to take it back?

What then? Because, let me remind you, Lyla, he is bigger and stronger than any of us. Bigger, stronger, and more psychotic. And *then*, if you, Lyla, *finally* decide that it is morally okay for us to defend ourselves and kill him—by then it will be too late. The sleeping tablets will be gone—and our last chance also. Conor will not give us two chances. You know it."

I opened my mouth to reply—and then shut it again. The problem was, she was right. I did know it. There was no way Conor would give us two opportunities to overpower him. It was now . . . or never.

But how I wished it could be never.

"So we're decided, yes?" Santana said, looking from me to Angel. "Tonight, Angel will give Conor four tablets, and two to Zana, and then we wait for them to fall asleep. When they're out, I'll creep over to the villa and administer the insulin."

"We are decided," Angel said firmly. "Now, all that is left is to get the coconuts."

CHAPTER 30

IT WAS ALMOST nightfall when we finally made our way down to the cabana, Santana and I carrying two coconuts each, and Angel holding one. We had already punched holes into them, and Angel had spent a long time grinding the pills into a fine powder we hoped would be undetectable and poking it through the small aperture. Angel was holding Conor's. Santana was holding her own and the one meant for Zana.

My heart was thumping in my chest so hard that when I looked down I could see the pink laces on my bikini top trembling with each beat—but I was no longer sure if that was fear of Conor, trepidation at what we were about to do, or just the physical side effects of extreme dehydration. We were all light-headed with it, sick and dizzy with lack of food and water, and Santana's blood-glucose monitor had been going haywire all day, with spiking highs her pump no longer seemed to control, and lows that even glucose tablets didn't seem to affect.

When we came into the cabana clearing the sun was several inches past the water palm, and Conor was already there, resting nonchalantly against the table as if he didn't have a care in the world, holding a jug of water. It was all I could do not to fall on him and tear the container out of his hands, but we stood there, almost shaking with anticipation, while he measured it carefully out into the three cups. He set them on the table, and we gulped the liquid down. The water stung the bloody cracks on my lips and smelled of flat plastic from the container, but nothing had ever tasted so good. When it was gone, it took everything I had to push the cup away and not plead with him for more.

"We brought coconuts," Santana said, her voice hoarse. She picked up the one that Angel had set down in the sand while she drank her water. "Only five I'm afraid, the last one split. But this is for you."

Conor nodded, but he didn't snatch at the coconut the way we had done at the water. Seeing him in the flesh, up close, it was more abundantly clear than ever that he was not holding himself to the same water rations he was giving us. Where Santana and Angel looked dangerously dehydrated, their lips cracked and dry, their skin clinging to their muscles, their veins standing out like cords, Conor looked sunburnt but relatively fresh.

Instead, he took the coconut and wedged it back in the sand, beside the others, then reached into the pockets of his board shorts and pulled out some packets of pretzels, a bag of cookies, and three bananas.

"Pretzels?" Santana said despairingly. "Are you serious? They're full of salt. We can't risk even more dehydration."

Conor shrugged.

"They're all that's left. And the fish weren't cooperating. I spent four hours baking under the sun earlier today, but if you want to try catching some, be my guest." He waved at the dark ocean, its turquoise hue turning deeper as the sun sank below the horizon. For the first time in a long time I saw there were clouds there, turned to flame by the sunset.

Santana shut her eyes. I thought if she'd had the moisture in her body, there would have been tears pricking there.

"Where is Zana?" Angel said, and now I realized something—if Zana wasn't here, we had no way of controlling which of the two drugged coconuts she would end up with.

"She's not feeling well," Conor said. "Headache, from when she fell and banged her face." *Contradict me*, his expression said, *and see how far it gets you.*

I saw Angel open her mouth and I knew, suddenly, that I couldn't let her finish what she was about to say. That if she said what she truly thought of Conor, of what he'd done to Zana, that might be the end of it, the end of *her*.

"Listen," I said hurriedly. "Thank you for the water, Conor. And for all the fish you've caught so far. I appreciate it's not an easy task. And I know— I know today hasn't been easy. For any of us. But we're only going to survive this if we stick together. So . . . cheers."

I picked up a coconut, one of the ones I had been carrying. I recognized the little chip on the lip.

"Here's to cooperation."

Santana looked at me, startled, and then realized what I was doing and why. If we didn't get Conor to drink his coconut now, we would never be sure that Zana wouldn't end up with both of them.

"To cooperation," she echoed, and gave Angel a look that was almost a death glare. For a moment I thought Angel was going to tell us all to fuck ourselves, that she would never raise a toast with Conor, let alone to something as poisonously ironic.

But then, suddenly, something seemed to click, and she nodded.

"Very well. To cooperation," she said stiffly, and reached out and took a coconut. "Conor?"

There was a long pause. Then Conor's mouth split in a wide grin, so close to the smile he'd worn in the headshot on that handout we'd received that first day on the boat, that my stomach twisted. When I had seen that headshot, when I'd met him for the first time, I had thought what a nice smile he had—how open he seemed, how sincere.

But now, that wide, warm smile that didn't reach his extraordinary ice-cold eyes, it seemed the most frightening thing in the world.

"To cooperation," he said. He picked up the two remaining coconuts, the one intended for him, and the one we'd meant for Zana, tucked one under his arm, and tipped the other back. The movement, in the dying light, was so quick that I wasn't sure which one had ended up under his arm. I was 90 percent certain that he had drunk the right one, but I wasn't *sure*, and now I found I was staring, mesmerized, as the muscles in his throat worked, draining the thin, sickly liquid. I saw that Santana was staring with the same intensity, and knew that she was trying to figure out the same thing and probably wishing, like I was, that we had drugged both of them to the same level.

Conor wiped his mouth, set down the coconut, and grinned.

"It's been a pleasure doing business with you. Now, if you'll excuse me, I'd better head back to Zana."

He turned and began walking back towards the jetty, his silhouette dark against the lemon-yellow remnants of the sunset that still stained the sky.

We watched him as he stepped from plank to plank, nimble as a goat.

We watched him as he stepped onto the veranda of the water villa, opened the door, and closed it behind him.

And then we turned and made our way back to Forest Retreat, the bananas and pretzels in our hands, and a feeling of foreboding in our guts.

IT WAS MAYBE an hour later, and we were getting ready for bed, shaking out sheets that were now sweat-soaked and dank, and chasing the last mosquitoes out of the room, when I realized something— I had forgotten to fill up the bucket of seawater for sluicing the toilet.

And Angel was in the bathroom. In fact, she'd been in there for a long time. A *really* long time.

"Angel?" I said. I knocked on the door, and when there was no reply, I tried again. "Angel, are you okay? I forgot to fill up the seawater bucket earlier. Do you want me to do it now?"

There was no answer. Just the sound of the wind outside. It had been picking up all day, and now I could hear it rustling in the trees.

I looked at Santana, who frowned, clearly making the same calculations I had over the length of time Angel had been in there.

"Angel?" she said, coming across to stand by me. "Angel? Can you hear me? Can you say something?"

No reply. I was getting seriously concerned now. Had Angel passed out from dehydration? Hit her head?

"Angel," I said. "Angel, we're coming in. If you don't want us to, say now."

There was still no answer, but I did hear something from behind the door . . . a strange kind of rattle that made my stomach flutter uneasily.

Santana looked at me and nodded, and I set my hand to the knob.

The door was locked, but the latch was flimsy and it took only a shove from my shoulder to displace it. We were inside within a few moments, but it took our eyes longer to adjust to the darkness, which was even deeper than the main room.

When they did, I saw Angel sitting, slumped on the toilet, her head lolling on her chest.

I gave a choking cry, ran across to her and began shaking her by the shoulders. She fell slowly forward, slithering down in my arms to land on the floor. I only just managed to catch her head, stop her hitting it on the hard tiles.

"Angel!" A feeling of panic was rising up to engulf me. I shook her shoulder again, harder this time. "Angel, are you okay?"

Stupid question. Of course she wasn't.

"Oh my God," Santana was gasping. She was standing in the doorway, her hands clasped over her mouth. "Oh my God, Lyla, is she dead? Please tell me she isn't dead."

But when I put my fingers to her neck, I realized she wasn't dead. And more than that, with the next slow, shuddering breath she drew, I realized what the sound was that I'd heard from outside the bathroom. It was a snore.

"She's—she's asleep," I said, looking up at Santana. Her expression changed instantly to one as confused as I felt.

"*Asleep*? Has she passed out?"

"I have no idea. Angel!" I pulled her half-upright and slapped her gently on the cheek. "*Angel.*"

"Laisse-moi tranquille . . ." Angel said, though her voice was slurred so that I could hardly make out the words. "J'suis fatiguée . . ."

When I let go of her shoulders, she slumped back down and curled herself into a ball, clearly intent on going back to sleep.

"What the fuck?" I turned to Santana. "What on earth is going on?"

"I have no idea," Santana said. Then she put her hand to her mouth. "Oh bloody hell, Lyla . . . you don't think . . . you don't think she took the wrong coconut? The one meant for *him*?"

There was a long silence as I processed this suggestion. Angel had been carrying Conor's coconut—she had insisted on it. There was no way she could have drunk that one, it was the one coconut we had all been fixated on, and Angel of all of us was the person in the best position to notice where it ended up. But it was *just* possible that she could have drunk Zana's.

"I don't think she could have taken his," I said at last. "But you were carrying Zana's—and we were all so focused on forcing him to pick up the drugged one, I think maybe . . . maybe she wasn't paying attention when you and I set ours down. Fuck, we should have made sure we each had one of the safe ones, so we could be sure of where they were."

"So does that mean Conor might be wide awake when I go out to the villa?"

"It's possible," I said. I shut my eyes, trying desperately to visualize the moment when Conor had picked up the two coconuts, slipping one under his arm. My fear had been that he'd drunk the less drugged one. But what if it hadn't been drugged at all? "I honestly don't know. I *think* he drank the one he was supposed to, but it was so quick, and the light was so bad—did you see?"

"Not enough to be sure. And we clearly fucked up one, didn't we? So it's fifty-fifty we screwed the pooch entirely."

"Shit." My voice sounded tremulous. "So what do we do?"

"We have to go ahead with the plan, surely?" Santana said. "I mean—we don't have any more sleeping pills, so it's now or never. And if even *one* of them is asleep, it's better than the alternative."

I nodded slowly. I knew she was right. But I also knew that she could no longer do this alone.

"You're right. We should go tonight."

"We? I thought the plan was for me to go alone."

"Not anymore. I'm coming with you."

"Lyla, darling, I know you didn't want to do this. And what about Angel?"

"I'm *coming*," I said, with more firmness than I really felt. "Angel will be fine. But if Conor's not drugged, there's a good chance he'll wake up, and I'm not sending you out there alone to deal with that possibility. No, we both go, or neither of us."

There was a long silence. Then Santana nodded.

"Okay. So how do we handle this? What do we do with her?" She jerked her head at Angel, still snoring on the floor. "Is it safe to leave her? Should we try to make her throw up?"

I considered the question and then shook my head.

"I think it's too risky. The pills are already in her system, so chances are they've already been mostly absorbed. And in the state she's in, there's a good chance she'd choke on her own vomit if we tried to stick something down her throat."

"But can we just leave her?" Santana said doubtfully. "Is it safe?"

"We pull our sheets into the bathroom," I said. "We tuck her up to try to make sure she's lying in the recovery position, doesn't choke on her own vomit or anything. And then we climb out through there." I nodded at the bathroom window. "In a way, this is a good alibi. If anyone checks the cameras, all they'll see is us heading into the bathroom to check on Angel, and then spending the night in there to keep an eye on her. We can say she was sick or something. It fits with the dodgy fish story."

"But won't the cameras see us climbing out of the bathroom window?" Santana asked. "That'll look worse than just walking out the door, won't it?"

I shook my head.

"There's no cameras in the bathroom, Camille told me. And if we skirt around the back of the villa, the bedroom camera won't catch us going past the window. If we stick to our story—that we both spent the night nursing Angel in the bathroom—I can't see how anyone can disprove that."

"*If* Conor's asleep," Santana said. "And if he disabled the camera in the water villa. That's a lot of ifs."

I nodded soberly. It *was* a lot of ifs. But there was nothing we could do about most of them except hope.

Working quickly now, we stripped the beds and dragged the sheets into the bathroom, where we tucked them around Angel, trying to wedge her on her side so that if she threw up while we were out, she wouldn't suffocate. As we worked, I kept trying to talk myself down from my fear that we'd come back and find her dead. A double dose for someone young and healthy—it surely couldn't be that big of a deal. Medicines with such a narrow gap between the toxic and therapeutic dose were rare for obvious reasons. But Zana, on the other

hand . . . the speed at which Angel had passed out had rattled my confidence in our calculations, and if Zana had drunk the coconut meant
for Conor, then a quadruple dose, for someone of her body weight . . .

I swallowed, my throat dry. Our actions suddenly felt grossly
irresponsible, and I tried not to imagine what would happen if we
went out to the villa and found her lying dead beside Conor.

When Angel was as safe as we could make her, I bent down and
shook her shoulder.

"Angel," I whispered. "Angel, we're going out. Try—" I stopped. I'd
been going to say, *try not to fall asleep*, but she was already snoring.
"Try to stay safe," I said instead. "Okay?"

"Shh . . ." Angel said. Her voice was slurred and she shrugged her
shoulder, trying to shake off my hand. "Je dors."

I sighed. At least she was still able to talk. That seemed like a
good sign. I just had to hope she wouldn't slip any deeper.

"Come on," Santana said. "I think we should get going. If Conor
is drugged, then we don't know how long it'll last. And the sooner we
get this over, the sooner we can get back to Angel."

I nodded, and we climbed out of the bathroom window and made
our way into the forest.

CHAPTER 31

THE WIND WAS picking up as we made our way through the trees and down to the beach, and as we walked slowly along the pebbled path, the undergrowth whipping back and forth in the breeze, I had a sharp flashback to the night of the storm, the night I had run out to the radio shack to try to call for help. If only someone had picked up then. If only I had caught the boat before it went out of radio range. How different everything might have been.

Santana was holding the syringe full of insulin clenched in her fist. She had filled it to the brim before we left, sucking up every drop of what was left in the vial.

"Do you think it'll still work?" I asked, watching her tap the syringe gently, pressing out the air. "I mean, the vial was open. It's been in the sea."

Santana just shook her head.

"I don't know. I just know we have no other option."

Now, I watched her as we walked, side by side through the swaying trees. She looked like a different woman to the one who had come here just a few weeks ago. Her beautiful hair was matted and ragged where her extensions had been pulled out. Her skin was burnt and peeling, and she had lost more weight than seemed possible in the short time we'd been here—although I suspected most of it was water. Even her face was different, her cheekbones sharper, her eye sockets deeper, her lips cracked—but most of all, it was her expression that was changed. Gone was the lazy, drawling amusement of the girl I had met. Now, all I could see was a grim determination to survive at all costs.

"You okay?" she asked as we rounded the corner of the path and came out onto the beach. She looked at me curiously. "Are you having second thoughts?"

I shook my head. These weren't second thoughts, they were first thoughts. I had never wanted this plan, had never wanted it to come to this. But I'd accepted that it was Santana's right to do this, and if it was Santana or Conor, I was going to choose to protect Santana every time.

"No, no second thoughts," I said. "You have to do this. I understand. I just wish . . ."

I trailed off. Santana nodded. She didn't need to finish my sentence. We both knew what I was thinking. I wished it hadn't come to this. I wished that radio call had gone through. I wished we'd never come to this island, any of us.

And yet, if we hadn't . . .

Maybe this was how it was meant to be. Maybe this was the only way it could have ended.

We had reached the jetty now, and I watched as Santana set one foot gingerly onto the planking.

"Christ, this is rickety," she whispered, and I realized that she'd never been out to the water villa since that first day. I'd gone out a couple of times, and Angel at least once, but Santana, never.

"Are you going to be okay?" I asked. The thought was turning uneasily in my mind—what if Santana couldn't make it across? What if I ended up having to administer the insulin? Could I do it? Could I kill someone in cold blood?

But Santana only nodded grimly, and stepped onto the next board.

The waves were lapping against the jetty, not as fiercely as the night of the storm, but with an energy that was closer to it than anything we'd experienced since, and when I set my own foot onto the walkway, I felt the same trepidation I'd seen in Santana's face. The planks were as unstable as they had been the day I went out to confront Conor, and now they were wet with salt spray as well, the waves just licking up to splash the planks with spume.

Ahead of me I could see Santana edging from plank to plank, almost crouching against the wind, trying to keep her center of gravity low, and I followed her example, bending my knees and shading my eyes against the spray. The one advantage to this weather was that if Conor wasn't drugged, it would make it harder for him to hear us coming. Our footsteps on the jetty and the sound of the door sliding open would be drowned under the splash of the waves.

When I finally set foot on the veranda, I realized that my teeth were clenched with concentration, and I had to make a conscious effort to breathe and shake out the tension that was locking my shoulders and jaw. Santana caught my eyes and pointed at the door, then did a little thumbs-up, her expression interrogative. The meaning was clear—ready?

I nodded, took a deep breath, and then we walked together towards the Ever After Villa.

Through the big glass window, I could just about make out Zana sprawled on the bed, and beside her Conor, apparently dead to the world. Which one of them was drugged, if either, was impossible to tell. There was a coconut propped in the corner of the room, but there was no way of knowing if it was empty or full, or even the one that Santana had given Conor.

Up against the far side of the room I could see the stacks and stacks of water bottles—and beside it the crushed empties. It was hard to make out in the darkness, but the number of empty containers looked much higher than I thought it should have. We were down to less than one bottle a day, if everyone stuck to their rations, but the number missing looked much higher than that.

On the other side was the food, a much smaller pile, mostly boxes and tins.

And in the corner . . . I looked automatically up at the place where the camera should have been and let out a shuddering breath.

In the corner there was no camera. Conor had taken it down. Which meant . . . it meant that we were really going to do this.

Santana was holding the syringe, so as my hands were free, it made sense for me to be the one to open the big double doors—and they weren't locked. They squeaked a little as I pulled them aside, the runners crunching with sand, but neither Conor nor Zana stirred as we stepped across the threshold, holding our breaths.

Inside, the sound of the waves was muffled, and we could hear only Conor's gentle snores, and a muffled whimper from Zana as though she was having a bad dream. Silently, I moved to Conor's head, not touching him, but ready to try to hold him down if he woke and struck back at Santana. If the person who woke was Zana . . . well, we didn't really have a plan for that. We'd have to cross that bridge if we came to it.

Gently, very gently, Santana pulled back the sheet, exposing Conor's long tanned thigh, dappled with blond hair. I remembered her saying that you were supposed to inject insulin into fatty tissue— and Conor's thigh looked more like a slab of pure muscle. But then, he'd been as lean and hard as they came two weeks ago, and all of us had lost weight since. There wasn't an ounce of fat on him anywhere. His thigh would have to do.

She took a deep breath, holding the syringe up, and I could see that her hand was shaking. It occurred to me that although this was routine for her in a way it wasn't for most people, it was still probably the first time she'd ever done it to someone else.

We had talked about it in the bathroom before we left. In and out, as fast as you can—like administering an EpiPen. Stab it in, press, and run.

"Ready?" she mouthed, and I nodded. "Three." She was staring intently down at Conor's thigh, her lips moving soundlessly. "Two."

On *one*, she stabbed the syringe into his thigh.

What happened next was too fast for me to see, too fast for me to react, too fast to make out whether Santana had had time to press the piston.

I heard Conor let out a great bellow, like a wounded boar, and saw him rear up from the bed. Before I could move, let alone restrain him, he struck Santana full across the face, sending her flying backwards onto the tiled floor, where her head hit with a sickening sound. Still, she got up, blood pouring out of a wound on her temple, and began staggering for the door, but Conor was faster. He scrambled off the bed, on all fours like an animal, and grabbed her around one ankle. She went down, slipping on her own blood, and he hit her again, punching her in the back so that she crashed to the floor with a moan of pain. As she lay there, unconscious, he laced his hand into her hair, lifted up her head, and then with a calculated violence, he smacked it deliberately into the floor.

Santana lay still.

For the first couple of seconds, I had been too frozen with surprise to move. But with that last, horrible *smack*, my limbs seemed to unlock and I launched myself across the room to grab Conor from behind, my arm around his throat.

It was a stupid move. I should have gone for his eyes, or his balls. But I'd never studied self-defense and I suppose I was mimicking what I'd seen in the movies. Conor, on the other hand, was a fighter, a trained one, and my attempt at holding him back didn't give him more than a few seconds' pause. Reaching back over his shoulder, he grabbed hold of my hair and then flipped me, bodily, over his shoulder to crash to the floor, half-in and half-out of the water villa.

For a moment I couldn't move, I couldn't even breathe. I was so badly shocked and winded it was all I could do to lie there, choking, trying to catch my breath as Conor hauled himself to his feet, kicked Santana in the head, and pulled the syringe out of his thigh. He gave a snarl of fury, then began staggering towards me.

I couldn't seem to inhale. I couldn't get any air into my lungs, but somehow, with a huge effort, I rolled over onto my stomach, pulled myself to face the sea, and began dragging myself across the veranda, away from the villa. I'm not sure what I was trying to do, or where I was going. There was no way I could have managed to cross the jetty to the mainland on my hands and knees. I only knew that Conor was going to kill me, kill us both, and I had to get away—even if that meant drowning, I had to get away.

"San—" I managed, my voice strange and strangled. "Santa . . . you . . ."

Are you okay, was what I was trying to ask. I was too winded to complete the sentence, but even just a whimper from her would have told me whether she was alive, whether it was worth my while trying to get her out, or whether I could only save myself now.

"Santa—" I tried again.

But before I could get any more words out, I felt Conor's hand close on my leg.

Desperately, I dug my fingers into the edge of the veranda, trying to pull myself away from him, haul myself to standing, but it was hopeless. I hadn't even got a knee under myself when he flipped me over and straddled me, one arm crushing my windpipe.

"You little cunt," he snarled. He was holding the syringe in his free hand, brandishing it close to my face. "What is this? What have you bitches done to me?"

I couldn't answer. I could only gasp helplessly. His weight was immense, unbearable. It felt like my ribs might crack, my heart was hammering helplessly, hopelessly, desperately trying to get oxygen to my brain, but Conor's thighs were squeezing all the breath out of lungs, and his forearm was pinning the arteries in my throat so that even if I had been able to breathe, no blood would have been able to make it past.

I could feel my limbs going numb as my body fought to survive, fought to pull back every atom of oxygen to the only thing that mattered—my brain. My vision was splintering into shards of light and dark.

"San—" I tried again. "Sa—"

Was she alive? Or had she already bled out on the villa floor, her body as limp as mine was fast becoming?

Because I was dying. I knew that, with absolute certainty. My thrashing limbs were barely twitching now. My vision was a mist of firework fragments and blurred darkness.

And then, through the scattered motes of blackness, I saw it, over Conor's shoulder. The dark shape of someone staggering towards him. It was a woman, her arms raised, with something in them. It took me a moment to make out what it was—a water bottle—a big five-liter water bottle, that she was brandishing like a weapon.

"Sa . . ." I managed, and it came out like a death rattle, like the last gasp of someone with nothing else to give.

But it was only as she swung the bottle down towards us that I realized who was holding it. It wasn't Santana. It was Zana.

CHAPTER 32

THE HEAVY WATER bottle met the side of Conor's head with a crack that sent his skull jerking to one side, and then, before he could do more than turn towards her, his face blank with shock, Zana hit him again, this time swinging the heavy bottle into his gut.

He tumbled backwards, and before I had fully processed what had happened, there was an almighty splash, water spraying up and over the jetty. Conor had fallen into the water.

Desperately, doggedly, I tried to force my limbs to work, tried to drag some air back into my lungs, tried to make myself turn and get to my knees and stagger towards the water. Because one thing I was sure of, if Conor made it out of the water, we were dead. We were all dead.

But I couldn't. I couldn't seem to do more than roll onto my side, holding my ribs and gasping against the tearing pain in my bruised throat.

Through blurred tears, I could see Zana standing on the edge of the jetty. She had her eyes closed and she looked like she was praying. Her lips were moving, but I couldn't make out what she was saying.

And then she jumped.

God knows what it cost her. I had seen her trembling in fear enough times as we simply sat at the edge of the veranda. I remembered her words, that first day. *I always think there might be something down there, waiting. In the darkness. Waiting to . . . grab me.*

To force herself into that black, choppy water, with Conor thrashing and gasping . . . that took a kind of courage I knew I didn't have. But Zana did it.

There was a splash, and I saw her swimming through the waves towards Conor. For a moment I honestly didn't know what she was going to do. Was she trying to save him? To drag him back to the jetty? It was only when she reached him, when she stretched out her arms towards him, that I knew.

She put both hands on the top of his skull and pushed his head underwater.

She was trying to drown him.

But it was clear it wasn't going to be that simple.

Conor, in the darkness, was fighting back. I couldn't make out much, but I could hear Zana's sobbing, panting breaths, see Conor's limbs thrashing the surface. Once, he broke the waves and let out a great shout of fury, and Zana pushed him back down with a cry that was half anger and half a kind of desperate, tearing grief.

They were fighting, and it was increasingly clear they were fighting to the death.

I had dragged myself to kneeling now, and I was trying to figure out what to do. Inside the villa was Santana, lying in a pool of her own blood, possibly hanging between life and death, for all I knew.

But in front of me was Zana, fighting for her life with a man who would certainly kill her if he got the upper hand. A man she was trying to kill to save us. But I wasn't sure if I could help her, physically. My breath was still rattling in my throat. My legs would barely let me crawl. I wasn't sure if I could walk, let alone swim. But I had to try.

Slowly, painfully, I dragged myself to the edge of the jetty and then, knowing I was possibly doing something very stupid, I lowered myself into the water and began trying to swim to where Zana was still wrestling with Conor. He had stopped breaking the surface now. He was still fighting. I could see Zana struggling, her head going under the waves, as he pulled her down, and then resurfacing with a gasp. They seemed to be getting farther and farther away. Was Conor trying to swim away from Zana?

I wasn't sure. But either way, he was losing strength. Whether it was the blow to the head or the insulin starting to take effect, I couldn't tell. But Zana was winning.

There was just one problem, and I realized it when I looked back over my shoulder to the villa, now surprisingly far back.

They were being pulled out to sea. They were in the rip. And if I swam any farther, I would be too.

"Zana," I yelled, but my voice was so hoarse that it came out as barely a croaky whisper, and she didn't hear me. "Zana, let him go."

She was being pulled out, away from the shore, and I would never catch up with her unless I swam into the current too.

I'm not a religious person; I never have been. But if I had been, I would have prayed in that moment.

Instead, I took a deep breath, and gave myself up to the rip.

At first it was strangely calming. The sea in the rip current was noticeably less choppy, the waves more subdued, and I could see why people swam for them, as Joel had said, mistaking them for calmer waters.

It was only when I glanced over my shoulder at the shore and saw how terrifyingly far it was that I began to panic. If we got pulled out beyond the reef, where the sharks were, where the waves battered onto the coral, pulverizing everything it carried into a bloody mess, all bets would be off. "Zana!" I called again, when I was closer, and this time my voice was stronger. Zana's head turned, and I saw her surprise turn to shock as she registered two things—me, and the distance we'd come from the shore. "Zana, we're in the rip. You have to swim sideways. Along the shoreline."

I pointed with a shaking arm, and saw Zana nod. I was feeling increasingly exhausted, and now I began to wonder what I had done, whether there was any way out of this, for either of us.

Conor was no longer fighting, he was drifting, a dark shape in the waves, and for a moment I saw Zana close her eyes, gather him to her, and I thought for a second she was going to try to drag him back to the beach. But then she let go and began to strike out sideways, along the shore.

WE SWAM. WE swam and we swam, until my arms ached and my breath tore in my bruised throat. And finally, we were out of the rip-tide and drifting in the ocean, but terrifyingly, incomprehensibly far out, with waves that were far larger than I had ever swum in.

Zana trod water for a few minutes, watching me, then called out, "Are you okay?" Her face was white, and I saw the way she kept glancing down at the dark waters beneath us, but she was holding up. Better than I was, if I was being honest.

"I think so," I yelled back, but it wasn't true. I wasn't okay at all. I had no choice though. I had to do this. There was no other option.

Together, we turned our faces to the shore and began to strike out for the beach.

It was about halfway when I knew I wouldn't make it. I was just too tired, my limbs too bruised, my lungs too exhausted. I had fought for my life once already today, and I couldn't do it again. I had to keep swimming. I had to keep swimming. But the prickles were back in my arms and legs, the creeping numbness I had felt when Conor had strangled me, and once again my vision was breaking up into shards of light and dark.

I thought about calling out, but Zana was far ahead of me now, forging through the water with a stroke that made this look almost easy. I didn't blame her for going on ahead—with her fear of the sea, I knew how badly she must want to be out of the water, safely back on dry land. But I knew she was too far off now. She'd never hear me, not with the waves breaking on the shore, and my bruised, broken voice.

When the first wave closed over my head, I fought back. I struggled to the surface, gasping and choking. But when the second wave claimed me, I knew it was all over. I knew that this was how it ended. I knew I was going to die.

CHAPTER 33

WHEN I OPENED my eyes, I was on a beach. Our beach. The white sand was soft and warm under my head, and in the sky I could see the first pink rays of dawn beginning to break.

I rolled over and coughed up what felt like a gallon of seawater, but was probably no more than a teaspoon, mixed with phlegm. My lungs felt raw and scoured, my throat hurt every time I coughed from where Conor had strangled me. But I had never felt more alive.

"Lyla?" I heard, breathlessly, from behind me, and as I tried to turn my head, I saw Zana leaning over me, her face anxious. "Lyla, thank God. No, don't try to sit up—"

But it was too late. I was pulling myself upright, my head thumping with every movement.

"Where's Santana?" I managed. "Is she okay?"

"She's alive. Angel's with her up at the cabana—and she's got her insulin. She's pretty banged up, but she's talking and lucid. I think she's going to be okay. We were more worried about you, to be honest. You were out for a long time."

"I'm okay," I said, but my throat was so mangled the words came out almost comically hoarse and croaky, and Zana gave a little tremulous laugh. Then she began to cry, and I felt my own tears rise up in sympathy, in spite of the pain each sob was giving me. A few minutes later we were holding each other, my face in Zana's hair.

"You were so brave," I was saying. "Did you come back for me?"

"Of course," she sobbed. "Of course I did. Fuck, you saved me, Lyla. If you hadn't swum out when you did—"

She stopped, but I shook my head. I hadn't saved her. She had saved herself. She had saved all of us.

"DO. NOT. MOVE." It was Angel's voice, peremptory as always, addressing Santana, who had made the mistake of reaching out for the water bottle. "I am telling you, your head is basically held together by that bandage at the moment." She waved her hand at the strip of bloodied sarong tied around Santana's head. "If you want something, you ask me and I get. Okay?"

"Okay," Santana said meekly, and she subsided back onto her pillow as Angel carefully measured out a cup of water from the big bottle.

Somehow, I still had no idea how, Angel and Zana had managed to guide a dazed, bleeding Santana across from the water villa before I woke, and now all four of us were camped out up at the cabana, our mattresses under the shade of the palm umbrellas, trying to work out what to do.

Out of the four of us, Santana looked unquestionably the worst. My throat still felt like I was swallowing razor blades, and I could feel the bruises coming up under the skin, where Conor had tried to strangle me. But Santana looked like a survivor of the Texas Chainsaw Massacre, blood streaking her matted red-blond hair, and a giant purple swelling on the side of her head where Conor had struck her.

But it was Zana who looked the most shell-shocked.

After the first burst of energy—getting me out of the water, rescuing Santana from the water villa, dragging us both up the beach to rest at the cabana—she had sunk into herself, and now she sat, hugging her knees to her chest and staring fixedly out to sea with eyes that were both watchful but strangely unseeing. I didn't know what she was looking for—a boat, maybe? Or something else. Conor's shape—cutting through the still choppy waves with his powerful crawl. And I didn't know whether she was hoping, or fearing, for that outcome.

Angel, however, had woken up fully recharged and ready to fight someone, and she was fussing around us like a mother hen, as if somehow her innate bossiness could make everything okay for us all. It was strangely relaxing to have someone telling us what to do. Well, someone who wasn't Conor. The memory of him shouting out orders gave me a cold feeling, and I shivered in spite of the heat of the sun.

Now, she topped up my water glass alongside Santana's.

"Drink it!" she said, and I obeyed, thinking, not for the first time since we had made it back to the safety of dry land, that I would never take fresh water for granted ever again. It was the most delicious thing I had ever tasted. Santana had her eyes closed as if she wanted to savor every ounce of sensation. Only Zana was sipping hers as if she really wasn't thirsty, though I knew she must be. When the cup was empty, she set it down in the sand and then got up.

"I'm going to see if I can find any fruit," she said. "We're really low on food."

"Shall I come and help you?" Angel asked, but Zana shook her head.

"No, I'm okay. I'd rather you stayed here with Lyla and Santa."

The meaning was clear—to look after us, to make sure neither of us did anything stupid, though I didn't really think we would. But I thought the truth behind Zana's words was different. She wanted to be alone.

We waited until she was out of sight in the trees and then Angel
let out a long sigh.

"I am worried for her. She looks like a zombie."

"I mean . . . she's been through a lot," Santana said, reasonably.
"The poor girl—" She stopped and lowered her voice, though I was
fairly sure Zana was too far away to hear and wouldn't have cared if
she could. "The poor girl killed her boyfriend, for God's sake. That's a
fuck of a lot to process."

"Her *abusive murderous* boyfriend," Angel put in. "Let us not forget."

"Still though," I said. "I agree with Santa. How do you cope with
something like that? The fact that he was an abusive piece of shit
doesn't change the weight of what happened."

"Maybe the opposite," Santana said quietly. She touched the swollen side of her face as if remembering how it had felt when Conor hit
her. "I mean . . . think about how controlling he was. Think about
living with that, day in, day out, and suddenly . . . he's gone. I think a
hole that size . . . that would be hard to come to terms with."

"Legally though," Angel insisted. "Legally it changes things.
Legally what she did was self-defense."

But her words were greeted with silence, and Santana and I
exchanged an uneasy look.

It was something none of us had really spoken about—in part
because we hadn't wanted to talk about it in front of Zana. But the
question of what would happen when we were rescued, *if* we were rescued, had started to weigh heavily on my mind, and I knew I couldn't
be the only one. How would we explain Conor's death? And Bayer's,
and Dan's? And then there was Joel, whom Angel had found hanging
from a palm tree halfway up the coast, a bed sheet tied around his
throat. How to explain the dizzying, terrifying sequence of events
without implicating all of us? Because the truth was, it hadn't been

self-defense. Not really. Zana had been defending me. And I wasn't sure where the law stood on that. Not least because I had no idea what legal jurisdiction we were in.

"Well, I hear you, Angel, but we have to get rescued before any of that is even a consideration," Santana said at last, and Angel nodded.

"I keep thinking about the radio," she said. "About the battery. Surely there is a way to charge it?"

She was looking at Santana, who in turn looked at me, and I held my hands up.

"Don't look at me. I'm a virologist. I know fuck all about electricity. That's physics. Or maybe chemistry. Either way, it's about as far from what I studied as English Lit."

"I know I asked this before," Santana said a little helplessly, "but is there *any* mileage in trying to warm it up? Do you think that works with car batteries?"

"Have you been in that hut lately?" I asked. "It's hotter than the seventh circle of hell when the sun is beating down on that tin roof, so no, short of actually combusting the battery, I don't think we could make it any hotter."

"*Could* we combust it?" Santana asked. She sounded almost as if she were pleading. "I mean, we're fucked now, so is it worth a try? We could make a fire in the sand and then when it dies down, we could bury the battery in the hot sand and see if we could get a tiny bit more charge out of it before it melts."

"Maybe," I said doubtfully. "I mean, you're right, it could be worth a try. But is this even the same kind of battery? I don't know if car batteries work the same way as normal AA ones."

"C'est une batterie au plomb," Angel said, frowning to herself, and then realized that she had slipped into French and translated for us. "What is the English word—a lead battery. They are filled with acid. The charge comes from the reaction between the lead and the acid, so I imagine if you heated the acid, it could be possible to encourage a little bit more reactivity. . . . It would depend why it has stopped working. If the lead is covered in sulphate . . ." She trailed off.

"If the point is the reaction between the acid and the lead . . ." I said slowly, "is there any way we could get more acid into the battery?"

"It is supposed to be sulfuric acid," Angel said. She pronounced it like a French word—*suul-four-eek*, with the stress on the last syllable. "Fin, a mix of sulfuric acid and water. I am not sure where we could find something equivalent on the island."

"Angel," Santana said, "how do you *know* this? Sorry, but you've suddenly turned into Bill Nye the Science Guy, and it's a bit disconcerting."

"I do not know this Bill, but my father owned a garage," Angel said. She looked down at her formerly pristine acrylic nails, now snapped to stumps, and sighed. "When I was a little girl, I would help him in the repair shop at weekends. I was obsessed with cars—it was my father's pride and joy that I could change a tire faster than any of the men he employed."

I had a sharp flashback to Angel at the meet and greet, telling us that she had wanted to be a Formula One racing driver when she grew up—and how we had all laughed at the incongruous image. Now I understood—and I saw the little girl staring out of Angel's tear-filled eyes. I reached out and held her hand.

"I'm sure you still are his pride and joy, Angel."

She shook her head, smiling too, though the tears still glistened on the edges of her lashes.

"Non. My father loved me very much, but he is dead. And I have forgotten almost everything he taught me. But I do remember a little about batteries. And lead batteries, they are not sophisticated. They are designed to make a chemical reaction, then you reverse the reaction with electricity, and repeat. It is not rocket science."

"Well, look," I said. "You clearly know more about this than any of us. And if there's anything Santa and I can do to help you, just say it. But I think this is on you, Angel. You're our best chance."

"Dieu," Angel said. It had been supposed to be a compliment to cheer her up, but it was plain she hadn't taken it like that. In fact, her face was more somber than ever. "What a terrible thought."

CHAPTER 34

THAT NIGHT WE slept up at Forest Retreat, Zana taking the mattress Joel had dragged across, Santana on the bed. She had become feverish over the course of the day, and now Zana and I lay, listening worriedly to her ragged breathing, and her voice muttering words we couldn't fully make out.

Only Angel wasn't here. She had spent all afternoon over at the staff quarters, hunting in the wreckage of the cabins and the broken-up desalination plant for something, anything she could use to repair the battery, and she had gone back there after supper to eke out the last of the daylight.

"I am not a nurse," she had said privately to me, taking one look at Santana's flushed face and glazed eyes. "But this I can do."

She came back after dark had fallen, her clothes smelling of chemicals, and her shoulders bowed in a way that told me that she hadn't achieved what she set out to do. When I saw her fumble with the door handle, I got up and opened it for her, putting my finger to my lips to signal that Santana was asleep. But it was me who broke the silence when I saw the burns on Angel's hands.

"Fuck, Angel, what happened?"

Angel shrugged.

"The acid was still reactive."

"You opened up the battery?"

"I tried. It is difficult without tools. I will need to try again in daylight."

From across the room Santana called out, stirring restlessly in her sleep, and we both stilled. When she was calm again, Angel whispered, "She is no better?"

Zana shook her head.

"We've been trying to get ibuprofen into her, but she threw up the pills. She's very hot."

Angel swore in French, words I didn't understand but which sounded filthy even in another language, and then sank to her mattress, her head in her hands.

"Fuck, will it never end? Will we never get a break?"

I swallowed against the pain in my throat. I wanted to tell her everything would be okay. But we both knew that was a lie.

Instead, I watched as she lowered her head wearily to the pillow and closed her eyes. She looked exhausted, and the faint snores a few minutes later backed that up.

I should have been equally tired, if not more so. Out of all of us, Angel was the only one who'd had any sleep last night, while I'd spent the intervening hours fighting for my life, first half-strangled, then half-drowned. But I couldn't seem to let go. I lay there, listening to Angel's gentle snores and Santana's shallow, feverish breaths, and then I realized something—only Zana was as quiet and watchful as me. When I raised myself on my elbow to look across at her, I could see her lying there, curled on one side, staring into the darkness. And as I watched, I saw a single tear roll down her cheek, to soak into the mattress.

I opened my mouth to say something—*Are you okay? Is there anything I can do?*—and then I closed it again. There was nothing I could do. Nothing I could say.

As quietly as I could, I let myself down onto the mattress, and then turned, trying to make it seem as if I was simply tossing in my sleep. Then I closed my eyes and waited for the real thing to come.

WHEN I WOKE the next morning, there was dawn light streaming through the windows and I saw that Santana and Zana were still out cold, but Angel was awake and up. She had wound a sarong around her hips, twisted her hair into a top knot, and was hunting for her shoes.

I stood up, pulled on the shirt I'd been wearing last night, and whispered, "Can I help?"

Angel looked across at Santana and Zana and shrugged, raising both eyebrows. I knew what she was asking. Was I needed here?

As silently as I could, I tiptoed to the side of the big double bed and touched Santana's cheek with the backs of my knuckles. Her skin felt cool, after the damp heat of last night, and the hectic flush had gone from her cheekbones.

"I think she's okay," I mouthed to Angel, who shrugged again, but this time in an indefinably different way that clearly meant, *okay, you do you.* She rubbed the last dregs of sun cream into her shoulders, and we set out into the forest.

Somehow, I don't know why, the staff area always felt like the hottest part of the island, maybe because the trees were fewer and more widely spaced, or maybe because the concrete soaked up the heat of the day in a way that the forest floor didn't. By the time we broke out of the trees into the staff clearing, both Angel and I were sweating, in spite of the breeze coming off the sea.

I could smell the battery acid even before we had crossed the clearing, and when we got to the shade of the radio hut, I could see what Angel had spent all day yesterday doing—hacking through the thick outer skin of the cell with a mixture of nails, screwdrivers, and a broken kitchen knife. She had managed to get a corner of the top cover almost free, like a partly open sardine tin, and you could just make out the liquid gleam of the acid inside. You could also see where quite a lot of it had spilled out onto the concrete—and presumably onto Angel herself.

"It was not easy," Angel said unnecessarily, and I nodded. The fumes were overpowering, and every time I breathed in, they caught in my bruised throat, making me want to cough.

"Should we take it outside?" I asked. "I can't imagine it's very safe to breathe."

Angel nodded, and together, carefully, we dragged the battery out of the hut and into the shade of a tree, where Angel began attacking it again with a nail and a makeshift hammer, trying to widen the aperture she'd already made. But her burned hands made her clumsy, and after a few minutes she missed her mark and hit the battery casing, making the acid inside slosh. A few drops sprayed up and landed on her fingers and she winced, sucking in her breath as it stung her raw skin.

"Christ, Angel, stop," I said, realizing what was happening. "Let me."

"I am fine," Angel said through gritted teeth.

"Clearly you're not. Your hands are already in shreds. Seriously, let me do this part. What are you trying to do?"

"I'm trying to create a hole large enough so I can attack the lead inside," Angel explained. She showed me the holes she'd already punched along the top of the battery, like perforations in a sheet of stamps. "I am trying to join these. I was using the knife, but it broke. I think if we can get it to there"—she pointed about halfway along the perforations—"we can peel back the metal, you see?"

I nodded.

"And then when it is open, I will try to scrape the sulfate from the lead. If we can expose enough fresh lead, perhaps we can create a little more charge."

"Okay." I took the nail and the screwdriver she was using as a hammer and began to try to join up the dots.

It was more difficult than it looked, and I began quickly to see why Angel's hands were so ragged. First, without a proper hammer it was extremely difficult to hit the nail hard enough without jolting drops of acid everywhere. Second, if you missed, the ragged edge of metal was apt to skin your fingers. Soon my hands were as red and swollen as Angel's, in spite of rinsing them with seawater, and my mouth was dry and bitter-tasting from inhaling the chemical fumes.

But at last, after what felt like hours of hammering, the jagged cut extended halfway down the side, and I was able to push the screwdriver under the flap of metal and force it back, exposing a good third of the interior of the battery and the lead sheet inside.

"Angel!" I called. She had gone down to the shore, by the wrecked desalination plant, and was soaking her sore hands in the water and gazing out to sea. "Angel, what's next?"

She turned, shading her eyes against the sun, and then her expression changed, and she got hastily to her feet and came running across the clearing.

"Wow! You have it open!"

"Is it enough?"

"Yes, it's enough." She took back the screwdriver and peered into the inner workings of the battery, looking at the pleats and folds of metal inside. "God, I hope this works." She wiped her brow, and for the first time I saw how exhausted she looked. Of all of us, Angel had always seemed the least defeated by the island, her defiant beauty and regal bearing surviving sunburn, thirst, and despair better than any of us. But now, even her veneer was beginning to crack, the desperation beneath clearly showing through.

I crouched beside her and watched as she began painstakingly scraping at the metal folds inside the battery. It was fiddly work, the lead packed so tight it was hard to get to parts of it without deforming the sheets. The whole point, I realized, was to create as much surface area as possible for the lead to attack, and so crushing the sheets together would be counterproductive. But Angel worked at it deftly and patiently, scraping and scratching until the lead showed shiny through the dulled surface, and then moving onto the next patch.

After a while I realized there wasn't much I could do to help, so I went back to the villa to check on Santana and Zana. When I arrived, I found Santana still lying on the big bed, Zana crouched beside her, trying to make her drink.

"How is she?" I asked, and Zana's head came up, her expression changing from surprise to resignation in a moment.

"I don't know. I can't get her to properly wake up. Santana." She slapped Santana's cheek gently. "Santana, honey, come on. You need to wake up. You need to drink something."

Santana's eyes opened for a moment and she slurred something, but then her lids drifted back shut. I looked at Zana, whose expression was close to despair.

"Fuck. What do we do?" she asked. "Do you think it's a concussion?"

"I have no idea." I squatted beside Santana and touched her forehead, which was no longer hot, but cold and clammy. The bright, feverish flush had left her cheeks, and she looked pale and bloodless. I picked up her hand. Her fingers were like ice. "I don't think so. I don't think a concussion would give you chills like this." Then I saw the blood sugar monitor on her arm and my heart sank. "Wait, it could be her blood sugar. She barely ate yesterday."

"Of course." Zana bit her lip. "You're right. God, I don't know why I didn't think of that. What do we do?"

"I have no idea. We should try to take a reading. Where's her . . . her reader thing?" I was hunting in the bed, and then I found it—the little digital box I had seen her checking every few hours during the day. The number on the display didn't mean much to me—I had no idea whether 2.1 was good or bad—but there was no mistaking the little graph at the bottom of the screen. The small digital line had been steadily dropping for the last few hours, until now it was right at the bottom of the chart.

"Fuck. She's low. I think she might be really, really low. You're supposed to give hypoglycemic people sugary drinks; juice or Coke, something like that. But we don't have anything like that."

"Is there any tinned fruit salad left? That has juice."

I shook my head.

"I don't think so." Then something occurred to me. "She has glucose tablets. I saw her taking them once when she went low. Where would they be?"

I began rummaging through Santana's belongings, but Zana had gone pale.

"Do they look like sweets? A bit like big versions of those Pez things little kids have?"

I nodded.

"Oh God, I'm so sorry. Conor took them. They're out at the water villa."

"I'll go," I said, but Zana shook her head.

"No. I have to go. I know where he put everything." She looked sick.

"Zana, I'll go. Just tell me where they are."

"No, I have to do this." Her face was white, but her expression was set. "Do you understand? I sat by and let him do this. I let him starve you all and take away your water and put Santana's life in danger. It's my fault she's in this situation. I *have* to make it right."

I took a deep breath, ready to argue, to snap that Zana had been as trapped as the rest of us by Conor's actions—and then realized there was no point. Because at the end of the day, it didn't really matter what I thought. What mattered was what Zana felt. And she felt she had to do this.

"Okay. I understand," I said at last. "Go. But . . . be quick."

Zana nodded.

"I will."

And then she disappeared.

I don't know how long it took. I only know that it felt like the longest time of my life, sitting there holding Santana's icy hand, listening to her shallow, fluttering breathing and wondering if each breath might be the last. I was beginning to despair, to wonder if something had gone wrong, when I heard the sound of feet running on sand, far away but coming closer. The person was running, and I could hear the crack of branches as they swiped them impatiently aside. I gently let Santana's hand go and stood up.

But it wasn't Zana who appeared in the clearing, face scarlet and chest heaving. It was Angel.

"Lyla," she gasped. She bent double, hands on her knees, trying to catch her breath. "Lyla, I got a signal. I have spoke to someone. There—" She broke off, her breath catching in her throat, making her retch silently into the dirt. "There is a boat."

CHAPTER 35

"**WHAT DID YOU** say?"

The voice came from the other side of the clearing, and we both turned to see Zana standing there, a tube of glucose tablets in one hand, a pack of cookies in the other, her face white and shocked.

"Zana," Angel said, her face splitting with a huge grin. "Zana, there is a *boat*. I made contact with a boat. We are going to be rescued!"

"Oh my God," Zana said. She moved to the veranda and then sat on one of the cane chairs as if her legs wouldn't hold her. "Oh my God. Did you really? Is this real?"

"Yes, it is real. We were cut off when the battery died again, but they knew where we were. They knew the island. They were too far away to come themselves; they are just a small boat and did not have enough fuel to get to us and get back, but they will radio for help. We are going to be rescued!"

She grabbed me and began dancing me around the clearing. I let her pull me around, but I felt strangely numb. Zana, still sitting silent on the wicker chair, looked similarly stunned.

Then she seemed to shake herself back to reality and stood up.

"Santana."

"Shit." I pulled myself away from Angel. "Angel, I'm sorry—it's Santa. She's not well. We were trying to get some glucose into her."

We both followed Zana inside the villa, where Santana was still lying on the bed, her face waxen now. Zana sat down next to her and began gently shaking her shoulders. "Santana. Santana, come on, wake up. You need to eat this." She held the tablet to Santana's lips, but Santana didn't do anything, just lolled in her arms, her eyes moving uneasily under her closed lids.

"Crush it," I said anxiously. "Crush the tablet against her teeth, rub it into her gums, maybe it'll dissolve in her mouth."

Zana broke off some fragments and tried to push them between Santana's lips, but Santana only moved her head away.

"Santa," Angel barked, making us all jump. Santana's eyes opened briefly and she focused on Angel momentarily and licked automatically at the chalky-white fragments on her lips. "Santana, don't fall asleep. Do you hear me?" She moved across, pushing Zana and me out of the way, shoved the rest of the tablet between Santana's teeth and then held a cup of water to her lips. "Drink this, okay?"

Santana took a sluggish sip, and I heard the slow crunch as she chewed the rest of the glucose tablet and then swallowed.

"Give her another," I said. I had been reading the packet Zana had left on the bed, and now I held out another tablet. "She needs at least three, maybe more."

"Don't like them . . ." Santana said thickly. "Taste . . . chalk . . ."

"Santana, you *will* eat this," Angel said fiercely. "I do not want to hear any of this bullshit. You *will* eat this tablet." She had been crushing the tablet I'd passed her between her fingers, and now she forced the shards between Santana's lips. "And you *will* swallow this water." She held the cup to Santana's lips again, and Santana made a face but swallowed obediently like a little child. Her eyes were fully open now, a little glazed, but focused. "And another," Angel said sternly. This time Santana nodded and took the tablet from Angel's fingers, chewing it. She swallowed and sank back on the pillows, but this time her eyes didn't slide shut. I felt the panic dammed up inside me begin to seep away, leaving my knees weak and trembling.

"Jesus." I thought my legs might give way, and sat heavily on the end of the bed. "Santana, don't *do* that, do you hear me? I really thought—"

"It's not exactly by choice," Santana said, a little croakily. Some color had returned to her cheeks, and she managed a smile. "But yeah . . . I should have noticed I was going low. Silly of me not to eat anything last night."

She picked up the glucose monitor I'd left next to her pillow and looked at the screen, and then made a face.

"Yikes. God, that was really low. Shit."

"Is it climbing?" I asked. Santana nodded.

"Yes. Give me the rest of the glucose tablets. I might need more."

I handed them over and Santana took another swig of the water, and a fourth tablet, then picked up the glucose blood strips from the bedside table.

"Did you hear the news?" Angel demanded as Santana stabbed her finger with a lancet. With the panic over, her eyes were shining again. Santana shook her head, puzzled, and Angel smiled like the cat that got the cream. "The trick with the battery worked. I made contact with a boat. They spoke English. We are going to be rescued."

There was a long, disbelieving silence. Then Santana's face broke into a huge grin.

"Are you kidding me? We're going to be rescued? We're really going to be rescued?"

"Don't speak too soon," I said warningly. I don't know why, but it felt like tempting fate to be too sure, after everything that had happened. "They've got to find another ship, locate the island . . . I mean, don't get me wrong, but I won't believe it until we actually see the rescue boat for ourselves."

"Did they say how long they would be?" Santana asked. Angel shook her head.

"No. They said they were at least three hours away from their home port. So I suppose it depends on if they manage to radio ahead."

"And even if they do," I said, thinking slowly, "that boat will have to travel at least three hours back to where you radioed them, probably, and then locate us from there. We're probably looking at at least . . . what . . . four hours? Five? Maybe more."

"Five hours," Santana said. She spoke as if she was savoring the words. "Five hours. We have only five hours left on this fucking island."

But then Zana spoke, and her voice was like the sound of a stone dropped into a well; hollow, chilly, bleak.

"So I have five hours left."

"What do you mean?" Angel looked at Zana, and then across at me, puzzled. "Five hours left of what?"

"Five hours left of freedom. I mean, I killed him. I killed my boyfriend. There's no way around that."

There was a long silence. Then Santana spoke.

"Zana, as far as we're concerned . . ." She swallowed and looked at me and Angel, seeking backup.

"As far as we're concerned," I said, "it was an accident. Conor fell into the sea during high winds. We all tried to save him. You and I got swept out to sea and barely made it back alive. Right?"

I turned to Santana and Angel, and they both nodded vigorously.

"Absolutely!" Angel said. "That is what happened."

But Zana was shaking her head. There were tears in her eyes.

"There are bodies all over this island. Not to mention the massive concussion on the side of Santana's head. How do we explain all that? How do we talk about what happened—about the water and the hoarding and Santana's insulin—without them figuring it out? It's all on camera, for God's sake!" She waved her hand at the unblinking black eye in the corner of the room. "What, you went out to confront Conor in the one place that doesn't have CCTV and he just *happened* to fall in the sea and drown while I stood there and watched? They're never going to believe that in a million years, not even if we all swore it on the Bible and our mothers' lives."

"But doesn't that make our case for us?" Santana said. "If we explain what he was like—"

"If I tell them what he was like, I'll be signing my own confession," Zana said bitterly. "You think some Thai or Indonesian court is going to care whether he hit me? Or that he put spyware on my phone? Or that he cut up my credit cards and made me resign from my job and burned me with spent matches? What I did, it's still murder!"

We all flinched. Santana looked stricken. Angel looked murderous.

"Look . . ." I said slowly. "Zana's right. The problem is that we have a motive to want to harm Conor—not just Zana, we all do. To the point where no one will believe us if we say that we didn't, even if we back each other up. So that's what we have to fix. We have to make it so that Conor is a person no one would want to hurt."

"What do you mean?" Zana said. She looked puzzled.

"We have to create a record of our time here, something that explains everything that happened—Bayer's death, Dan's, Joel's disappearance, all of it—but doesn't pin it on Conor. Something that explains about the food and the water, but makes it sound like we all agreed. Something that turns him into a man no one would want to kill. And we've probably only got six hours to do it in." I looked up at the sky. The sun was already above the palm trees. "Does anyone have paper? And a pen?"

"I do," Santana said. She pointed at the front pocket of her suitcase, and I rummaged inside and came out with a lined notebook, and a pencil. I handed them to Zana.

"I think you need to do this, Zana. Yours is the account people are most likely to believe. What day was the storm again?"

There was silence while everyone tried to remember.

"I think it was the fourteenth," Zana said at last. "Didn't someone mention Valentine's Day?"

"Yes, it was," Santana said. "I remember Dan making a joke out of it. But I can't remember what day of the week, if that's what you meant."

"It was a Wednesday," Zana said. "I got my period. I remember thinking it was a day out, that I must be stressed."

"Okay, then let's start the day after the storm," I said slowly. "Dear Diary, today is Thursday, fifteenth of February. Something like that."

"But why?" Zana asked helplessly. "Why would I do this? We're stuck on a bloody desert island, for God's sake. Am I really going to start keeping a diary? What would've been the point when we thought we were all going to die?"

"To keep track of time?" Santana suggested.

"For mental health," Angel said, a little sarcastically.

"Maybe that's the point," I said in a low voice. "Maybe the fact that we all thought we were going to die is the point—you're writing this to leave a record of what happened. In case we didn't make it off the island alive."

Zana nodded at that. Her face was somber.

"Okay. Yes, you're right, I could imagine doing that. All of it, but particularly the last one, but maybe I shouldn't say that yet. I mean, we were still hoping to be rescued at that point. Okay . . . so . . ." She began to write, slowly, reading the words out as she did. "'Today is Thursday, fifteenth February, and I have decided to write a diary— my head is so full of everything that's happened since the storm last night, and I needed some way to make sense of it all.' Is that okay?" She looked up at the rest of us and we nodded.

"What else happened that day?" Santana asked. "I don't remember much from those first couple of days, just how much my leg hurt, and how scared I was of dying." She put her hand to the scar on her thigh, as if reliving those first few days of pain and confusion.

"We buried Romi," I said. "That first day— That was the day we buried Romi. And the producer."

Zana rubbed her eyes.

"God, of course." Her voice cracked. "I can't believe I didn't remember that. It seems like a lifetime ago."

It did. It was only a fortnight, but it seemed like something that had happened on another planet, to a distant set of people only slightly related to us, and much more innocent.

"'We are all reeling,'" Zana said aloud, writing the words as she did. "'From the storm, which seems to have blown our boat off course, but also from the terrible shock of poor Romi's death—she was killed when a palm tree came down on her villa, crushing it to bits.'"

"You should put something in about Joel," I said slowly. "About how upset he was. But you should make it sound like Conor was the one who took care of him. The camera up at Joel and Romi's villa was destroyed, so there's no evidence who dug her out. You should make it Conor. Set it up so he's starting to be a hero from the beginning."

Zana nodded and carried on, writing slowly, pausing sometimes to consider a word, and then she got to the end of the first page, where she stopped, as if stumped.

"I should put something to finish up the day," she said, looking up. "Some kind of conclusion. I'm just not sure what."

"It should be something positive," Angel said. "Something that makes it sound like we were all united."

Even though the cracks had already started to show, I thought, though I didn't say the words aloud. I knew we were all thinking it.

"You should say how many of us were left," Santana said softly. "And that we were injured."

"You should say that we were looking after each other," Angel said.

"'Eight of us,'" Zana said, as she wrote. "'Just eight. And two injured.'" She looked up, and then swallowed, and I saw there were tears in her eyes. "'It feels more vital than ever that we take care of each other until the boat gets back for us. . . . We just have to stay strong.'"

I'm not sure what day it is anymore. 27th? 28th? I've lost count, I don't care. Because the worst thing in the world has happened, and now I'm not even sure if I want to be rescued anymore.

Conor is gone.

It happened so fast. It was late, and we were out at the water villa. Santana was there, and Lyla. Angel wasn't well and they'd come over to ask whether I had any painkillers left.

In the end they decided they had to leave, and they got up to make their way back to Angel, check she was okay.

The wind had picked up over the course of the evening and when they got to the jetty, Santana hesitated.

"Is this thing safe?" she asked, and I could see why. The waves were buffeting it in a way that made the planks shudder and creak. Conor shrugged. It was as safe as he could make it, but nothing on this island is safe—the deaths of our friends have proven that.

"I don't know," he said. "Do you want to wait until it calms down?"

But Santana shook her head.

"We need to get back to Angel, make sure she's okay."

Conor and I nodded, and they began walking across the jetty.

They were only about halfway across when something happened. I still don't know what—maybe a plank tilted, or maybe a wave hit them when they weren't expecting it, but suddenly Santana's feet went out from under her and she fell, hitting her head hard against one of the posts.

She grabbed at Lyla as she fell, more by instinct, I think, than deliberately, and the two of them went over—and were in the water before Conor or I could react.

For a second I wasn't sure what to do. They're both strong swimmers, and they weren't far from the veranda. I knelt by the edge, holding out my arms to try to pull them to safety, but then I saw the blood in the water, and I realized what had happened—Santana must have cracked her head when she fell, and was barely conscious. Lyla was struggling to hold her up in the water, struggling against the pull of the current, which kept trying to suck them out to sea with every wave. And before I could protest, Conor dived into the water.

He got to Santana fast and managed to tow her out of the pull of the current and get her to me, and somehow—I still don't know how—I dragged her up onto the veranda. But then he went back for Lyla—and I saw that they were both in the pull of the riptide.

Beside me, Santana was choking out seawater. She was conscious at least. But Lyla was struggling. She was far out to sea, and Conor was going after her. I saw them swimming, swimming—and then, and I still don't know what happened—Conor was gone.

Was it a shark? Baz told us ages ago that they couldn't get inside the reef, but I don't know if that's true. He was wrong about so much, poor Baz. All I know is that one minute Conor was there, cutting through the water towards Lyla with his powerful crawl, and the next minute he was gone. And Lyla was still being pulled out to sea.

It was probably the worst moment of my life. Conor was gone, Santana was choking on the deck—perhaps dying, for all I knew—and Lyla was being swept out to sea. I didn't know if I could save her. I didn't know what to do. I wanted to fall on my knees and cry out to God, ask him why he kept punishing us like this.

I couldn't save Conor. I couldn't even tell where he had gone under anymore.

But I saved Lyla. I saved Lyla, and Santana lived. And Angel woke up today and she's okay. But oh God, Conor is gone. Conor—my rock, my love, my life—he is gone. He is gone. Perhaps if I keep saying it, I can make it feel real.

Conor is gone, and I don't know how I can carry on.

CHAPTER 36

ZANA WAS CRYING when she finished the final diary entry. She closed the notebook, and I wondered if she was going to let us see what she'd written.

I would have understood. What we were asking her to do—mine her own fears and feelings to save us all—it was a lot for anyone. But we had to know what she had said, we had to be able to back up her story if we were questioned on it.

I opened my mouth to say something—ask if she was okay, perhaps—but before I could speak, she shoved the book towards me, across the floor of the villa, and then stood and walked outside, her back to the door, facing the forest as if she couldn't look at us while we read it.

I picked it up, glanced at Angel and Santana, and then began to read.

Bayer's death . . . our growing thirst and desperation . . . Dan's drowning . . . the water rationing . . . Joel's disappearance . . . and then finally Conor's own death. Seeing them all laid out like that, one after the other, was a visceral reminder of all we'd been through. But there was a strange distortion to it, reading them through the lens of what Zana was trying to do. It was like picking up the wrong glasses—everything was familiar, but wrong. The perspective was wonky, the distances false. Everything she wrote about had happened . . . but not quite as she had explained. In her version, Bayer had had some kind of fit. Dan's death was an accidental drowning. Joel had committed suicide, survivor's guilt, with no reference to what he'd done. Somehow, Zana had shifted the narrative to one where Conor was the hero, the person keeping it all together.

It was the last entry that had the greatest ring of honesty to it—in spite of it being the most false. But perhaps that was because the lies were stitched together with painful truths. Zana's love for Conor, her grief, her guilt . . . all of that was real.

Conor is gone, and I don't know how I can carry on.

I could hear the truth in those words, and the agony too.

When I had finished, I found there were tears in my eyes, and I pushed the book to Santana, wiping my eyes with my sleeve and swallowing hard.

Santana read it silently through, and then handed it to Angel, who read it in turn, and then nodded.

"Yes," she said. There was a catch in her voice as if she too were fighting tears. "Yes. That is good." She cleared her throat. "It was hard to read. It must have been hard—hard to write."

"She's bloody clever," Santana said. "I mean . . . it's all there, isn't it. If the cameras turn out to be working, it's all explained. The water rationing, Dan standing up to Conor—there's an explanation for everything. It's just . . ."

"Twisted," I finished. "Yeah."

And it was. Twisted into a narrative where Conor was the hero, not the villain. A hero who had sacrificed his life for the rest of us.

We were all sitting around, contemplating what Zana had written, when suddenly we heard her voice through the trees. It sounded a long way off, but it was coming closer, her words jerky, as if she was running.

"What did she say?" Angel said plaintively, and I shut my eyes, the better to listen.

". . . here!" I heard. And then, much louder. "It's here! The boat is here!"

I opened my eyes. In front of me, Angel was grinning like she'd just won the lottery, and Santana let out a whoop and punched the sky.

"It's here." Zana burst through the trees, into the clearing. She stood there, her hands on her hips, and for a moment I saw her, really saw her, as the sailors would have; her salt-matted hair, the sheen of dust and dirt, the scars on her arms and legs, the bruises and the black eye, and the way her skin cleaved to her sinews, every vein standing out of her water-starved muscles. She looked . . . wild. Emaciated. Like a survivor. But then she smiled, and her grin was as wide as Angel's. "The boat. It's here. We're saved. We're going home."

CHAPTER 37

HOW TO DESCRIBE the long, slow boat ride back to reality? How to describe the first shower, better yet the first *bath*, the sheer, unimaginable luxury of being able not just to drink as much as we wanted, but to immerse ourselves in water, wallow in it, drench ourselves in it. To feel it running over our skin—pure, clean water. I never wanted to get out.

How to describe the first meal that wasn't forest-scavenged fruit, or moldy pastries. How to describe crisp mouth-melting fries, and ice cream, and Coca-Cola, with the ice cubes chinking and the perspiration dripping gently from the glass.

There were other things too, that none of us knew how to describe. The news that the *Over Easy* was gone, lost at sea in the storm. They didn't tell us at once, perhaps they didn't know, I'm not certain. But after a few days a man from the British Embassy in Jakarta came to our hotel and told us gently that there was very little hope, that the *Over Easy* had likely foundered in the storm. The marine transponder, the ship's equivalent of a black box, had cut out in the middle of the deep ocean, and there was no wreckage to be seen. We might never know for sure what had happened.

And then there was the first sobbed phone call with my parents, over a crackling long-distance line. And the first Zoom call with Nico's mother, dry-eyed and racked with a pain she hadn't fully begun to process.

What could I say? What could I do to make her loss bearable? There was nothing.

They had offered us a room each, when we were released from hospital and our paperwork and passports were sorted out—but it was Santana who had said she didn't want to be alone, and when I heard the words, I realized they were true for me too. After so long spent sleeping, eating, fighting to survive together, I didn't want to be shut in a room by myself—but I wasn't yet ready to face the outside world. Not until some of the scars had healed.

So we had ended up with a family apartment, two bedrooms, linked by a little sitting room. Santana and Angel in one, Zana and I in the other. In the air-conditioned cool of the evenings we came together in the little communal area in the middle to eat the miraculous room service food, and drink all the water we wanted, and we talked. We talked and we talked, as we somehow hadn't been able to on the island.

I told them about Nico, about the growing rift between us, and the fact that I wasn't sure we would have survived the experience of Ever After Island, even without the storm. I told them how I lay awake at night, wondering if Nico knew that, wondering if his last thought before he died was of me, and whether I loved him.

Angel told us about her childhood, her father who had died when she was just seventeen, and how much she missed him. About her Parisian mother, who told her every time she saw her that she had gained weight, and that no man would want her if she let herself go. And about her abusive ex, and how long it had taken for her to find the strength to leave him, to come to London—where she had met Bayer, and where, for a while, everything had seemed good. "Perhaps I will go back to Paris," she said with a shrug that verged on hopelessness. "I do not know."

Santana talked about Dan, mostly. About their time together at school, funny anecdotes about how he cheeked the teachers, and the time he dressed up in women's clothes and asked for a tour of the school for his supposed son, Anthony. It was the art teacher who had taken him around, a man in his seventies who had taught at the school since the 1980s, back when it was all boys, and who kept peering at Dan shortsightedly through his bifocals, murmuring, "I'm sure I know you, my dear. Did I teach your father?"

And Zana . . . Zana talked about Conor. About how he had reached out to her on Instagram when she was just seventeen, and they had messaged back and forth, flirting, joking, and finally met up in a bar in London on her nineteenth birthday. She'd taken friends—she wasn't an idiot—but she didn't talk to any of them all night, just sat there, enraptured by Conor, dazzled by him like there was no one else there. She told us how wonderful it had been at first, and how bad it had become later. She told us how scared she had been, towards the end, of what Conor had done—might still do.

"It's my fault," she choked out, her hand over her face. "All of this. If I hadn't agreed to come, if I hadn't let him do everything he did—"

"It is not," Angel said, and there was nothing but compassion in her voice. "It is not your fault, chérie. I promise you. And how could you have known, how far he would go? We have all known a man like him. Sometimes it is all you can do to survive."

But as Santana nodded sadly I realized . . . it wasn't true. Not really. Not for me, at any rate. The only man I had known like Conor was Conor himself. Nico and I might not have been the perfect couple, but he had been sweet and funny and gentle, and had loved me with nothing but respect and kindness.

But Angel, and Zana, and Santana—they had all known a man like Conor. Some of them had known several.

And as I thought about that, something else floated up from the back of my mind, something that had been scratching there for a long time, perhaps ever since that first day on the boat, when I had met Joel, and he had told me about his job.

"I've been thinking. . . ." I said now, a little tentatively. Santana looked up from where she was rubbing Zana's back. Zana wiped her eyes, and I swallowed, and began again. "Ever since we got back from the island, I've been thinking about this whole thing. The whole *One Perfect Couple* setup. There was something Joel said . . . it puzzled me at the time. About seeing the handout and trying to get his job correct. And then Dan mentioned it too. Do you remember?" I looked at Santana. "He said something about looking Conor's videos up, back when you got the information pack. Did you know what he was referring to?"

Santana nodded.

"Yes, that kind of dossier thing. We got it about three or four weeks before we left."

"Yes, but *we* didn't," I said. "Nico and me. We didn't get one. We only signed up a couple of weeks before we set sail."

For a moment all three of the others looked puzzled, and then Angel's face cleared.

"Of course! I had completely forgotten. You were not in it. It was another couple . . . what was it . . . he had a stupid name. Hunting, or something."

"Hunter," Santana said. "Hunter and Lucy. I'd never heard of him, but I actually know her slightly. She's a friend of my cousin, and I when I realized they weren't on the boat, I texted her to find out what happened."

"And what *did* happen?" I asked.

"Apparently her boyfriend pulled out when he got the dossier. He had a massive problem with one of the other contestants. Lucy didn't say which one."

"I know which one," Zana said in a low voice. She looked at me. "It was Conor, right?"

I nodded.

"I think so. Did you know Hunter, Zana?"

Zana shook her head.

"No, but Conor did. He saw his name in the dossier, and I got the impression he was looking forward to seeing him. In fact, he was the first person he asked about when we got to the boat. He asked Camille whether Hunter was here yet. When Camille said Hunter and Lucy had dropped out, Conor laughed. He said something about it, something like, *Hunter always was a pussy.*"

"I do not see the point of this," Angel said, but not dismissively. She sounded puzzled. "You have lost my thread."

"Think about it," I said softly. I was answering Angel, but I was looking at Zana. "Think about what all the couples have in common. Everyone except me and Nico. Really think."

Angel looked surprised.

"Chérie, we have nothing in common. Isn't that the point? We are all so very different. Models. Actors. Fitness coaches. Teachers. Scientists. The whole idea was to have a diverse cast."

"No." I shook my head. "Everyone had one thing in common. At least, one person in each couple did. You all had some kind of history with Conor."

Santana frowned, and I pressed on.

"Santana, you were at school with his ex-girlfriend, the one who killed herself. You could speak to his past as an abuser. Romi was a victim of his YouTube channel, all his followers descending on her to call her a body-shamer or problematic, or whatever it was. Hunter— well, I don't know what happened there, but clearly there was something. Maybe Conor had screwed up someone he loved."

"And what about me?" Angel said. She sounded skeptical. "I had never met the guy."

"No, but you did have personal experience of being in an abusive relationship. Is there any way Baz could have known about that?"

"I mean . . . I have tweeted about it," Angel said with a shrug. "I did a thread about relationship red flags that went viral."

"Well there you go," I said. "You were the ideal person to recognize Conor for what he was. And Bayer—well, *he* was the perfect person to rile Conor up, to get him to drop the nice-guy act and show his true colors. Which was exactly what he did, the first moment there was any kind of tension. You, Santana, Bayer, Romi—practically everyone on the island was hand-picked to either speak to Conor's past or make him come clean about his present. Nico and I—well, we were dropped in at short notice, so there was no time to research someone with a link as good as Santana's. The best they could do was find someone like me, someone who might clash with him politically." I remembered Baz's questions at the interview, the ones that had puzzled me so much. *Would you call yourself a feminist? And your politics. Would you say they're left of center?* Now I understood. He'd been trying to find someone Conor would butt heads with—and ideally a woman. "Add in plenty of booze to oil the wheels, and some stressful tasks designed to make everyone lose their rag . . . The storm was never part of the plan, of course. That was just horribly bad luck."

"But why?" Santana said, her voice bewildered. "Why would Baz go to all this trouble to take down a total stranger, however much of a shit?"

I shook my head again.

"I don't think they *were* strangers. Dan told me, right back at the beginning of all this, that Baz knew Conor. He said that Conor had dated Baz's niece. And I started to wonder . . . What if she didn't walk away unscathed either?"

There was a long pause. I could see the other three thinking about my words, turning them over in their heads. Then Santana's face changed. A kind of horror came over her expression.

"Wait a minute, what was his name?"

"Baz's?" Angel asked, puzzled.

"Yes." Santana was tapping frantically on her new phone—part of the emergency package the British Embassy official had arranged for us, so we could contact our families. "What was his surname? He only ever introduced himself as Baz to me. Baz from Effing Productions."

I pulled out mine too and began searching back through the emails from Ari. It was true that Baz only ever signed off with his first name—his surname wasn't even in his email address. But finally, deep down in one of the contracts, I found it.

"Basil Ferrier," I read out. "Sounds kind of posh, doesn't it? Not really in keeping with his man of the people act. No wonder he preferred going by Baz." And then, as I realized the connection. "Oh, I get it now. Effing Productions. *F* for Ferrier."

"Exactly. And—that was *her* name. The girl I went to school with —Cally. The one who killed herself. Her full name was Calista Ferrier. She told me once she had an uncle in Australia. *She* was Baz's niece."

I stared at her, and Santana stared back—holding each other's gaze as the final pieces slotted into place and I felt a profound, terrible compassion for Baz sweep over me, in spite of his stupidity, in spite of the way he'd lied to us all.

It must have been bad enough for your beautiful, nineteen-year-old niece to kill herself after breaking up with her boyfriend, but to watch that boyfriend go on, year after year, growing bigger and bigger and more and more famous. To watch his YouTube subscribers tip a million, and then two and then ten million—to watch his followers lapping up his rhetoric, more and more of them hitting that *like and subscribe* . . . I had watched some of Conor's videos since getting off the island, sitting on the toilet with the door locked and the shower running to cover the sound, and I had become more and more disturbed. Beneath the faux-reasonable tone was a vein of poison that his supporters celebrated openly in the comments. Yes, I could imagine that a man like Baz would not be able to stand by and watch that.

"Car crash TV" was what Joel had called *One Perfect Couple*, and he'd been more right than he knew. A car crash was exactly what Baz had been aiming for—an engineered one, with Conor at the wheel. But with Conor's supporters weighing in on social media, it wouldn't have been just car crash TV, it would have been *viral* car crash TV, and a double win for Baz: a ratings bonanza for him, and a career-destroying meltdown for Conor. Baz would have walked away a made man—the hero who exposed a YouTube guru for the problematic misogynist he was, and created the must-watch show of the year. The rest of us . . . well, we were just cannon fodder.

There was a long silence. I could see the other three women slowly turning my suggestions over in their heads.

"It would explain why they hadn't sold it," Santana said slowly. "If the draw was going to be this prominent YouTuber melting down on-screen . . . well they'd kind of have to wait for that to happen before they could present it as a USP. But . . . God. Could it be true? It seems . . . it seems crazy."

I shrugged.

"I don't know. But it's the only way I can make sense of all these threads leading back to both Conor and Baz. I mean, your friend Cally—I don't think that's a coincidence, do you?"

Santana shook her head. Her face was pale.

"And I don't know much about reality TV, but it seems to me that what Baz was attempting, it's kind of just an extension of what they *all* do, isn't it? They pick volatile people, people who're going to perform for the cameras, they wind them up as tight as they can, they engineer a bunch of high-stress situations that are practically guaranteed to make someone lose their shit, throw in some alcohol—and then they sit back and let the cameras roll and the tweets pour in."

"Fuck," Angel said. "I mean, it is crazy, but you are right—all these links to Cally, they don't make sense otherwise. So Baz destroys his enemy, and creates the TV événement of the year. And fuck the rest of us in the process."

"Jesus," Santana said. Her jaw was clenched, a muscle there ticcing. When she spoke again, her voice sounded like it was coming through gritted teeth. "Jesus *Christ*. I knew this whole thing was shitty from the start. I didn't even want to do it, it was Dan's idea. He's never wanted to be 'just' a model." She put air quotes around the word. "He's always wanted to be an actor or a presenter. I mean . . ." She trailed off, realizing her mistake. "He always wanted."

"Fuck him," Angel said. There was a contained fury in her voice that I'd never heard before. "L'homme de ma vie—my poor Bayer, he is dead. And for what? For nothing! For Baz to make his stupid plan! Seriously, fuck him!"

Zana was bent forward, and her hands were over her face. I couldn't tell if she was crying, and if so whether it was with shock, grief, or relief. Maybe all three.

But when she sat up, I saw that she was laughing—laughing through her tears with a kind of bitter, mirthless fury.

"If this is true—" She was struggling to get the words out. "If this is true, then you know, you know the fucking worst thing?"

She gave a kind of hiccupping gulping laugh, and I shook my head. Angel and Santana were looking at her with a mix of horror and sympathy.

"We've made a fucking *hero* out of him," Zana managed. She was rocking back and forth, almost crouching, her head in her hands, but now she threw back her head. "That diary—that fucking diary I wrote. We've made him into a *saint*. Have you seen the headlines?"

She dug in her pocket for her phone, tapped something into the search bar and held it out.

"Look. *Look*."

I leaned forward, peering at the tiny screen. And there it was in black and white, headline after headline—most of them illustrated with Conor's charming, grinning face.

YouTuber's Tragic Death Saving Pals

*Co-Bros Mourn the Loss of Their Hero as British
YouTuber Conor Brian Reported Dead*

*Conor Brian: A Remarkable Life. A Selfless Death. A Last
Gift to the World.*

I pushed the phone away.

"*That* was what Baz achieved," Zana spat. "He put us all through hell, just to canonize his enemy. And now we all have to live with this—this *lie* forever. And I have to live with what I did—with what I let happen."

There were tears streaming down her face, and I didn't know whether it was because of Conor or everything else. Maybe all of it.

"Look," I said. I took the phone out of Zana's hand, switched off the screen. "Look, Zana. Baz is dead, Conor is dead—they're all dead." A lump rose in my throat, thinking of Dan, of Joel, of Bayer, of Romi, and the poor, nameless producer—and of Nico, of his last words to me. *You set me up. This wasn't what was supposed to happen. This wasn't what we agreed!* And it was true—more true than any of us could have known at the time. We were all set up. None of us had agreed to Baz's stupid, stupid plan. "They're dead," I said again, my voice more vehement than I had meant it to sound, "and there is nothing we can do to change that. We can't help them. We can't fix what they did or change what they suffered. All we can do is protect the living—protect *us*." I looked around the circle. "And that is what I'm going to do. No matter the cost. Okay?"

There was a long silence. Then Angel nodded.

"Yes. Fuck Baz. Fuck Conor's legacy. So it is a lie. So it is of lots of people. The living is what matters. Agreed?"

"Agreed," Santana said. Her face was wet, and she dashed at her eyes. "Zana?"

"Okay," Zana said. Her voice was low. "But I hate that you're doing this for me."

"We're not doing it for you," Angel said. Her voice was hard. "We're doing it for us. For *all* of us. For the survivors."

She picked up the beaded glass of lemonade sitting in front of her.

"To survival."

"To survival," Santana echoed.

"To survival," I said. We turned and looked at Zana.

"To survival," she said softly. And then she smiled.

CHAPTER 38

THE REPLACEMENT SIM came in the post. New phone, since my old one was at the bottom of the South Pacific. But the same number. I'd had enough people frantically trying to contact me via friends of friends that I knew I needed to reactivate my old number to reassure them that I was okay.

I was alone when it came, in our—my—flat. It was still strange being there without Nico. I still found myself looking for him when I turned over in bed, my breath still caught in my throat when I came through the front door, about to call out to him, *Honey, I'm home!*

It was a Saturday, and not so long after we got back from Jakarta—my mum and dad had finally gone home, reassured that I was eating, and sleeping, after a fashion at least, and wasn't about to slip through their fingers once again. But my hands were still gaunt and sunburnt, still covered with cuts and acid burns that were only partially healed. I remember looking down at them as I tore open the envelope and cut my thumb on the flap—thinking about how much it hurt, and how ironic it was to mind about a stupid paper cut, when we'd all been through so much.

I opened up my phone with a paper clip, slipped in the SIM, and then waited as the texts came through. Dozens . . . and dozens . . . and dozens of them, ramping up as word of the shipwreck had filtered back to the UK, and friends began hearing of my disappearance.

Most of the people had found me via email or through my mum, and as I scrolled down the list, I unmarked the ones I knew I didn't have to respond to and sent a quick "hi, I'm back—I'll be in touch as soon as I can" to the people who might not have heard. The worst ones were Nico's friends—knowing that I was going to have to break the awful news to them again and again. It was like going back in time. Back to a time when everything was okay.

And then, finally, I reached the very last text of all . . . or maybe the very first, though it was last on the list. Judging by the date stamp, it must have been sent just a few hours after I switched my old phone off and put it in Baz's safe, and it had presumably been sitting on the server ever since, waiting for my SIM to reconnect.

It was a text from Nico.

At first I didn't understand. His phone had been inside the locker along with mine—I had seen Baz put it there. How had he managed to text me? And *why*, when he of all people would have realized that I couldn't answer it?

And then I realized—he must have been given his phone back when he got on board the *Over Easy* for that final journey. And he had sent this, so that it would be the first thing I read when I picked up my own phone, when I too was kicked off the island.

It wasn't just one text. It was several, in fact, one after the other. A little number thirteen hovered by the preview of the most recent one.

Thirteen texts. That sounded like he'd had a lot to say. A *lot*.

My finger hovered over his name, my stomach shifting uneasily, wondering whether I had the courage to open this thread now, with everything so raw. I kept remembering Nico's bitterness that last night on the island, his wild accusations, *you sabotaged me . . . what game are you playing?*

But I couldn't leave the chain there, unread, tormenting me. I had to face whatever he'd wanted to say, and whatever his last words were, they couldn't be worse than the ones ringing in my head. And the beginning, the bit I could see in the preview, didn't look too bad. "hey lil," it began, in Nico's characteristic unpunctuated stream of consciousness, "well im back on the boa—"

That was where the preview cut out.

I took a deep breath. I clicked.

hey lil. well im back on the boat and had a chance to cool off and fuck im sorry. i was a dick

worse than a dick

i guess if ur reading this youve been kicked out too. or maybe youve won!!!! i hope u know i didnt mean any of that stuff i said when i left. i was just angry. and maybe scared too. i felt like this show was my last chance and i let myself down. both of us down. because heres the thing—you didnt. you came thru like you always do. because ur amazing and clever and a good person and

fuck pressed send by mistake. i dont know what else. i just know i dont deserve you and ive been feeling it for a while. you deserve someone whos gonna work hard and give u kids and all the stuff i dont know if i really want. i love u lil and i feel like you love me too but i dont know. maybe its time for me to let u go

fuck i shojldnt have text that sorry im drunk. ive had a lot of bear

*beet

*beer

a lot to drink

i love u and i hope you win. i hop you get the whole prize pot nad you do something amazing. life changing i know u will

u deserve it

i love you

ps I hope you beat connor. baz says he dated his neice or someting and hes kind of a shit

I don't know how long I sat there, staring at the screen. I only knew that there were tears rolling down my face, and that when my phone beeped again with an incoming text, the screen lit up like a candle, illuminating the room with a ghostly glow.

I wiped my eyes and scrolled back to the top of the list, where a text from an unknown number sat in my inbox.

Hey, the text said. *It's me. Santana. Testing your new number. Old number I mean. Stupid question but... are you going to be ok?*

I closed my eyes. Took a deep breath. Tried to figure out what to say.

Then I simply typed, *yes*.

And pressed send.

ACKNOWLEDGMENTS

I don't typically thank my family very much in my acknowledgments because they very rarely have anything to do with writing my books, apart from tactfully keeping out of my way when it's going badly. However, this one is an exception as Lyla's career as a virologist is directly inspired by my own husband's job in science, and the many hours he spent early on in our relationship splitting cell lines and generally abusing his long-suffering cultures.

Writers have a terrible habit of marrying other writers but I'd like to make a strong case for marrying a scientist. There's something comforting about having a spouse who doesn't really understand your job, just as you don't really understand theirs—and it forces you to leave your work worries behind when you sit down at the kitchen table. But more than that, scientists are generally extremely intelligent, competent, curious people who are very interesting to live with, and who help you remember there are worse things in the world than using less when you mean fewer.

I have never really understood what my husband does. I used to make a pretty good fist of explaining the difference between viruses and retroviruses, but I've forgotten even that. But what I do know is how passionately he feels about his work, how important the pursuit of truth and scientific integrity is, and how hard he's tried all his career to put the data first. Ian, I love you, and your qualities as a scientist are one of my favorite things about you, and I hope that this comes across in Lyla.

I need to extend a heartfelt thanks to Ivan Brett for letting me quiz him about the emotional side of being a reality-TV contestant, and for advising me on the plausibility of some of the details I wanted to include. I must however make it clear that the slipshod attitude to health and safety displayed by Effing Productions in *One Perfect Couple* was entirely my own invention and not based on Ivan's experience! Courtney Robertson's fascinating memoir *I Didn't Come Here to Make Friends*, about her time on *The Bachelor*, provided behind-the-scenes insights on a very different kind of show.

A huge thank-you also to Sally, Gus, and Robyn for putting up with endless questions about what it's like to live with T1 diabetes, and the minutiae of pumps and insulin. Any mistakes are my own fault!

And enormous thank-yous to Chris Moore and Sabrina Chapman for help with the French dialogue.

My lovely agent, Eve White, and her brilliant assistants Ludo and Steven are always by my side and I'm beyond grateful to them for shepherding my books through the years. And I also owe many, many individual thank-yous to the indomitable and indefatigable teams at Simon & Schuster in the UK, US, Canada, and Australia, and at my publishers in other languages and abroad. To Alison, Jen, and Suzanne, I am thankful every day for your joint editorial brilliance and the faith you've shown in me and my characters. And to Ian, Jessica, Sydney, Sabah, Katherine, Taylor, Kevin, Mackenzie, Gill, Dom, Nicholas, Maddie, Heather, Gail, Hayley, Sarah, Harriett, Matt, Francesca, Richard, Genevieve, Louise, Jennifer, Aimee, Sally, Abby, Anabel, Caroline, Jaime, John Paul, Brigid, and Lisa—I owe all of you heartfelt thank-yous for the care and attention you've lavished on my books. I am so very grateful for all you've done for me!

To my dear family and friends, including the increasingly obstreperous Colin Scott, I love you all, and I couldn't have done it without you.

And to my dear reader, if you've made it this far—thank you. You make it all worthwhile.

ABOUT THE AUTHOR

Ruth Ware worked as a waitress, a bookseller, a teacher of English as a foreign language, and a press officer before settling down as a full-time writer. She now lives with her family in Sussex, on the south coast of England. She is the #1 *New York Times* and *Globe and Mail* (Toronto) bestselling author of *In a Dark, Dark Wood*; *The Woman in Cabin 10*; *The Lying Game*; *The Death of Mrs. Westaway*; *The Turn of the Key*; *One by One*; *The It Girl*; and *Zero Days*. Visit her at Ruth Ware.com and follow her on X @RuthWareWriter.